S0-BDR-289

"Mad, Bad, and Dangerous to Know"
Mary Jo Putney

After the death of her no-good husband, a broken woman surrenders to a night of passion with a gambler sentenced to hang—an innocent man whose dying wish will give her a brand-new life. . . .

"The Antagonists"
Joan Wolf

A headstrong beauty must face her true feelings for her childhood nemesis when she prepares for her come-out in society—and marriage. . . .

"Buried Treasure"
Edith Layton

When a man is stabbed by pirates and left for dead on the shore, a sheltered Long Island woman heals his wounded body—but must fight the lure of the sea for his wild heart. . . .

"Fathers and Daughters"
Patricia Rice

A reformed spendthrift struggles to repay a loan to the father of his former fiancée—and a debt of love to the woman he could never forget. . . .

"Precious Rogue"
Mary Balogh

Though practically invisible to her aunt's wealthy guests, a quiet orphan catches the eye of an unprincipled rogue—and makes him see the error of his ways. . . .

Captured Hearts

Five Favorite Love Stories

Mary Jo Putney
Joan Wolf
Edith Layton
Patricia Rice
Mary Balogh

A TOPAZ BOOK

TOPAZ
Published by the Penguin Group
Penguin Putnam Inc., 375 Hudson Street,
New York, New York 10014, U.S.A.
Penguin Books Ltd, 27 Wrights Lane, London W8 5TZ, England
Penguin Books Australia Ltd, Ringwood, Victoria, Australia
Penguin Books Canada Ltd, 10 Alcorn Avenue,
Toronto, Ontario, Canada M4V 3B2
Penguin Books (N.Z.) Ltd, 182–190 Wairau Road,
Auckland 10, New Zealand

Penguin Books Ltd, Registered Offices:
Harmondsworth, Middlesex, England

Published by Topaz, an imprint of Dutton NAL,
a member of Penguin Putnam Inc.

First Topaz Printing, February, 1999
10 9 8 7 6 5 4 3 2 1

Contents

Mad, Bad, and Dangerous to Know

by Mary Jo Putney

He was going to be hanged on Tuesday.

Andrew Kane supposed that he should be contemplating his imminent demise, but the misery of the present left no room to worry about next week. The scorched plains of Texas were dismal at the best of times, and in his present situation, they were a fair approximation of hell.

The horse ahead of him kicked up a swirl of dust and Kane began to cough with parched painfulness. If he didn't get water soon, he wouldn't live long enough to be hanged. No point in asking his escorts for a drink, though. When Kane had done that yesterday, Biff, the more vicious of the two, had knocked him to the ground, sneering that he wasn't gonna pamper no low-down, murdering son of a bitch.

While Biff underlined his remark with a kick in the ribs, the other of the temporary deputies, Whittles, had chimed in. "Witless," as Kane mentally dubbed him, had waved a tin cup of water and said that mebbe they'd give the prisoner some if he got down on his knees and asked for it real purty.

Kane might have complied if he thought it would do any good, but he knew his guards were just looking for entertainment. After a good belly laugh over his groveling, Witless would have poured the water on the ground just out of reach.

Tiredly, Kane raised his handcuffed wrists and wiped his sweaty forehead with one sleeve. In a couple of hours they would be in Forlorn Hope, the last night's stop before reaching their destination, Prairie City. He supposed that in the interests of keeping him alive for his execution, the sheriff in Prairie City would give him water. It wouldn't do to deprive the crowd that would turn out to see justice visited on the ungodly.

Kane had been to a hanging once, when he had been such a young fool that he'd thought it would be entertaining. The convict had been a skinny little fellow, too light to break his neck when the trap fell away under his feet. The poor devil had swung back and forth for quite a spell, gasping and kicking. Kane hadn't seen the end; he'd been behind the livery stable, spewing his guts out. He never went to a hanging again. And, though he was no saint, he sure as hell hadn't expected to end on the gallows himself.

He ran a dry tongue over his cracked lips. As a boy he'd wanted an exciting life, and he'd gotten it. Maybe he should have wished for a little less excitement.

Elizabeth Holden wearily contemplated the yellow dust that saturated her mourning gown. Black wasn't a very practical color in a dry Texas summer, but with both her husband and her father dead in the last month, she didn't have much choice about what to wear. And heaven knew that black suited her mood. She shifted in her saddle, hoping to find a more comfortable position.

A soft southern voice said, "You feeling poorly, Miz Holden?"

Liza managed a smile for her escort. Since there wasn't anything he could do for what ailed her, there was no point in making him worry. "I'm fine, Mr. Jackson, just a little tired. I'll be glad to reach Forlorn Hope. As I recall, the hotel there is a good one."

Tom Jackson nodded, but his dark eyes were still concerned. "Mebbe I can hire a wagon to take you the rest of the way. Mr. Holden will have my hide if anything happens to you."

Liza felt a chill, as if clutching hands were closing around her. Determinedly she shook off the image, not wanting to think of the dreary future that stretched before her. "Truly, I'm fine. The road is so bad that horseback is easier than a wagon would be."

Mr. Jackson nodded, accepting her decision, but the compassion in his eyes almost reduced her to tears. He'd worked for the Holdens for years and must have a fair idea what her life had been like as bride of the late Billie Holden. Not that he could know the worst; even Billie's parents hadn't known just how difficult their son had been. They hadn't wanted to know.

The rest of the ride was accomplished in silence. The town of Forlorn Hope was better than its name, but not much. Besides the hotel, there were two saloons, a handful of stores, and a couple dozen straggling houses. The town was on the route between Liza's girlhood home in Willow Point and her in-laws' ranch outside Prairie City, but with her father dead and his general store sold, she'd probably never come this way again. No great loss, she thought dully as her companion helped her from her horse.

After he carried her luggage into the hotel and located a clerk to register her, Liza said, "Didn't you mention that a cousin of yours lived here, Mr. Jackson?"

"Yes, ma'am, the blacksmith." He smiled reminiscently. "His wife Molly is the best Alabama cook in Texas."

"Then take the rest of the day off and go see them," Liza suggested. "Spend the night if you like. We came through in such a hurry two weeks ago that you didn't have time for a visit, so you should make up for that now."

Mr. Jackson hesitated, clearly tempted. "I should stay in the hotel bunkhouse so's I'm nearby if you need anything."

"I won't need anything. I'll take a bath, have some food sent up, and go to bed early," she assured him. "Think of the time off as a thank you for all the help you were with my father's funeral and all."

He surveyed her face, then nodded. "If you're sure, Miz Holden. I'll come for you at nine in the morning."

The hot bath was wonderful for Liza's sore muscles. After she'd soaped and soaked, she lay back in the tin tub and studied her body, trying to see if her abdomen was starting to enlarge. But she could detect no change. If anything, she'd lost weight in the last weeks. Hard to imagine that a baby was growing inside her.

Not a baby—her jailer.

Desolation swept through her, but before tears could destroy her fragile composure, she climbed from the tub and briskly toweled herself dry. She must not allow herself to sink into melancholy, for she needed all her strength.

Thinking that she'd read a bit before going to bed, Liza donned her other black dress, which was wrinkled but clean. Then she began brushing out her wheat-blond hair. It was still light outside, so she drifted to the window and gazed absently down into the street. A half dozen people were in sight, none of them in any great hurry.

Her eye was caught by the wreckage of a recently burned building. Thinking back, she recalled that there had been a combined town office and jail on the site before.

She was about to turn away from the window when three dusty riders appeared. Curiously she saw that one of the horses was on a lead, and the black-clad rider on its back was slumped forward as if barely able to stay upright.

When the newcomers were opposite the hotel, the heavyset man in the lead saw the charred ruins of the jail. Scowling ferociously, he halted the group right under Liza's window, so close that she could see his small, piggy eyes. After asking a question of an idler sitting in front of the hotel, Pig-Eyes dismounted and tethered his horse to the hitching rail. Then he went to the led horse, whose rider wore the characteristic black suit, ruffled shirt, and brocade waistcoat of a gambler.

Pig-Eyes grabbed the gambler's arm and jerked him from his saddle. The man in black pitched heavily from his mount, barely managing to catch his saddle horn in time to prevent himself from crashing to the ground. As he regained his balance, Liza saw that his hands were cuffed together. A prisoner. She wondered what he had done.

The third rider, a thin, weasely fellow, dismounted and laid a rough hand on the gambler's arm. In spite of his physical condition, there was defiance in the prisoner's posture as he raised his head and answered back.

The results were explosive. With a snarl of fury, Weasel drew back his fist and slugged the other man in the stomach. As the gambler folded over, he lashed out with one foot at his tormentor, his boot connecting just below the knee. Weasel howled and almost collapsed. When he recovered, he and Pig-Eyes began beating and kicking the prisoner. Even when he fell to the ground, the kicks and blows continued, right under Liza's horrified gaze.

Fury blazed through her, burning away her fatigue and depression. Without waiting to see more, she raced from her room, taking the stairs two at a time, her loose hair flying behind her. When she reached the street, she saw that a half dozen townspeople were watching the beating. Though most wore uncomfortable expressions, no one intervened. It wasn't healthy to come between angry, armed men and their victim.

Liza was too incensed to feel such compunction. Furiously she cried, "Stop that this instant, you brutes!"

From sheer surprise, Pig-Eyes and Weasel obeyed, both of them turning to stare at her. Liza took advantage of the pause to say fiercely, "You should be ashamed of yourselves, beating a man who is bound and helpless."

Weasel shifted uncomfortably, his bravado vanishing in the presence of a lady. "Beggin' your pardon, ma'am, but Andrew Kane ain't helpless. He's quicker'n a snake and twice as mean."

"That doesn't give you the right to beat him to death," Liza retorted. "What kind of men are you, to attack someone who can't defend himself?"

She looked down at the gambler, who lay still in the dusty street, blood flowing from numerous cuts. Under the dirt and bruises he looked young and vulnerable, not mean at all. Not that Liza was much of a judge of character; when she'd met Billie Holden, she had thought he was kind and honest.

A lean man with drooping mustaches and a tin badge

on his vest pushed through the small crowd of silent on-lookers. "I'm Sheriff Taylor," he barked. "What's going on here?"

Pig-Eyes said, "My name's Biff Burns. Me and my partner Whittles are temporary deputies who are taking this murderer to Prairie City for hanging." He prodded his prisoner with one booted toe. "We was gonna put him in the jail for the night, but I see it's burnt down."

The sheriff scowled. "It was fired by some folks from Rapid City. They want to see their town made county seat, so they burned down our public building."

Uninterested in local politics, Burns said, "Where can we put this son of a bitch tonight?" The weasel hissed something and Burns flushed, then glanced askance at Liza. "Beggin' your pardon, ma'am."

After giving him an icy glance, she knelt by Kane. Burns exclaimed, "Don't get so close, ma'am. He's dangerous."

Ignoring the words, Liza took her handkerchief and began blotting blood from a slash on the man's forehead. Long, dark lashes flickered open to reveal eyes of piercing blue—gambler's eyes, that saw everything and gave away nothing.

For a long moment their gazes held. She saw intelligence, shrewdness, anger, and determination in the blue depths—the qualities of a man used to living on the edge of danger. It was suddenly easy to believe that he was a murderer. Disconcerted, Liza sat back on her heels.

Yet when he spoke, Kane was polite enough. "A pleasure to make your acquaintance, darlin'." He had a crisp accent that she couldn't identify because his voice was a barely audible rasp.

Seeing his cracked lips, Liza asked, "Do you need water?"

Desperate longing flared in his eyes, though he tried to keep his voice steady. "I'd be much obliged."

She glanced up at Burns. "Give me your canteen."

Biff started to protest, then subsided, unwilling to argue with a lady in front of a steadily growing audience. He untied the canteen and handed it to Liza. She opened it and dribbled a few drops into Kane's mouth. His tanned throat moved convulsively as he swallowed. Slowly she poured more, careful not to give him more than he could manage. From the way he drank, she guessed that it had been a long time—too long—since he had been given water. Her anger rose again. He might be a murderer, but even a mad dog didn't deserve such treatment.

The sheriff said, "You can put your prisoner in the hotel storeroom, Burns. It's got a solid door that locks and a window too small for a man to get through. Won't be the first time it held a prisoner. He'll be safe there for the night."

Burns cleared his throat. "We'll put him in as soon as the lady gets out of the way."

Liza glanced up, her gaze going to the sheriff, who seemed reasonable. "This man needs medical attention."

Sheriff Taylor shook his head. "There's no doctor in Forlorn Hope."

Liza got to her feet and gave Burns a challenging glance. "Then I'll tend him myself."

Outraged, Biff said, "Nothin' wrong with that son of a . . ." Remembering his language, he coughed. "He's not bad hurt, ma'am, and 'sides, in a coupla days it won't matter. A lady shouldn't concern herself with trash like him."

Liza's eyes narrowed. "Sheriff Taylor, the constitution forbids cruel and unusual punishment. Doesn't that mean that even prisoners deserve food, water, and medical treatment?"

The sheriff shrugged. "If the lady wants to play nursemaid, let her. Most gamblers have a soft spot for women, so he probably won't hurt her, though you might want to chain him up, just in case."

Burns and Whittles grabbed Kane by the upper arms and hauled him to his feet. Not wanting to watch, Liza stalked back into the hotel. She didn't understand her need to champion a criminal who probably deserved everything he got, but the impulse was too strong to deny. Perhaps it was because she felt so helpless about her own life. By taking shameless advantage of the reverence westerners had for women, she could do something to help a fellow being.

It was a nice bonus that her good deed would also keep her too busy to think about her own problems, at least for a while.

Liza spent the next half hour collecting what she would need to treat Kane's wounds, plus food and drink since the deputies couldn't be trusted to feed their prisoner. It was almost dark by the time she made her way to the storeroom, which lay behind a larger chamber which was used as a second dining room when the hotel was busy. At the moment, the only occupant was Biff. His chair was tilted back and his booted feet rested on the edge of a table while he idly shuffled cards and looked bored.

When Liza entered, the deputy's expression bright-

ened and the front legs of the chair hit the floor with a
bang. The frank admiration in his gaze made her grateful for the fact that she was wearing mourning; even the
Biffs of the world would seldom force unwelcome flir-
tation on a new widow.

She nodded toward an unused lantern sitting on the
sideboard. "Will you light that and bring it in, Mr.
Burns?" As he hastened to comply, she murmured,
"You're very kind."

The deputy opened the door to the storeroom and she
stepped inside. It made a good cell, for the only window
was high on the wall and too small to be used by anyone but a child. The walls were lined with shelves, and
sacks, barrels, and boxes were stacked around the
perimeter of the room. The prisoner had been dumped
unceremoniously in the middle of the plank floor.

Though Kane had been lying motionless, his eyes
flickered open when they entered. Accompanied by a
metallic rattle, he pushed his battered body up so that he
was sitting against a sack of flour. Liza saw that his right
handcuff had been removed from his wrist, then locked
to a chain that looped around a supporting post in the
corner. Though he had one hand free and the chain was
long enough to allow some movement, she disliked seeing a man treated like a dog on a leash.

Wanting to get rid of the deputy and his hungry stare,
she said, "You've had a long, hard ride, Mr. Burns." She
set her tray on the floor near Kane. "There's no need for
you to stay here if you'd rather go to the saloon for a bite
of supper."

Biff licked his lips as duty wrestled with desire. "I
shouldn't leave you alone with him, ma'am."

She made an impatient gesture. "Your prisoner is in

no condition to hurt anyone. And if he does get rambunctious, I'll just move out of reach."

"I'll have to lock you in," Biff warned. "Can't risk letting him break out."

She shrugged. "As you wish. It's going to take time to clean his wounds. You can let me out when you've finished your own dinner."

"That's what I'll do, then," Biff decided. He hung the lantern from a nail so its soft rays illuminated most of the storeroom, then turned and left.

Kane had been watching in silence, but as the key turned in the door, locking them in together, he drawled, "He's right, darlin'—you shouldn't be here. Twelve good men and true have decided that I am mad, bad, and dangerous to know."

Her eyes widened, and not only because of his cool English accent. Who would have thought a murderer would be so well-educated? Well, she had had a decent education, too, reading every book that had come through her father's store. "Don't try to convince me that you're Lord Byron," she said briskly, "because I am certainly not Lady Caroline Lamb."

Startled pleasure lit Kane's tanned face and his tension eased. "If you're not Lady Caroline Lamb, who are you?" He examined her with appreciative interest. "Guardian angels aren't supposed to be so lusciouslooking."

She found herself coloring under his scrutiny. Not wanting to use the married name that she had come to hate, she replied, "My name is Liza. You're an Englishman?"

"I was born in England, but I'm an American now. I came here when I was twenty-one."

"Are you a remittance man?"

"Well, my family didn't actually pay me to keep out of sight," he said with a crooked smile, "but they did heave a vast sigh of relief when I decided to see the world after I was sent down from Oxford. That means I was thrown out," he added when he saw that she didn't understand the term. "The professors said that I lacked a proper respect for rules and tradition. They were right."

"Many of your countrymen must feel the same way, because there are plenty of them around." She'd always enjoyed the Britons who stopped by her father's store, and had encouraged them to talk just so she could listen to their lovely accents. Kane himself spoke with a delicious blend of English crispness and American idiom.

After dipping a pad of cotton into the bowl of warm water, she began cleaning the lacerations on Kane's face. Under the cuts, dust, and several days' growth of beard, she discovered that his features were strongboned and handsome. She guessed that he'd broken his share of female hearts. His intense blue eyes were disturbing at such close range.

He winced when she touched the deepest gash, which started on his forehead and curved down his left temple. Thinking that conversation would distract him from the discomfort, she asked, "What made you decide to stay in this country?"

"When I first reached Denver, I went to a livery stable to rent a horse. The only man in sight was a rough-looking chap sitting on a stump, so I asked him where his master was. He spat a stream of tobacco juice that just missed my foot, then said that the son of a bitch hadn't been born yet." Kane chuckled. "I knew instantly I'd found my spiritual home." His amused glance went to Liza. "Excuse the profanity, but cleaning up the fellow's language would dilute the flavor of the encounter."

Liza smiled, unoffended. She was tolerant of ungenteel language, for her father's customers were frequently profane. She had found it touching when tall, bristly cowhands blushed and apologized with the shyness of little boys. But Kane was another sort of man entirely, one who was completely sure of himself, even now, when he was on the verge of execution.

The thought produced a jolt of disorientation. It was impossible, obscene, that the man beneath her hands would soon be dead. He was too alive, too vividly real. Distressed, she bowed her head and moistened a pad with whiskey, then patted the cuts she had already cleaned.

Though the alcohol must have stung like blazes, he endured it stoically. When she had finished working on his face, he remarked, "A pity to waste good whiskey on cleaning wounds when I'm going to die anyway."

She chuckled and reached for the china mug. "I should have guessed you might want a drink more than nursing."

"A sign of weakness on my part," he said with self-mockery, "but the last fortnight has been . . . difficult. I wouldn't mind a bit of oblivion."

"I don't think there's enough here for oblivion," she said as she poured whiskey from the small bottle. "Will you settle for relaxation?"

He laughed out loud. Strange. He hadn't expected to laugh again before he died. Nor had he expected to be alone with a beautiful young lady. He feasted his eyes on her, for she was the loveliest sight he had seen in years. The loveliest he was likely to see for the rest of his life.

To his regret, she had pinned up the thick fair hair that had danced loose around her shoulders when she had come charging out of the hotel, but a few wheat-colored tendrils still curled temptingly around her face. And what a face it was—heart-shaped, with delicate features and wondrous gray eyes that regarded the world without flinching. The women were one of the things he liked most about America. The best of them were direct, confident, as strong as a man, not at all like the simpering misses he'd known in England.

After putting the mug into his left hand, Liza turned her attention to his right wrist, the one that was still handcuffed. Her lips pursed when she pushed the cuff up and discovered that the metal had gouged a circle of ugly lacerations. Without comment, she began cleaning the raw flesh. Her light, cool fingers were soothing as she cleaned and bandaged his right wrist, then the equally damaged left one.

He sipped the whiskey slowly, wanting it to last. It hit hard on an empty stomach. He welcomed the harsh burn, for it eased the aches and pains he'd suffered at the hands of the deputies. The whiskey affected him in other ways, too, and when Liza bent forward, he had to fight an impulse to pull out her hair pins.

Yet much as he would have enjoyed releasing the sunstreaked brilliance of her hair, he restrained himself. He daren't alarm her, for he needed her kindness too much. Already he hated the knowledge that soon she would leave.

Indicating the widow's weeds with his forefinger, he said, "You've had a loss?"

She went still. "Two," she said quietly. "Several weeks ago, my husband was killed. Right after we buried him, I received word that my father had also died. I'm returning to my in-laws' ranch from my father's funeral."

"I'm sorry," he said, knowing how inadequate the words were. Needing to know that she would be all right, he continued, "Your husband's family will look out for you?"

"Oh, yes," she said with a trace of bitterness. "Since I have something they want, I'll be very well cared for."

When her hand unconsciously went to her belly, he realized that she must be with child. It was a surprise, and not only because of her slimness, for she didn't have the glow common to expectant mothers. He supposed that the tragedies she had experienced were enough to extinguish joy. "At least you'll have something left of your husband," he said, wanting to offer comfort.

Her face tightened and she almost spoke. Then she gave a faint shake of her head and glanced up. "Are you hungry, Mr. Kane? I brought some food."

Her face was only a foot from his, close enough so that he could admire the creamy texture of her skin and the alluring fullness of her mouth. A wave of desire swept through him, so intense that he had to bite his lip to prevent himself from reacting. In a detached corner of his mind, he knew that what he felt was not simply normal male yearning for a lovely woman, but a desperate desire to bury himself in passion; to obliterate, for a moment, the terror of knowing how little time he had left.

Exercising all of his will, he said steadily, "It's been so long since I ate that I've forgotten what food is, so I reckon that it's time I had some. And if I'm to call you Liza, you must call me Drew." His smile was a little crooked. "Normal manners don't quite seem to fit present circumstances."

"Very well, Drew." Her tray included slices of cold

fried chicken and slabs of fresh bread, which made a tasty sandwich. As he ate, he felt strength flowing into his exhausted muscles. He hadn't realized how much hunger was affecting him.

When he finished, Liza said, "Would you like more?"

He shook his head. "That's all I can manage at the moment, but I thank you kindly. Amazing what food can do for one's state of mind. I feel better than I have in days."

As she covered the rest of the food, a gunshot punctuated the night air. Kane frowned as he realized that the noise outside had been steadily increasing. "From the racket, it sounds like every cowhand in fifty miles has come to town to celebrate payday."

Liza jumped when an exuberant bellow sounded right under their window. "I hope Sheriff Taylor can handle them."

"He seemed like a capable man." Kane cocked his head, trying to decipher the conflicting voices. "My guess is that hands from two or three rival spreads are entertaining themselves by trying to rip each other's heads off."

She shivered and glanced at the door. "They wouldn't break into the hotel looking for food or whiskey, would they?"

"Even if they do, we'll be safe here. Besides the key lock, there's a bar for the door. Whoever built this hotel was a cautious soul." He got to his feet and went for the wooden bar leaning in a shadowed corner, only to be pulled up with a painful jerk when he reached the end of the chain. He swore under his breath; in the pleasure of Liza's company, he had forgotten his restraints. "I'm afraid that if you want the extra protection, you'll have to do it yourself."

She retrieved the heavy bar, then dropped it in place with a solid thunk. "This will stop any drunken cowboys who might want to get too friendly."

A burst of shots sounded from the direction of the saloon, followed by the tinkle of breaking glass. The sheriff would have his work cut out for him. Kane frowned. "Since Biff and Witless are acting deputies, Sheriff Taylor will probably enlist them to help him whip that lot into line. Might be hours before you get let out. Sorry."

"No need to apologize." She gracefully seated herself on a sack of flour. "It's not your fault."

"Maybe I'm apologizing because I'm not sorry you're marooned here," he said in a burst of candor. After days of having to maintain a stiff upper lip while surrounded by enemies, the need to have one last real, human conversation was overpowering. "Thanks for helping a dangerous, unworthy stranger, Liza. It . . . means a great deal to me."

She tucked her feet under her, carefully covering her ankles with her skirt. "You don't seem very dangerous. And I'm not being entirely unselfish. It's . . . been hard making it through the nights. Distraction is welcome." Then, speaking quickly, as if she had said too much, she continued with deliberate lightness, "Are you a gambler, or do you just dress like one?"

Kane was still standing, for now that he was stronger he felt restless. Accompanied by a soft clinking of chain, he began to pace back and forth within the limits of his tether. "I was a gambler for years, but I'd about given it up."

"Why did you do that?"

"I wanted something different. Better." He stopped in front of the small window and gazed out, seeing not the clear night sky but the long, winding road that had led him to this impromptu cell. "I come from a long line of English squires, respectable folk who wanted nothing more than to work their land, raise another generation of little Kanes, and be buried in English soil. If I'd been in line to inherit the estate, I expect I would have been exactly like all my ancestors. But by custom the land goes to the oldest son, and I was the younger."

He turned and leaned against the wall, his arms folded across his chest. "I couldn't have the estate and didn't have the patience for the church, the army, or the law, which are the usual choices for younger sons. So I became a hellion instead. After being sent down from Oxford, I came to America, which suited me right down to the ground. For years, I lived in saloons, moved from one town to the next when I got bored, saw the world and lived high. I gambled with some of the best, and won more often than not."

He smiled a little. "Though I always played straight in an honest game, if I sat down with a bunch of crooks, I could cheat as well as any riverboat gambler. It was a point of pride." His smile faded and deep weariness showed. "But after seven or eight years, I'd had enough. Too much time in dark, smoky, noisy saloons, living on black coffee and hard liquor. Too many sore losers who'll pull a gun rather than admit that they played their cards badly. It got downright tedious."

He looked down at his hands and fiddled absently with the metal cuff. "It's ironic. I was the family rebel and black sheep. I traveled thousands of miles to the wild frontier, braving Red Indians and Lord knows what else—my mother says that my letters are a source of shocked fascination to the whole county of Wiltshire. But when my thirtieth birthday showed on the horizon,

I learned that at heart, I'm exactly like all my respectable ancestors—what I really wanted was a piece of land to call my own." He fell silent.

Liza waited patiently for him to continue. When he didn't, she asked, "Have you been looking for a spread to buy?"

"I already found one. Bought it with the proceeds of a four-day poker game in Leadville." He smiled wistfully. "It's up in Colorado, in the foothills above Pueblo. A valley with plenty of water, mountains all around— the most beautiful place I'd ever seen. And only a couple of hours from a railroad—I can be in Denver in a day when I feel a need for civilization."

His voice flattened. "At least, I could have if I wanted to. Only lived there for six months—not long enough to get bored." He shrugged indifferently, as if being a condemned man was of no more consequence than a horse with a loose shoe. "I won't be seeing the Lazy K again."

Liza regarded him with wide, compassionate eyes. "You don't look like a murderer to me. Were you falsely convicted?"

He laughed bitterly. "Oh, I killed a man right enough. Everyone in the Gilded Rooster that night agreed that it was self-defense, but the fellow I shot was a rich man's son, so justice didn't have a chance."

Her eyes widened and the blood drained from her face until she was pale as a death mask. *"What was the name of the man you killed?"*

"Holden. Billie Holden." He frowned. "Did you know him?"

Looking ill, she buried her face in shaking hands. "He was my husband," she said dully.

Dear God, this lovely girl couldn't have been that brute's wife, he thought with horror. Instinctively, he retreated as far from her as the chain would allow. He would have given everything he had ever possessed to be somewhere else—any place on earth where he wouldn't be causing Billie Holden's widow more pain. "I'm sorry," he said helplessly. "So damned sorry."

She raised her head and regarded him with wide stark eyes. "How did it happen?"

Hesitantly, he said, "It was quick. Your husband didn't suffer any. Beyond that . . ." Kane shook his head miserably. "You don't need to know more than that, Mrs. Holden."

"Liza. My name is Liza." She got to her feet and approached him, eyes dry and implacable. "And I do need to know. All his father said was that Billie had been gunned down in a saloon called the Gilded Rooster, but there's more to it than that, isn't there?" When he still hesitated, she said tensely, "I *must* know, Drew."

He released his breath with a sigh. "Very well. I'd come down into Texas to look over some fancy new stock I'd heard about, and was on my way home when it happened. I stopped for the night in Saline. After dinner, I had a friendly game of poker at the Gilded Rooster with a couple of locals.

"I was about to call it a night when there was a row at the bar. A chap who'd had too much to drink— Holden—took a fancy to a girl. Not one of the regular sporting girls, who'd have been happy to accommodate him, but a little Chinese kitchen maid who'd brought out a tray of clean glasses. Mei-Lin couldn't have been more than fourteen or fifteen. Holden—" He broke off. "Are you *sure* you want to hear this? Only a man who was dead drunk and crazy could even think of looking at another female when he had a wife like you waiting at home."

Grimly she said, "Keep talking."

"Holden wouldn't take no for an answer, and he was scaring Mei-Lin half to death. The other men in the saloon didn't like it, but none of them dared interfere," Kane said. "One of the bar girls, Red Sally, tried to break it up. Even though she looked almost as scared as Mei-Lin, she said she'd be happy to go upstairs with such a fine gent. Holden ignored her. Said he'd never had a Chink, so he was going to have this one. He grabbed Mei-Lin by the wrist and started to drag her away.

"When she began crying, I ambled over and suggested that it might be better to choose a lady of experience. Instead of answering, Holden hauled off and slugged me in the stomach. I went down hard, and the next thing I knew, I was staring at the business end of a Colt.

"As I rolled away, Holden put a bullet into the floor where my head had been. I had a derringer in my pocket, so I shot back before he could try again." Kane fingered the scorched hole in his coat where he had fired through the fabric. "If there had been any warning, I'd have tried to wing him rather than shooting to kill, but it all happened so fast . . ." His voice trailed off.

"If it was self-defense, how come you were convicted?"

His glance was sardonic. "You probably know that your husband was visiting his uncle, Matt Sloan, who pretty much owns Saline. Sloan decided that his nephew had to be avenged, so he sent a posse of his hands after me the next day. I was easy to catch, since I thought I'd been cleared and wasn't trying to hide. When they caught up, they took me back to Saline, where Sloan called a court in the bar of the Gilded Rooster. The saloon owner, who was a crony of Sloan's, sat as judge."

Kane's mouth twisted. "No witnesses were called, and whenever I tried to talk myself, I was ruled out of order—with a fist. I was tried, convicted, and condemned in ten minutes. Sloan sent word of what he'd done to Holden's family. Your father-in-law requested that I be sent to Prairie City so the family could have the pleasure of seeing me hang. Biff and Witless are a couple of Sloan's hands who were deputized to take me back. The hanging must have been organized after you'd gone to bury your father. It should be quite an event." His agonized gaze caught hers. "I wish I could change what happened, but I can't. I'm sorry."

She turned away from him and leaned against the wall, wrapping her arms around herself as if she were freezing. After a long, painful silence, she said, "Don't blame yourself. Billie was a walking calamity. If it hadn't been you, sooner or later someone would have had to kill him." She gave a shuddering sigh. "His parents spoiled him rotten all his life. He was always nice as pie to them, and they thought he could do no wrong."

Knowing that it was none of his business, Kane asked, "Why did you marry him?"

She smiled sadly, her mind in the past. "He could be charming, and of course he was handsome as sin. When he came to Willow Point three years ago, he seemed like every girl's dream come true. My father wasn't so sure, but I was so crazy in love that Papa was afraid I'd run off if he didn't let us get married. And he'd heard of the Holden family, so he knew that I'd be marrying a man who could support me.

"But things started going wrong as soon as Billie took me back to Prairie City. His parents were furious that he'd married a nobody—they'd had hopes of matching him up with the daughter of another big rancher. Still, since the deed was done, they had to accept me. They were civil on the surface, but except for his sister Janie, it was like living in an icebox. Worst of all, Billie changed. Sometimes it was like when we were courting, but more often . . ." Her voice trailed off.

"What was he like then?"

Haltingly she said, "About six months after we married . . ." She stopped, her face white, before finishing in a rush of words. "At a church social, Billie saw me laughing with a neighbor. He pulled me away, and as soon as we got home he went crazy. Claimed I'd betrayed him, then he beat me to within an inch of my life."

She bent her head, tears glinting in her eyes. "I was laid up for a long time. There was no one I could talk to. When I tried to tell his mother what happened, she wouldn't listen. Billie had said I'd fallen down the stairs, and that was that."

Kane swore with suppressed violence. "Where was your husband when you were half-dead from what he'd done?"

"Billie was very apologetic," she said in a brittle voice. "Got down on his knees and begged my forgiveness, swore he'd never hurt me again."

"Did he keep his word?" Kane asked cynically, knowing the answer.

"He never got so crazy again, but whenever he drank, he'd knock me around," she said painfully. "He started taking long trips, supposedly doing business for his father. And . . . and he began seeing other women. He didn't try to hide it from me."

If Billie Holden had been present, Kane would have broken the polecat's neck with his bare hands. "Did you consider leaving him?"

"I did, but . . . well, he was my husband, for better and for worse. Sometimes he wasn't so bad, and I kept thinking that if I tried harder, was a better wife, he wouldn't be the way he was."

"No! Don't blame yourself. Any man who'd treat his wife like he treated you is crazy or evil."

She looked down at her fretfully twisting fingers. "I expect you're right. No matter what I did, it didn't make a difference." Silent tears began flowing down her face. "God help me," she whispered, "when I heard he was dead, my first reaction was relief."

Kane had never been able to stand seeing a lady cry. Without conscious thought, he reached out and stroked her bent head as if she were a hurt child. It wouldn't have surprised him if she had jerked away, but she didn't. Instead, she turned into his arms with a muffled sob.

He held her close while she wept as if her heart was breaking. He wondered when she had last been able to cry. Living in a house where she was despised, with a brutal husband who didn't appreciate the treasure he had married—God, it was enough to convince a man there was no justice in the world.

When her sobs began to diminish, he said quietly, "In time the nightmare will be over, Liza. When you leave the Holden ranch, you'll be able to build a new life—to find the love and happiness you deserve."

She made a choked, hysterical sound. "It will never be over." Her hand went to her abdomen. "I'm pregnant. His parents will never let me go, because they want Billie's child. I'll be trapped in that house until I die."

Kane was silent for a long time. Then he sat down against the wall, bringing her with him and arranging her across his lap so that her head was resting against his shoulder. She was soft, so soft. "It's a bad situation, Liza, but not hopeless," he said as he circled her with his arms. "You don't have to go back to the Holdens. There's plenty of ways a hardworking woman can support herself. And when you're ready to marry again, there will be no shortage of decent men who will treat you right."

"I've thought of all the possibilities," she said bleakly. "I've thought of nothing else. If I didn't go back, or tried to leave with the baby, they'd hunt me down no matter where I went—I'd never have a moment free of worrying when they'd find us. And with his money, sooner or later Mr. Holden *would* find us. He'd never stop until he did."

Kane's arms tightened around her. "You don't have to stay after your confinement. Though it would be a hard, hard thing to do, you could leave and let the baby be raised by its grandparents. Or would they insist that you stay, too?"

"The Holdens wouldn't mind if I left after the baby is born—in fact, they'd be delighted to see the last of me. But how can I let them raise my child? Billie was probably born with a mean streak, but they made him worse." She swallowed hard. "Though it's a terrible thing to admit, I don't even want this baby. I've had a feeling of doom ever since I found out. What if the child turns out like Billie? Even if I'm there, I might not be able to make a difference. Yet I can't abandon my own child—I *can't*."

"Life is harder for good people," he said sadly, unsurprised at her answer.

Liza closed her eyes, her grief ebbing away. Shouting and occasional gunshots rattled in the distance. She hoped the trouble would last all night, because when the town quieted down, Biff Burns would surely return and she would have to leave.

Strange that in the arms of her husband's killer, she was finding peace. Strange, yet it felt utterly right. She couldn't blame Andrew Kane for what had happened in the Gilded Rooster. He was a decent man who'd helped a terrified girl, and was going to pay for his decency with his life. Thinking about it, she realized that she and Drew were both victims of Billie's craziness. Maybe that was why she felt so much kinship with him.

No, it was more than that. Drew was special. She would have thought so under any circumstances. "Thank you for listening," she murmured. "My problems aren't much compared to yours. Your courage sets a good example for me."

There was a harsh edge to his laughter. "You think I have courage? Believe me, it's as fake as a wooden nickel. Though I've faced death before, it's always been a sudden thing, with no time to think. That's not so hard, but having to sit and wait to die . . ."

He inhaled, then said in a rush of words, "I'm scared, Liza. Not only of death, but of having to die in front of a crowd of strangers. I'm terrified that when they take me to the gallows, I'll break down and bawl like a wounded steer, begging for my life like the yellow-bellied coward I am." His voice broke. When he spoke again, it was with hard self-mockery. "Pretty stupid to worry about whether I'm going to die with a proper British stiff upper lip. But with death the only thing left to me, how I do it seems powerfully important."

She raised her head and studied Drew's face. In the dim golden lamplight, the planes of his face seemed unyielding as granite. She guessed that when the time came, he would not disgrace his solid Wiltshire ancestors; instead, he would face death with composure, perhaps even a dry joke. Yet she understood his fear. Merciful heaven, how she understood it.

On impulse, she leaned forward and touched her lips to his, wanting to convey her sympathy, her gratitude, her belief in his courage. After a startled moment, his arms tightened around her waist and he kissed her back, crushing her against the hard angles of his body.

Liza was not surprised by the sweetness, but she was shaken by the fire that flared between them. Even when she was an adoring bride, she had not felt like this. Her mouth opened under his and her head tilted back as she lost herself in the depths of his kiss.

It ended when he lifted his head, saying hoarsely, "It's . . . it's time to stop, darlin'."

She opened her eyes, disoriented by the hammering of her own heart. Or perhaps it was his heart she felt, beating in tandem with hers. "I don't want to stop," she whispered, knowing that what she was suggesting should have been unthinkable. Would have been, before tonight, but the last hour had stripped them both down to raw emotion. She knew that he wanted her, for desire was blazoned across his face. If her body would give him solace, she would give it freely.

More than that, she wanted the closeness of being lovers; she wanted a man's touch to obliterate the failure and pain she had too often experienced in her marriage bed. And, ironically, her unwanted pregnancy meant that she could give herself to Drew without fear of consequences.

"Are you sure?" he asked, a hard pulse beating in his jaw. "You've been hurt too much, Liza. I don't want to add to that."

"You won't." She managed a shaky smile. "I'm

afraid of what lies ahead, Drew, but maybe I'll be able to face it better if I have something happy to remember." She raised her hands and slipped her fingers into his hair. "Let's forget the world outside this room for as long as we can."

Wordlessly he raised his left hand and began tugging the pins from her hair. One by one, the heavy coils fell around her shoulders. "You are so beautiful." He buried his hands in the tangled, silken mass. "As beautiful as life itself." Leaning forward, he pressed his lips to her throat through the shimmering strands.

She inhaled sharply, startled at the sensations that flared through her as Drew's firm, knowing lips drifted up to her ear, then back to her eager mouth. Slowly, as if they had all the time in the world, he laid her back against the floor, improvising a pillow from two empty burlap sacks.

As he lay down beside her, the chain on his wrist rattled against the planks in an unbearably poignant reminder of what the future held. With sudden desperation she drew him into her arms, tugging up his shirttails so she could touch the warm bare skin of his back. The only thing that mattered was now, this precious, fleeting moment. Though the world would judge her wicked, she could not believe that what they were doing was wrong. Yes, Kane was a stranger, a convict who had killed her husband, but their pain made them kin, and the tenderness between them was balm to her bruised soul.

What followed astonished her. Three years she had been married, and she had thought that she knew all about what a man might do to a woman.

But now, as Drew worshiped her with hands and mouth, she discovered what it was to make love. He kissed every sensitive bit of exposed skin—her throat, her palms, the fragile flesh inside her wrists. And as he did, he whispered how lovely she was, how much joy she was giving him.

She wished that they shared the privacy of a bed, with loose garments that might be pushed aside so that flesh could press flesh. That wasn't possible, not when Biff might return and start pounding on the door at any moment. Yet even through the sober layers of her clothing, her breasts came to yearning life when he caressed them.

She tensed when he unbuttoned her drawers and tugged them off. In the past, intimacy had often meant pain, and the taut hunger on his face frightened her a little. But to her surprise he did not immediately mount her. Instead, he pleasured her with slow, expert fingers that created embarrassing amounts of heat and moisture. Only when her hips began to move involuntarily did he unfasten his trousers and lift himself over her.

They came together easily. Not only was there not a hint of pain, but she found that his weight and warmth brought the most profound sense of completion she had ever known. Delighted, she experimentally moved against him.

Her action was like a spark to tinder. He groaned and thrust deeper, and suddenly they were fiercely mating, becoming one with sweet, desperate savagery. Her nails curved into the hard, flexing muscles of his back. There were no words, for none were needed. Until, at the end, her body spun out of her control and she cried out with wonder and joy.

As she did, he groaned and drove into her again and again, with a primal rhythm that shattered them both. When he had nothing left to give, he eased forward, surrounding her with his warmth, resting his face in her hair.

When she could speak, she said with awe, "I didn't know it could be like that for a woman."

"You've never . . . ?"

She shook her head, feeling ridiculously shy. "Never."

Selfishly, he was glad. Though he wished her a happy future with all his heart, he hoped that she would not forget the man with whom she had discovered a woman's passion.

He rolled over and sat back across the sack of flour, then lifted her so that she lay across him, one bare leg between his, her skirts rippling about them. "Thank you, Liza, for a gift beyond price," he said softly. "You've put the heart back in me. Whatever happens in the next few days, I think I'll be able to face it like a man."

Her fingers curled into the ruffles at the throat of his shirt. "I feel the same way. No matter how bad things get in the future, I'll always have tonight to remember," she said tightly. "If only . . ." She stopped, unable to continue.

"Don't say it, sweetheart," he murmured as he stroked her nape with gentle fingers. "Don't even think it. Be glad we're together now. There will be time enough for grief later."

He still didn't quite believe the miracle in his arms. Liza was a lifetime of joy compressed into a handful of minutes. She, who had so little reason to trust, had given herself with brave honesty, and the poignancy of their union was like an arrow in his heart. He wished that he could stop time, with her forever in his embrace.

But that wasn't possible. The din from the riotous

cowboys was fading. How much longer would they have? He offered a fervent mental prayer that Biff would do some drinking in the saloon before remembering that he must release the lady from the convict's cell.

Knowledge that time was running out was like a clock ticking in the back of his brain. Reluctantly he said, "Better put your hair up, Liza. Anyone seeing you would have a pretty fair idea of what you've been up to."

Blushing, she sat up and began combing her fingers through her hair in a doomed attempt to straighten it. "I must look like a saloon girl."

Enjoying her less-than-successful efforts to look prim, he said with a faint smile, "Not at all. You look like a woman who has been well loved."

Her blush deepened, but she didn't avert her eyes.

When she began pinning her hair back, he said, "Liza, I've a favor to ask."

"Anything," she said simply.

"It's a pretty big favor. Someone will have to notify my family of my death. I should write myself, but I can't. Saying, 'By the time you get this, I'll be dead . . .' Well, I've tried again and again in my head, and I can't get it right. Cowardice again." After a long pause, he said painfully, "When I bought the Lazy K, I thought that in a year or so, when the place was fixed up the way I wanted, I'd invite my parents for a visit. I wanted them to see that the prodigal son hadn't gone as thoroughly to hell as they had feared. But it looks like their fears weren't misplaced."

"Where should I send the letter?" she asked, wanting to lift the darkness that had settled on his face.

"Sir Geoffrey Kane and Lady Kane, Westlands, Amesbury, Wiltshire, England," he replied.

After repeating it twice, she said, "Your father's a lord?"

"No, just a baronet. Sort of a jumped-up ranch owner, English-style."

She smiled a little at the irreverent description. "Do you want me to tell them the truth?"

"No!" he said harshly. "Tell them that a horse threw me, or that a fever carried me off. Anything but that I was hanged for murder. No point in their suffering more than necessary."

"Do you have any special messages?"

The muscle jumped in his jaw again. "Just . . . just say that I sent them my love."

With a flash of absolute certainty, she knew that his death would break his parents' hearts, for like the prodigal he called himself, surely he was much loved. "I'll do as you wish," she said quietly, not daring to carry the thought any further. "What will happen to the Lazy K?"

"Lord, I don't know." He rubbed his jaw, the whiskers rasping against his palm. "I haven't wanted to think of it." Abruptly he raised his head and stared at her, his gaze sharpening. "I know—I'll leave it to you."

She gasped and dropped the last hairpin. "You can't mean that. We scarcely know each other!"

He gave her a smile of great sweetness. "I'd say that we know each other rather well."

She blushed again. "When you put it like that . . ." She retrieved the hairpin and stabbed it into the coil at the nape of her neck. "But what would I do with a ranch?"

"More than I'll be able to do," he said with bone-dry humor. "Perhaps it will let you escape the Holdens.

Change your name and they'll never find you there." He began rummaging through his pockets, eventually producing a somewhat grubby piece of paper and a stub of pencil.

"Good thing there isn't anyone who would challenge this," he remarked as he began writing. "Pencil on the back of a hotel bill isn't exactly correct form for a man's last will and testament." He wrote a few lines, folded the paper, and wrote more, then handed it to her. "The foreman, Lou Wilcox, and his wife, Lily, will help you run the place if you decide to live there. They'll need to be notified of my death, too. I wrote their names and the ranch location on the outside."

She accepted the paper gingerly, as if it were about to explode. She wasn't as sure as he that she would be able to elude her in-laws, but she didn't want to extinguish the light in his face. "I . . . I don't know what to say."

"You don't have to say anything." His brow furrowed. "Do you have any money?"

Confused, she said, "A little from my father, but Billie didn't leave much of anything. The money all belongs to his father, Big Bill. Do you need some?"

"Not unless I figure out a way to take it with me between now and Tuesday." The chain on his wrist rattled as he pulled off his right boot, then wrenched off the thick heel. Inside were gold coins packed in raw cotton to prevent clinking.

As Liza watched, bemused, he emptied out the money, replaced the heel, then repeated the process with his left boot. "I've always liked to travel with an emergency stake, in case I run into thieves or a bad run of cards," he explained as he scooped the coins up. Offering them to her, he continued, "You can use this better than I."

She stared at the gold as if it were a nest of scorpions. "I hate the idea of benefiting from your death."

"Personally, I'd like to think that someone will benefit. I sure as hell won't," he said. "I understand your scruples, Liza, but if you decide to leave the Holdens' ranch, you'll need running-away money. Matt Sloan's kangaroo court appropriated the rest of my cash, but this should be enough to take you far and fast if you want to escape."

She couldn't refuse a gesture that was clearly important to him. More than that, it was undeniable that the money might prove useful. She accepted most of the coins, but handed some back. "You may need this for bribes or food or something."

As he pocketed the gold, she added in a low voice, "Thank you, Drew. Your generosity may give me a future."

"I hope so." He gave her a light kiss. "I truly hope so."

He reclined against the flour sack again and drew her down so that she was sprawled on top of him. She relaxed, content to be in his arms.

As she half-dozed, her soft weight a delicious burden, he wondered how much longer would they have.

Not long. Not nearly long enough.

Soon after the night fell ominously silent, he heard heavy footsteps approaching the storeroom. Liza inhaled sharply, then scrambled to her feet, separating them with harsh finality. Cheeks burning, she scooped up the crumpled drawers which she hadn't gotten around to putting on, and jammed them in a pocket. "How do I look?" she hissed as she smoothed down her skirts.

Kane rose more slowly, buttoning his trousers as he

did. "Every inch a lady," he assured her, knowing it was what she wanted to hear. Brushing her cheek with the back of his knuckles, he added softly, "Also every inch a woman."

The key turned in the lock and Biff attempted to open the door, only to be blocked by the bar. "Open up!" he bellowed. "Are you all right, ma'am?"

"She's fine, Burns," Kane called. "Safer in here than out there, by the sound of it."

He and Liza stared at each other. The end had come and there was too much to say to even attempt words. Fiercely, she threw her arms around his neck and gave him a bruising kiss. As he crushed her pliant body to his, he wondered despairingly how he could let her go.

Somehow he managed to do it. When his arms dropped, she stepped away, eyes bright with unshed tears as she whispered, "You will always be in my heart."

Biff roared. "Kane, if you don't open this door, I'll blow it off!"

Turning, Liza bowed her head and pressed her hands to her temples for a moment. Then she straightened and stepped forward to lift the bar. Kane retreated to the back wall, then slouched on the floor as if he had been peacefully dozing.

Accompanied by a haze of whiskey fumes, Biff entered the storeroom, his suspicious gaze going to his prisoner. "Sorry to leave you with this trash for so long, ma'am, but there was trouble and the sheriff needed me and Whittles. Did Kane bother you?"

"Not in the least," she said stiffly. "It was a most uneventful interval."

Kane made a sound that might have been a laugh that was hastily turned into a cough. Then he drawled,

"Make it quick, Biff. A condemned man shouldn't have to have his sleep disturbed by a face like yours."

The deputy scowled and took a step forward, then stopped, remembering that a lady was present. Liza guessed that Drew had deliberately insulted Biff to draw attention away from her. Trying to look casual, she stooped and lifted the tray she had brought, her brain and heart numb. Already the interlude with Drew seemed incredible, dreamlike—but the warmth in his eyes was as true as anything she'd ever seen.

Biff shifted his befuddled gaze to her, and his expression changed. With heavy gallantry that made her nervous, he said, "Lot of purty ladies in the saloon, but none as purty as you, ma'am. Real fine hair." His hand moved vaguely, as if he was considering stroking it.

Kane's voice sliced across the room. "Biff, if you touch the little lady, or upset her in any way whatsoever, I'll find a way to kill you before we reach Prairie City. I swear it."

Biff jerked, sobered by the icy menace in the prisoner's voice. "Didn't do anything," he mumbled. "Come on, ma'am, time you was away from that no-good varmint."

Liza's gaze went to Kane once more. Silently she mouthed, "I love you."

A muscle in his rigid jaw twitched. It was the last thing she saw before she turned and walked away.

Liza had thought her feelings would be too turbulent to permit sleep, but to her surprise, as soon as she went to bed she fell into a profound slumber. The next morning she awoke clear-eyed and refreshed after the best rest she'd had in years.

Her sense of well-being vanished when she remembered the events of the night before. She supposed that she should despise herself for her immorality, but she didn't; guilt didn't have a chance compared to her searing grief at Andrew Kane's fate.

She washed and dressed mechanically, her mind going round and round, torn between memories of Drew and the sick knowledge that he was doomed. Deciding that she felt well enough to face food, she was about to go downstairs for breakfast when she heard the soft jingle of bridles. She went to the window and saw that the skinny deputy, Whittles, had brought around the three horses and Biff was leading the prisoner out of the building.

The night appeared to have helped Drew as much as Liza. No longer worn down by thirst and exhaustion, he walked tall, looking like a lord among peasants in spite of his handcuffs. As she looked down, hoping for a glimpse of his face, she remembered how he had been deprived of water during the long ride.

She would not allow it to happen again. Seizing her own canteen, which she had refilled the evening before, she dashed downstairs, across the lobby, and into the street. All three men were mounted and the party was on the verge of leaving, but she defiantly walked in front of Whittle's horse and handed the canteen to Drew. "It will be a hot day, Mr. Kane. I believe that you need one of these."

He inclined his head. "So I do. Thank you kindly, darlin'." Though his tone was negligent, his gaze was a caress.

Under her breath, so that only Drew could hear, she said, *"Vaya con Dios."* She had often used the words, but never had she known anyone who so much needed to go with God.

Unable to bear the expression in his blue eyes, Liza turned and channeled all her anger at the situation into a furious scowl at Biff. "I trust that your journey to Prairie City will be entirely uneventful, Mr. Burns, and that your prisoner will arrive in the same condition he is now."

Even as the deputy stumblingly reassured her, she turned and went back inside. As the door closed behind her, her stomach turned sickeningly. She barely made it back to her room before she was violently ill in the chamber pot.

She lay down, hoping that her nausea would pass quickly. Inevitably, her thoughts returned to Drew's impending execution. No honest judge or jury would have condemned a man who had killed in self-defense, but Holden money and influence were going to hang an innocent man, and there wasn't a thing Liza could do about it. Even if she got down on her knees to her father-in-law and pleaded for justice, it wouldn't help. Big Bill Holden was not a reasonable man at the best of times, and his grief and rage demanded that someone pay for the death of his son.

The problem was that Drew had not been tried by an honest judge. Federal judges were few and far between, so makeshift courts like the one Matt Sloan convened in the Gilded Rooster were common. Generally such courts did a decent job of determining guilt, but because of Matt Sloan, that hadn't happened in the case of Andrew Kane. If a federal judge was notified, maybe he could overrule what was clearly a miscarriage of justice. The trick would be to find a judge and persuade him to intervene soon enough to make a difference.

Liza caught her breath as she realized that Prairie City was in the same judicial district as Willow Prairie and

Saline—and she was acquainted with the judge. Albert Barker had sometimes stopped by her father's store, and even held court there once or twice. At first she'd been surprised at Judge Barker's mild appearance, for he had a fearsome reputation for upholding the law. Then she'd looked into his implacable gray eyes, and believed everything she'd ever heard about him.

And Barker wasn't just a hanging judge; he believed it was his job to free the innocent as well as to punish the guilty. If he could be reached in time and persuaded to intervene, he might be able to save Drew. A new trial, with witnesses and an honest judge, would surely acquit him. But how could she reach Judge Barker, who spent most of his time traveling and could be anywhere in his far-flung district?

Ignoring her nausea, Liza got up and wrote a letter to Judge Barker, reminding him of their past acquaintance, then relating what Drew had told her of the circumstances of Billie's shooting. After expressing a pious wish that the tragedy of her husband's death not be compounded by hanging an innocent man, she had named the two women whom Drew had mentioned. Perhaps Mei-Lin and Red Sally would have the courage to testify to what happened, even if none of the men who had been present would.

She sealed the letter and addressed it to the judge and had just scrawled URGENT across the envelope when Tom Jackson knocked. Now came the hard part.

She admitted Tom, who had a wide smile on his face. "Morning, Miz Holden. Hope you had a good night's rest. It was purely good to see my cousin Jacob and his family."

He was crossing the room to pick up her baggage

when she said bluntly, "How do you feel about innocent men being hanged?"

His expression went blank and he regarded her warily. "Ma'am?"

"Something bad's going to happen, Mr. Jackson. I don't know if it can be stopped, but I want to try, and I can't do it alone." She wiped her damp palms on her skirt. "You may want to refuse, because Mr. Holden won't like what I have in mind one bit, and if he finds out, it could cost you your job." Then she outlined what she had learned from Andrew Kane. Tom simply listened, his head bowed and expression inscrutable.

When she was done, he said, "You believe this Mr. Kane was telling the truth when he said it was self-defense?"

"I believed him." Her mouth twisted. "You know how Billie could be."

"I surely do. Sometimes I used to wonder how you stood . . ." Tom cut off his sentence.

She smiled humorlessly. "Sometimes I wondered that myself." Falling silent, she waited for his decision.

Tom gazed at his battered hat, turning it around and around in his hands. After carefully pushing out a dent in the crown, he said softly, "My brother was lynched ten years ago in Alabama because someone thought he was an uppity nigger." Raising his head, he looked Liza in the eye, his face set. "So to answer your question, no, I don't hold with hanging innocent men. What do you want me to do?"

"I've written a letter to Judge Barker," she said eagerly. "Do you think you could find out where he is now and take it to him? It will have to be done quickly—the hanging will be Tuesday in Prairie City."

Tom frowned. "I can't leave you alone."

"I'll be fine," she said. "I can stay right here in the hotel."

"Wouldn't be right," he said firmly. "Mr. Holden would have my hide for neglecting you, and rightly so."

Her eyes narrowed. "If I have to, I'll go after the judge myself."

"You can't do that, not in your condition," he said, scandalized. "Don't think I haven't noticed how tired you get riding, even slow as we've been going." He rubbed his chin, considering. "Mebbe my cousin's oldest boy, Jimmy, could go. He's smart, and a good rider."

"Then let's go ask him." Liza tied her bonnet and prepared to go downstairs. "Oh, before we leave, I'll need to stop at the general store and pick up a new canteen. I gave mine away."

Tom gave her a quizzical look that made Liza wonder if he guessed that her interest in Andrew Kane was more than an abstract desire for justice, but he said nothing. As they went outside and headed toward Tom's cousin's blacksmith shop, she gave thanks that she had confided in him.

Jacob Washington proved to be a giant of a man with a booming laugh and massive blacksmith muscles. His wife Molly laughed with equal ease, dispensing food and hugs to her active brood. Jimmy, the oldest, was a tall, slim youth of about eighteen, with steady eyes and a shy smile.

After Tom introduced Liza and said that she had something serious to discuss, she was invited into the family kitchen and the smaller children were chased away. Then, while Molly plied her with fresh cornbread and scalding coffee, Liza went through her story again. The question of whether or not Jimmy would go was never even raised. The youth simply looked at his father and asked, "Has anyone passing through mentioned where Judge Barker is holding court now?"

Jacob rubbed his chin. "East of here, I think. Least he was a couple of weeks ago."

Molly frowned. "He'll have moved on by now, probably to the north. He usually goes that way."

After a discussion of the judge's possible whereabouts, Jimmy glanced at Liza. "I'll be on my way within the hour, ma'am."

She closed her eyes for a moment, so overcome with relief that she was almost dizzy. It was still a long shot that the execution could be stopped, but at least something was being done. She rose and handed the letter to Jimmy, then reached into her pocket and brought out Drew's gold. "You'll need this."

For the first time, Jacob scowled. "We don't accept money for trying to save a man's life."

"Of course not," she said quietly. "This isn't for your help—it's for Jimmy's expenses. There's no telling what he might run into along the way."

After a moment's hesitation, Jacob nodded and Jimmy accepted the handful of coins.

"God bless you, Jimmy," Liza said unevenly, "and be careful traveling."

"I will be, ma'am," he said. "And if Judge Barker can be found in time, I'll find him."

She prayed that he was right. After bidding the Washingtons farewell, she and Tom started back to the hotel. The excitement that came with action faded as they walked the length of Forlorn Hope's dusty main street. She had done everything in her power. Now she could do nothing but wait and see if it was enough.

It would be the easier to wrestle a cougar barehanded.

*   *   *

The last leg of Kane's ride was blessedly uneventful. The fury of a virtuous woman had subdued Biff and Witless; not only did the deputies let Kane keep Liza's canteen, but they gave him some of their food. Still, it was a relief to reach their destination. Kane thought it doubtful that the deputies' improved behavior would have lasted through another day.

The Prairie City sheriff, Bart Simms, proved to be an acquaintance of Kane's. They had met in El Paso a couple of years back, played some poker, shared a few bottles of whiskey, and told each other tall tales. Since then, Simms had grown a drooping, lugubrious mustache and acquired a tin star on his chest. In Kane's jaundiced opinion, the result was not an improvement.

Simms' shaggy brows rose when Kane was brought into the jail, but he said nothing, simply locked the prisoner in the cell in the back room. The two deputies left, with a cheerful promise to Kane that they'd stick around to see him on the gallows.

When they were alone, the sheriff asked, "Did you do it?"

With equal terseness, Kane said, "Self-defense."

Simms chewed his tobacco for a time. At length, he asked, "Then why're you here?"

"Because Billie Holden's uncle owned Saline, and his father owns Prairie City."

The sheriff shot a wad of tobacco juice into a spittoon. "A pity. Billie was a no-good skunk."

"I couldn't agree more." Kane regarded Simms narrowly, wondering if the sheriff's sympathy might extend to being careless enough that a prisoner might escape.

Accurately guessing Kane's thoughts, Simms said, "Sorry about this, but the law's the law."

"The law is an ass."

"Sometimes it is," the sheriff allowed. "But it's my job, and I aim to do it right." He withdrew to the front office.

Kane was unsurprised that the sheriff didn't recognize the quote; Simms wasn't the sort to spend his spare time reading Dickens. Wearily, Kane stretched out on the narrow, lumpy bunk, his hands folded beneath his head.

One of the cracks in the ceiling reminded him of the way Liza's hair fell. Actually, just about everything reminded him of her. With a faint smile, he set about recalling the time they had spent together, from the moment she had roared out of the hotel to stop the deputies from beating him to death, to the heartstopping expression in her gray eyes when they parted.

He couldn't think of a better way to spend the last four days of his life.

The Prairie City jail stayed boring but peaceful until the next morning. Then the door to the back room was thrown open with a force that crashed it into the wall. A heavy-set man stepped through, growling, "So this is the son of a bitch who shot my son."

Jerked out of his daydreams of Liza, it took Kane a moment to react. Big Bill Holden was broad as a barn, with a furious gleam in his small eyes and the face of a man who assumed that getting his own way was divine law. Kane felt a pang for Liza, who had lived under this man's roof for three years, and maybe would be trapped there indefinitely.

The thought made him angry. Instead of standing, Kane stayed sprawled on the bunk, as relaxed as if he were fishing on a riverbank. "So I am," he said in his most infuriating tone. "The little bastard deserved it. You should have taught him not to bully defenseless women. Better yet, you should have told him that if he was going to try to kill a man for no good reason, he should pick someone who wouldn't shoot back."

"You'll pay for that!" Holden roared with a rage that made Kane flinch involuntarily. A good thing that steel bars separated them.

As Holden reached for the Colt holstered on his hip, Kane said cordially, "Go ahead and shoot. The good citizens of Prairie City will be deprived of their show, but I'll be spared three more days of jail food. With luck, you might even be convicted of murdering an unarmed man."

After a precarious pause, Big Bill's hand dropped away from the revolver. Breathing heavily, he said, "I can't wait to see you swing."

"I'm afraid you'll have to, but when the happy moment arrives, I shall try to live up to your expectations. In the meantime"—Kane pulled his black hat from under the bunk and lazily set it over his face—"leave me the bloody hell alone."

After more snarling and threats, Big Bill stormed out.

Kane exhaled slowly and laced his fingers over his midriff. He wasn't sure whether he was glad or sorry that Holden hadn't gunned him down on the spot. It would have been a quick death—better than hanging. But it was against nature to want to die, even though his prospects of survival were nonexistent.

So far, he wasn't doing badly at showing coolness in the face of death. He rather thought that the Kanes in the portrait gallery at Westlands would approve.

*   *   *

By the time she reached the Holden ranch, Liza was so tired that she scarcely had the energy to be depressed. At least there would a clean, quiet bed waiting for her.

After Tom Jackson helped her from her horse, she climbed the wide steps of what Big Bill boasted was the largest mansion between St. Louis and Denver. Perhaps it was; certainly it was the gaudiest. Once inside, she removed her dusty bonnet and rubbed her aching temples. Strange to think that when she married Billie, she'd been excited at the prospect of living in such a fine place.

Alerted by the housekeeper, Adelaide came to greet her daughter-in-law. A beauty in her youth, she was still handsome; Big Bill would never have married a plain woman. "It's about time you got back." Adelaide's assessing gaze swept over Liza. "Have you been taking care of yourself?"

Liza was unsurprised that there were no questions or sympathy about her father's death. "Yes, ma'am. We rode very slowly. Mr. Jackson was most considerate."

"You need some tea as a restorative," Adelaide announced.

"Most of all, I need sleep," Liza said wearily. "If you'll excuse me . . ."

Adelaide raised her hand. "Very well, but before you go, I want to tell you the good news. Billie's murderer has been caught and convicted. Mr. Holden has arranged for the revolting creature to be hanged here on Tuesday."

Unable to conceal her bitterness, Liza said, "Is another death really good news? It won't bring Billie back."

"My son's death must be paid for," Adelaide said grimly. "The Bible says an eye for an eye."

Liza's face tightened. "I hope you don't expect me to watch."

"Of course not," Adelaide said, shocked. "It might mark the baby."

Her status as brood mare firmly established, Liza excused herself and went to the bedroom she had shared with her husband. Yet, in spite of her exhaustion, she halted on the threshold, her stomach twisting. She had vaguely assumed that Mrs. Holden would have packed away Billie's possessions, but everything was still in place, as if he might return any minute. It was just like Adelaide to leave the place as a shrine to her dead son.

Sadly, Liza leaned against the door frame, thinking of the charming young man who had courted her. The charm had been only a small part of Billie, but it had been real, and so had her love. Where had it all gone? Perhaps if she had tried harder. . . .

Quite clearly, she heard Drew's voice in her head: *Don't blame yourself. Any man who'd treat his wife like he treated you is crazy or evil.*

His words were like a splash of cold water on the embers of her guilt. Her back straightened and she turned away. There was no point in brooding. She'd rather think Billie had been crazy, not evil. But in either case, it wasn't her fault. Moreover, she wasn't going to sleep in this room.

With a wintry smile, she headed down the corridor to the guest room. No doubt Adelaide would be happy that the shrine wouldn't be sullied by Liza's unworthy presence.

Dawn slowly lightened the cell. Kane tried to ignore it, preferring to remain in the dream, where a soft, loving female nestled in his arms. Wheat-colored hair, un-

flinching gray eyes, delicious curves. He'd have enjoyed taking off Liza's garments one by one and dis-
covering exactly what was underneath. He'd have liked
waking up in his own bed at the Lazy K with her beside
him. He'd have loved sitting by a fire with her while the
bitter wind whistled off the mountains and snow piled
up around the ranch house.

With a sigh, he pushed the blanket back and sat up,
running his fingers through his hair. There were a hell of
a lot of things he'd have liked to do that he was never
going to get to. He'd always assumed that someday he'd
settle down and marry, have a family. Why hadn't he
done that already? Because he had never met a girl like
Liza—who could be both friend and mistress—until it
was too late.

He felt a piercing sorrow. With youthful arrogance
he'd always assumed that eventually he'd get around to
everything he wanted to do. But today, time ran out.

He drew on his boots with an odd feeling of unreal-
ity. At heart, he couldn't quite believe that he wouldn't
live to see sundown. He felt too alive, too healthy.

It took only an instant for a man to die.

He looked at his hands, glad to see that they were
steady. He hoped that would still be true at noon, when
he was taken to the gallows.

Sheriff Simms ambled in. "Anything special you'd
like for your last meal?"

Kane raised a sardonic brow. "So condemned men
really do get their last request."

"If possible. What's your choice?"

"A woman?"

Amusement gleamed in the sheriff's hazel eyes. "In
Prairie City, last requests only cover food, boy. The

good ladies of the town wouldn't hold with such goings-on in the jail."

Kane shrugged, not having expected any other answer. It didn't matter, since Liza was the only woman he would have wanted. But it wouldn't do to waste a last request. He pondered. Unaccountably his mind leaped back to a hunt breakfast in Wiltshire. "Kippers," he announced. "I want kippers."

Simms blinked. "What the blue hell are kippers?"

"Herring that's been salted and smoked," he explained. "Delicious."

"Mebbe I can find some salted cod," the sheriff said doubtfully.

"Do your best." Kane lay back on his bunk again. "Just make sure there's a bottle of whiskey on the side."

He stared dry-eyed at the ceiling after Simms left. Three more hours.

Fighting a feeling of unwellness, Liza swung her feet from the bed. As she stood, a cramp deep in her abdomen caused her to double over with pain. It passed quickly, leaving her shaky. Probably the pain was because she was so upset. She'd been hoping to hear of a miracle, but the day of Drew's execution had arrived and nothing had changed. Jimmy must not have been successful. *Ah, Drew, I did my best. I'm sorry—so sorry.*

After breakfast, Big Bill and Adelaide set off for town, identical expressions of ugly satisfaction on their faces. Liza was left alone with Janie, her sixteen-year-old sister-in-law. Since Janie had always been overlooked in favor of her brother, the two young women had become allies and friends.

The morning passed with agonized slowness as they sat in the parlor and sewed, making desultory conversation that never touched on the subject that dominated their thoughts.

As noon approached, Janie set her sewing aside and got restlessly to her feet. "I'm glad you didn't want to see the hanging, Liza," she confided. "Gave me an excuse not to go. I don't care if that fellow Kane did kill Billie, I couldn't have stood watching a man die."

Liza stared sightlessly at her embroidery. "On my way back from Willow Point, I heard it said that Kane killed Billie in self-defense."

Janie turned and stared at her, distressed. The girl had her mother's good looks, but a far sweeter nature. "Merciful heaven, that's dreadful if it's true." Her voice quavered. "And Billie being Billie, it could be true, couldn't it?"

"It certainly could." As Liza stuck her needle into the fabric, a sick dizziness engulfed her and the point stabbed into her finger. Confused, she watched her blood stain the white linen with crimson. There seemed to be too much blood.

Janie said sharply, "Liza, are you all right?"

She raised her head and tried to say yes, but she couldn't make her voice work.

The mantel clock began striking with deep, melancholy tones. High noon. At this very moment, Andrew Kane was dying in agony. As the last hollow boom died away, she closed her eyes and shuddered. It was over. Drew was dead.

Knowing that she should lie down, she tried to stand, but her legs wouldn't obey her. She pitched to the floor, a vicious pain clenching her abdomen.

Janie's voice came from a great distance, screaming for the housekeeper. As Liza slid through the pain into darkness, she thought with anguish, *Vaya con Dios,*

Drew—I hope you died the kind of death you wanted. And may God have mercy on your soul.

Simms hadn't found any salted cod, so Kane's last meal was a large steak, pan-fried, with lots of gravy and a mountain of potatoes and onions on the side. Tasted a damned sight better than kippers would have. The bottle of whiskey provided had been aged for at least a month—prime sipping whiskey by local standards. Nonetheless, Drew had only had a couple of shots. While the thought of drinking himself into a stupor had a certain appeal, it seemed foolish to obliterate his last minutes of life. Besides, if he was drunk, he'd be a lot more likely to lose control and disgrace himself.

The noise outside indicated that quite a crowd had gathered. There was even a brass band playing—badly. Drew concentrated on picking out the wrong notes, preferring that to thinking the unthinkable.

All too soon Simms and a deputy with a shotgun entered the back room. The sheriff slid the key into the lock. "It's time."

Drew stood and put on his hat, tilting it forward a little, as if he were going into a poker game with unknown opponents and wanted to look nonchalant. Then he walked out of the cell and stood still while Simms tied his hands behind his back. Gruffly the sheriff said, "Sorry."

"You're just doing your job."

A phalanx of deputies fell in around him as he stepped outside into the fierce noonday sun. Several hundred people had gathered for the show, and their shouts struck him like a bullwhip. As his escorts forced a path through the crowd, Drew studied individual faces. Some were avid, some curious, one or two sympathetic.

Then he saw Big Bill Holden. He and Matt Sloan were standing right in front of the gallows with a well-dressed virago between them. Mrs. Holden, no doubt, and one of the few women present.

Drew inclined his head at her with mocking courtliness just to see the outrage spring into her eyes. But as he climbed the steps to the gallows, he told himself that that was not well-done. Though the woman might be a virago, she had just lost her son, and her pain was as real as anybody's. He hoped she'd be kind to Liza and Liza's child.

The crude planks of the platform creaked under his footsteps, and the death that he hadn't quite believed in became horribly real. Fear pulsed through him, making his heart hammer and his breathing turn rough. Before fear could blaze into panic, he summoned up Liza's image—her quiet courage, her clear gray eyes that made a man feel so much a man.

He swallowed hard. He was damned well not going to die in a way that would make her ashamed of what she had given him.

The crowd was so loud that the hangman had to shout. "Any last words, Kane?"

He had to swallow again before he could reply. "Too much noise to be heard. I'm not going to die with a hoarse throat."

The hangman removed Kane's hat, then dropped the noose around his neck. The rope scratched as the noose was tightened until the knot was snug beneath his left ear. How long now? Less than a minute. Good-bye, Liza. If there's any justice, maybe we'll meet again, when there's more time.

He took a deep breath, trying to take his mind as far away as possible. Thank God his parents need never know how he died.

As the hangman prepared to release the trapdoor, the noise increased still further, with an ugly edge of excitement. Then a rifle fired, cutting through the din like a wire through butter.

In the startled silence that followed, a ferocious voice bellowed, "Hold it right there! This man's not for hanging!"

A babble of excitement rose, and a murmured name that sounded like Parker. Not daring to hope, Kane stared at the eddy in the crowd that was a man fighting his way toward the gallows.

When the newcomer reached the steps, he took them two at a time. He was a short, broad fellow dressed as soberly as a preacher, but he had an air of authority that didn't need the rifle he carried in one hand. Turning to face the crowd, he raised his arms and the noise died down.

"I'm Judge Barker," he boomed in a voice that could quiet the rowdiest courtroom, "and evidence has come to my attention that this man was not properly tried— that he killed Billie Holden in self-defense. I'm here to see that he goes back to Saline and gets a fair trial."

"No!" Furiously Big Bill forced his way to the steps and bounded onto the platform. "Kane's a murderer and the bastard's going to hang right now!"

Unintimidated even though he was half a head shorter, the judge retorted, "I'm the law in these parts, you son of a bitch, and I'm not going to see an innocent man hanged."

Big Bill's hand hovered near his Colt. Then Sheriff Simms climbed onto the platform. "I wouldn't do that,

Mr. Holden," he drawled. "The law's the law. If Kane's guilty, justice will be done in Saline." He glanced at Drew, and one eye closed in a slow wink.

Holden's bravado crumbled into confusion. The judge took advantage of the lull to loosen the noose around Kane's neck, then flip it over his head. "Time to make tracks, young man."

Stunned though he was by events, Kane knew enough to follow Barker off the platform and into the crowd. By sheer force of personality, the judge cleared a path as they moved away. A few disappointed citizens looked inclined to finish what had been started, but no one had the nerve to go against the judge. No one until they came across Biff Burns on the edge of the crowd.

With a growl, Biff grabbed at his former prisoner. His balance hampered by his bound hands, Kane almost fell as he twisted away from the other man's grip. "Biff," he snapped, "I've got just one thing to say to you."

"Yeah?" Biff sneered as he tried again. "What's that?"

Kane pivoted on his left heel and swung his right foot in a ferocious kick that landed where a man would least want it. As Biff shrieked and doubled over, Kane said coolly, "Next time you take someone to jail, show some decent manners."

The judge grabbed his arm and hustled him along. "Now that you've had your fun, boy, get your tail moving."

Two minutes later they reached the livery stable. A slim black youth waited in front with three horses, one of them Drew's. With a flashing smile, he said, "Looks like the judge was in time, Mr. Kane."

"Only just." Barker pulled a razor-edged Bowie knife from a sheath under his coat. "Kane, do you have enough faith in your innocence to give me your word of honor not to try to escape between here and Saline?"

"I do," he said promptly.

"You'd better keep it. Try to run away and I'll slice you into coyote bait myself." The judge circled behind Drew and started sawing at his bonds. It didn't take long to cut through the rope and give Drew the use of his arms again. He rolled his tight shoulders, then swung onto his horse.

Barker did likewise. "Now, gentlemen, we'll be on our way before Holden forgets that he's a law-abiding man."

They wheeled their horses and galloped out of town. After several fast miles, the judge pulled his horse back to a trot. "That should do it."

Still not quite believing that he'd escaped, Drew said, "Don't think I'm not grateful, Judge Barker, but how the devil did you happen to show up at such a propitious moment?"

"You have a young lady to thank for that. Billie Holden's widow had Jimmy here bring me a letter. I figured if the dead man's widow thought you might be innocent, the situation was deserving of my attention."

My God, Liza had done it, Kane thought, amazed. Not only had she given him the happiest hours he'd ever known, but she'd saved his life. Oh, Liza, sweet Liza, will I be able to save you from your captivity? He thought of her sharing a house with Big Bill Holden and the virago, and scowled. When he was cleared of the murder charge, he'd look into that. If she wanted to run away, he'd see that she made her escape safely.

Touching his heels to his horse, he said, "Onward to Saline, gentlemen. The sooner we get this over with, the better."

*   *   *

Liza remembered mercifully few of her nightmares. She knew that Janie was sometimes with her, and other shadowy forms, but when she finally returned to full consciousness, Adelaide was the woman sitting by the bed.

Her voice a thread, Liza asked, "The man who killed Billie—they hanged him?"

Adelaide swallowed hard, a strange expression on her face, then said stiffly, "Yes."

Liza closed her eyes and tears spilled from under her lids. "I . . . I lost the baby, didn't I?"

"You did," Adelaide said, not trying to conceal her bitterness. "But the doctor said *you* would be fine, and there was no reason why you couldn't have children in the future."

"I'm sorry," Liza whispered. She felt empty, too hollow even to grieve.

"So am I." Adelaide stood and gazed at her with hooded eyes. "He should have married a woman who was stronger."

Once again, it was all Liza's fault. Her voice choked, she said, "As soon as I'm able, I'll leave the ranch."

"As Billie's widow, you're entitled to live here as long as you want."

Adelaide would always do her duty, no matter how little she liked it. "You're very generous," Liza said wearily, "but I think it would be best for everyone if I left."

"Yes, it would."

As her mother-in-law turned to leave, Liza said, "You've had two great losses, and I truly grieve for you. But don't forget that you have another child, and she needs you."

Adelaide stopped short. Then, after a half dozen heartbeats, she gave an infinitesimal nod.

Alone again, Liza turned her face into the pillow and let the tears come. She had the freedom she had craved, but at such a price! It was the freedom of absolute aloneness. *Oh, Drew, if only you could be here for five minutes, to hold me in your arms and tell me that someday things would be better than they are now.*

She couldn't have him, but she could go to the home that he had loved. There, perhaps, she could find a measure of peace.

Liza probably should have rested longer after her miscarriage, but the atmosphere at the Holden ranch was unbearable. Neither a wife nor mother, she had no place there, so she left as soon as her strength started to come back. Apart from Adelaide's token offer of a home, no one tried to prevent her from leaving, though Janie shed heartfelt tears.

Just before departing, Liza said a quick good-bye to Tom Jackson. Neither of them referred to the attempt to save Andrew Kane; she couldn't have borne it.

The only possessions she took away from her marriage to a rich man's son were the fine mare that had been Billie's present to her their first Christmas, and as much clothing as would fit into her saddlebags. Dressed like a man, Elizabeth Baird Holden, unsuitable wife, failed brood mare, unfortunate reminder, vanished from the Triple H ranch as if she had never set foot there.

In spite of her fatigue and the emptiness inside her, Liza's bleakness began to lift as she rode north. Though she still wasn't sure she could accept Drew's legacy of the ranch, she looked forward to seeing his home. There

she would write the letter to his parents that she had
been delaying.

Mentally she had tried again and again to compose
the letter, and the task was proving as hard for her as
it had been for Drew. How should she start? *Dear Sir
Geoffrey and Lady Kane, your son is dead. He was a
gambler and maybe a bit of a rogue, and the kindest
man I ever met. He left a ranch that he loved. It should
go to you, but since you probably won't come to Colorado, maybe I'll keep it myself and try to run it as he
would have liked.*

With a sigh, she put the project aside. She'd worry
about it when she got to Colorado.

Even though Liza had been pretty sure that her fast,
grain-fed mare could outrun trouble, she fortunately
didn't have to prove it. She took the long ride in easy
stages, and by the time she reached Pueblo, she was almost her old self, at least physically. An inquiry at the
general store gave her directions to the Lazy K, and she
headed up into the hills.

When she reached the top of the last ridge and gazed
down into the valley, she saw that Drew had told the
truth: it really was the most beautiful place on God's
earth, with spectacular mountains above and greenery
marking the path of a swift creek. So this was the place
that had changed Drew from a ramblin', gamblin' man
to a landowner like his stuffy ancestors. She smiled.
Maybe some of those ancestral Kanes were less respectable than they had appeared in their portraits.
She'd like to think so.

She rode into the valley slowly, feeling as if she was
completing a pilgrimage. The long, low ranch house
was built of stone, so it would be cool in the summer

and stand firm against the winds of winter. As she approached it, she saw a stocky middle-aged man coming from a smaller building to the left. Guessing that it was the foreman, Lou Wilcox, she squared her shoulders and prepared to deliver the bad news.

Kane's second trial at the Gilded Rooster lasted considerably longer than the first. Led by Red Sally and the halting, accented words of Mei-Lin, the parade of witnesses attesting to his innocence was a long one. Cynically, Kane ascribed the testimony of the men to the fact that Matt Sloan was still out of town. The women, he guessed, would have testified at the first trial if they'd been allowed to.

After the last witness had spoken, Judge Barker banged his gavel on the bar. "A clear case of self-defense. Mr. Kane, you are acquitted of all charges."

Kane checked the coins in his pocket, calculating how much he'd need to get back to Colorado. A good thing Liza had suggested he keep some of the money. Taking out what he could spare, he slapped the gold coins on the bar. "Ladies and gentlemen, in honor of the fact that justice has been served, the drinks are on me until this runs out."

A cheer went up. The saloon owner, the very man who had presided over the first trial, shrugged and started setting out bottles and glasses. Business was business.

Drew picked up a bottle and two glasses and made his way to the judge. "Thanks again, Judge Barker. You're a credit to the federal judiciary." He poured two drinks and handed one over.

Being off duty, Barker beamed and accepted the whiskey. "A pleasure, my boy. I never could stand Matt

Sloan or Big Bill Holden—the bastards think they're above the law." He raised the glass and drained it in one swallow. "And I got a bonus out of your case. That Jimmy's a clever lad. He's going to be my clerk and read law with me."

"Excellent." Drew emptied his glass, then set it on the bar. "Give him my best wishes. Now I'm going home."

The judge peered over his spectacles. "I suggest that if you're riding north, you give Prairie City a wide berth."

Drew nodded, accepting the wisdom of the advice. He'd have to wait until he got back to the Lazy K before trying to find out how Liza was. He'd send someone to make discreet inquiries, since showing his own face in Prairie City would be distinctly unhealthy, and not just for him. It wouldn't do for Liza to be seen communicating with him, and the last thing he wanted was to cause her trouble.

As he collected his horse at the livery stable and turned its head north, he gave serious thought to the question of what it would be like to raise Billie Holden's child. Liza would be the mother, so the kid couldn't be all bad. Likely Kane and Liza would have children, too. He hoped so; his close brush with death made him want a family as he never had before.

Such thoughts helped the long miles pass more quickly.

Summer was almost over and fall was on its way. The nights were cold at this elevation, and as Liza lay sleepless, she could hear the dry rustle of the first fallen leaves.

She'd been at the Lazy K for a week, long enough to

fall in love with it. Even though she had never seen Drew here, his books and clothes and occasionally whimsical possessions created a vivid sense of his personality. And his bed—it was all too easy to imagine him in his bed. That's why she was having trouble sleeping. Strange how a man whom she had known for such a short time could have imprinted her soul so thoroughly. She wondered whether the tragic circumstances of his death meant that he would become a ghost and haunt the living. If so, his ghost would be welcome here any time.

Since she couldn't explain the exact nature of their relationship, she had told Lou and Lily Wilcox that she and Drew had been planning to marry, and that was why he'd left her the ranch. They had never questioned her story. As soon as he had seen the crude will on the back of the hotel bill, Lou said that he'd recognize that fancy English handwriting anywhere.

As Drew had promised, Lou and Lily did everything they could to help her learn about the ranch. The Lazy K was a well-run spread, larger and more prosperous than she had expected. His parents would have been impressed if they had ever visited.

Liza's eyes began to sting, and she blinked rapidly. With a sigh, she swung her feet from the bed to the bright Indian rug that warmed the floor. She couldn't put it off any longer—she really must write Drew's parents, and she might as well do it now since she was already in a weepy mood.

It was too chilly to sit up in her shift, so she donned a robe of Drew's. It was black velvet with flamboyant scarlet and gold trim, exactly what she would have expected a successful gambler to wear. Though she suspected that it was not entirely wise to take such pleasure

in wearing his clothing, she loved the feel of the robe,
and the faint, masculine scent that was uniquely his.

Sadly she slipped on a pair of warm wool socks, then
padded into the study to write the most difficult letter of
her life.

A smart man would have spent the night in Pueblo,
but then, a smart man would have stayed in England and
become a solicitor. Taking advantage of the full moon,
Kane pushed on through the night. He was too close to
home to be satisfied with anything less, even though he
was aching with fatigue from the hard riding he'd done.

It was well past midnight when he reached the Lazy
K. He took his horse into the stables quietly, not wanting to wake anyone. Greetings could wait until morning.
After bedding his horse down for the night, he crossed
the yard to the house, drinking in the familiar scene. The
moonlit mountains and valley were even more beautiful
than he remembered.

The front door was unlocked, which didn't surprise
him, but a faint glow of lamplight did. Since the
Wilcoxes had their own house, his place should be
empty.

Curiously he followed the light to the study. Then he
stopped in astonishment in the doorway, wondering if
his imagination was betraying him because he had
thought of Liza so often. But he'd never thought of
putting her in his own black velvet robe, which fit her
slim frame like socks would a rooster.

His shock was nothing compared to hers. She had
been frowning over a letter, her face deliciously intent,
but she glanced up when he came to the door. With a
horrified gasp, she dropped her pen, black ink spraying
across the paper. Her face went dead white.

They stared at each other for what seemed like forever. In his dreams, Drew had assumed that if—when—they met again, they would go straight into each other's arms. Instead, he was painfully aware that in many ways they were strangers. With a crooked smile, he said, "I know that I've been wearing the same clothes for a month, but surely I don't look that frightening."

Disbelieving, she got up and walked toward him, the hem of his robe trailing across the carpet. "Drew," she whispered. "Is it really you? Not a ghost?"

He began to laugh, and as soon as she came within his reach he caught her in his arms and pulled her close. "What do you think?"

She began shaking. "M-Mrs. Holden said that you had been hanged."

With a happy sigh, Drew leaned against the door frame and rested his chin on her head. She felt even better than he remembered, probably because she was wearing a lot less clothing. "The lady should have known better. She had a front-row view when Judge Barker stomped up and said that he was going to take me back to Saline for a new trial."

Liza's head shot up, her gray eyes wide. "Then it worked—Jimmy Washington found the judge in time?"

"That he did, though he and the judge cut it pretty close." Drew made a rueful face. "Even two minutes longer and it would have been too late. Scared me out of five years' growth."

Liza's brows drew together as she thought back. "Mrs. Holden looked odd when I asked her if the execution had taken place. She must have assumed that I wanted Billie's killer dead, and since I was ill, she told me what she thought I wanted to hear. Probably the one and only time she tried to be considerate to me. And

Tom Jackson must have thought that I knew what had really happened." She gave a choked giggle. "I was sitting here trying to write the letter to your parents that you asked me to send. Lucky I was so slow."

"I'm glad to hear that," he said wholeheartedly. "But you say you were ill?" With a frown, he put his hands on her shoulders and studied her critically. "You do look a bit peaked. What happened?"

Her gaze dropped to the limp ruffles of his shirt. "I—I lost the baby."

He wrapped his arms around her again and began rocking her gently. "Oh, Liza, sweetheart. You lost so much, so quickly. That must have hurt dreadfully even though you were unhappy about the prospect of having to stay with the Holdens."

She began to cry, his sympathy causing all of her sorrows of the last weeks to pour out uncontrollably. Only when her tears began to subside did she realize the strangeness of the situation. Breaking away from his embrace, she said shyly, "It must look odd to you, me acting as if I own the place."

He smiled and took off his hat, then skimmed it onto a chair with a flick of the wrist. "Well, you thought you did. And that robe looks better on you than it ever did on me."

Self-consciously she drew the velvet panels together, because the shift she wore underneath was very thin. "I'll get out of your way tomorrow."

He straightened, his humor dropping away. "Why would you do a silly thing like that? Where would you go? It would make a lot more sense for you to stay here." His voice softened. "I'd like it if you did. Time I married and settled down and became respectable."

Her mouth dropped open. "How can you talk about

marriage? We hardly know each other. My husband has been dead only a few weeks."

"And I killed him," Drew said flatly. "Is that an impassable obstacle?"

"I'm not blaming you for that," she said in a frantic bid for sense. "But there's plenty of other reasons not to marry."

"Such as?" He studied her face, his expression sardonic. "I think I understand. It was one thing to have a quick tumble when we were strangers in the night, both feeling desperate and lonesome, but that doesn't mean I'm good husband material. Mad, bad, and dangerous to know. A lady smart as you could certainly do better."

"You've got it backward!" she said, outraged. "You're a rich, handsome man with a ranch and a fancy pedigree. What would you want with a penniless widow whom you've only known for a few hours?" She blushed furiously. "A woman who behaved in a manner that must have given you an extremely low opinion of her morals."

His tension eased and he smiled, with devastating effect. "The way you behaved gave me an extremely *high* opinion of you. You're brave, lovely, and kind, and you saved my life." He reached out and began playing with her hair. "You're a dangerous woman, Liza. Not only have you got me roped and tied, but I can't wait to be branded."

She shivered as he stroked the lobe of her ear. "You don't have to marry me because you're grateful for what I did, or because you feel guilty about shooting Billie."

"Neither guilt nor gratitude come into it." With his dark tousled hair and rogue's charm, he looked like every mother's nightmare, and every girl's dream.

"What did you tell Lou and Lily when you turned up here?"

"The truth, except that"—she hesitated—"well, I said that you and I were engaged to be married and that was why you left me the ranch. It was the simplest explanation."

"Splendid!" he said enthusiastically. "That means if you try to run away, I can sue you for breach of promise."

She glared at him. "This is not a joke. Just because we—we helped each other when we were at the end of our tethers doesn't mean there should be anything more between us."

His fingers skimmed down her throat, warm and sensual. "Is that all that was between us, Liza—a little shared misery?"

Why did his delicious English accent have to make her bones feel like butter? Her pulse was pounding and she was having trouble thinking. "It . . . it meant a lot more to me."

"It was more than just a night to me, too," he said pensively. "I think I would have fallen in love with you under any circumstances, but since we had so little time, it happened in an instant. To me, it felt as if we skipped right over the usual courtship and went directly heart to heart."

His hand curved behind her neck and a gentle pressure urged her closer. "You and I have both suffered some terrible things in the last few weeks. You lost a husband, a father, a child. I killed a man, which I'd never had to do before, and almost lost my life." He tilted her chin up. "The only good thing that happened was our meeting. Don't we have an obligation to take that seed of goodness and help it grow into something that's even better?" He bent his head, and his lips met hers.

His kiss was everything she remembered, and more, a promise of both passion and protection. She leaned into his embrace, loving the feel of his warm, muscular body. "Oh, Drew, I'm not very good at being noble. If you aren't careful, you'll be stuck with me for life."

He gave a gusty sigh of satisfaction. "Now there's a life sentence I can live with." Circling her shoulders with one arm, he turned her and guided her down the hall toward the bedroom. "If necessary, we can continue this discussion in the morning, but at the moment, I would dearly like to go to bed." He cocked a mischievous eye at her. "Preferably with you."

When she halted in midstride, he said hastily, "Just to sleep. I imagine that after what happened, you're not ready for anything more." His voice became intense. "But, Lord, I'd like so much to spend the night with you in my arms, and wake up and find you there."

In a flash of pure knowing, the last of Liza's doubts vanished. Maybe they had started their relationship in the middle, rather than the beginning, but that didn't make this any less right.

"I'd like that, too." She slipped her arms around his neck. "Did I mention that I love you?"

For a suspended moment, there was silence. Then he said quietly, "The feeling is entirely mutual."

This time she started the kissing, losing track of time and place in a rush of joyous emotion. Vaguely she became aware that they were wrapped around each other like squash vines, her back was flat against the wall of the corridor, and the velvet robe had fallen around their feet.

Lifting his head, he said hoarsely, "We're not making much progress toward that bedroom."

She laughed and started unbuttoning his dilapidated shirt. "I'm feeling fit as a fiddle. We could see how it would go. Of course, if you're too tired. . . ." Her voice trailed off provocatively.

"Not that tired." He swooped her up in his arms and carried her, laughing, to the bedroom where he deposited her gently on the bed. Then he bent over her, his arms braced on either side of her head. "A good thing you didn't manage that letter to my parents. Now when I write, it will be good news instead of bad." He kissed the tip of her nose. "Won't it?"

She slid her arms around his neck and pulled him down beside her. "The best, my dangerous man. The very best."

The Antagonists
by Joan Wolf

One of the greatest misfortunes that can befall a young man in his formative years is for him to become an earl. Perhaps there are some tempers that would not be spoiled by such an experience, but when the young man is a top-lofty boor to begin with, the addition of an earldom can be fatal.

This is what happened to Hugh Lesley St. John Lydin, sixth Viscount Coleford and fifth Earl of Thornton. I shall tell you about it.

When his heir was but sixteen, the fourth Earl of Thornton was killed in a hunting accident. The earl's death left his son, then Viscount Coleford, and his daughter, Caroline, as the sole family inhabitants of Thornton Manor, the Lydin estate in Derby. The death of his father also transformed Hugh from Viscount Coleford into the fifth Earl of Thornton.

Shortly after the fourth earl's death, the entire Lydin family held a meeting in order to decide what was to be done about the orphans, as the countess, unfortunately, had died at Caroline's birth. My mother was one of those summoned to attend this meeting, and before she left she explained to me that the official guardian and trustee for the new earl and Caroline was their uncle, the Honorable George Lydin. My mother further explained that although the Honorable George was will-

ing to see to the business aspects of the Thornton fortune and property, he did not desire to move his trunks
to Derby. It seems that George Lydin was accustomed
to spending most of his time in London, where he was
a member of the government.

The purpose of the family meeting was to find someone to live at Thornton and be a mother to Caroline.
The family was not so concerned about the new earl,
my mother said. He was away at school for most of the
year. It was Caroline who needed a mother, and the
mother the family eventually came up with was mine.

Mother, unfortunately, is a widow. Also unfortunately, she is not very plump in the pocket. The opportunity to live at one of the country's greatest estates was
too tempting for her to resist, and almost before I knew
what was happening, I found myself being driven up a
seemingly endless graveled drive on my way to meet
the cousin my mother insisted on referring to as "darling Caroline."

It seems that "darling Caroline" was just my age,
eleven, and, owing to this stupid coincidence, the entire
family had assumed that the two of us were bound to
become bosom friends. Which just goes to show you
how amazingly idiotic adults can sometimes be.

Though I would have died before admitting it out
loud, I was very impressed by my first view of Thornton Manor. The house is *enormous*. Mother and I had
been living in a small cottage in Wiltshire, and the sight
of the great stone mansion, with all its hundreds of windows sparkling in the sun, did truly inspire awe.

I suppose I ought to say here, in case you are interested in that sort of thing, that Thornton Manor is a rel-
atively new house, built by the present earl's
grandfather in what my governess, Miss Lacy, calls the

Paladian style of architecture. Also according to my governess, "It is classically proportioned, with a central part that is three stories high flanked by matching wings at either end. The rows of identical windows are punctuated by a pattern of pillars and pilasters, which stand in graceful contrast to the smooth pale stone of the building."

Such a mouthful of words to say that it is an excessively lovely house!

"Are we actually going to live here?" I breathed, staring out the window of the coach. The coach, I might add, belonged to the earl, had been sent to transport us in comfort and style, and was exceedingly elegant. I had been afraid to put my feet up on the squabs the whole day.

"Yes, Dinah, we are." Even my mother's voice sounded hushed. We are not noble folk ourselves, and are not accustomed to such grandeur. Mother always said that her cousin, the one who had married the fourth earl and had so inconveniently died when Caroline was born, had stepped considerably above herself with the match. My own father had been a simple army officer, of good though not noble birth. I had always thought Papa was noble in every other way, however. And he was brave. He had been killed in the Peninsula two years before, and I still missed him.

As the carriage pulled up before the steps of the house, the great door opened and a liveried servant, of scary-looking dignity, descended the stairs. Lackeys scurried to open the coach door and put up the wooden stairs. Mother and I got out.

My mother is rarely frightened by this sort of thing. She was not nobly born, true, but she has gone through life with one very useful advantage. She is beautiful.

"Mrs. Stratton," the majordomo said deeply. He bowed. "Welcome to Thornton Manor."

My mother smiled. "Thank you, Edwards."

I stared at her in surprise. How had she known the man's name was Edwards?

My mother returned my look and frowned slightly. "This is Miss Dinah," she said.

The powdered head inclined my way. I almost curtsied, he was so dignified. Then I had to suppress a grin at the thought of what kind of an impression that would have made!

We proceeded up the stairs and into the front hall. Coming down the stairs as we entered was a young girl who looked to be about my age. She had long blond hair and large blue eyes and was dressed in an immaculate white frock.

Caroline, I thought. Darling Caroline.

"How do you do, Aunt Cecelia," a softly pretty voice was saying. "I am so happy you have come to live with me."

"Darling Caroline," my mother said. "My dearest child. How good it is to see you again."

Mother and Caroline had met before, though this was my first introduction to my new little friend.

"See whom I have brought," Mother was going on. She was using her warmest voice. I thought she sounded like a pigeon cooing. "A new friend for you. My daughter, Dinah."

Dutifully I stepped forward. Politely I murmured, "How do you do."

"I am so happy you have come," Caroline said, and smiled as if she meant it.

I gave her a half-grin in return. Then, getting right to the heart of things, I asked, "Do you like dogs?"

"Yes," Caroline said.

I turned to my mother. "Then we can send for Sergeant, Mother. I *told* you Caroline was sure to like dogs."

"Is Sergeant your dog?" Caroline asked. "Of course you must send for him. You must miss him terribly."

As I had been parted from him for only a day, I had scarcely had time to miss him terribly. But I appreciated the thought and allowed my grin to widen a little. "He's a wonderful ratter," I volunteered.

Caroline's celestial-blue eyes widened.

"That is quite enough about that wretched animal, Dinah," my mother said briskly. "Darling Caroline, would you be kind enough to show us to our rooms?"

I am happy to be able to report that none of my worst fears about the move to Thornton Manor came true. Caroline turned out to be a very pleasant girl, and I did not at all mind sharing my time or my mother with her. We had a governess whom we had lessons with every morning. The lessons were very dull. At home I had studied with our old rector, who was much cheaper than a governess, and he had given me books you could actually think about. Miss Lacy liked to skim over the surface of things, and every time I asked her *why,* she got flustered and told me to look it up.

I discovered that there was a splendid library at Thornton, and I soon got into the way of bringing my own books to our lessons. I think Miss Lacy was relieved not to have me asking questions anymore.

But by far the best thing of all about Thornton was the stables. The last earl had been a keen hunter, and the stables were filled with beautiful, well-conditioned horses. I had adored horses all my life, and when Papa was alive he had always made certain I had a pony. He was a great horseman himself, even though he was not in the cavalry. It costs a great deal of money to be in the cavalry, you see, and so unfortunately Papa had been forced to settle for the infantry. But he had taught me to ride when I was three years old, and I had had my own pony until Papa died. Mother could not afford to keep a pony for me on her widow's pittance, and I had been horseless for the last two years.

Caroline had two lovely ponies, and she let me ride one. The only drawback to this otherwise splendid arrangement was that I had to go out riding with Caroline, whose speed in going cross-country was far slower than what I liked. I soon found a remedy for that particular problem, however. I got up at five in the morning and rode out with the stable lads, who were exercising the earl's big hunters. Lucky, my pony, loved it, and would tear along on his sturdy little legs beside the big horses, blowing through his nose in sheer delight.

I think I was happy for the first time since my Papa died. And then summer came, and the new earl came home from Eton.

For as long as I live I shall remember my first view of the fifth Earl of Thornton. The entire staff had lined up on the front steps to greet the new master. I thought privately that it was a silly way to greet a sixteen-year-old, no matter what his title, but I kept my thoughts to myself. Mother, Caroline, and I were poised by the front door, waiting to offer our own welcome. News had come to the house five minutes before that the earl's coach had been sighted on the main road, and the notice had given us time to get into position.

We waited. Finally, through the trees on the lower

half of the drive, I could see the horses. Then the coach was out onto the open drive, and in a minute it had come to rest before the front stair. Edwards descended to greet his master. The door to the coach opened, the wooden coach stairs were set, and finally the earl came out.

The first thing I noticed about him, the first thing I think anyone would notice about him, was the fairness of his hair. It was purely flaxen, a color rarely seen on anyone older than six or seven years old. He was tall and slim, and the smile he turned upon Edwards was just beautiful.

I thought he looked like an angel.

Which only goes to show that appearances are not to be trusted.

A husky brown-haired boy was getting out of the coach next. The earl had written to my mother that he would be bringing a friend home with him for part of the summer holiday, and this, obviously, was the friend. The two boys started up the stairs.

The servants were all bobbing curtsies and bows and the earl grinned and tossed a word here and there to faces he recognized. Then he was standing before us.

"Aunt Cecelia. How lovely to see you." And he gave Mother that beautiful smile. His eyes were a very clear, very brilliant blue.

Mother smiled back. "Thank you, Thornton," she said in her prettiest voice.

Caroline pushed forward and reached up her arms. He stooped to give her a brisk, businesslike hug. He said something into her ear that made her laugh. Then he looked at me.

The blue eyes widened as he took in my hair. "What a fiery head!" he said. Then, "You must be little

Dinah." And he gave me the most top-lofty, the most patronizing smile I had ever received in all my life.

I stared up into his face. My palm itched to smash across one of its hard cheekbones. I *hate* to be teased about the color of my hair. Nor do I appreciate being called "little."

"I am Dinah," I said. "And I am not little. I am just the right size for my age. And it's rude to comment on the color of a person's hair."

"Dinah!" My mother was appalled. "Apologize to Thornton at once."

I gritted my teeth.

"It's quite all right, Aunt," said that top-lofty voice. "Perhaps she will learn some manners by the time she turns twelve."

You didn't. But I kept the thought to myself.

"Dinah is very sensitive about her hair, Cole," Caroline said. Then, in confusion, "Oh dear, I suppose I can't call you Cole anymore."

"No, he is 'Thorn' now, Lady Caroline," said the earl's friend, whom he had introduced to my mother as Mr. Robert Merrow. "It took us a few weeks to grow accustomed to it at school, but it seems quite natural now."

Caroline said, in a puzzled voice, "No one ever called Papa 'Thorn.'"

A strange look came across her brother's face. "No one ever called Papa anything other than 'my lord.'"

"That is true," my mother said. "He was a most aristocratic man. Shall we go into the house, Thornton? You will like to show Mr. Merrow where he is to stay."

I arrived at the stables early the following morning, ready to ride out with the hunters as usual. I was surprised, and not pleased, to find Thornton there before me.

"Dinah!" he said, staring at me in surprise. "What are you doing here?"

"I come every morning to ride exercise with the stable lads," I answered. I took care to speak politely. I was rather afraid that I had been rude the day before, and I was determined not to put myself in the wrong again.

"*You?*"

That top-lofty look was back on his face. My palm itched.

"Yes, I," I replied with great dignity. Imitating Edwards, I raised my chin and gazed off into the distance. "The lads don't mind, and it is good for Lucky to stretch his legs. We don't go above a slow canter when I ride with your sister."

"Caroline is chickenhearted," her brother agreed. "She took a bad fall a few years ago and was laid up in bed for three months. She's been afraid to ride ever since."

"Considering that your father was killed by a fall from a horse, perhaps she has cause for her fear," I snapped.

His eyes widened with surprise. I had a sudden suspicion that very few people ever snapped at Thornton.

I resumed my gaze off into the distance. He said, "That expression you're wearing makes you look just like Edwards."

I could feel myself flushing with annoyance. My skin is very pale and has an irritating habit of revealing feelings I would much prefer to keep hidden. I glared at him and caught him staring at my legs. "What," he asked with greatly exaggerated astonishment, "is that suit you're wearing?"

To my fury, I could feel the blood rush once more to my cheeks. "It is not a suit!" I gritted through my teeth. "It is a riding costume." I followed his eyes and looked down at my person. I was wearing boy's breeches, actually. My mother would have swooned if she knew. When I rode with Caroline I wore the habit my mother had had made for me when we came to live at Thornton Manor.

"Good God," Thorn said, his eyes swinging next to a spot beyond my shoulder. "What is that?"

It was Sergeant, who had been visiting in the paddock and had now come to join me for our morning ride.

Sergeant was a large dog. In fact, he was not a great deal smaller than Lucky. And, to be truthful, I suppose he was rather homely. *I* thought he was beautiful, but I loved him. Upon first glance, I had to admit that he was not . . . ah, taking.

"This is my dog," I told the earl. I fondled the too-large brown ears. "His name is Sergeant."

"What a dreadful-looking creature," Thorn said, and snapped his fingers. Sergeant, the fool, went immediately to have his ears scratched.

The head groom came up to us. "The horses are ready, my lord," he said. "And Lucky is ready for you, Miss Dinah."

"Does this baby really ride out with the hunters?" Thorn asked insultingly.

"Every morning, my lord." The head groom's name was John, and he was one of my particular friends. "She's a neck-or-nothing rider, my lord. Just like you was at that age, if I may say so."

My cousin and I looked at each other, equally re-
volted by the comparison. "She's a girl," Thorn said,
curling his lip.

"I can ride every bit as well as you can," I shot back.
"Even if you are five years older."

"Ha." We eyed each other. "We shall see about that,"
Thorn said.

"Now, my lord," John said placatingly. "Let's not
have any accidents."

"Accidents?" Thorn raised fine golden eyebrows.
"How could we possibly have an accident? Miss Dinah
rides like a centaur. She just told me so herself. And
you agreed."

My papa had told me about centaurs. "I ride better
than a centaur," I said.

We glared at each other. Then he gave me a very
nasty grin. "Come along, Red," he said, "and we shall
see."

I followed his back toward the paddock, inwardly
vowing to show him even if it killed me.

It almost did. In my zeal to show off my horseman-
ship, I put Lucky at a fence that was too high for him.
As was to be expected under the circumstances, we
came to grief. I collected some notable bruises and
sprained my ankle. Lucky, thank God, was all right.

The only bright light in the morning was that Thorn
got into trouble with John, who told the earl he had
"provoked" me into it. He had, of course, and the reprimand was fully justified. Thorn was absolutely furious at being in the wrong. Typically, however, he was
not furious with himself, but with me. Over the years,
one thing I was to learn about Thorn: he never, ever
thought he was in the wrong. And he usually was, even
though he always tried to put the blame on me.

*   *   *

The years went by. Thorn left Eton and went to Cambridge, where he did odiously well. During the holidays he would return to Thornton Manor and let my mother and Caroline feast upon his meretricious charm. Very often he would bring a friend with him. His friends were usually quite nice, although they all had an unfortunate tendency to fawn upon Thorn. Of course, he was an earl, and, according to my mother, very rich.

To give his friends their due, however, I don't think it was entirely Thorn's title or his wealth that impressed them and made them worship him in the most odious way. Thorn never suffered from any of the usual trials that beset adolescent boys. His complexion was never marred by a spot; he grew evenly and gracefully, with none of the awkwardness that marked so many other boys; he could ride and shoot and wrestle better than anyone else at school. All these things impressed his friends, and they deferred to him in the most revolting manner.

The fact of the matter is, everyone around Thorn spoiled him to death. He was so accustomed to being toad-eaten that when he met up with someone who was not inclined to worship at his shrine, he became insufferable.

I hated to argue with him. He had an unfair advantage, having been to Eton and Cambridge and having learned all sorts of things I knew nothing of. It made me livid to have him quote Latin at me. He knew that, of course, and used to quote it at me all the time.

And he called me Red.

Let us get one thing perfectly clear. My hair is not red. It is strawberry blond. When I was little, Papa would call it red-gold, but when I grew older he was forced to admit that it was really strawberry blond. My mother said it was strawberry blond. Caroline said it was strawberry blond. Only Thorn insisted that it was red, and he did it simply because he knew it annoyed me.

Despite Thorn's holiday visits, however, I found the years I spent at Thornton Manor exceedingly pleasant. Caroline and I had scarcely a thought in common, and yet, despite our differences, we liked each other very well. Perhaps it was our very differences that kept us such good friends. We did not tread on each other's toes.

Caroline was talented musically, and she also had a gift for drawing. Neither of these subjects interested me in the slightest. I did like learning a new language, however, and it was not long before I could speak French and Italian as well as Miss Lacy. I was certain that I could learn to speak both languages even better than she, but there was no one to teach me. Until, that is, Mother brought in the Italian dancing master.

His name was Signore Montelli. He came in the autumn of the year that Caroline and I were to make our come-outs. The come-out was actually to be in the spring, but Mother wanted us to attend some local parties over the winter—to acquire some "polish," she said. And so the dancing master came to Thornton Manor.

That was the same year that Thorn came down from Cambridge, the year that he turned twenty-one and officially entered into his inheritance. No longer would Uncle George have to approve anything Thorn might wish to do. He was his own master now, Mother said. She also said that I ought to be nicer to Thorn, that he could turn me out of the house if ever he decided he wanted to be rid of me. And turn her out too!

The scene she painted was quite pitiful. Where would we go? How would we live? My beautiful come-out (which Thorn was going to pay for) would be lost. No more horses. I should have to become a governess like Miss Lacy, and Mother would probably end up in the workhouse.

I didn't believe a word of it. Thorn would never put himself so far in the wrong as to turn a widow and her child out of his house. I knew him too well. Such a gesture would not accord at all with his sublime picture of his own nobility. Mother was perfectly safe.

When I explained all this to her, all she did was give me an exasperated look and totter off to pour out her troubles to the housekeeper.

To return to the Italian dancing master. He arrived at Thornton Manor in September to teach Caroline and me the intricacies of the various dances we would be expected to know when we went to parties. Mother was most particular that we must learn to waltz. It would be utterly mortifying, she said, to be asked to waltz and to disgrace ourselves, and her, by clumsiness. The other dances did not present such a challenge, but one was held so closely against a gentleman in the waltz that Mother was certain it would be quite difficult to keep from treading on one's partner's toes.

Signore Montelli had flashing white teeth and was quite nice. He was particularly nice to me. He talked Italian to me, and it was extraordinary the progress I made in the language when I had the stimulus of actual conversation.

Needless to say, neither Caroline nor I was ever left alone with Signore Montelli. Either my mother or some other chaperone was always present, so it was not until the wily Italian caught me unawares in the library one day that I realized his dastardly intentions.

He kissed me. He grabbed me by the shoulders, pushed me up against a wall of books, and pressed his drippy wet mouth over mine. I was so astonished I could hardly move.

The man, after all, was *old*. He had to be thirty, at least. Far too old for this sort of thing, I thought.

"My little Titian beauty . . ." he was mumbling. He actually began to kiss my neck. "Such hair . . . such skin . . . such magnificent eyes . . ."

He raised his head and looked down into my face. "You like me, yes?" he said. "You press yourself against me in the waltz . . ."

I had thought that was what you were supposed to do in the waltz. He had told me that was what you were supposed to do in the waltz.

"No." I said. "I do not like you. And if you kiss me again I shall tell my cousin Thornton. He is the best shot in the country and he will kill you."

The warm Italian skin turned pale. He was so close I could see where the beard was beginning to grow under his skin. He stared at me, his mouth a little open. He looked so like a fish that I almost laughed.

"You would not do that," he said.

"Not if you give me your word never to touch me again," I said. "Or," I amended, "at least not to kiss me. I suppose you have to touch me if you are going to dance with me."

"My perfect little Titian," he breathed and, leaning closer, he touched my cheek. "You would not tell your cousin."

"Who the devil is this Titian?" I demanded, slapping his hand away. "And I most certainly will tell him."

He stared at me as if I were a barbarian. "Titian is a painter," he said. "A very great painter. He is famous for painting ladies with red hair."

"My hair is not red. It is strawberry blond."

"No, *cara,*" he said. He smiled at me almost tenderly. "It is red. Red like copper, red like firelight, red like—"

"That is quite enough, *signore.* Do I have your word, or do I tell my cousin?"

Well, after a bit more discussion, he gave me his word. He kept it, too. Thorn actually did have a reputation as a marksman, although it was highly inflated. He had won some sort of silly wager at one of the London clubs. We had heard about it all the way up in Derby. It sounded to me as if Thorn were utterly wasting his time in London, but I forbore to say a word. In my opinion, anything that kept him away from Thornton Manor, and hence out of my way, was all to the good.

Mother spent the entire winter preparing Caroline and me for our come-out in society. For those of you who are not familiar with what a come-out entails, I will describe it.

First and foremost, the purpose of a come-out is for a girl to find a husband. Girls, you see, must have husbands. If a girl does not have a husband, she must: a. become a governess (if she is poor); b. go and live with a relation and become a drudge (also if she is poor); or c. set up her own establishment and scandalize everyone (if she is rich).

I was poor, otherwise the last option might perhaps have interested me. I was most emphatically *not* interested in becoming a governess or a drudge, and so it clearly behooved me to find a husband. Thus, the come-out.

There were, however, two great drawbacks to success in my quest. The first, and by far the more important, was the fact that I was poor. In general, men do not like to marry poor wives. They like to marry wives with money. But Papa had been only an infantry officer, and Mother had only a small portion of her own, so neither of my parents had been able to provide me with the all-important marriage portion or dowry.

This was a distinct problem. Mother kept telling me stories about these poor girls she had heard of who had made brilliant marriages, but I had a healthy skepticism about these stories. The thing Mother didn't seem to notice about all her fairy tales was a very important point: all of the brilliantly married heroines had been beautiful.

The problem of the dowry was actually solved the month before we left for London. And it was solved by, of all people, Thorn. He offered to provide me with a dowry.

Mother was speechless with gratitude. "It is just enough, Dinah," she told me breathlessly. "Enough to make you respectable, enough to make you acceptable. Oh, bless the boy!" A repressive look at me. "Considering how rude you always are to him, Dinah, I think it is absolutely princely of him to do anything for you at all."

"Nonsense," I said. "There is nothing in the least princely about it. Thorn is simply terrified that he will have me on his hands for life if I can't find a husband. This dowry is purely in his own self-interest, Mother. Don't be fooled."

So was solved problem number one, the matter of the

dowry. Problem number two was a trifle more difficult. It had to do with my hair.

In our world, red hair is not considered attractive. Not that I have red hair, mind you. It is strawberry blond. But I am forced to admit that to some people it might appear red.

The color is bad enough. It is also very, very fine, and very, very curly. In fact, it is so fine and curly that it is impossible to confine it into any semblance of order. It just sort of floats around my face and shoulders in a cloud of rosy ringlets.

I hate it. I cut it all off once, when I was fourteen, but it looked worse. It was grown in now, to touch my shoulders, and it did what it wanted to.

Caroline had beautiful hair, smooth and straight and properly blond. Caroline also had beautiful big blue eyes. My eyes are gray-green in color. They are all right. Not beautiful, like Caroline's, but acceptable. I will never have my mother's beauty, but as I have grown older I have begun to look more like her. I am not unpleasing. Except for the hair. And the hair, unfortunately, is not something that one can easily overlook.

It was probably a very good thing that Thorn had come up with a dowry, otherwise he might very well have been stuck with me for life!

To continue about the come-out: one comes out during the Season. The Season traditionally begins with the opening assembly at Almack's, which event usually takes place on the Wednesday following Easter Sunday. The Season then continues until the summer, at which time the *ton,* that is, the fashionable set, deserts London for the country or for Brighton.

In the fall the *real* hunting season begins, when one goes out on horseback after foxes. During the social season in the spring, the hunting is aimed at finding a mate. Young girls look for husbands, bachelors look for wives, married people look for lovers . . . you see the picture I am painting.

A great deal of the hunting—at least the husband-hunting—takes place at Almack's. This is a social club that holds assemblies every week and attracts only the *crème de la crème* of the *ton*. You must be given a voucher by one of the patronesses of the club in order to attend an assembly. Almack's is very exclusive. According to my mother, it is also known as the Marriage Mart, so you can see what its function in society is.

Caroline and I, of course, had vouchers to Almack's. The sister and the cousin of the Earl of Thornton would be acceptable anywhere, so my mother informed us grandly. Before we went to Almack's, however, there was to be a great ball held in London at Thornton House in Grosvenor Square. The purpose of this ball was to "present" us to society. My mother had schemed to make this ball the grandest, most-talked-about event of the Season, and Caroline and I were beginning to be sick of the very subject when the time finally came for us to depart for London and our fates.

Thornton House was the town house of the earls of Thornton. It had been built by Thorn's grandfather, the same earl who had built Thornton Manor in Derby. Thornton House was generally referred to as the "town house" or "Grosvenor Square," as it became too confusing to speak of both Thornton House and Thornton Manor. The town house had actually been closed up since the death of Thorn's father, but it was opened up for Mother and her charges, and on the day of our arrival it looked very grand indeed. Mother had explained that previous to our arrival, Thorn had lived in just a few of the rooms during his sojourns in London. Apparently he had eaten and been entertained elsewhere. However, now that there would be more than just himself in residence, the town house had been fully staffed and cleaned and stocked and Thorn himself would join us when he returned to London from Scotland, where he was visiting a friend.

My bedroom was very pretty, with freshly polished furniture, fresh flowers, and old chinz coverings. I liked it immediately, and helped Liza, the maid who came to unpack for me, fold my clothes into the enormous wardrobe that took up almost an entire flower-papered wall. Actually, I had not brought too many clothes. Mother planned to buy new wardrobes for both Caroline and me, with Thorn once more putting out the blunt—he was certainly anxious to be rid of me—and so we had left home with only the bare necessities. Our old clothes, according to Mother, were all right for the country, but would not *do* for London.

I was not overly concerned about my clothes. I was concerned about my horses. It's not that I doubted that the Thornton House stables were anything less than first-rate. The house had been closed up, but Thorn had opened the stables the first time he had come to London. Thorn might be a pain in the neck in most ways, but one can always count on him to see to the welfare of his cattle. No, it was not that I doubted the excellence of the stables, but, like myself, my horses had never been away from home before and I hoped they were not feeling too strange. They had been sent on a day ahead of us, and I was concerned about them. As soon as I decently could, I made my way to the stables.

The first person I saw when I got to the stables was Kevin. Kevin was one of the grooms from Thornton

Manor who had accompanied the horses to London; he was about my own age and was a particular friend of mine. He grinned when he saw me.

"Do you not be fretting, Miss Dinah. The horses are grand."

I heaved a sigh of relief. "No problems on the road, Kevin?"

"None at all." His grin widened. "Well, almost none. Sebastian was after making a bit of a scene flirting with a good-looking black mare at one of the inns we stopped by, but otherwise all went fine."

I sighed again. "I wonder when Sebastian is finally going to realize that he's a gelding and not a stallion?"

"Some of them never realize it," Kevin said. "Particularly those that are gelded late. Truth to say, from the looks of her, the mare didn't know the difference either." Kevin grinned wickedly, and I grinned back. My mother would have had heart palpitations if she had been able to hear our conversation. She has a very odd notion of what is "suitable" for a young girl to know. If I hadn't spent half my life hanging about the stables, I would have been appallingly ignorant about the entire business of reproduction.

As you may have guessed, Sebastian is my horse. He is an extremely handsome chestnut thoroughbred, just under sixteen hands in height, and not of a placid disposition. If he had not been gelded, he would have been completely unmanageable. I really should not have brought him to London, but I would have missed him dreadfully if I had left him home. A horse that could learn not to kick a hound could learn not to spook at city traffic; or so I reasoned.

"And how is Max?" I asked next, referring to Caroline's horse. Max is an enormous bay gelding that had

had a long and illustrious career before moving into semiretirement as my cousin's mount. Max had done it all: he had raced and won, and he had hunted for years with the best hounds in the country. Now, at the age of sixteen, he lived off the fat of the land at Thornton Manor, and carried Caroline with grace and safety wherever she might wish to go. He was a marvelous old campaigner and I adored him. It was I, in fact, who kept him in condition. The amount of riding Caroline did would not have begun to exercise him properly. If the truth were known, I always thought of Max as my horse too.

I produced a bunch of carrots. "I brought some treats," I said.

"Come along," Kevin said, "and I'll show you over the place."

I spent a very pleasant two hours chatting in the stables with Kevin and the other grooms and helping to hay the horses, and then I made my way back to the house. Unluckily, the first person I met as I came in the side door under the stairs was my mother.

She glared at the pieces of hay that were sticking to my green traveling dress. "We will be dining in less than half an hour, Dinah," she said. "Get dressed."

"Yes, ma'am," I said. I have ever found that the best way to handle my mother is to agree with everything she says. It makes life much easier, and once her back is turned, I can do as I please.

I was hungry, however, and so this time I did as I was told.

We spent the next two weeks shopping. At first it was fun. I like a pretty dress as well as anyone else, but after one week of it I thought that enough was enough. In fairness, I suppose I must say that my mother and Caroline did not get bored; but I most certainly did. Such a fuss about clothing!

"Well, Dinah," my mother said when I commented upon her obsession with our wardrobes, "you are just as boring when you begin to prose on about horse feeds."

I must confess she had a point. I find the subject of horse feeds utterly fascinating; I suppose Mother feels the same way about clothes.

Two days before the great day of our come-out ball, Thorn finally put in an appearance at Grosvenor Square. Mother was furious with him for not having arrived earlier. I cannot imagine what she expected him to do that she should have wished for an earlier arrival. I could quite understand that it was important for him to be there on the night of the ball, but he was only bound to be a nuisance in every other way. I was rather hoping he wouldn't show up until the afternoon of the ball itself. I had a feeling he would not be pleased that I had brought Sebastian to London.

Sure enough, the first thing he did when he arrived was to go check the stables.

"Dinah!" he shouted, charging into the hallway after he had been gone only fifteen minutes. "What the devil do you mean by bringing Sebastian to London? I told you to bring Anicet. Sebastian is much too hot to trust in the streets of a large city."

He *had* told me to bring Anicet, and I might even have indicated to him that I would bring Anicet. But even though Anicet is a very nice mare, I just had not been able to bring myself to leave Sebastian behind.

I said airily, "He is doing just fine, Thorn. There is no cause for worry, I promise you. I take him to the park very early for a nice long gallop, and that shakes the fidgets out of him. He has been very mannerly, I assure you."

"So mannerly that Kevin tells me he almost put you under the wheels of a coach yesterday," returned my cousin.

Blast Kevin, I thought. "The stupid coachman blew his horn almost into Sebastian's ear!" I said. "I jumped myself." I tried an ingratiating smile. Thorn's eyes had grown very blue and he had that look he gets on his face when he is contemplating a particularly unpleasant course of action. I would die if he ordered me to send Sebastian home. "If I get killed, think of the money it will save you," I said.

"Dinah!" That was my mother's horrified voice.

"Don't talk like that." That was Caroline's soft-hearted protest.

Thorn grinned. "You have a point," he said, and I knew that I had won. Sebastian wouldn't be sent home—at least, not immediately.

Thorn had arrived in London accompanied by the Scottish friend he had gone to visit. The friend's name was Douglas MacLeod, he lived on an island called the Isle of Skye, and he was very nice. Thorn had met him only a few months before, at some party or other they had both attended. Douglas—he told me to call him Douglas—was a few years older than Thorn, but Thorn often fools people with the fake maturity he can assume. A number of his friends were older than he.

The two of them went out after dinner to some club or other, but before they left, Thorn said to me, "I will accompany you to the park tomorrow morning, Red. Do not leave without me." This statement was accompanied by the chilling look that he always hopes will cow me. Actually, I do not much like it when Thorn looks like that, but I would die before I let him see that he had intimidated me.

I gave him a sunny smile. "Are you really prepared to arise at six in the morning?"

His lips tightened. "Yes," he said baldly, gave me that look again, and left.

"Oh, dear," said my mother, "I knew Thornton would not approve of your bringing that horse"—Mother always referred to Sebastian as "that horse"—"to London. Now he is angry. Really, Dinah, *why* must you always be at loggerheads with him?"

You can imagine my indignation. *"I?* I am not the one at loggerheads, Mother. All I have done is to bring my own horse to London. I cannot understand why Thorn is behaving as if I have stolen him!"

"It is just that he fears for you, Dinah." It was Caroline's soft voice. She gave me a rueful smile. "Someone has to fear for you. You certainly have no fear for yourself."

"I have fear when it is sensible to have fear. There is nothing to fear in Sebastian. As Thorn will see for himself tomorrow morning. *If,* that is, he can rise with the dawn after having been on the town all night."

On this parting shot I adjourned to my own room to send a quick note to the stables telling Kevin to cut back on Sebastian's grain so that he would not have too sharp an edge on him in the morning. I had no real doubt that Thorn would miss our appointment. He had never needed very much sleep.

The early-April morning was soft with pale post-dawn light when I met Thorn in the stableyard the following day. He was dressed as he would have dressed for an afternoon outing on Rotten Row: blue riding coat with brass buttons, leather breeches, polished top boots, and a crisp, perfectly tied cravat. His uncovered head reflected the light of the morning. He tapped the rim of my riding hat with his crop and said lightly, "You've hidden all your hair. Good. If you make a cake of yourself, no one will know who it is."

I glared at him. "I will not make a cake of myself."

There was the sound of iron-shod hooves on cobblestones, and our two horses, fully tacked, were brought into the stableyard. Sebastian looked to be on his best behavior, thank God. The only other horse he liked was Thorn's big gray gelding, and he seemed pleased to be with Gambler again.

Thorn had a stableful of horses at home, but Gambler was his favorite, one of the horses he usually took when he went to hunt with friends. Gambler was nearly seventeen hands of pure power, but his disposition was amiable. This is not to say he was an easy horse to ride. In fact, in his own way Gambler could be as big a problem as Sebastian. He didn't explode into fireworks, à la Sebastian; Gambler was more subtle. When he didn't like his rider, he simply dropped all his considerable weight onto his forehand and lumbered like an elephant. When Thorn rode him, Gambler strode forward from his hindquarters and looked marvelous, but put a less competent rider on his back and he died. Spectacularly. Thorn liked him because he had wonderful spirit, and would jump anything. He would jump anything for Thorn, that is. I have been a witness at what he would do for someone else. It was not an edifying spectacle.

Spookiness was not one of Gambler's problems, however, and his big, calm presence was a decided help to Sebastian. Someone from home was out on this terrifying, strange street with him, and it made him feel much more confident. He jumped and bucked only a half-dozen times before we were in the park.

We opened up the horses almost immediately and let them stretch out into a full run. As usual, Gambler went just slightly ahead, and Sebastian hung very comfortably at his big gray shoulder. The chill April wind brought tears stinging to my eyes, and I laughed out loud in pure delight. At the sound of my voice, Thorn turned his head. I saw the white flash of his teeth. Probably the only time we two were in accord was when we were out together on horseback.

Finally the path began to wind into the woods, and Thorn sat down in his saddle. The horses slowed, first to a canter, then to a trot, and finally to a walk. The birds were calling in the trees, the sky was a brilliant clear blue, the exact color of Thorn's eyes, and Sebastian snorted loudly with the sheer pleasure of the day. I heaved a hearty sigh myself, counterpoint to Sebastian's snort. Thorn chuckled.

"Every time I want to strangle you, Red, I force myself to remember that you are probably the best rider that I know. It almost makes up for all your other failings."

Fierce pleasure scalded my heart. Thorn never complimented me. "Better than you?" I asked.

"Of course not." A small, superior smile curled the corners of his mouth.

Prudently I refrained from the comment that hovered on my lips, and said instead, "Then I may keep Sebastian in London?"

"Small chance I ever had of getting you to send him home," my cousin retorted.

"Well . . ." I murmured. I couldn't suppress a grin. "True."

"How are things going for the ball tonight?" he asked after we had ridden in silence for several minutes.

"Thank God this wretched ball is finally going to happen, Thorn!" I exclaimed. "Mother is a madwoman on the subject. She has talked of nothing else for the past month, at least. If I don't attach at least three eligible suitors who will propose to me within the week, I shall feel as if I've been a failure as a daughter."

He gave me a sideways flash of blue. "You don't have to pick out a husband within a week, Red. Take a month, at least."

I sighed. "Perhaps there will be an eligible gentleman in London who is blind to colors," I said gloomily.

"Why should you say that?" He sounded surprised.

"Well . . ." I certainly didn't think I would have to point out my defect to Thorn of all people. He was the one who insisted on calling me "Red" all the time. "Don't be dense, Thorn," I said crossly. "You know what I mean."

He halted Gambler, and Sebastian, the adoring follower, stopped also. Thorn reached over and put a hand on my arm. "No," he said, "I don't know. Tell me."

I scowled at him. "My hair, stupid. Who will want to marry a girl with hair the color of a sunset?"

I looked away from the astonished expression on his face. I could feel that my cheeks were the color of the sunset also. I hated Thorn for making me say my most secret fear out loud, and I pulled my arm away and nudged Sebastian with my leg to make him go forward. I suppose I nudged him too hard, for he bucked and then bolted. It took a few minutes to get him back to order again.

Thorn said to me, as our horses walked side by side

back toward the gate, "Dinah, I had no idea you felt this way about your hair."

"Mphh," I said.

"I hate to have to say this." His voice had an odd, rueful note to it. "I must confess that I have enjoyed teasing you about your hair for years."

"I noticed," I said in a muffled voice. To my absolute horror, I was feeling a little teary. I really was dreading this night, when I would have to stand in front of half of London in all my flaming glory.

"Dinah," Thorn said, "your hair is beautiful."

"Mphh," I said again.

"Listen to me, you little witch." He reached out and took hold of my arm again, and both the horses stopped once more. Reluctantly I looked at him. He was the one with the beautiful hair, I thought, watching it shine, thick and flaxen in the sunlight. If only I had hair like that.

"Listen to me," he said again. "Your hair is beautiful. In fact, it is the most beautiful hair I have ever seen in my life. The men will be lining up to dance with you."

I suppose my face conveyed my skepticism, for his fingers tightened on my sleeve. "Do you know that there is a great Italian artist who is famous for painting ladies with hair not half as beautiful as yours?"

"I know," I said, nodding wisely. I was so pleased for once to be able to show him I was not an imbecile. "Titian. Signore Montelli told me about him."

"Who is Signore Montelli?" Thorn asked.

"The Italian dance instructor Mother engaged," I replied. "He kissed me in the library and called me a little Titian."

"He *what?*"

Too late, I realized my mistake. "It was just a little

kiss, Thorn. He caught me unawares. I told him he had better not do it again or you would shoot him. He never did."

Thorn rolled his eyes upward toward the heavens. It is a particularly irritating mannerism of his, supposed to indicate that I have said or done something outrageous.

"He surprised me," I repeated. "He was really quite old." I thought back upon that moment in the library. "And his mouth was wet," I added in disgust.

Thorn snorted. "How old?"

"He must have been thirty, at least."

"Good God. Dinah, you are impossible. Thirty is not old!"

"It is old to me," I replied with unimpeachable logic. "I have yet to turn eighteen."

Thorn took his hand off my sleeve, straightened up, and began to walk his horse forward. "Well," he said, "this Italian dancer may have been old and wet-mouthed, but he certainly wasn't put off by your hair. Have you ever thought of that? Did he try to kiss Caroline?"

I could feel my eyes widen. "No," I said.

"There you are," he said.

I thought for a few minutes. "Perhaps I shall have to look for an Italian gentleman," I said at last. "They seem to have a penchant for red hair."

"I think you will find that a number of English gentlemen will have a penchant for red hair as well," Thorn said.

"Do you really think so?"

"Yes."

We continued along the path in silence. I was feeling considerably better. Of course, my mother and Caroline had been telling me for years that my hair was not so bad, but I hadn't believed them. Thorn was a different story. He would die under torture before he flattered me. If he said my hair was all right, then it was.

I turned to look at him. He was watching the path before us, his tall body erect and easy in his saddle, his rein long enough to allow Gambler to stretch his neck. Thorn was twenty-two. That was the age man I should be looking for, I thought.

He must have felt my eyes, for he turned his head. I was feeling unusually kindly toward him, and I gave him a big smile. He blinked. "What was that for?"

"You made me feel better about my hair," I said. "Thank you."

He blinked again. "I am going to write this down in my appointment book when I get home: 'TODAY DINAH SAID THANK YOU.'"

"Why should I even try to be nice to you?" I demanded. "Every time I make an effort to be civil, you make fun of me."

He surprised me. "Sorry, Red," he said. Then, with the ghost of a grin, "It was the shock of it, you see."

I stuck my nose in the air and refused to talk to him for the rest of the ride home.

I shall tell you about the come-out ball.

It began with a dinner party for what my mother called "a few select persons."

These persons numbered twenty-six.

Chief among the dinner guests were Uncle George and Aunt Harriet. The Honorable George Lydin was not actually my uncle, though he had graciously given me permission to call him thus shortly after I had come to stay at Thornton Manor. He was the younger brother of

Thorn and Caroline's father, was a minister of some kind in the government, and had been the administrator of Thorn's fortune until Thorn had turned twenty-one.

He was rather stuffy. Thorn said he was a quintessential Tory (Thorn being a Whig). However, he had always tried to be kind to me. He had once even brought me a doll. I never played with dolls, and would much rather have had a new bridle, but I never told him that. I had given the doll to Caroline to add to her considerable collection, and Caroline had given me a new bridle for my next birthday.

Filling out Mother's table in addition to Uncle George and Aunt Harriet was an assortment of their friends. Mother, you see, knew no one in London and had had to rely heavily upon the Lydin family connections in the matter of establishing herself in society. The biggest coup of the evening, according to Mother, was the presence of Lady Jersey, who was a friend of Aunt Harriet's. Lady Jersey was the patroness who had procured us vouchers for Almack's, and her sponsorship was evidently a very desirable thing.

The dinner was excruciatingly dull. Thorn sat at one end of the table, and Mother sat at the other. Caroline and I were squashed in the middle of the highly polished mahogany board, but, needless to say, not next to each other. I was placed between a red-nosed old earl and a young man who kept telling me about some bet he had placed at White's. I was utterly uninterested in this silly bet, but I did my best to be polite, and smiled and nodded as if I were listening to him the whole time he was prosing on. I fared better with the red-nosed earl, who turned out to be a fanatic huntsman. We exchanged hunting stories for the remainder of the dinner, both of us enjoying ourselves more than we had expected to.

After dinner we all went up the staircase to position ourselves in the small anteroom before the ballroom to greet the guests.

Mother had done wonders with the ballroom. It was decked with fresh flowers and smelled perfectly lovely. The polished wooden floor shone like glass. There were mirrors on some of the walls, and the mirrors reflected the crystal of the chandeliers and the points of light that were the candles in the crystal wall sconces. It truly did look lovely. And so, I must confess, did Caroline and I.

Caroline was always a beautiful girl, but tonight she looked breathtaking. Her gown was the traditional white, laced with blue ribbons the exact color of her eyes. The high-waisted cut of her dress accented her tall slenderness. I had always begrudged Caroline those two extra inches she had on me. Her blond hair had been cut to lie in light feathery curls around her face, and then was swept up in a sleek and stylish arrangement at the back of her elegant head. I grinned at her as we were taking our places, and she reached out to squeeze my hand.

"You look beautiful," she whispered to me.

Caroline is a very generous girl. "So do you," I whispered back. We assumed our places between my mother and Thorn, and as we waited for the first guest to be announced, I looked down at my own person.

My gown was white over a pale green underdress and it was quite the prettiest dress I had ever owned. The London hairdresser who had done my hair as well as Caroline's had caught it back behind my ears with pearl-encrusted combs and cut it so that it looked more like a cascade of curls and less like a wild bush. I had a string of pearls around my throat, and small pearl earrings in my ears, and though I would never be a beauty like Caroline, I thought I looked very well.

In fact, I was feeling better about this come-out than I had ever thought I could. Thorn had told me before dinner that all of his friends had promised to dance with me, so I was certain of spending at least part of the evening on the floor. This was an enormous relief; I had spent a few sleepless nights imagining my mother's disappointment if I were not asked to dance at all.

"Viscount Eddington," the majordomo intoned, and a young man who turned out to be one of Thorn's friends came down our line.

"Lord and Lady Rivers," the majordomo said next, and two more people started down the line.

At the height of the arrival period, the staircase was jammed with people waiting to be announced, and the entrance hall inside the front door was filled to capacity. They were even queuing up in the street! Mother was in heaven. The ball was already being labeled a "sad crush," which is apparently the highest accolade any hostess can achieve.

The worst part of the ball for me came when Caroline and I had to open the dancing. It was very frightening, having to go out on the floor in front of all those strange people and dance under the scrutiny of so many critical eyes. I would far rather have faced a six-foot gate on Sebastian than have ventured out onto that floor! Thorn danced with Caroline, and Uncle George danced with me. Thank heaven our solitary demonstration did not last long; after about a minute, at the orchestra leader's urging, the floor began to fill with other couples.

Uncle George saw the look of relief on my face and smiled. "You dance very well, Dinah," he said kindly. "And you are in particularly good looks tonight. I have always thought you to be a very pretty girl."

"Thank you, Uncle George," I said.

"And how are you enjoying London?" he asked.

The dance was soon over, and then I was surprised to see Thorn bowing before me. "Your turn," he said when I just stared at him.

"Oh," I said. "Are you going to dance with me now?"

"No," he answered with awful sarcasm. "I am going to dance with the Queen of Sheba. Come along, Red, and stop being so stupid."

He took me by the hand and towed me out to the floor to join a set. I glared at him, but we were too close to other people for me to give him the set-down he deserved. He placed his hands upon my waist and I lowered my glare to his cravat.

It has always annoyed me that he is a full head taller than I.

The music started, our feet moved in rhythm, and we danced.

Neither Caroline nor I was allowed to waltz at our come-out ball. This is a very strict, and I think very silly rule of the patronesses of Almack's. It seems they have decreed that one of them must formally give her permission before a young girl is allowed to perform the waltz.

So I did not dance any of the waltzes at my own ball, but to my utter astonishment, I danced every other dance of the evening. My card was filled in the first ten minutes of the ball! Nor was it only filled by Thorn's friends, who rallied round with great loyalty. A great number of other gentlemen, some of whom Thorn did not even know, asked to dance with me.

It was a great relief. Caroline danced every dance also, but that was not a surprise. My mother was beaming. I was so pleased for her. She had worked so hard, poor thing. It would have been dreadful if I had had to spend the night sitting with the chaperones.

We did not get to our beds until three in the morning, and I must admit that I did not arise the following morning to take Sebastian for his daily gallop in the park. When I finally opened my eyes, the bright sun streaming in my window told me it was much later in the day than my usual six-o'clock awakening time.

"Why did you not wake me?" I demanded of Liza, who was the housemaid who brought me my morning tea. "I *never* sleep this late."

"His lordship said to let you sleep, miss. He said you were not accustomed to going to bed as late as you did last night."

"Blast Thorn," I muttered under my breath. Sebastian would probably be kicking his stall down by now. There were no pastures for turn-out in London, and he was not accustomed to standing in a stall for such long periods of time. Much as I hated to admit that Thorn was right about anything, I was beginning to think he had been right about bringing Sebastian to London. It was not fair to the horse to confine him the way he was necessarily confined in the Grosvenor Square stables. The grooms hand-walked him around the stableyard for a few hours every day, but it was not the life he was accustomed to.

In my own defense, I must point out that I had not realized how much time Sebastian would have to spend in his stall.

I finished my tea and got out of bed. "Put out my habit, please," I said to Liza, who was now standing in front of my wardrobe.

"Your riding habit, Miss Dinah?"

"Yes."

"But it will be the calling hour shortly," the maid said. "Surely you will want to be home to receive any gentlemen who may call?"

"What I want to do," I said evenly, "is exercise my horse. Put out my riding habit, please."

I had finished washing my face and hands and was about to get dressed when a very young maid came in with a note for me. It was from his lordship, she said shyly. It contained one sentence: "I rode Sebastian for you this morning. Thorn."

Well, part of me was grateful to him, of course. I really was worried about Sebastian. And part of me was furious with him. It was owing entirely to his orders that I had not been awakened at my usual time so I could exercise my horse myself.

On the other hand, I still felt tired. I could imagine how I would have felt if I had arisen four hours earlier.

I decided I would ignore the whole situation unless he brought it up first. If I thanked him, it would appear as if I had been glad of the extra sleep, and if I upbraided him, I would appear churlish. How typical of Thorn, I thought with exasperation as I told Liza to put out one of my new day dresses. He always managed to put me in the wrong!

Liza had not been mistaken about the calling hour. At least a dozen gentlemen called to see Caroline and me during the course of the morning. Before I had quite realized what was happening, I had promised to ride with Viscount Eddington in the park that afternoon, and to

go see the wild animals at the Tower with Mr. Richard-
son the following morning.

April passed in a whirl of this kind of activity. There
were dances, assemblies, routs, theater parties, opera
parties, Venetian breakfasts, musicales, rides in the
park, and drives in the park. Mother had been right
about our clothing. One needed an enormous wardrobe
in order to keep up with the endless chain of social en-
gagements one seemed to have in London.

I am also pleased to report that I even collected some
potential suitors. There were three of them whom Caroline and I labeled as definite "possibles."

One was Thorn's friend Viscount Eddington. He was
a good-looking, good-humored young man of twenty-
four. He had a nice smile, some fairly decent property,
although not in a county notable for its hunting, and apparently was comfortably rich.

Then there was Douglas MacLeod, who had been
staying with us at the Grosvenor Square house until he
removed to a cousin's. I liked Douglas very well, even
though he was a trifle too serious-minded to make for
easy company. He was a second son, which had kept
him off our original list since I was aiming for a husband with a nice estate and horses, but according to
Mother, who had had Uncle George check his creden-
tials, Douglas had an independent fortune from his ma-
ternal grandfather. Caroline and I then put him down as
a distinct possibility.

Last, but certainly not least, was Lord Livingston.
Lord Livingston was certainly older than the husband I
had envisioned. In fact, he was almost as old as the dastardly Montelli, but he was excessively handsome and
excessively rich. He was a prime "catch" on the Mar-

riage Mart, and it was a definite feather in my bonnet that he appeared to be interested in me.

I might mention here that *the* biggest catch on the Marriage Mart had turned out to be none other than Thorn!

Caroline also had a flock of admirers, but we never bothered to make a list of "possibles" for her. She had known whom she wanted from the first week of our stay in London. The moment she and Lord Robert Dalviney had laid eyes upon each other, it had been decided. I had never believed in love at first sight, but the fact of the matter is, it happened to Caroline. I saw it. Everyone saw it. And everyone knew it was merely a matter of time until their engagement would be made official.

With Caroline settled, the attention of the family naturally turned to me. I quite understood that, considering the amount of money that Thorn was expending, I was expected to catch a husband. I can assure you that I did my best.

I went driving with Lord Livingston, riding with Douglas MacLeod, and to Gunther's for an ice with Viscount Eddington. I danced with them all at every ball and rout and assembly I attended. I tried very hard to notice only their good points.

They all had distinct drawbacks, of course.

Viscount Eddington was an unimpressive rider, and if the horse he rode in London was any indication, he was no judge of horseflesh either. Of course, this could prove to be a positive factor. With such a husband I should probably have a pretty free hand in the stables. On the other hand, it would be nice to be married to a man one could ride out with for a morning's gallop without fearing that he would fall off and have to be carried home on a hurdle.

Douglas MacLeod was a decent horseman, but he was terribly intense. He took everything I said so seriously! You may not have noticed, but I have a tendency to exaggerate. With Douglas I was always watching my tongue so as not to alarm him unduly or hurt his feelings. I was beginning to fear that a lifetime of watching one's tongue could prove to be a trifle tedious. It would be nice to be married to a man to whom one could speak one's mind without fear of his brooding upon your words for half the afternoon.

Then there was Lord Livingston. He was probably the best of the lot, but I wasn't certain if I could bring him up to scratch. According to my mother, he had a reputation for breaking hearts. I could quite understand how that might happen; he was a terribly attractive man and a dreadful flirt. He certainly flirted with me, but I didn't know if he meant anything beyond the flirting. Livingston was a man of the world, and men of the world were utterly beyond my experience. To tell the truth, he sometimes made me a little uncomfortable. One never knew what he was thinking. I like to know where I stand with people, and I was beginning to think it might be uncomfortable to find oneself married to an enigma.

Caroline thought I should aim for Douglas. My mother was in favor of Eddington. I myself rather favored Livingston (I have always liked a challenge). When my mother consulted Thorn, she said he was quite rude on the subject and told her I should take whomever I could get.

He probably thought I couldn't get any of them. Of course, this only fired me up to try even harder.

The husband hunt came to a climax in mid-May, at a garden party given by one of society's leading lights, the Duchess of Merton, at her beautiful home just outside of London. Merton House is situated on the Thames, with acres and acres of gardens and lawns and summerhouses and even a maze almost as large as the one at Hampton Court. The duchess apparently has this garden party every year and it is one of the highlights of the London Season. I can quite understand why. Everything about the day was perfect: the beautiful setting, the delicious food, the elegant company; even the weather cooperated by being warm and sunny. It must be nice to be a duchess, I thought, and so be able to order everything to your requirements.

Mother and Caroline and I all attended, and Thorn escorted us. He had been out of London for a week visiting a friend in Hampshire, but he had returned in time for the Duchess of Merton's garden party. Thorn had been a heroically good brother this Season, escorting Caroline to a large number of affairs that he obviously found very boring. He escorted me too, of course, but that was because I always went along with Caroline.

Truth to say, as the Season had advanced, Thorn's temper had noticeably deteriorated. As usual, he had taken his temper out on me. Even Caroline had commented upon his irritability.

"Every time Dinah opens her mouth, you jump all over her," she had told him before he had left for Hampshire. "Whatever is the matter with you, Thorn? If London is preying on your nerves, please don't feel you must stay for my sake. Aunt Cecelia is a perfectly adequate chaperone, and you know that Robert and I have settled things between us. It is just the lawyers who must arrange about the settlements."

Released from duty, Thorn had promptly produced
an invitation to visit a friend and had left for Hampshire
two days later. We hadn't seen him until his arrival at
Grosvenor Square the previous afternoon. He had insisted upon escorting us to the garden party, "to see
what you have been up to in my absence," as he put it.

"Are you certain that it is not to see Rosamund
Leighton?" Caroline teased. Rosamund Leighton was a
girl who had, like Caroline and me, made her come-out
this year. She was odiously beautiful, with smooth
black hair and big blue eyes. She fawned all over
Thorn, and he adored it. When I accused him of liking
to be toad-eaten, he said it was a nice change to have a
girl appreciate him instead of vilifying him all the time.

I hated Rosamund Leighton and her smooth black
hair with a passion. She probably would be at the garden party, and the prospect of seeing her gazing wor-
shipfully up at Thorn for the entire afternoon cast a pall
of gloom upon the whole day for me. I can assure you,
it was an utterly sickening sight for sensitive persons to
be forced to behold.

It was hard to stay gloomy for long, however, when
once I was out in the beauty of the duchess's gardens.
My three suitors were supposed to be in attendance
also, and I thought that if I saw all three of them in a
countrylike setting, it might give me a chance to decide
which one I liked best.

The program for a garden party is very simple. One
strolls about the gardens, admires the views, eats and
drinks in the dining room of the house, and talks to
one's friends and acquaintances. On a warm mid-May
afternoon it can be quite a delightful way to pass the
time.

I spent the first hour we were at Merton House

strolling about on the arm of Douglas MacLeod, who listened to every word I spoke with such an expression of intense interest that it depressed me unutterably.

Then I was claimed by Viscount Eddington. Viscount Eddington is a light-hearted young man, and I quite enjoyed the hour I spent walking about on his arm. If I had never seen the man on a horse I might have been more enthusiastic about him as a prospective husband. Unfortunately, I knew how he looked on a horse. The thought was inexpressibly discouraging.

Then I caught a glimpse of Thorn parading about with that odious Rosamund Leighton on his arm. The silly cowlike look on her face was enough to cast any-one into a fit of the dismals.

In fact, by the time I was claimed by Lord Livingston I was feeling very glum indeed. This business of suitors was not at all what it was cracked up to be, I thought. It was all very well to play games and make lists and gossip with one's friends about them, but the reality of having to spend one's entire life shackled to a strange man was . . . well, frightening.

Lord Livingston put my hand upon his arm and began to walk me firmly down a long path that I had not seen before. He chatted to me lightly, and I smiled and nodded without really listening.

Lord Livingston's looks are rather in the style of a romantic hero, which is one of the reasons he has broken so many hearts. His hair is dark and it dangles on his forehead in an unruly curl. His smile usually has a mocking edge to it. His conversation also had a mocking edge to it. It was that edge that so confused me. I never knew if he meant what he was saying or if he meant the opposite of what he was saying. He was rather exhausting company, if the truth be told.

"Lord Livingston," I said when we had reached a very pretty little arbor and he showed signs of wanting to stop, "don't you ever grin?"

His magnificent dark eyes widened with surprise. "Grin?" he said.

"Yes. You know—a big smile. A really *amused* smile. A smile that lets people know you are happy."

He lifted a well-marked black eyebrow. "I smile, little one."

"I know. But your smiles are so confusing," I said. "They never look happy."

He gave me one of those mocking smiles. "They don't?"

"There," I said, pointing to his mouth. "You just did it. That is not a happy smile, my lord. *This* is a happy smile," and I gave him a huge, radiant grin. "See?"

He was looking at me with a very odd expression on his face. He often looked at me like that. I never knew what it meant. Today was my day for clearing up mysteries, so I asked, "What are you thinking when you look at me like that?"

"I am thinking," he answered promptly, "that you are a most beautiful girl and that I want to kiss you." And then he did.

This was not at all like Signore Montelli's kiss. This kiss was serious business. Lord Livingston had me grasped firmly in one arm while his other hand held the back of my head so I couldn't pull it away. His mouth was hard and bruising. I couldn't breathe. I pushed against his shoulders with my hands, and couldn't move him. I was beginning to be frightened as well as disgusted, when a cold, furious voice ripped across the silence of the arbor.

"Get away from her, Livingston. Now."

It was Thorn.

Lord Livingston loosened his grip enough for me to pull away from him. I ran across the arbor to Thorn as if all the hounds of hell were at my heels.

"There's nothing to be upset about, Thornton," Lord Livingston said. His voice sounded oddly thick and he paused to clear his throat. Then he added, "I have every intention of marrying the girl."

Thorn turned to look down at me. "Is this true, Dinah?" he asked. "Did you agree to marry him?"

I stared up into his face. I had never seen Thorn look like this. His eyes were positively glittering with fury. There was a white line about his mouth. Even the tip of his nose looked white.

I shook my head so hard my hair floated. "No, Thorn," I said. I swallowed and then I whispered, "Please don't make me marry him."

I hate to admit it, but I sounded almost pitiable. But the thought of spending a lifetime submitting to that suffocating kiss! I shuddered at the very idea.

Thorn said to Lord Livingston, "If I ever find you within ten feet of my cousin again, I'll shoot you dead."

Lord Livingston was at least seven years older than Thorn, and certainly more a man of the world. However, it didn't surprise me at all when he decided not to pursue the discussion. The expression on Thorn's face was absolutely terrifying. After the briefest of hesitations, Lord Livingston turned on his heel and strode away.

We listened to the sound of his feet crunching on the graveled path. Then he had passed out of our hearing.

Silence reigned in the arbor.

Finally Thorn said, "What the devil possessed you to

come to this secluded place with a man of Livingston's stamp?"

"I didn't know he was taking me so far away from everyone," I protested.

"You have eyes, don't you?" He still sounded very angry.

I said, trying to introduce a note of humor into the atmosphere, "That is two men now who have kissed me, and you have threatened to shoot both of them."

He swung around so he was standing directly in front of me. "I never met the Italian dancing teacher," he said.

"Oh, that is right." I attempted a placating smile. I was uncomfortably aware of being in the wrong, and was doing my best to slide out of it. "*I* was the one who threatened that you would shoot Signore Montelli."

Thorn's blue eyes were searching my face. "Dinah. . ." he said. "*Were* you thinking of marrying Livingston?"

I don't know why, but I could feel tears begin to rise in the back of my throat. I shook my head.

"Then what of Eddington?" he asked. "Or MacLeod?"

I wet my lips with my tongue and tasted blood. That blackguard Livingston had cut my lip with his teeth!

"I am trying very hard to like them, Thorn," I said. "I know I must get married. Perhaps you had better make the choice. You know them better than I do."

There was a very long silence. Thorn's face was as unreadable as ever Lord Livingston's had been. Finally I said, "Do you have a handkerchief, Thorn? I fear that Lord Livingston cut my lip."

His eyes began to turn dark blue. Without speaking, he removed a square of white linen from inside his coat, took my chin into his hand, and dabbed the handkerchief gently against my lower lip. I stood very still and looked up at him. Then, after he had taken the handkerchief away and put it back into his pocket, he bent his head and very slowly, placed his lips lightly on mine.

Their touch was infinitely sweet. I think I must have swayed a little, for his hands came up to grip my shoulders and support me. The pressure of his lips increased. I tipped up my face and let my head fall against his shoulder. I know I closed my eyes.

And then we were kissing, deeply, intensely, our bodies pressed into each other, my arms around his waist, his hands spread on my back to hold me close. It was wonderful to be held so close to him. His long, lean body felt so strong against mine. I loved the familiar smell of him. After a while he moved one of his hands to touch my hip, my waist; it came to rest upon my breast.

I quivered with delight under his touch. His mouth was moving on mine, asking for something. . . . I opened my lips and felt his tongue come into my mouth.

I had never known kissing could be like this!

It was a rude awakening a few minutes later, to feel him take me once more by the shoulders and bodily lift me until I was set on my feet a good arm's length away from him. I blinked at the sudden separation.

"Dinah," he said in a rough-sounding voice, "this has got to stop or I won't answer for the consequences."

I stared at him. His hair was disordered and spangled his forehead with threads of gold (had I done that?), and his eyes were brilliantly, blazingly blue. "What consequences?" I asked.

"The consequences that you are likely to find yourself lying on the ground there with all your clothes off," he answered bluntly. "There is a reason, Dinah, for the rule that a young unmarried girl ought not to be alone with a man."

It sounded an attractive prospect to me, but I didn't dare say so. There was no humor about his mouth; in fact, he was looking oddly grim. A terrible fear smote my heart. Perhaps that was all it had been to him? The excitement of being alone with a girl? And now he was afraid I would take it to mean more than it did? I dropped my eyes and stared at the ground.

"You don't have to marry anyone you don't want to," he said. His voice was harsher than it usually was. "I never wanted you to think that."

I shrugged and still did not look at him.

"I thought you were enjoying yourself." Now he sounded as if he were accusing me of something.

I shrugged again. "I was just trying to do what was expected of me. It wasn't so bad at first. It was like a game. But then . . . when I realized that I would actually have to marry one of them . . . a man who was a stranger . . . a man I could never love . . ." To my horror, my voice had begun to shake. I stopped talking and drew a deep, long breath.

"Dinah," Thorn said. "Dinah, darling. Don't look like that." His feet crunched on the hard-packed dirt of the arbor and then he was taking me into his arms.

I huddled against him. I said into his shoulder, ". . . a man who wasn't you."

I felt his mouth on the top of my head. "All this Season I have been feeling like doing a murder," he said. "Isn't it amusing? I had no idea at all that I loved you until we came to London and I saw you dancing with another man. I wanted to go up to you, rip you out of his arms, and shout, 'Hands off. She's mine!'"

I gave a delighted chuckle.

"I thought you thought I was an arrogant boor," he said into my hair.

"Well," I said, "I do." I lifted my face out of his shoulder and looked up at him. "I also think that you are wonderful. For years I have nearly killed myself trying to keep up with you, trying to get you to notice me. I've spent my entire life comparing other boys to you, and none of them ever began to measure up."

He looked fascinated. "Well, this is certainly news."

"This is very bad for you," I said. "You are spoiled enough by everyone else without my beginning to add to the problem."

The amusement left his face, to be replaced by a look of intent seriousness. "Spoil me, Dinah," he said softly. "I would love to have you spoil me." And he bent his head and kissed me again.

Ten minutes later he was towing me along the path toward the terrace of the house. "You are a menace, Red," he said as I bleated a protest that I needed to button the top of my gown, which had somehow come undone during the course of an extremely pleasant embrace.

"I?" I said with great indignation as I redid my buttons. "*I* am not the person who unbuttoned this dress, Thorn. It was you. Stop trying to blame me. You *always* try to blame me."

"It is usually your fault," he said. Then he grinned. "Stop flashing your eyes at me. It *is* your fault for being so damned irresistible. Now, be a good girl and come along before your mother and Caroline call up a search party to find us."

The following day, Thorn called a meeting of the family to tell them the news of our engagement. The general reaction was one of stunned stupefaction.

"You are marrying Dinah?" Uncle George said incredulously.

"Are you joking us, Thornton?" my mother asked doubtfully.

"But you two dislike each other!" Aunt Harriet said.

It was Caroline who was the surprise. She smiled and said, "Well, I am glad that is settled at last. I was beginning to wonder how long it would take you two to resolve matters."

Everyone, Thorn and I included, stared at her.

"Do you mean you expected us to become engaged?" I asked.

"I thought you might."

"And what brought you to that interesting conclusion?" Thorn asked in that odiously polite voice he uses when he doesn't believe a word you are saying.

"You have been like a bear with a sore toe ever since we came to London," his sister told him. "You have been consistently rude to all of Dinah's suitors. You were so rude that Douglas moved out of the house. And you watch Dinah all the time." She smiled at him. "I'm in love myself," she said, "so I noticed."

I hadn't noticed a thing.

"You made a list of suitors with me," I accused her, "and you never once mentioned Thorn!"

"She probably thought you'd laugh in her face," Thorn said.

Caroline looked at him with those smiling blue eyes. "Dinah has always worshiped the ground that you walk on," she said. "It wasn't Dinah's feelings that I was unsure of."

Now, in a deeply private moment I *might* perhaps be willing to admit such a thing to Thorn, but to have it said out loud, in front of all the family! I could feel my cheeks flaming.

There was a moment of amazed silence. Then my mother said, "I suppose we could have a double wedding."

"No," Caroline said immediately. "I love Dinah dearly, and have been very happy to have her company during the Season, but I will not be married with her. The only one who will look at me is Robert."

Caroline is such a generous girl, but even so, I thought it would take some time for me to forgive her for that remark about my worshiping the ground Thorn walked upon. He was looking overly pleased with himself at the moment.

"Dinah and I are going to be married immediately," he announced. "I see no need for the sort of delay Caroline is certain to insist upon. Dinah doesn't care about bride clothes and things like that."

This, of course, was perfectly true. It would have been nice to have been consulted, however.

Mother said, "Of course she must have bride clothes!"

Thorn said, "Dinah, come over here to me."

Normally, of course, I would never have jumped to his command. But there was a note of such heartstopping tenderness in his voice . . . Well, I was beside him before I quite realized I had moved.

He put his arm around my shoulders and bent his head close to mine. "Are you missing Thornton Manor?" he asked softly. "Wouldn't you like to just go home and be married without any fuss?"

I think that was the first time the reality of what had happened really struck me. Home. Thornton Manor would be my home forever. I wouldn't have to leave my horses and my dogs and my friends in the stables and the kitchens. I would marry Thorn, and live with him, and perhaps have a flock of blue-eyed children, all with his beautiful hair. I sighed with the sheer bliss of it and smiled up at him.

"Yes, Thorn," I said meekly. "I would like that very much."

Buried Treasure

by Edith Layton

June, 1699
Glen Cove, Long Island, New York

The path of moonlight on the water shone silver as pieces of eight. The water in the Sound was dead calm. The night was still, except for the men's harsh breathing and the scuffed sounds of their footsteps as they struggled through the sand to the land beyond. Their dirks, swords, and pistols were snugged secure in their belts, and although their bright earrings swayed to their steps, they were silent as bells without clappers. Even the parrot that rode a shoulder of one of the men was still as a jade statue. No other ship except the one that had brought them could be seen in the waters beneath that luminous moon tonight. But still, no one spoke until they let down the heavy chest they had staggered under—and that only when they were under a sheltering tree at the edge of the beach they'd come upon.

"Gawd! Weighs a ton," one man sighed as he finally straightened his aching back. "Mebbe two. We should of had more men with us. Me back's broke entirely."

"Aye, Master Quickwit," another scoffed, "so there'd be more to share with?"

"Ye mean fer the cap'n to worry about," the first man said with a sneer.

"Oh, I don't think so," a bulky man said as he

stepped from the shadows to stand over the chest. "I don't worry about any of you. Should I?"

The silence was profound. Then the first man spoke up again with a great deal of false gusto. "Nah. I never meant that, Cap'n. Trust me wi' your life, ye can."

"No," the captain said quietly, "I believe it is you who trust me with your lives, isn't it? Of course," he went on as the silence deepened, "you all have been at this business longer than I. I might not have it right. But I believe that I am the one with the power to leave you all here to guard the chest for me for eternity, if I so chose. Am I not?"

"No need to talk like that, Cap'n," another man said, shifting his boots as he spoke. "No need a'tall. Sure, you're cap'n, and we do as you says, we do. Jewel here, 'e's just gibbering in 'is beard, is all."

"Jewel," another of the men said with humor in his voice, "complains like other fellers sneeze, Cap'n. Were he not kickin', we'd wonder were he breathin'."

"You lookin' fer trouble from me?" Jewel asked the man menacingly, his hand flashing to the dagger he had thrust into the sash belted across his wide middle. Then he crouched and spread his bandy legs apart and glowered at a muted sound he heard coming from a man leaning against the tree. "And you. You laughin'? Mockin' me, Dancer, eh?"

"Relax, Jewel," one of the men said, "it were only a jest."

"Were it?" Jewel asked, his small eyes narrowing more. "Or were it that he wants somethin' of me?"

"When I want anything from you, you'll know it, I promise," the man he'd called Dancer said. "But don't wait on it. I wouldn't want ice from you in Hell."

"*I* want only that you fellows plant that chest for me,

and plant it deep," the captain said. "And now. Of course, if you don't wish to . . ."

The men fell silent and picked up the shovels they'd brought with them. They began to dig.

The captain strolled behind the lean man called Dancer. "I'd advise you to keep your laughter to yourself, lad," the captain said softly, "do you wish to end this journey all of a piece, that is."

Dancer shrugged, and then got to digging with the rest of them.

When the hole was deep enough, they lowered the chest in. Then they stood in a ragged ring and looked down with satisfaction. They were a colorful company, even in the moonlight that bleached them all to the colors of sand. They wore long frockcoats, flowing shirts, and had wide sashes over their ragged trousers. Their soft boots were cuffed high on their legs, and they wore their hats or kerchiefs low over their tanned foreheads. Their hair was too long for any fashion but their own. Some had eyepatches, most had scars, and all were tanned the color of teak. Their captain was dressed as a prosperous man of business, the only concession to his livelihood the many rings that glittered on his fingers.

The captain paced off the site, back to the beach and the rowboat they'd come in. Then he paced back again, muttering to himself and nodding. He was memorizing the number of steps he'd taken, and in what direction, when he heard the men begin to argue again.

It was done before he got back to them, though he hurried.

He saw only the flash of steel. The man he'd called Dancer stood with his hand on his heart, staring at Jewel in astonishment. Then he turned and looked at the captain.

"I—I didn't even have my knife in hand!" he said in amazement, looking at his blood, black as midnight in the moonlight, as it poured between his fingers. Then he fell.

The men stood still, in shock.

"He were only jesting!" one of the pirates said, looking at Dancer and the dark pool spreading beneath him in the darker shadows as he lay before them.

"One time too many," Jewel said. He was still crouched for the kill, and his small eyes scanned the others. "Who's next? C'mon," he said, waggling the fingers of his left hand, his knife glinting in the bright moonlight in his right one. "Who wants to argue wi' me? Eh? I had a grievance, din't I? I done what I had to. He goaded me, he vexed me sore. But I waited. A man can't fight 'board ship. I knows the rules of the Brotherhood. But he can on land. On land is where we are. C'mon, who wants to take issue wi' me?"

"What 'e says, 'tis so," muttered one pirate, eyeing the still form on the ground before them.

"So it is," the captain said on a sigh, looking down at Dancer.

"But 'tis a hard thing. He had no warning, did he?" another said.

"Was I s'posed to send him a letter, eh?" Jewel asked. Looking around and seeing their averted eyes, he grinned at last, showing all his yellow teeth to the night. "Well, well," he said jauntily, sheathing his dagger in his sash again. He sauntered around the fallen man, and prodded him with one foot. "No more jests, Dancer, eh? Be tellin' them to the Devil now, I s'pect. Eh? Be *wishful* I'd give you ice now, I s'pect, eh?" He laughed and kicked the body.

"Leave him be!" the captain said harshly.

It was an odd thing for a pirate captain to say, because most wouldn't have minded if Jewel had torn the fellow's guts and gizzards out and made a necklace of them on the spot. But Kidd was new to the sea, and every man jack of them knew it. He was also on the run for his life, and in no position to lose them now, and every man jackal of them knew that too.

"O' course, o' course," Jewel said generously. "Leave him be, right here, and forever. Let's bury him wi' it. On it. Many's the cap'n who leaves a body to guard his treasure, Cap'n. Ye said it yerself, and I seen it done. Trust the captains to get a body to work for them forever, eh, lads?"

He laughed uproariously. But the others didn't. The lad had been a handsome one and no mistake, and no few of them knew that was really why he'd grow no older than the night now. They'd heard him reject Jewel's offer of friendship when he'd first appeared among them—and after too. But work was work, and theirs was a hard life. They looked at the captain.

"No time for anything else," he admitted. "Let it be done."

The rowboat left the island as quietly as it had come. Nothing stirred in the sea but the oars as they bit deep and surfaced again, as the little boat sped to join the great ship waiting for them near the horizon. Some of them gazed back at the rapidly diminishing sight of the island where they'd left the treasure, and the dead man who would guard it for eternity now.

But a light breeze had picked up, and the island was a welter of shadows. They were too far, in any case, even to see the spot where they'd buried their treasure. Or the hand that clawed up from out of the sand there.

And then shot up in the air, wavering frantically—almost as though it was waving farewell to them.

There had been sand in his eyes and his ears. He'd opened his mouth to scream and could not. It had to have been a nightmare. No man could live so. No men could let another die so. He remembered trying to scream; he remembered the panic that set him clawing and scuttling and writhing to find air to fill his lungs. He had, somehow he had. But then he had no breath left to scream. He'd only strength enough to squirm and twist and pant until he'd freed himself from his grave. Or so, at least, he must have done. Because he wasn't dead now. The pain made him wish he were. But when he closed his eyes and sought sleep, he remembered the nightmare and came awake again. This, he thought, remembering a sermon he'd once heard when he'd been young, must be neither death nor life, Heaven nor Hell. Dark and painful, and wracked with equal parts remorse and horror: he must be in Limbo.

But were there voices in Limbo?

"Poor fellow," one voice said, "poor lad."

"But he's a pirate, Father. Just see how he's dressed!"

"We can't know that."

"We saw the ship sail off."

"He could have been a captive on that ship," a gentle woman's voice argued.

Dancer tried to open his eyes. It had been a long while since he'd heard a woman's voice.

"And he could have been a cutthroat."

Dancer froze. He was aware enough to understand they were talking about him, and hard experience had taught him to be still when that happened.

"But someone tried to cut his throat, poor fellow,"

another woman's voice said, "or at least, his heart out. And he's so young. Have some charity. He might be your age, Jeffrey."

"He might be a killer," the voice said stubbornly.

"Softly, softly, lad. He might be dead by morning," another voice said with sorrow. " 'Tis a wonder he got so far as it is. They must have dumped him off the ship, and the tide did the rest. Because the men found him half in the water, and more than half dead too, poor soul."

He struggled to open his eyes, to tell them he'd be damned if he'd die, in more ways than one. Someone put a cool hand on his forehead. It comforted him. They didn't do that in Limbo, he thought.

"Poor fellow," the gentle voice said, "sleep, sleep."

He didn't want to, he wanted to see who spoke such sweetness.

"There, he's resting easy."

No! He tried to cry. And heard the voice fade as he fainted.

When he opened his eyes again, it was morning—on this earth, he thought with relief. But it might as well have been another one because he'd never woken to such comfort in all his life. Not even in the best bordellos in Hispaniola. There were no gilded chairs and feathery palms. He lay on plain cotton sheeting, not satin. But he stared around the room and felt the peace and plain comfort of it soothe him.

The bed he lay in was huge, with posts at the foot and head. It was intricately carved and polished to a high sheen, and he could see it was made of solid mahogany. If there was anything his life at sea had taught him, it was the appreciation of good wood. The fittings in the room were also stoutly made, the chests and chairs fashioned of thick oak. White curtains shaded the sunlight that flowed in through the big windows, but let in enough to show the varied colors on his coverlet, and all the bright hues of the rag carpet that covered the wide-planked floor. It smelled clean. It was quiet. He was alone. It was, he thought, as he watched a slight breeze make the curtains belly out like clipper sails, a sort of heaven, after all.

The door opened and he quickly closed his eyes. It was better that a man knew what he was opening them to before he did. Both his life at sea and the one he'd led before he'd ever set sail had taught him that.

She opened the door and peered in. He lay still as one of the carved figures on his headboard, she thought. In fact, he lay so still that she caught her breath and hurried to his bedside to put a hand on his forehead. He was warm, but it wasn't the hectic heat of fever anymore. It was a healthy warmth; he glowed with the banked fires of life. He rested easily at last. And so she gazed her fill at him for the first time without fear of looking her last at him.

She lived in a place where men went to sea to earn their livelihoods and protect their families. But still she'd never seen his like before. He seemed a creature of the sea, not just a man from it. His chest was covered with bandaging and he wore one of her father's nightshirts, but still it was clear he was lean and well made, with wide shoulders and a strong young neck. His skin was dark against the white sheets, the total tropical brown of a man who had lived outdoors beneath alien suns. His overlong crop of shaggy hair was wheat at its roots, and there were strands of purest gold and platinum where the sun had bleached it. His face was young, but even in repose it was not a boy's. He had high, sharp cheekbones, a sharp, straight wedge of a nose, and far too much jaw for true handsomeness. But that strong chin was graced with a cleft. And his face, with its light stubble of golden beard grown since he'd been put in the bed, fascinated her more than any handsome man's ever had.

She was used to rescuing the creatures from the waters that surrounded her island. It was a wild coast, where northeast storms and the rag ends of tropical tempests that strayed up from the south often signaled the change of seasons. She'd weathered many storms in her short life and nursed many wild seaborne creatures before freeing them to ride the tide again. But he, she thought with a shiver, was as alien and exotic as any bird that had ever been blown off course and brought in to their safe harbor.

He'd been in bed nearly a week. Her mother had tended him most of the time, with her father doing the more intimate duties for him. But she'd watched over him every day since the morning they'd brought him in too, and had never seen him conscious. Now he was still inert and silent before her. He lay in the second-best bedroom, with the early morning sunshine shining in on its familiar trappings, and a soft morning breeze puffed at the curtains. Nothing could be more familiar, safer, homier. And yet she found herself hesitating to come close enough to him to straighten his sheet. It was foolish, she scolded herself, to feel so wary around him. He was completely at her mercy.

Until he opened his eyes. She gasped.

He knew why. It had happened before.

"Hello," he said, his low voice rusty from lack of use. "Do I live? Are you real? Am I?"

"Oh," she said, her color rising, because his voice was only that of a man's, and a tired, weak one too. "Yes, you're certainly alive," she said briskly, to cover her embarrassment at her fear of him. "How do you feel?"

"But are you real?" he asked, so he could see the charming color climb in her cheeks again. He'd known women whose cheeks were the tints of wild rose, sunny sienna, and all the hues of scarlet from hibiscus to poppy. But he couldn't remember when he'd last seen a lass blush. Or seen a maid's pale complexion turn pink and not stay that way until the color was removed with soap, or water, or tears.

She was young and pretty although she was plainly dressed and wore no paint at all, and that too was a novelty to him. He was used to women whose colors screamed their sex from half a tavern away. He was used to more spectacular ones too, but she was indeed a pretty woman. Slender and shapely, her hair was smooth and straight and seal brown, and her eyes hazel and sheltered by long lacy lashes. She had a small, straight nose and warm pink lips. He noticed there were freckles on the bridge of that little nose. The sight of them filled him with a queer tenderness that tempered his lust. But not for long.

The modest green-striped cotton gown she wore didn't flatter her. But it couldn't conceal the lovely shape of her high breasts and small waist. He only glanced away from that entrancing sight when he realized she was backing tiny steps away from him. It was wise of her, but it would never do. He hurt, and had no more energy than a flea. But he breathed. And he'd endured worse. Still, he sensed he'd be a long time healing. He'd no intention of spending all that time in bed alone.

"Oh!" he gasped, putting his hand to his heart as though he was stricken, and lay back and closed his eyes again.

She stepped back to him quickly. He saw, through half-closed eyes, that she was alarmed. Better, he thought with an inward smile as she came closer. She bent toward him. He scented flowers.

"Mother!" she cried.

Damnation, he thought on a resigned sigh. He'd overplayed his hand. But it was a poor one anyhow, he reminded himself ruefully. He didn't know what he could have been thinking of—well, he did, but it was folly. Having been so close to death made him want to prove he was alive, and he knew no better way than with a lass. But his chest *did* hurt, and he didn't know who she was or where he was. It was no time to be thinking of lasses, pretty little ones who blushed or not. It wasn't like him either. He was a man who always used his head. It must have been the injury, he thought. Thinking of that, and how narrowly he'd escaped being buried alive, he grew solemn.

So he looked gray under his tan, and grim, when the older woman who must be her mother came hurrying into the room.

"What's amiss? Has he taken a turn for the worse? I thought he was on his way to healing," the older woman said as she bustled to his bedside.

"He was—he woke. He spoke," the girl said in confusion, "but then he gasped and closed his eyes again."

"Don't fret yourself on my account," he said weakly, struggling to rise and catching his breath sharply as he failed. This time he wasn't shamming. He looked up at the women. "It's only that I tried to move and discovered myself unable. I'm not used to being an invalid.

I . . . ah . . ." He paused and saw how the older woman was looking at him. The younger kept her eyes averted this time. A faint resigned smile was etched around his hard mouth, "Don't worry, mistress. It takes some folks like that. I'm used to it. Besides, I only see myself when I'm shaving, and only in a dim mirror at that. The sailors on that accursed ship that stranded me sometimes called me 'Shark.' I see you can see their point."

"Fiddle," the older woman said briskly, "they're lovely eyes, silver as Spanish coins."

But "shark" was exactly right, Hannah thought, looking at him again. She'd never seen a live shark that close, of course. But they too must have such eyes when they coursed the seas in search of prey: eyes the color of their skins, bright and silver, glinting with danger and knowledge men didn't possess. The stranger's were tilted and shining, beautiful and odd, and terrifying. And so attractive that she avoided them now.

"Spanish coin?" he asked with a hint of weary humor. "False as that? Is that what you think of me, mistress?"

"I think you're a fine rogue," Hannah's mother said, "to jest and flirt like a cavalier when you've a dagger wound deep as my hand in your chest. And just waked to find yourself in a strange place too. Well, we've passed a week trying to get you to the point of realizing that. So let me introduce ourselves. You're in the house of Jedidiah Jenkins, of Glen Cove. I'm his wife, Rachel, mistress of this home. And this is my daughter, Hannah. And you, sir?"

He answered, but he was obviously still confused, she thought. Because he stammered, and had to catch himself and think before he even got his own name right.

"I give you thanks for all your efforts, Mistress Jenkins. I am Danc— Dans— Dan Silver," he said.

"Before I tell you the way of it, I've an odd question to put to you," he said.

The wounded man sat propped up on pillows in his high bed. The morning sun showed him pallid beneath his tan and yet he seemed restless, though they knew he hadn't even the strength to sit up by himself yet.

The four members of the Jenkins family filled his sunny room.

Mistress Rachel sat in a chair by his bed, her tall, broad, genial husband Jedidiah, beside her, puffing on his pipe. Lanky young Jeffrey, whose face showed he was hovering between suspicion and fascination as much as he was between boyhood and adulthood, lounged in the doorway—too interested to leave, too embarrassed about his interest to come all the way into the room. And the lovely Hannah sat by the window wreathed in morning sunlight.

They'd come into his room to hear his story. They were his rescuers, they deserved a tale about his plight. He'd make it a fair one for them. Whatever he was or had been, he knew the value of a fair trade. But first he needed some answers. They were folk who lived by the sea. Before he told them anything, he had to know what they knew of it.

"They say when a man faces the worst there is, sometimes kind nature hides it from him if he survives," he began. "I woke with a pain in my chest, to find I'd escaped death. But how did you find me?"

"Some boys were putting out for lobsters. They found you on the beach, half in the water and half out, and with half your blood gone, or so it seemed. It was the cold water kept the rest in you. So it often happens," Jedidiah said wisely, "salt and the cold seal it in.

"Many's the hook I've set in my own hand, and many's the time I've healed the wound that way," Jedidiah mused. "I was a fisherman before I quit the sea to do my trading from a desk. But it's done me well. I've the biggest house hereabouts. That's why they brought you to us. You were so mazed with pain you were actually trying to crawl out to sea instead of the shore. You may thank Providence the tide was coming in, and you were too weak to fight it. You were taken from the sea covered with sand and blood, and brought straight to us. We can't tell you more than that—and the fact that a privateer was seen sailing out of the sound the night before."

Dan Silver nodded his shaggy head. "It's a wonder, then, that you took me in," he said. "Weren't you afraid you'd taken in a pirate?" he asked flippantly. But he watched them closely.

"Even had we, we had little to fear," Jedidiah said, "seeing as how near to death you were. But are you telling us now that you are of that persuasion?"

"Why, were I, I'd be a fool to tell you, wouldn't I?" his guest said with a bitter smile. "But they're not so cruel to those of their number as they were to me. Still, I can't ask you to take my word for what I am, friends, since you don't know me. I owe you my story. What I am, I shall tell you now. And leave it to you to believe what you will."

His odd silver eyes filled with a faraway look.

"As to how I came here—you know almost as much as I do," he said on a long sigh. "As for my life before that? I'm a common seafaring man, and have been since I was a lad. I was born in England and stayed there only until I was old enough to get my feet wet. I've seen seven and twenty summers, and in that time I've traveled six of the seven seas. There's many an entertaining tale I could tell you. But not today. That tale begins when I set sail last year from London town."

They nodded. He had the accent, and there was no sense denying it.

"I hired on a fine merchantman bound for the Caribe Indies to trade in spice and fine cloth," he went on. "Alas. We never got so far. Not a month out, we were hailed by cutthroats. We tried to outrun them—"

"Ah, there's folly," Jedidiah said on a puff of fragrant tobacco.

"Just so," Dan sighed. "For they took it much amiss, I can tell you. I'll not go into details," he said with a significant glance toward Hannah, "but I tell you, they were not pretty, not at all. They did board us. I survived, to be sure. As did most able-bodied men—who were not officers. That's their way, you see. I'm by nature a survivor. It occurred to me that were I a good sailor, I could sail on with them until I could win my way to freedom. I *am* a good sailor, though they didn't want me as such. But I can stroke an oar as well as any living man. So I did. It was hard work, but a man may work hard for many masters. While I was prisoner they didn't seek new booty, so my conscience didn't hurt so much as my body."

He chuckled as they did. But then his long face grew harsh shadows, his eyes grew a flat silvery sheen like water before a storm, and his voice roughened. "Ah, but not a month past, I overheard a conversation below decks. Then I knew I had to escape while I still could. They were going to Madagascar to sell all their ill-got gains, you see . . . including me."

Hannah gasped, but her mother and father only nodded.

"The beys, they do say, buy men of Christian flesh as slaves," Dan explained.

"This is so," Jedidiah said on a sigh.

"Aye," Dan went on, "and once a man is sold into bondage there, he never sees freedom this side of Heaven again. Since I wasn't at all sure I could gain admittance there, I tried to escape."

He waited while the women hid their grins and the men were done laughing. But then Jedidiah looked at him shrewdly.

"But the ship that was sighted in the sound the night before we found you was the *Antonio.* That's Captain Kidd's. He's no corsair. He's a New York merchantman known from Manhattan Island to Oyster Bay."

"Merchantman turned pirate," Jeffrey spoke up from the doorway.

"Aye, more's the pity," his father said. "But even so, the beys get their Christian slaves from the Barbary Coast, not Long Island Sound, lad."

"True," Dan said quickly, "but a privateer will take on any sort of merchandise if there's a profit in it. And a man on the run lightens his cargo where he can and when he can. All I know is that when I heard I was bound for Algiers, I knew I had to try to escape if an opportunity presented, whether it was a false rumor or no. No, I reasoned that even if I died in the attempt, it would be better than living with the Turks with a collar around my neck and hot coals on my feet—that much I knew. Kidd's wanted for piracy in London and is all a pother to escape with his name *and* his treasures."

"So it *was* Kidd's vessel you were on," Jedidiah said.

Dan sat up straight. The effort made him wince, and his face grew ashen beneath his tan.

"My illness has loosened my wits along with my tongue," he said quickly. "I owe my life to you good people, I'll not risk yours. There are things it's better not to know. So I'll only say I was discovered trying to escape. I remember fighting. I felt a knife thrust, and then a long fall to the water. After that I remember nothing until I woke in this bed. More than that—I cannot say. Forgive me. Or turn me out. But that is all."

He sat back with the air of a man who has just thrown the dice and waits to see how they fall.

"Aye, toss you out, and we'll have the bother of burying you," Jedidiah said.

His wife shot him an angry look, but before she could say what she'd opened her mouth to do, her husband went on. "No, the only thing worth burying here is fish heads. Keep your secret, Master Silver. There's little we can do with it anyway, were you pirate or not. Kidd's sought wherever he goes, and it's not Long Island fisher folk will take the prize money for him. But they say he's burying his treasure from here to Gardiner's Island so that it won't fall into the hands of the English. I don't suppose you know ought of that, do you?"

"Of course I do," Dan said, grinning. "Pirate captains always tell their prisoners the why and where of it. Sometimes they give them maps to their treasure as well. It helps to pass the long evenings between the dancing and pipe music, don't you know."

When they were done laughing at him, he said more seriously, "But I wish he had. Seriously, my friends, I am only a poor seafaring man, with no more worth in life than the wages due me at the end of a voyage. My voyage has ended beforetime. I have nothing but my thanks for you. How can I repay you?"

"Get well," Jedidiah said as he rose to his feet. "We ask nothing else."

"Done!" said Dan so fiercely he started coughing.

"Not quite," Jedidiah said with a wry smile.

"Are you sure we're wise to keep him here?" Rachel Jenkins asked her husband when they were alone. "We know nothing of him, after all. And we do have a daughter."

"What, then? Throw him out? And our daughter is a clever girl," her husband answered comfortably.

They sat in their bedroom and talked as they always did when they prepared for bed. It was their only true quiet time together, when she was too tired to knit or mend and he, too weary to whittle or tinker with his fishing gear or rifle any longer.

"Yes, she's clever but moral, I remind you, Mr. Jenkins. He looks a lusty lad," she said as she brushed out her hair.

"Lusty but not likely. The fellow was near death the other day."

"But don't you wonder why?" she asked, putting down her brush.

"What's eating at you, my dear?" he asked, marking his place in the Bible with one finger as he gazed at her. "Out with it."

"You know me too well, Mr. Jenkins," she admitted with a sigh. "Here it is, then. There was a privateer in the sound the other night. He came off it and doesn't deny it. I know he told a good story, but he may be a pirate. That is what he may have been."

"Yes. Maybe so. But so have many of our friends and

neighbors been. Or do you think old Bellamy got all his gold from catching cod? Or Mr. Wickham his money to start his dry-goods store from picking winkles? No, no. We live off the sea in many ways, and there's many a man of our acquaintance who's gone a'pirating. And do we blame them for it? No, we look away and pretend they were common sailors or whalers. But no honest tar can come up with the sort of money that so many of our leading citizens have. You know it well, Mrs. Jenkins. The sea is a hard master, worse for those lads who take the king's coin. Worse still for them who didn't mean to. You know how it is when a captain needs a full roster by the next tide. Then a crew is kidnapped—'impressed'—well, call it what they may, it's the same thing. The men they need are carried off from the streets to the ship, and all in the name of the king's navy. Men—and boys—sent to sea for years when all they want is to stay at home with their loved ones. Sometimes it's not much better for those who sign on with pirate masters thinking it will be a fine, free life and finding it little better than slavery. And not at the hands of the beys, neither."

He sighed. "For some, being on a privateer means being free. But the wise ones chart a course to the land soon as they are able. I don't hold with pirates. Some are the scum of the earth. But some are men looking for freedom, and some just lads gone wrong looking for the light. There's too many boys who think it's a life filled with adventure too. We thank God on bended knee each night our Jeff hasn't felt Jolly Roger's lure, don't we?"

She sighed. "You're right on all counts, Mr. Jenkins. But what about our Hannah?"

"Why, what about her? It's not as though the fellow is in any condition to do any damage in this house."

"That's not the sort of damage I was thinking about," she said as she lay her brush down. "I've never seen a prettier fellow."

"Pretty?" her husband asked in astonishment. "The fellow's about as pretty as a shark."

"You men don't understand," she complained as she tugged on her lace nightcap.

"Oh, but we do and better than you think, Mrs. Jenkins," he said on a chuckle, coming up behind her to lift the lacy thing off her head so he could run his hands through her hair. He smiled down at her. "Far better than you think."

It was much later, as she curled against his side in their big feather bed, that she spoke again. "It's not what the lad might do that I fear," she fretted. "It's what a lad like that might make a girl do."

"Not our Hannah," he muttered sleepily.

"Well, I suppose not," she said doubtfully before she closed her eyes to sleep. "She is a very sensible girl, to be sure.

". . . and," she reassured herself a half hour later before she finally allowed herself to sleep, "it's not as though she's alone in the house with him, is it?"

Hannah paused at the door to his room and frowned at the sound of laughter. It didn't sound the least bit funny to her. Because she recognized whose it was. Molly's laughter was girlish, and Sal's was muffled because she always covered her mouth with one hand. But both maidservants were supposed to be working— not laughing. Molly was supposed to be in the kitchen getting dinner ready. Sal was only supposed to be making the bed up around him. Whatever they should have been doing, neither was supposed to be smothering giggles.

It stopped when she walked into the room.

"Oh!" Sal said, her hand flying to her mouth in midgiggle. "S'cuse me, I'm sure, Miss Hannah, I was only just going."

"So I see," Hannah said. "But what were you only just doing?"

"Ah, helpin' poor Moll here with the linens," Sal said, and dropped a quick curtsy before she fled the room.

"I were just finishing," Molly protested as she scurried out after Sal.

Hannah turned to see the patient.

Her father had said that even if he was a pirate, he'd be no harm to anyone until he could move out of his bed. Her mother agreed, but she had looked a little worried. Now Hannah knew why. Maybe men couldn't see the danger in the fellow. But he had only to look at a girl for her to know exactly how dangerous he was. Especially propped up in bed, looking so tan and fit and comfortable. Hannah had grown up in a community where half the men worked the sea, and a man's bare chest was as common a sight as a storm cloud to her. But she's never seen his like before.

He should have looked like an invalid, with that great white bandage wrapped around his chest. But he lay back against his pillows, his nightshirt open, and all a girl saw was the tanned skin where the bandage wasn't. Skin and the taut muscle beneath that moved when he shifted his position and smiled at her. And then all a girl saw was the white of his teeth against the tan of his face and the creases the smile made in his lean cheeks. And that only because she was trying so hard to avoid looking at the knowing smile growing in those amazing eyes. He looked about as helpless as a sting ray.

Hannah had a youthful father, a younger brother, four uncles, and three male cousins. She had beaux all over the island and one in Manhattan too. She never lacked for a dancing partner at a party, and her parents were always warning her to be careful in her choice of a husband because a husband was forever. She didn't need their warnings. She loved flattery and attention, and got it in plenty, but she often wondered how much flattery a married woman got. No fellow so far had tempted her very much. In truth, now that she was one and twenty, she'd started worrying about that, wondering if there was some fault in her. All her friends were wed, or engaged to be. But she couldn't get up much enthusiasm for any lad. It seemed that every man she knew was someone she had known forever.

This man was an unknown, and so was the fluttery feeling in her stomach when he smiled his dangerous smile at her.

"How are you this morning?" she asked abruptly.

"Better . . . now," he said, on a grin.

She ignored the insinuation and came to his bedside. But there was nothing for her to do for him. His sheets were crisp and clean, his bandage snowy, there was a carafe of water and a tumbler by his bed, and an untouched bowl of fruit besides.

"Is there anything I can do for you?" she asked anyway, moving the bowl of fruit an inch so as to have something to do. And to avoid seeing speculation in those knowing eyes that followed her every step.

His smile was so bright it bordered on bold. But just as she was about to walk from the room, he said seriously. "Aye. There be. There is a thing, if you would, Mistress Hannah.

"I've been here three days that I know of, and a week, they tell me, before that. I've no complaint about my treatment," he said earnestly. "Truly. How could I? Your family kindly saved me from the sea and nursed and fed me too. I'm a lucky fellow indeed, and well I know it. Were I to live to a hundred I couldn't thank you enough. But there is a favor. . . . It's not that I'm ungrateful, mind. But I'm unused to biding in one room, all pent up. One room that doesn't move, at that. So, could you bide with me a while, mistress, and tell me about the day? I have a window, to be sure. But your mother is afraid I'll take a chill, so it's sealed as tight as a mermaid's purse. And lying here as I must, I can't see out it. Might you tell me something of the weather and the tides too? Or news from the town, or country? I feel quite out of it, you see."

"But Molly and Sal were just here . . ." she said and stopped, blushing, remembering how one look at her face had chased the pair of them back to their chores.

"And fine lasses they are too," he said enthusiastically. "But more interested in giggles than conversation. And who else is there to talk with? Your mother has her duties cut out for her, as does your father. Your brother, I fear, does not trust me entirely. Not that I blame him," he said quickly, "coming to you from the sea like a bit of driftwood as I did, why should he? But I mean no harm—'deed, I couldn't do any did I mean any," he chuckled. His handsome face grew grave again. "I hoped you, Mistress Hannah, might have time for a chat. I must truly be getting better, because an invalid doesn't care about the world around him—and the truth is that I'm restless as a crab on a hot deck."

It was a reasonable request. For all he looked magnificent in his nest of white linen, he also looked sorely out of place. He was too vital a man for the room itself. But he didn't look threatening. Only ill at ease. There wasn't a trace of anything piratical in his face now. Instead, he looked so humble that her fear of him was replaced by concern for his feelings.

"No one's brought you a newspaper?" she asked. "But that's no problem. Father gets the paper once a week. I'm sure he'll share it with you."

"Thank you," he said after a moment of silence, "but that would never do. I chose the sea too young, you see. I can read the stars and the clouds, the wind and the tides. But I can't read a paper of any kind. I'm sorry," he said, and he seemed to be, "but there it is. But if you . . ." He gazed at her and it seemed his tan grew a little ruddier, "that is to say," he said quickly, "might *you* consider reading it to me? I dislike to ask, but it's a thing I'd hardly ask of your father," he added with a crooked smile.

"Why, but I'd be pleased to," she said, trying to hide the fact that she was shocked. He spoke like an educated fellow—and every man she knew, fisherman or merchant, could read. Not bondsmen or hired hands, of course. But even the poorest fellows in town went to school until they learned that, at least.

"Or maybe even show me the way of reading the letters, so I could do it for myself and not be such a bother to you," he said carefully. "I haven't the art of it, but maybe that's because I was never really shown the way of it. I can try, if you would care to try me . . . I understand if you cannot," he said quickly, looking away, smoothing the patchwork quilt at his chest with one big tanned hand. "Forgive me my presuming, mistress."

"Well, but I wouldn't understand if I could not!" she said angrily, because she was vexed with herself for her confusion. "I'd be glad to, Mr. Silver. And I'll start as soon as you feel able."

"Mistress Hannah, behold me able," he said. "I sorely need to exercise something, if only my poor brain. Ah, but only if you call me Dan. Because it would be a hard thing, I think, for you to say, 'Look again! That's a *A* not a *Z* Mr. Silver, you blockhead!"

"Very well, but then I must be Hannah too. Because Mistress Hannah makes me feel like a schoolteacher. And mine was a caution, and two years younger than Moses too!"

"Very well, Hannah," he said, so softly she colored up and ducked her head.

"I'll just get a primer. I still have mine. And a slate, with some pencils, I think. Yes. Paper and ink wouldn't be a good idea if we are going to work while you are abed. And we can," she said with sudden inspiration, her eyes gleaming. "I'll get a board, we can lay it across the bed. Oh, this will work wonderfully."

He smiled at her enthusiasm. And his smile remained, although it was different, as he watched her trim figure as she left the room.

"You're doing wonderfully well," Hannah said an hour later. She sat back and looked at him suspiciously. "Are you sure you're not teasing me? I could swear you know your letters."

"Don't jeopardize your soul, Hannah," he said with a laugh, lying back against his pillow again. "I know the shape of them, and the name of some, to be sure, but I never stayed long enough to know all that they can do. It hinders a man to be ignorant. This is a wonderful opportunity for me. I could almost thank the villain who laid me low."

"Can you remember more about that now?" Hannah asked eagerly.

"They say the mind heals itself by covering over such pain until it can be dealt with, so it must be with me. I can't remember more than I woke with. It seems—sometimes, in the night, that I dream of it. Because I awake in terror. I will tell you that. But I remember nothing when I do. Just as well, I think. But here, no need to mourn me. As you can see, I thrive now. And I know my alphabet, and in the correct order too, do I not?"

"But I don't understand, you speak so well," she said, brushing aside his question. Because he did, she thought, he spoke like a man of learning.

" 'Deed, I hope so. I've an ear. It's so with many men who have no letters, Hannah. We learn to read faces and voices as other men read books, and we do it well— perhaps because we have nothing else in our minds," he laughed. But then he grew serious. "Early on, I learned that a man is marked by his speech as surely as by his clothing. A man who speaks well does well. So I copied the men who owned the ships, not those who sailed them. I was a poor lad, Hannah. I intend to be a richer man someday. I'll do anything I must to be that," he said, and he said it like a vow. "So thank you. This is a rare opportunity. There's not too many teachers sailing the seas. And none half so lovely on land either, I daresay."

His compliment would ordinarily have turned her pink. But she was thinking too deeply to be self-conscious. "Did you never think of quitting the sea?" she asked.

"Oh. Yes. Many times. But I don't know the land as I do the sea. And only a fool jumps in with two feet without knowing where he's going. But now? Well. I am learning—many things. And perhaps now I've more of a reason to look to the shore," he said gently.

They were close. She'd set a board over the coverlets on his knees and established a makeshift desk there. But she had bent from her chair to see what he'd written, and so their faces were very close now. She heard the hesitation in his deep voice at the last. When she looked up, startled, she could see that his odd silver eyes were fixed on her face, and there was a look in them she couldn't look away from. Although she should, she thought with an odd sense of panic. Oh, heavens, she should.

Her face went pink, then pale, except for her lips, he thought. They remained pink, though they parted in surprise. They looked soft and plush and were so close. Close as his hand, as he reached to her. He touched her cheek with the tips of his fingers and felt how soft her skin was, and heard her next indrawn breath. And leaned forward to claim her lips, because he knew to the second when they would part farther for him. But so, it seemed, did she.

Because she gasped and moved back at the last second. He would have fallen on his nose if he hadn't been watching for her slightest movement. As it was, he couldn't control the slight gasp of pain he felt as he overbalanced and met nothing but air.

"Oh! Are you hurt?" she cried, ashamed of what she'd expected. The man was an invalid, in her care. She rued her wild imagination as much as her unruly thoughts. He'd looked at her so intently she thought he'd moved close—but he couldn't have meant to kiss her. The poor man must think her mad. She swept the improvised desk from his lap, and pushed him back against his pillows. "Should I call Mother?" she asked in dismay.

His eyes were closed against the knowledge of his folly, not the pain. He'd moved too fast for his purposes, not his healing body. But he knew how to make the best of the worst. He'd spent his life trying to do that.

"No," he groaned, "it was only a spasm. There," he said, opening his eyes, " 'tis passed."

But her hands were already undoing his shirt as she anxiously examined his bandages. They were still snowy. Her eyes went to his, and then slewed away in embarrassment. Away—to the side. She looked at his cheek and then his ear, and stared. Because she saw the hole in his earlobe. It looked like it had been pierced for an earring. And though many a seafaring man had tattoos, and many more bore the teakwood tan his skin did, only a pirate wore jewelry in his ear.

She was afraid of more than his kiss now, he saw.

"Yes," he said quickly, "I see you see it. One of their little jests. They did it one night when there was little other sport offered. With a hot needle, and a bottle of rum—for them, not me—and many a rude quip beside. I can only hope time heals it. I bear enough damage on this poor old hide of mine."

He gave a shaky laugh and shrugged. But he also turned slightly as he did, so that the opened shirt fell from his shoulder and she could see part of his back. She gasped, as he knew she would. Only then did he straighten and begin to button his shirt with carefully trembling hands. "Sorry," he muttered, "I'd have spared you that."

Her hands covered his, but they were shaking too. "Did they do that too?" she demanded, furious at seeing the obscenity of the many long, white, welted scars that streaked across that smooth, tanned back.

"It doesn't bear speaking of," he said.

It didn't. He'd earned them from many masters. Until he'd learned that a lad with wits was best off pretending he had none if he was a lad aboard ship with no name except for his own to save him from the lash. They'd served their purpose, and fixed his goals. They served him again now. Because she'd forgotten his ear by looking at his back.

"No more lessons today," she said shakily.

He nodded in agreement. There would be time enough for them tomorrow. Those she'd teach him, as well as those he was determined to teach her.

He tried to come to dinner the next night.

"I'm tired of being such a deadweight," he argued. "Bad enough I came to you in such a state. But now I can feel my energy returning. I don't want to lie like a stump and be waited upon. I can't think of a worse burden than a guest who cannot dine at table with you," he protested.

He wavered where he stood at the foot of his bed. But he stood tall. He wore his host's castoffs. And though he was an invalid and Jedidiah was a tall man, his broad chest strained at the buttons of the old broadcloth shirt. Jedidiah noted that strong chest and the bandages still wrapped around it. Then he saw his guest's strained face. He nodded. And had to bite his lip as he watched the big man walk, slowly and stiffly and with obviously stifled pain. But though everyone in the family held their breath, their guest made it unharmed to the big, warm kitchen where they ate their daily meals.

He sat with care, and folded his napkin and laid it in his lap. His big, tanned hand shook as he lifted his soup spoon. The serving maid held her breath. Hannah held her tongue. Rachel Jenkins and her husband winced, and even their son grew still in the face of such obvious courage. They watched him look down at his plate, and wondered if he'd collapse in his soup bowl.

Jedidiah rose from the head of the table. But not to propose a toast.

"You'll dine in bed, lad, until you can do a jig," he commanded.

His guest looked downhearted, but he was forced to take his host's arm again when he staggered back to his room.

But as soon as he was alone in it, with the door closed behind him, he straightened. And grinning, danced a little jig around his bed. It winded him and left him aching, so that he was pale and winded when the maid came with his dinner tray. He accepted it humbly, but he was delighted. Because pain was such an old companion of his he didn't pay attention to it unless it stole his thoughts. This was merely hurting, and so endurable.

Everything was as he needed it to be. He needed only time. And solitude. And the complete trust of these good people who sheltered him.

"Would you like me to write a letter for you?" Hannah asked idly a few mornings later as she gathered up her teaching tools. "Oh, I know you're getting better and better at it," she added quickly. "But I could do it for you in no time, and it would get out faster that way.

There must be someone who would like to know you're all right."

Maybe one or two, he thought, but they couldn't read. There were definitely some others who would sleep better knowing the opposite. But it was better for him if neither friend nor foe knew how or where he was at the moment. But that wasn't a thing he wanted her to know.

She held her breath as he withheld his answer. She had never let herself think it, but now she had to: a wife would want to know where he was.

"No," he said, and she let out her breath, "I doubt there's a soul who'd care. Truth is, I've wandered this far from home because there was no home to wander from." It was the truth, but his smile was twisted because truth wasn't something he was used to telling women. But truth to tell, he realized with some shock, he couldn't remember discussing much with any of the women he'd met before—apart from the price and quality of the services they provided, of course. Still, this lovely creature was as pretty to look at as she was easy to talk with. Since he couldn't do much more than look yet, talking was pleasurable. And it would make what would come after even more interesting, he decided.

"My family died of a contagion, it took half our street," he went on. "All my brothers and most of my mates too. It was odd I took the fever so lightly since I was the youngest, and always running after them all with my nose running, or so they always jested. Aye," he added in a colder voice, "it was odd—so odd that no one would take me in after. It's why I first signed on at sea. A captain who needs a crew is not too particular.

Nor does he care so much about a lad's history as he does his future."

"How old were you?" she asked.

"Ten," he said with a shrug.

She clucked her tongue angrily, her expression thunderous.

"No, no," he said, holding up one hand, "don't blame them. I don't. Everyone has their superstitions. Sailors feel that way about albatrosses, you know. It's an ill-omened creature—as is any fish that's white when it's supposed to be silver, black, or blue. If a seaman happens to catch one, it gets thrown back with a curse, no matter if it's big enough for ten men's dinners. And the heartiest tar will shake in his boots if he sees St. Elmo's fire flickering in the masts. It does, you know, on some strange nights—it shivers up and down the masts like a web of lightning before it fades away. But if you touch it, it's cool and damp," he said with wonder. "Ah, but the sea's a strange place and no mistake. A man could sail it ten years times ten and never know the half of it."

"Oh," she said, bending her head and paying too much attention to the spine of a book she was holding, "so I suppose you can't wait to return to it?"

"Oh," he said softly, "I suppose it could wait awhile. It's not going anywhere, is it?"

She looked up at him with a radiant smile. He smiled back at her, and reached out a hand to touch a silken strand of her hair lightly with the tips of his fingers. She blushed.

He shook his head. Fish in a barrel, he thought with wonder. A pretty, shapely, sweet little fish swimming round and round in a barrel. Just waiting to be put on his plate. He was as amazed as delighted. He'd never met anyone, male or female, who was so unprotected.

Because take away her father and mother, slip her out from under her mother's watchful eyes—just winkle her out of her family's snug little house, and she'd be helpless as a clam out of a shell. And as tasty. It would have made him uneasy if it didn't excite him so much.

She lowered her eyes. Her heart was beating fast. He smoothed the strand of hair between his fingers, and she could swear she felt it to her toes. It was as if the surface of her hair suddenly had as much sensitivity as her scalp. She'd actually forgotten to be afraid of the look in his eyes until he touched her, and now she didn't know how she could raise her eyes to his startling, knowing ones again.

"I can't imagine not having a family. I've never even been alone," she confessed, "except when I've gone off berrying in the wood—that sort of thing."

"A woman shouldn't be left alone, not ever, there are too many dangers," he said, and meant it.

"But I don't know," she said slowly, raising her eyes, forgetting her fear of him in the need to explain herself to him. "I think sometimes that a person can't think so deeply when they're with people. Why, you know, I think that's why famous artists and poets and such are always men. Because people leave them alone if they want to be alone. Everyone worries so much about women, and there's always so much for her to do for other people, that she never gets a chance to listen to herself thinking for very long."

"I don't know if being alone is any great thing," he mused. "Some nights, when you're all alone at the top of a mast, with nothing above you but stars and nothing below but the watery deep, a man gets to feeling like he's nothing, nothing at all. Oh, he can put pictures in the stars, and make believe he knows everything going on beneath him in the sea. But alone like that, rocking in the darkness high above the deck and far below the moon, knowing how trifling a thing even the biggest ship really is—only wood on water, after all—it's no pleasant thing to think about. Then with only the wind in the sails to hear, because the water's too far beneath and there's no shore for it to lap at, he gets to feeling like he's the only one of his kind in the world, and that it makes no difference if he is. If he's not a poet or an artist, then what's he to do with all that emptiness?"

He was startled by what he said. It wasn't like him to share such thoughts. But when he looked at her there was no mockery in her eyes. There was no answer in them either. Only deep sympathy. That was such a peculiar thing for him to see that he refused to think about it. Instead he saw how fascinated she was by him and thought of how near she was to being netted by him. She was already caught. It was only a matter of being reeled in. His words were the lure, his smile the hook. And his touch . . . ? He closed his hand in her hair. And catching her by that silken strand, he slowly drew her face near to his.

He kissed her—lightly, briefly, as a brother might. "Thank you for caring," he said in a deep, sad voice. And waited to see what she would do now. Because he was in no hurry. A hasty man went hungry. He would never reel in his line until he was sure his hook was well sunk. And he knew full well that this was neither the time nor the place to enjoy his catch. But he wanted to see how well he'd judged his skill.

She didn't know what to say or do. But because she was a woman she didn't have to do anything, because they'd been alone a whole fifteen minutes and so now she heard her mother's voice in the hall. She backed away. His hand left her hair, but his eyes never wavered from her lips.

"It's nothing," she said, flustered.

But he smiled, content. Because he knew it wasn't.

"How is the patient doing?" Rachel Jenkins asked, looking from her daughter's flushed face to her guest's quiet smile.

"Fine," they both said at once.

And that was exactly what bothered her.

"I've wonderful news!" Hannah said as she came into his room. "Father says it's time for you to leave!"

His head swung around from the window, and his eyes glinted more brightly than the sunlight he'd been staring into. He looked dangerous in that moment. But she'd learned to disregard such looks. He'd been nothing but gentle and charming. It was only that his size and startling looks made her feel weak and frightened sometimes. She had learned to deal with it. The only trouble was that in the past week she'd learned it was impossible for her not to deal with.

She couldn't stay away from his room for very long anymore. He was the most exciting thing that had happened to her in her short life. He treated her parents with respect, her brother with amused patience, and Molly and Sal had nothing to complain of from him— except, Hannah thought with smug delight, for the fact that they'd nothing to complain of from him. He joshed with them, but never flirted. The only woman he ever treated like a woman was herself.

Those few of her girlfriends who were not married envied her fascinating guest. Those who were wed looked at her knowingly, until she blushed. Because she'd little conversation anymore, except about him. And she refused to let them come goggle at him.

"The man is an invalid, not a traveling medicine show!" she told them at church the first Sunday after he'd come to them.

"Oh, Lord, send me a tall, strong, broad-shouldered blond invalid," her old friend Rebekah had sighed, and they'd all laughed. But Hannah had hurried home after services to see if he needed anything.

All he needed, he told her with his quirked half smile when he saw her, was to see her again.

He altered everything. She'd been merely content before. Now every day was filled with anticipation. She woke in the morning rejoicing because she knew that when she finished her chores she could give him his lessons. And she went to sleep at night pondering the lessons he'd taught her. She taught him his letters, and he was learning amazingly fast. But so was she. Because when his lessons were done, it was time for hers. She'd discovered that if she asked prettily enough, he'd sit back and spin her stories about some of the places he'd been and some of the astonishing things he'd done. He had a way with a tale. In fact, his deep, smooth voice gave her chills even when he wasn't describing strange lands and people. She was very glad that Jeffrey, who had distrusted him so much at first, had now got into the habit of slouching into the room to listen to him too. Otherwise she feared she'd make a fool of herself because of the way he enthralled her.

"Of course," he said now as he rose to his feet, "I'll be ready to go in a moment. It's not as if I have to pack," he added on a strange laugh. "I'd just like to say good-bye to your parents and then I'll be on my way."

"What? Oh no, no, no," she said on a trill of laughter. "Not 'go' as in 'go'! Go as in 'go out and sit in the sun for a while.' Goodness! None of us think you're ready to leave. It's just that we thought you might like to get some fresh air and move about in the garden for a while. And get your tan touched up a bit," she said mischievously, "because you've faded to the color of tobacco, and when you first came you were pure teak!"

He relaxed, his eyes glinting with laughter now. "Teak, with a nice green finish, I think. It's very good of you, I'd like that very much, thank you."

They strolled in the garden. He walked without hesitation, but his stride wasn't as long as his long, muscular legs were capable of. That might be because he was walking in step with her, his sun-streaked head bent as he talked with her.

Rachel Jenkins saw them from her kitchen window and frowned.

"Jeffrey?" she said.

He rose from his luncheon and tugged on his coat. He looked over her head and stared out the window.

"They're walking. He's likely telling her a tale or two. I wish I could hear them," he said enviously. "But Father wants me at the office, to listen and learn. Old Tate is selling off his winter acres and we're high bid, we hope."

"I thought now that school's out you'd be with them every minute," his mother said fretfully. "We agreed to never leave them alone too long. But I have to go to Amy Fletcher's house. We're doing up that quilt for her wedding come September."

"Well, but I can't," he said. "Though I wish I were with them. It's true I didn't care for him being here at first. But he's a good fellow and he tells a rare tale."

His mother clucked her tongue.

"You still think he's a rascal?" Jeffrey asked curiously.

"I can't say what sort of a man he is," she answered, her face troubled, "but I know he is a man. And an attractive one."

"So he is," her son answered on a shrug. "But what can he do in the garden in plain sunlight?"

If Jeffrey didn't know, she certainly wasn't going to tell him. But she decided it was high time his father taught him about more than mortgages and crops. Still, it was noontime, and on Long Island, and the fellow had recently had a knife pulled out of his chest. But next week, Rachel vowed, there'd be no more strolling in the garden. If he was well, it would be time to set the fellow to some task to keep his mind—and his eyes— off her daughter. Her dratted picky daughter who had never looked at a man as she did at him, until her mother had almost given up hope because all her girlfriends were getting wed before her. But, Rachel thought with more pleasure, if he was as good a man as he appeared to be, and he was to become a man with a promising trade, why then . . . Mistress Rachel smiled as she bustled from her kitchen, full of dreams, to do her chores.

Hannah strolled on with her fabulous invalid. She looked up at him and saw how the light kindled his hair and gave color to his high cheekbones. His eyes were clear as the summer sky, or the sea itself. In fact, the day flattered him so much she could hardly believe that only a few weeks past they'd feared he might not live through the night.

"You're a way from the shore here," he remarked.

"Not such a long way," she said. "No place around here is. But we are far enough so that even the worst storm tides can't touch Mother's garden. That's why they built our home here. She refuses to grow pumpkins for King Neptune, she says."

She laughed up at him. The sunlight spun rainbows in her long, smooth brown hair because she'd taken off her bonnet and was holding it by its strings. That would win her a new freckle or two, he thought, and then thought of how he'd like to taste the few he saw sprinkled like cinnamon on the bridge of that saucy nose. He had known far more beautiful females, but none like her. Because she was a good girl, protected and cherished, and from a fine family. Pretty little creature, he thought with affection. Better still, she was bright and clever, and free with him now that she knew him. But not free enough.

He'd never been so close to a woman he wanted without having her, and it was as strange as it was exciting to him. He considered the frustration was well worth it. It gave him something to think about when he wasn't planning his revenge, and escape, and success. Because he never doubted he'd have all three—and her—before he was gone from here.

The house was at the end of the lane, and beyond that there was a path that led, she said, to the sea.

"But you're not ready for that yet. Not today," she said. "Father said a turn around the garden for a start. And that's all we shall do."

"Hannah!" he complained, stopping in his tracks as she turned back toward the house. "Am I a garden snail, to walk the length of a leaf and then back down again? Or a yard dog, to be kept on a tether? Oh, it would be a cruel, cruel thing to keep me from the sight of the sea when I can smell it clear and hear its roar."

"What a fib! That you cannot," she laughed. "It's a

long walk down the path, and up a hill and down another before you can even see the sound. And Father said 'the garden' clear."

"But the sea is God's garden," he protested. "Do you want me pining away? There are crabs—little blue ones with scarlet claws—that thrive on Carribean shores. If you take one a mile from its home it will die, do you pack it in seaweed, keep it in a bucket, or sluice it down with water from the sea—it makes no difference. Away from the pull of the tide where it was born, within a day it will die."

"But you, sir," she said with a grin for his foolishness, "are not a little blue crab."

"No, but I am a big blue fellow. Ah—please, just another step or two, out the gate and down the road, so that I can feel free even if I am kept imprisoned in a magic garden by a cruel jailer."

It was so silly, he so big and bold, calling her a cruel jailer, when it was clear she couldn't prevent him from anything he set his mind to. She giggled and followed as he opened the gate and led her down the path to where he wanted her. To the bend in the road where it was bordered by trees and bushes and wild grape, so that no one from the village or the house could see them.

Once there, in the dappled shade, he stopped, put his hands on his slim hips, and took a long, deep breath.

"Are you all right?" she asked at once. "Oh, see what you made me do? Now you've overdone."

"Nay, the trouble is that I haven't done enough," he said as he caught up her two hands in his. "That's been my trouble, gentle jailer, for many days now," he said, smiling down at her.

But it wasn't quite a smile. And he wasn't exactly

joking. She was trying to decide just what it was when he gave her hands a little tug, and she found herself drawn up close against him. She was just trying to decide whether she was embarrassed or thrilled by the feel of his long, hard body next to her own when he bowed his head and kissed her. And then she couldn't decide anything, because all she could do was feel.

She'd been kissed before. But that was like a drowning woman thinking she'd been in the water before. Everything about him flooded her senses: his sun-warmed, hard body, his strength, the gentleness of his mouth, the sweetness of it, the intense pleasure a touch on her lips gave to her whole body. . . . She was lost in newfound pleasure until his tongue slipped between her lips. The shocking newness of that, the fright and then the thrill of it, made her stagger. And so he drew her closer so she wouldn't have to trouble herself with standing. Only breathing.

Sweet, he thought with growing pleasure, sweeter than he could remember a woman's kiss being. Her body was soft and lithe and giving in his arms. He stood in the shaded sunlight with the free wind at his back, and held a willing woman in his arms, and felt right and good again. If he could take her somewhere and be alone with her for an hour he would be entirely healed. But he was no boy, and no fool. And no matter the sweetness and temptation, he never forgot he was a lone man on a strange shore. A visitor in an alien place had no right forgetting where he was, whatever he was doing.

"Oh, Hannah," he said with regret as his mouth left hers. Because he knew her name would bring her back to her senses.

"Oh, my!" she said, and blinked. And stepped back.

She didn't know where to look. Her face was pink and her eyes wide, and she looked so altogether shocked he found it very hard not to pull her back into his arms again. Because he knew he could make her forget her name again. But it wasn't wise right now. The time wasn't ripe.

And so he could have blessed the bird, although a moment later he damned it.

He spotted it from the corner of his eye. It flew down from a hickory tree, coming down from out of the deep green recesses of it like a bright-feathered comet, and landed hard on his shoulder. He didn't flinch. The sound of its wings were as familiar to him as the weight of it as it settled on his shoulder. It rubbed its small, warm head against his chin, and crooned deep in its throat.

But Hannah stared, her hand to her mouth in utter surprise.

"Pitheth of eight!" it said in its high, cracked voice. "Pitheth of eight!"

Hannah's eyes widened in childlike pleasure.

Dan shrugged. But he knew it would take more than that to dislodge the bird.

"Ah, me corithone!" it cooed as it bobbed up and down, rubbing its green head against his cheek. "My heart'th delight!"

But Mistress Rachel wasn't delighted. And Master Jenkins was so downright suspicious he didn't try to hide it.

Hannah explained.

"Dan said it was on the ship he was thrown off. He remembers it. It obviously remembers him. He had a kindness for it. The other men would have let it starve," she said indignantly.

The parrot sat on Dan's shoulder and stared down at them, its small black eyes unwinking.

"I don't know why it's here," Dan said, and the parrot rode out a shrug. "I wouldn't have credited it—for it seemed to belong to the ship rather than any one man. But I confess I appreciated its company when I sat alone in the night, staring at the stars. And so I often shared my breakfast with it. Which was more than most of the other men did. That's the only reason I can think for its preference for me. It was a marked preference, I admit. Still, I never thought it would follow me. Do you think it came off the ship when it saw me hit the water?" he asked as he scratched the small green head with one long finger and the bird closed its eyes in what looked like ecstasy.

Hannah felt a warmth in the pit of her stomach and almost envied the bird.

"Well, they do say the creatures think like men. They live as long as we do," Jedidiah said as he watched the small creature as it snuggled closer to the big man, "and wed each other for life, it's said. So it's only natural they could form a fondness for a human. I've heard stranger things. Birds of the land often do leave ships of the sea when they approach a pleasant shore. There's fruit trees down the coast too, at Wilson's place. The smell of the peaches might have carried on the wind and tempted the little fellow."

The bird shuffled its feet on a broad shoulder. "Ah, me corithon!" it cried in its creaky voice. "Me corithon!"

"Or something else may have tempted it more," Jedidiah said.

"If so," Dan said with a little smile, "it's a hasty heart we have here. I'm not the first this bird has loved. I think it was trained to speak by a Spaniard. It says 'my heart, my heart' in Spanish when it's happy."

"Pitheth of eight! Pitheth of eight!" the parrot croaked, bobbing up and down.

"And that," Dan said with less glee, "when it wants to make a fuss."

"Pitheth of eight, corithon. . . ." Hannah sounded it out, and then laughed. "It lisps!" she said with delighted discovery.

"Yes. Well, I said I think it was taught to speak by a Spaniard," Dan said.

"Aye. And 'pieces of eight' because it was a Spanish pirate that taught him, or maybe because he was stolen from a Spanish ship," Rachel said, watching him narrowly. "Because if they are loyal creatures, only death or theft could have separated it from its master."

"Yes. Likely," Dan agreed in the thoughtful silence that followed that.

They spoke about his future as well as his past in the dark of the night that night in their bed.

"No saying he was a pirate," Jedidiah said.

"No saying there's any harm even if he was," his wife agreed. "But he's up and about, and his eyes tell me what he's thinking about. And honest sailor or reformed pirate, he's no saint. Hannah's heart is in her eyes too—whenever she sees him. And to my mind, she sees him too much. We don't know where he's been, Mr. Jenkins. Nor where he's going."

"True," he said after a pause. "But at least, we can see that she doesn't go with him until we do."

"Good," she said with relief.

"And then we'll see what else we can do," he murmured before he turned on his side to sleep.

But his daughter couldn't sleep. Hannah lay in her bed, turning so often she tangled her sheets to ropes. Then she rose and paced, and looked out the window and saw nothing but the soft mists of a damp Long Island night. She thought she might as well abandon all attempts to sleep. She drew on a robe and decided to tiptoe down to the kitchens to find something to eat. Halfway there, upon the stair, she heard it.

At first she thought it was Dan's exotic green bird. It stayed in his room at night as by day, reluctant to go farther than his shoulder. But it was not the bird that spoke. This was a terrible sound, a smothered croak that came, however strange, from a human throat. And from his room.

She knew the halls of her father's house as well as her own heart, and ran to Dan's room quickly. She listened at the door and heard the sound clearer. He was muttering, "No, no, no," when he wasn't protesting something else wordlessly and with horror. She'd come into this room when he'd been helpless before, and so after only a second's hesitation she went in now.

He was alone. But he was clawing the air, straining, his eyes closed tight, his head thrown back against his pillows. He was bare to the waist, and his broad chest was damp with sweat. The parrot had flown to his bedstead, where it sat, agitated, flapping its wings, but silent.

"No, no, no," he muttered, turning his head, as he'd done when he'd burned with the fever that had followed his injury. But when she put her hand lightly on his forehead she found his skin chill and damp.

"No, no, no," she echoed with sympathy so great it

welled up in her throat and hurt. She leaned over him. She touched his arm, and he shivered. She held his clenched hand, and he startled. His eyes flew wide and he rose in one swift movement and caught her by the shoulders and pinned her down to the bed beside him.

"What?" he snarled. "Oh, Lord," he said, seeing her. He loosed her and fell back, dazed. "Is it real?" he groaned, still half asleep. "The sand around me: the more I dig, the more comes back. I'm digging my grave as I fight for the air. Oh, God, will I never get out!"

Before she could think of what to say to reassure him, he was upright beside her, his hand gentle on her cheek. "Did I hurt you?" he asked in his normal voice. "It was the dream again. Are you all right? Hannah, forgive me."

"I'm fine," she whispered. "But you? I heard you. I came to see."

"And see what you get for it," he groaned. "Lord, look at this! You're in my bed in the middle of the night! What will your parents say? Hannah, leave. Now. Go to your own bed. Never have I had to say a thing I meant less," he said with a shaky laugh, "but please—go. I'm fine now."

She rose and went to the door. She looked back.

"I'm sure," he said without her asking, "now, shoo!"

When she left and closed the door behind her, he fell back to his damp pillow, one arm across his eyes. He was a strong man, but he didn't know where he'd found the control to send her away. He'd woken from horror to find himself visited by a woman from the kind of dream that comes to men who have been at sea too long. Her hair had been loose, drifting in a perfumed, silken curtain to her waist. And her waist! She'd been soft and curved under his hand—all he needed. But all he needed was to be found with her in his bed.

He'd have her in his bed yet, but not now, and never where they could be found. But he would, he promised himself. The planning of it finally enabled him to relax. His pulse slowed, his breathing calmed, and, his desire banked, he lay back and waited for sleep. It was a long time coming because he feared it as much as he needed it. Because this wasn't the first night he'd clawed his way up out of sleep, covered with sweat and filled with stifled screams.

He didn't understand why. He should have rejoiced at his good fortune, and slept his usual deep and dreamless sleep. Because he had been lucky. They hadn't buried him deep. They couldn't have, because when he'd waked in pain in the damp dark, encased in sand, he'd immediately realized what they'd done. It was hideous, but it was a hideous profession, and he was lucky enough to know it. Another man might not have, and would have been doomed. As it was, he'd heard of such things, and so instead of wasting the last seconds of his life in confusion, he'd understood. His horror had given him the strength to scramble free. It had been a desperate struggle but not a long one. It had been easier because they'd obviously sat him upright on the chest—trust Jewel to have had the last laugh. But the last laugh would be his. That, he vowed. And finally, on that vow, he slept.

Hannah didn't. Not for a long while. She wasn't worried so much for him now as for herself. He was the most fascinating man she'd ever known, and every moment she spent with him fascinated her more. He looked like a bold corsair and spoke like an English gentleman. Yet he was humble as a boy because he didn't know his letters. But he learned so quickly, she almost believed he was teasing her by pretending to be illiterate. It wouldn't matter if he was. She was glad of any excuse to be with him. It was breathlessly exciting. Because although he was a perfect gentleman with her, the look in his wild eyes was as palpable as a touch—and the thought of his touch kept her tossing and turning in the night. But he never spoke of the future. And she hadn't the right—or the courage to ask him about it.

But her father did.

"You're mending," Jedidiah said, and puffed on his pipe before he spoke again. "We're pleased at your progress, to be sure. But it's that very progress that's the crux of the problem here," he said, staring down into his pipe so as to avoid his guest's brilliant eyes.

"As well it might be," Dan Silver said quietly. "An able-bodied man has no business battening on a family once he's on his feet again. I was meaning to talk to you about that myself, sir."

The two men sat in Jedidiah's parlor before a cheerful fire.

"I've been your guest for weeks now," Dan went on. "You gave me back my life. There's no way I can repay you. But I'd like to earn my way from now on, because I can. I think it would be more comfortable for everyone if I did."

Jedidiah didn't deny it. They both knew Hannah had been given chores to do, been taken on visits and told to visit others so often she'd not been alone with their guest since the day the parrot had found him a week before. Other things had changed since then too. The invalid had been allowed out. He disappeared for long hours each day, accompanied only by the uncanny green bird. He was seen trampling the shoreline, looking out to sea. He was obviously restless. Hannah was as obviously impatient to see him again.

"Widow Clark, down in town, and the Remsons, who have the farm out by the pond," Jedidiah said, "both say they'll be happy to board you in exchange for work received. Remson's got a bad back, and the widow could use a strong back on her place. They'll provide good meals and a snug berth until you find your way and know what it is you want to do."

Jedidiah busied himself by puffing his pipe to life again. He hated asking the fellow what was none of his business. His daughter was his business, but he couldn't even ask the fellow's intentions, because the lad hadn't professed to have any. Hannah was the one who couldn't take her eyes off him. It wasn't like her, and that wasn't a thing Jedidiah liked.

"I'm sure they would," Dan said. "But I was wondering . . . Ah, it's no secret I'm troubled by dreams, Master Jenkins. I hope I've not disturbed anyone in the night. I can forget what happened to me, but I remember in my sleep each night. It's best, I think, that I live alone until I can tame the dreams. And better still if I could live alone until I know where I'm going." He looked down at his clasped hands and said thoughtfully, "I couldn't help noticing there's an abandoned shack in the woods, by the sea, down near the point. It's a room, nothing more, but I'm a lone man, nothing more. I thought I could fix it up, make it sound. I'd like to bide there. That way I could work for both the widow and the fellow with the bad back. I'd take my pay in food. I could get my feet back on the ground without being beholden to anyone, and have privacy at night until I'm fit to live among men again."

"Don't see why you can't," Jedidiah said thoughtfully. "It's been empty long enough. The fellow who owned the place came here to see if he liked the land well enough to farm it. He gave up a few years back. . . . Do you know? It might be the very thing. We could give you a bed and some provisions. . . . Might well be the very thing," he mused.

Because once the lad was out of the house, he thought, Hannah wouldn't have to watch him so close. And they wouldn't have to watch her so close either.

"Thank you, I'd like that," Dan said.

"And after that . . . ?" Jedidiah asked, using their easy companionship to prod a little more.

"After that?" Dan said with a smile. "Many things, I hope. I never tried farming, but I can learn. Now I've my letters, I can learn more. I'm a good sailor too, and a good sailor can be many things in a thriving port." He lifted his brilliant gaze and looked straight at his host. "But a man must have hopes for a future before he speaks of it—especially to the father of the one he may harbor some hope for. Doesn't he? Or should I say, can he?"

"We'll see," Jedidiah said, greatly pleased.

"I can't ask more," Dan said sincerely.

He smiled, thinking that was true enough. But he certainly could take more. And certainly would.

The house seemed empty when he'd gone. He worked for the widow and Wilt Remson, and Hannah heard nothing but good of him. Sometimes she'd see him in the fields. Sometimes she'd hear of how he paced the water's edge at sunset, skimming stones and staring at the path of the sun on the sound. She'd healed enough wild creatures to know how they pined until they could return to the air or the sea. The thought of him readying to leave wounded her in ways she'd never felt.

She missed his bright jests as much as the solemn moods he'd try to conceal when he saw she noticed them. She missed his outlandish stories and the sly grin he wore to let her know he was joking—as well as the hungry look he had when he thought she wasn't watching. Her parents kept her busy, but busy as she was, her mind was always with him. She thought of him alone in the night in the woods, with nothing but the green bird and his nightmares for company. A week had gone by since he'd left, and she hadn't exchanged a word with him. But it was as if he'd called to her.

She had a basket of food to deliver to his door, and she'd been told to do it after she dropped off some yard goods for Mrs. Haggerty, down the road. That would make her delivery take place after noon, while he was still out in the fields. But she managed to get into a long chat with Mrs. Haggerty. In fact, she seemed so fascinated by that good woman's troubles with her daughter-in-law that Mrs. Haggerty, giddy with the unexpected pleasure of having someone interested in her troubles, invited her to tea. And was delighted when she tarried long after.

Hannah left with an earache, a frozen smile, and a vastly contented neighbor. And a guilty conscience. Because if she hadn't exactly deceived her mother, she knew very well that she wouldn't please her by appearing at Dan's door at dusk. But she thrilled herself.

He was genuinely surprised to see her. She was staggered by how wonderful it felt to see pleasure replace the surprise in his crystal, glowing eyes. Their brilliance illuminated his tanned face, and dried up all the conversation on her lips.

"I thought you were angry with me," he said.

"No, no," she managed to say, and tucked her chin down as though looking in her basket.

He put one finger beneath her chin and tilted her face up to his. "I haven't seen you in days," he said simply.

"Well, no, but you were working, and I was busy . . ."

"And your parents, rightly, didn't want me near you," he said on a sigh, and turned from her. He put his hands in his pockets and looked out to sea.

The hut he lived in was on a cliff overlooking the sound. It was a calm evening, and there was nothing to be seen but gulls on the sunset-bronzed waters below. She saw him staring out over the sound, his face still, his wide shoulders silhouetted against the vast, empty waters. She wondered what he saw there, beside the beautiful view. And never knew that he saw neither sunsets or birds but only a road. The one that had taken him here, and the one that would take him away. He turned back to her.

"I'm a vagrant, a vagabond, a fellow snatched from the sea, and owed to it forever," he said with a sudden burst of candor. "And you're a girl from a good family." He shrugged. There was nothing else to say. But he watched her closely. He had his plans for her and doubted she'd elude them. But he was a fair man. She should know it in some way. If she chose to stay despite it, so be it. He had little conscience, and so it needed little appeasement.

"So, does that mean I can't deliver a basket of good bread and cheese to you?" she said saucily, taking refuge in a jest.

But he wouldn't have it. He cupped her face in two hands and gazed at her steadily. The bright, burning look in his eyes held her as surely as his hands did. He nodded, satisfied with what he saw. And then he kissed her.

She was entirely lost. His mouth was hot and intoxicating, his hands were hard and soft on her body. She leaned in to him, too shy to put her hands on him, too pleasured to make him stop touching her. She never wanted his kiss to end. It almost didn't. But he never became so lost in the incredible sweetness of her mouth that he didn't remember he had no right to it. He released her.

"Fly away home, little ladybird," he said in a hoarse voice. "It's dusk, you shouldn't be out alone in the dark."

"But you are with me," she said.

"So I am. Wouldn't your father be pleased?" he said bitterly.

"Why shouldn't he be?" she asked, dazed with pleasure, terrified at her boldness, terrified lest he never be so bold with her again.

"Why, indeed? I have no family, no occupation, and nothing but my back and two hands to recommend me. Wouldn't any father be pleased with me being escort to his dear daughter in the dark?"

"Father doesn't judge a man for his past. Only his future," she said.

"Truly?" he asked. "And if that was to be with you?"

Her eyes grew wide. A faint tinge of wild rose appeared in her cheeks. "He wouldn't mind," she said faintly.

"Would you?" he asked and chuckled deep in his throat when she could only shake her head.

Their next kiss lasted until he knew he wouldn't be

able to contain himself much longer. Then he stepped away.

"Come, I'll walk you home," he said. He took her hand and kissed it before he put it in his, and walked her down the long path to her house.

He had to remind her to give him the basket when they parted at her gate. "Best you say nothing until I can say more," he told her soberly. "When I've a future and a date, that is to say. Please. I should be the one to have that pleasure. All right?"

She nodded. He took another long kiss from her, and then pushed her gently toward her house. " 'Til then," he said, and waved. When she looked back, he was gone again, into the shadows of evening.

He strolled back in the dark, pleased with himself. It wasn't as if he'd promised her anything but a word about his future, and a date. If she'd take him on that word, he'd take her. Even though the future he saw lay across the water, and the date when he'd stay with any one woman was one he couldn't count to—and he never had any trouble with his numbers.

He wanted her badly. The women he'd known had been hard and tart. She was sweet and yielding. He rose in the night from his nightmares, but also sometimes in a different form of excitation, with the taste of her still on his lips and the vision of her long dark hair and smiling lips still imprinted on his sleep-blinded eyes. Beyond her physical attractions, she was kindhearted and good, and he'd had little enough of that in his life.

Born in poverty, he'd run to the sea to find his fortune. He'd found pain at the hands of many masters instead. He'd decided to come ashore forever when he'd gotten drunk that night in Liverpool. And woke to find himself aboard a new vessel, laboring for the king—

and the king didn't care if he lived or died any more than any man ever had. He'd worked out his years before the mast, and then signed on with the only men the king's navy feared. Now he breathed deeply of the ferns and bracken on the path around him. The earth smelled sweeter than the sea, but the sea was his home. He'd be gone from this place as soon as events warranted. But before he left, he'd have her. He'd had small pleasure in his life, he thought. He deserved some now.

He'd leave her with the memory of pleasure, the knowledge that not all men were safe, and the wisdom to expect nothing more than what one could get for oneself. That wasn't a bad legacy. Because it was, after all, all he had.

He reached his doorstep and the green bird fluttered down to his shoulder.

"Thweetheart, thweetheart," it muttered.

He laughed and stroked its silky head. "A bird to love me, eh? Ah, well, why not? You screamed me out of my sleep in the sand, love. Yours was the voice that woke me to life. So I'm yours forever, then, is that it? Faith! You're possessive as any lass, aren't you? I'll bet you're ten times more faithful. Wait, I'll share a biscuit with you," he promised.

He shook off the bird, put two hands on his lean hips and stretched the work-weary muscles in his long frame. He'd eat and then sleep, and then rise to work in other men's fields until he found a way to return to his own. He yawned and stretched again. But then he froze, his hands still in the air, and stared out at the moonlight on the water. He had the eyes of a shark, they said. But his vision was that of a seabird. He lowered his arms slowly. He saw a tiny shape, a spot, a blotch, an absence of moonlight far out on the horizon. But he knew what it was. They were back.

His heart, the heart that a dirk had missed by an inch, picked up a new, heavy beat. They were back. That meant he had a chance to get the other things he wanted badly: a way to leave. And revenge.

But he would have to move quickly.

She paced the moon-shadowed path and looked back over her shoulder every so often in fear. Because every snapped twig and fallen leaf sounded like a footfall. There were no strangers here, except the one she was stealing off to see. And no wild animals except for fox and deer, raccoons and possum, who were more afraid of Hannah than she could ever be of them. But if her parents should rise and find her not in her room, where she was supposed to be . . . But why should they? They hadn't checked her bed since she'd been a little girl afraid of ghosties and terrors in the night. Now she feared nothing so much as not seeing him again.

He'd brought her back her basket at dawn, before he set off for work. Before he'd left, after he'd thanked her parents, he whispered to her.

"Come to me tonight, at eleven bells. Alone. Tell no one. I can say no more now. Only as you love me: come, love."

It had been hard to think, to talk and walk normally all day, just thinking of his voice as he'd said "love." Because he had sounded in need and forlorn. And though she'd never had a secret from her parents of any higher order than a smuggled toad in her bedroom, tonight she slipped through the wood to his house on the cliff without a backward look, except in fear of discovery.

"You're here!" he said, and took her in his arms, and closed the door behind them.

The little hut smelled of fresh-hewn wood, green pine, and the sea. It was swept clean and kept painfully neat. But that didn't surprise her. Many kinds of men were good sailors, but a good sailor was always a tidy man. There wasn't much room in the shack that he'd repaired, but every piece in it was stowed where it belonged. There was a bed with her mother's old patched coverlet over it, a chair, and a table. His coat hung on a nail on the wall. All his other gear was in an old sailor's bag near his bed. The one window that faced the sea was open. The other was shuttered. One lamp was lit.

She drew back from his kiss. "What is it?" she asked, her eyes searching his face in the dim shadows. "What's the matter?"

"Did you tell anyone?" he asked urgently.

She shook her head in denial until her cloak's hood fell back from her hair. He pushed the hood back farther and gazed down at her. His hand went to the buttons at her throat. She gazed at him with wide, fearful eyes.

"Dan," she said again, "what is it?"

"I missed you," he said.

"What?" She blinked. "You made me sneak away, you made me crazy all the day, and only because you . . . missed me?"

"There's no 'only' about it," he said. "I didn't think I could get through another long night without you. How many nights can a man go without sleep? I almost fell into the thresher today. The sun sets, and seals my doom. I wait out the night until the morning, and then waste the day dreaming of you—and hoping for a glimpse of you. I can't bear it, love."

"But tonight is Friday. We'll see each other in Church S-sunday," she said, stammering because he'd slipped her cloak off, and his hand was still at her nape, toying with the buttons of her dress now.

"In church," he echoed, "and shall I get to harmonize with you? What joy. Hannah, I need you closer than that. I'll swear you know that, love."

"Ah, me corithon, me corithon," the parrot piped.

Its harsh tones were ridiculous in light of what Dan had just said. Hannah laughed too loud. She was distracted, but relieved the strange mood had been broken.

But it hadn't been. Because without taking his eyes from her, Dan opened the door with one hand and the parrot flew out into the night.

"I need you, love," he said, and closed the door against the night.

His lips met hers, and then moved to her cheek, to her neck, as he loosened one button after the other, and saluted each new bit of her skin that was revealed. She shivered in his arms, and drew in the fresh, spicy scent of him, and held hard to his wide shoulders. He caressed her breast, and as she drew in her breath in shock, he took the rest of it away with his warm, searching mouth. The buttons opened, and he began to slide her dress away from her shoulders.

"Dan," she murmured in as much fear as delight, "we mustn't, you mustn't."

But she kept kissing him and burrowing into his arms. Because no man had ever done her an injury, and she couldn't believe the one she loved most would do anything that wasn't right. He would stop when the time came. She knew that as well as she knew she didn't really want him to.

He stopped, and she was lost. He looked down at her soberly.

"No. I must, you must. We must," he said. "You know that."

"But you said . . ."

"I said I'd tell you when the time was right. It is. You will be mine. And so why not tonight?"

She didn't know why not. They would be man and wife, wouldn't they? He'd declared himself. She knew no other man she wanted, and knew she'd want no other. Her parents weren't thrilled with him, but had allowed they might come to be if he got a regular job. She knew he would. He was no fool: there was no other way he could have asked for her, and he knew it. And above all these reasons, and beyond all reason, she knew he needed her now. As much as she needed him. They wouldn't wait on their wedding. She wouldn't make him wait now. She raised her lips to his.

He sighed against her mouth. She felt his lean, muscled body relax, and then coil into action again as he raised her in his arms and carried her the few steps to his narrow bed.

"Better," he whispered as he set her down in the fluffy coverlets. "Ah, better," he breathed as he settled beside her.

She turned to him without shame and with absolute trust. After all, she'd been waiting for him all her life, although never in her wildest dreams of love had she dreamed of a lover like him. Strong and gentle, wild and yet restrained, he was all she'd hoped for. His face was her mirror; she thought herself beautiful when she saw herself in his eyes, and was glad that she deserved him. Because she thought him so miraculously handsome she couldn't look her fill of him. She was thrilled

by the sight of his powerful body as he took off the last
of his clothing. But not so much as she was by the feel
of his naked form against her own. She was staggered
by the sensation but not afraid. How could she be? She
had discovered the other half of herself at last.

He took his time with her. He had the time to do it in.
The moon was rising. They wouldn't be here until long
after midnight. She'd stay until then. And then he'd
leave her. Forever.

He felt no guilt, he told himself. He'd won her fair
and square as rigging. He'd chosen his words carefully,
so she could never call him liar after either, even in her
thoughts. "The time was right for him to have her. She
would be his. And why not tonight? He *should* be the
one to ask her father." So he should be—if he ever did.

Everything he'd said was true. If it wasn't what she
thought, that wasn't his fault. Neither was the fact that
all the world wasn't filled with simple island folk. He
would give her a night to remember in every way. And
maybe, he thought as he felt her body warm beneath his
questing hands, she wanted no more than that. She'd
have no more, at any rate. He was a pirate and a rover,
a man whose road lay over the water, and tonight he
visited her as the tide visited the shore. He'd be gone by
dawn's light. Better for her that way too, he thought.

He'd had many women, and he'd left every one of
them. In that, she'd be no different from any of them.
Only better. Because her mouth was impossibly sweet
and her high, firm breasts even sweeter, and the damp
he eventually sought in her nether lips told him she was
ready for him, as every other woman's always had. But
she was different. She was Hannah, and he couldn't forget it for a minute, though he tried.

It was Hannah's long, dark, fragrant hair that he loosened to lay over his own shoulders now. It was Hannah's innocent mouth he tutored to expertise. It was Hannah who turned and twisted beneath his tender, insistent ministrations. It was Hannah's small, tentative hands that dared to touch him at last, drifting down from his powerful shoulders to his lean flanks. She shied away until he placed her hands on him again and then retreated, only to touch him once more until he groaned with the pleasure of it.

But still she was like no other he'd ever known. She bore the scent of soap and flowers, not harsh perfume and sweat. She muttered no curses, whispered no profanities, gave out no squeals women thought a man liked to hear. She only breathed, "Ah, Dan. Oh, Dan," again and again, until his heart nearly broke because he so yearned to have her call him by his real name.

So he stopped her mouth with kisses and bent to her. And realized he'd never caused a woman pain with his entry before either, not even for the second he saw Hannah open her eyes in surprise. But what undid him entirely was the thought—while thought was still possible for him—that no other woman had ever looked at him with love as he made love to her.

And Hannah held on to his wide shoulders and received him the way the shore receives the incoming tide: because it was inevitable, and right. She took the cresting of the wave of his pleasure as he pounded against her. And rose to meet it and heard the broken tumble of his ecstatic cry even as she took his body deep within hers.

He held her close long after, and that too was a thing that had never happened before. Because he knew he'd done an extraordinary thing. Now too he knew what he would do, if he could. But it was too late.

"Sleep now," he crooned to her as he petted her long silky hair. "I'll wake you and get you to your bed long before the light."

But long before that, when he saw her breathing was deep and even, he stole from the bed. He dressed in the dark and picked up his bag. And at the last he left her the note he'd so painstakingly written the night before. He put it on his table, where she'd find it with his last gift to her. He regretted only that he couldn't kiss her one more time. And then he crept from the hut and strode out into the night.

Her eyes opened as the door closed. She could no more sleep after the amazing thing they'd done together than she could fly. But he'd wanted her to, and there was enormous pleasure in just lying next to his warm, breathing body, savoring their intimacy. And then terrible pain, watching him through downcast eyes, as he'd stolen away like a thief in the night.

The bent tree stood at the seam of the beach and the land. The tide had eaten away half the earth at its roots, yet it flourished in the peculiarly aggressive way of all things that dare to live at the edge of the sea. Tonight the moon was almost full and gave off a translucent light. The pirate ship on the horizon was like a black cutout pasted on the margins of a molten silver sea. The light was bright but not quite like daylight, so the men who stepped from out of the rowboat that beached itself on the shore could see clearly but not with depth and accuracy. It was as though they were looking underwater.

Their stocky leader strode onto the shore and paced to the tree. He stopped and pointed. The men with him bore shovels, but they hesitated. A squat fellow among them laughed.

"Don't want to disturb dear Dancer, do ye?" he chortled. "But why not? I be sure he'll be glad of the company. Maybe he's waitin' with a quip fer us. Aye, he'll be grinnin' some, to be sure. He be grinnin' more in a month or so, but we'll see teeth enough tonight, I don't doubt. Come, let's see how the climate's improved his complexion, shall we?" he asked, and set to digging with zest.

"Get to it," the captain said glumly. "Ignore the body and bring me the chest. I need it sooner than I thought. Jewel's right, damn his eyes. Dig."

The other men picked up their shovels and joined in, but they were silent as the sea tonight. They dug for several minutes, but then, one by one, they stopped. Jewel dug on with increasing frenzy.

"They's naught here, Cap'n," one of the men said fearfully. "Nary a scrap."

"Aye, but moonlight's tricky," one of the men volunteered. "Want to pace her off again, Captain?"

"I know the tree. There's no other place it can be," the captain muttered, but he turned back to the sea and sighted the land again. He counted his paces and walked back, stopping in the same spot again. By now Jewel stood in the hole he was digging, and the only chest to be seen was his own, halfway above the sand.

"Leave off!" captain shouted. "There's nothing here! Someone's been here. It could have been any of you. I mind we made landfall thirty miles up coast from here not two weeks past. Some of you said you were restless and so were given leave to go ashore for a handful of days to raise some hell before we weighed anchor again. Now I wonder if anyone was raising something else . . . any man who knows anything would be wise to speak up now."

"Captain," one of the men called, and in the eerie light his eyes were wide and wild, "t'aint our way! Mebbe it be one of the locals. This ain't a wild shore. Some lucky fisher lad could be setting on yer treasure now."

"Aye!" another pirate agreed. "Mebbe we could start askin' questions in this town. Ask some sharper, get some answers, get back yer chest double quick. Chick here, he looks nachural. Got no scars, nary a tattoo. Speaks regular too. Got fist like iron, though. We could send him, couldn't we?"

"Mebbe Jewel too," another called. "Seein' as to how he's so quick and sharp wi' a knife."

"Aye," the men murmured among themselves.

"He be here!" Jewel protested. "He has to be. I planted him, and I knows it. Tide's might of shifted, land moves by the sea. I'll shift a bit left, then right, I'll find him—"

"If it takes all eternity, right, Jewel?" a lazy, mocking voice called from out of the shadows. "But what if he finds you first, murderer?"

They froze in place. Even Jewel did. A lean, long shadow stepped out of the woods.

"Looking for me, Jewel? Or pretending to? Since whoever took the chest would have to shift its guardian too, so men would doubt it was ever there. But why bother? Here I am, hot from Hell for you."

Jewel stared. But then he put his hands on the rim of the hole he'd dug, and levered himself up and out of it. He squinted at the figure before him.

"I don't think yer come from Hell, Dancer. But I be

glad to send ye there again," he said, crouching, his knife in his hand.

But the shadow held a knife too. And when it moved into a pool of moonlight, it was grinning. With Dancer's face. One of the pirates crossed himself, another blanched white as the moonlight. They all drew back, except for Jewel. And the captain.

"You're hard to kill, lad," the captain said with a smile in his voice. "I'm glad of it. You've brains, along with your brawn and courage. Much could be made of you, in trade or the high seas. I know merchants and pirates, but few who could be both. I've missed you sorely. But I miss my treasure too. I'm off to London sooner than I thought. Come, lead me to it."

"I was put in with it as caretaker, Captain, but I'm sorry. I abandoned the post. Well, not that sorry, actually." The shadowy figure showed a brighter grin. "Because I was saved somehow. I woke in a local man's bed. But I didn't wake for a week, and I'm not even sure I can help you dig for it now. Jewel's dirk was sharp but, like himself, slovenly. As now, he missed the mark. But it was close. So close as to bring me close to death's door and lying on my back for weeks wondering if it would open for me. So as to where the treasure is, I don't know."

"Aye, likely," Jewel snarled. "He woke in a strange bed and left a pirate's treasure to rot whilst he mended? Not he. He'd steal the coins off his dead father's eyes while he himself lay dyin', that one would."

"Possibly—if I'd ever known who he was," Dancer agreed. "But not this time. I couldn't. Your knife bit deep, Jewel, but as ever not true."

"Try me now," Jewel said, beckoning with his free hand. "I'll settle the matter clear. Or are ye goin' to jest yer way out of it, so none will see ye got more quips than courage, eh? Dancer, the handsome lad who dances his way out o' tight spots—but not this time, I vow. Come, test 'gainst my blade, if ye dare, if ye be a man a'tall."

Dancer threw his bright dagger into his other hand and crouched. "Oh, Jewel, you don't know what I dare when I've an enemy who dares face me when he knows I'm ready for him! I've laid awake nights dreaming of this."

"Don't be a fool, lad!" the captain shouted. "Jewel's a killer. You have the shark's eyes, but he has the temperament. Settle it later with sword or pistol when your blood's not running so hot—or you'll spill it out again. You've courage, true. But you've been ill and he's a devil with his dirk."

"I don't fear him," Dancer called, never taking his eyes off Jewel. "I don't use my dirk so often because I don't hate my fellow man so much. But I can slip through the shadows like my namesake, Captain, and I've a taste for blood tonight."

"Aye, c'mon, c'mon," Jewel said, grinning and beckoning.

Dancer stepped forward. The men fell still, because the deadly dance had begun and there was nothing anyone could say that would influence the outcome.

But then there was a screech, a flapping, and a compact ball of feathers came flying out from the forest. It landed on Dancer's shoulder with such velocity, he staggered. But he recovered quickly, and held his knife out high in front of him.

"Don't try it, Jewel," he warned his opponent. "Don't even think it. One time you had at me unprepared. It will never happen again. I was startled merely.

Let me rid myself of my friend and I'll be back for you."

"Thweetheart, thweetheart," the parrot cooed. But Dancer's grin was a thin line as he gave the bird his free hand to perch upon. Then he handed it to another pirate. "Take the green lad, Benson, and hold him tight. He might interfere, and I want no one on my side but the Devil himself now."

He stepped back in front of Jewel and nodded. "Have at me now, Jewel, or hold your peace forevermore."

"Not bloody likely," Jewel snarled.

They got in position again. And again there was a wild cry from the surrounding forest. But this time it was a girl who came flying from the wood. Her long hair floated free behind her, her feet were bare, and she ran to Dancer's side.

"Don't, oh, Dan, don't," she cried, her hand on his arm.

"Oh, good God," he sighed. "Hannah, what are you thinking of?"

"Don't fight," she begged him. "You're not yourself yet. You lost so much blood—you've just healed. Let him say whatever he likes, just don't fight him."

He looked over her head at the men standing in a circle on the sand. Even the errant moonlight couldn't conceal their interested stares. She was young and lovely, and alone with them in the concealing night. But not quite alone, he realized, thinking quickly.

"This lady is going to be my wife," he said, putting his arm around her. "I claim her as my own. He who touches her, whatever happens to me, violates the law of the brotherhood." They nodded, every man among them, and he breathed easier. He turned to her.

"Hannah, I must," he said quietly. "It's a debt, and a challenge, my fate and our future, all in one. It's not a thing I can avoid. Nor would I wish to." Saying it, he knew it, and felt a surge of happiness, and then a new, odd, and curious peace settle upon him.

She gazed into his silver eyes for a long moment. The moonlight showed matching silver tears as they began to course down her cheeks. But she nodded and backed away, step by step, from him.

Dancer stepped toward Jewel, on the sand beneath the tree where he had been left for dead a month past. And Jewel grinned and greeted him with a swaggering bow before he resumed his deadly stance. They fought in silence, the only sounds their feet scuffing the sand, their breathing becoming harsher and louder as they danced. Because it was a dance. A thing of side steps and feints, leaps and pivots, approaches and retreats, but a dance to no music but their own rapidly beating hearts. It could be over in a second, and they all knew it. But until it was, it was a thing of shifting shadows and racing hearts—until one of them was stilled forever.

And then there was a grunt. And a gasp. And it was done.

Jewel stood smirking until he looked down at his lifeblood spouting from his chest, and he shuddered, like a harpooned whale in its final flurry. It was the last thing he did. He crumpled to the sand.

Dancer ran lightly toward him and knelt at his side. He plucked the knife from Jewel's lifeless hand gingerly, the way a man might cosh a dying bluefish, so as to avoid being bitten in its death throes. Then he swiftly thrust his hand into Jewel's coat. And sat back on his heels, grinning brighter than the waxing moon. He held something that glittered even more brightly in the palm of his bloody hand.

"Ah, Captain. Just as I thought. See? This is why he wanted me dead again so badly. Because a dead man is the best man to blame your own crime on. See. Just as I thought."

The captain came close and picked the glittering jewel from Dancer's palm. It was an ornate stone in a baroque setting, heavily crusted with gold, pendant in shape, and it shone in the night like a star.

"The Princessa's Diamond!" Kidd exclaimed. "From the chest."

"Aye. A gem that couldn't be easily sold because it is so distinctive," Dancer said. "That's probably why he still had it on him. I couldn't have touched your chest, Captain. I was on my back in my sweet Hannah's father's bed. I admit, when I could rise from that bed I went looking—it was gone. Else," he said ruefully, "I wouldn't still be here. You know that."

The captain nodded and the men murmured among themselves. They all knew it was true. Jewel had been right about one thing. Dancer's odd eyes had always been fixed on treasure. The girl was a beauty, all right. But it was simple alchemy: mix Dancer with gold, and Dancer would vanish. The very fact that he was here this night was a sure sign he couldn't have known where the treasure had got to.

"But Jewel could get at it," Dancer went on, "and did. He wanted my heart on his knife to explain it. You're out a small fortune, Captain, unless you find where he's hidden it. But I bear him no grudge now. If he hadn't stolen your buried treasure, I wouldn't have stayed around to find mine."

He held out his arms to Hannah, and she rushed to

him. He held her so tightly it was almost painful, but not so painful as his absence had been to her. He dropped his head and buried his face in her hair, and she could hear his heart as it shuddered steadily against hers.

"Well, then," Kidd sighed, "I'm fair diddled, aren't I? I'll set a search, but my hopes aren't high. I'm off to London soon, to plead my case. If you hear aught of my treasure, lad, send word to my wife in Manhattan. If not—ah, but there's more where that came from. I've hidey holes along this shore from here to Gardiner's Isle, and I mean to empty them this night. And then there's others on the Connecticut side. I don't suppose you're coming with me, are you Dancer?"

"Thank you, but no, captain," Dancer said, his face serious and still. "I valued gold above all else, until Jewel almost took me from this life. I've had time to think. I've my life before me now—and it's here."

"Well, then, start it with this," Kidd said, and flipped the pendant to him. Dancer caught it in one hand and closed his fist over it. "You might not be able to sell it, but your children can," Captain Kidd said. "Count it as my wedding gift. That—and the damned bird. Good luck."

"And to you," Dancer said, because there was nothing else to say. If the captain was going to face justice in England, he knew he'd never see him on this earth again, no matter the treasure Kidd unearthed for influence and bribes. England had sent Kidd to harry pirates, not to become one. He had, and Dancer was sure he would pay for it. Dancer came from England, and knew too well its revenge on those it deemed enemies of the crown. Kidd would pay his last crew handsomely. But it was a waste of his money, and their time. The money earned would never be spent on pleasure. Dancer pitied those who followed him to his fate. He also knew he'd nothing to fear from them. They'd trouble him no more than Jewel did now. England would see to that.

And the other pirates he'd served with would soon scatter across the seven seas and never seek him further either. Because they saw for themselves that his treasure consisted merely of one pendant they couldn't sell in their lifetime, one lisping parrot, and one lovely girl.

But it was more than enough for Dancer.

The pirates buried Jewel beneath the tree and went back to their rowboat. Dancer and Hannah watched them disappear over the water and fade into the night.

"So now you know," Dancer said seriously when they turned to each other again. "My name isn't Dan Silver. I said it was because I was afraid someone might hear it and know me. I am called Dancer. If you want me, you'll have to give me a first name as well as a new name. But do you want me now? Listen well before you tell me. I was a pirate. Don't deceive yourself about that. True, I was many things before I became a pirate, things that made me become one—perhaps. And it's also true that I'll never sail as a privateer again, at least not willingly. But there it is. Jewel took exception to something I said—or wouldn't do for him before." He shrugged. "However it happened, he hated me. He saw an opportunity and attacked me before I could defend myself or anyone could prevent him. Thinking I was dead, they buried me here with their ill-got treasure. I escaped my tomb—and that life. I came tonight to end it for good, one way or another, because I knew that did I not, it would always be waiting for me. It's over now.

"I can change what I will be, but not what I was. Do you want a pirate, love?"

"I want no other," she declared.

It was a long while before either said anything again, although they communicated to each other beautifully without words.

"We'll marry by this week's end, come what may," he said when he finally left her at her door. "Tell your parents tonight. I'll speak to your father in the morning. I'll find a trade, and build you a fine house someday, you'll see. But I want my name on you before my babe starts growing in you. First things first."

She smiled through glad tears, and clung to him long after their good-night kiss. Because it tasted like a greeting instead of a good-bye.

It was. He stepped lightly into the wood. But he ran when he remembered what he'd left in the shack. When he got there, he breathed a deep sigh of relief. As he'd hoped, she'd been too intent on following him to read his note or unwrap his gift. He burned the note and slipped the pile of golden coins he'd left for her into his pocket.

Then he pushed his bed until it was away from the wall. Then he knelt, and whistling under his breath, set to prying up the floorboards there.

He'd burned the chest plank by plank. And pitched the iron staves into the sea. That he'd accomplished the first night he'd crept out of the Jenkins' house. There might have been blood on the wood staves too then— his, from his reopened wound. And his blood as well on the handle of the shovel after he'd piled the sand back into the hole that had been his tomb and his treasure trove. But the shovel had been broken and given to the sea. Then he'd poured the coins into the pillow slip he'd brought with him, and dragged it into the wood. When he'd got his breath back, he'd hidden his trove beneath last autumn's leaves, behind a rock by an old oak, until he'd been fit enough to bring it here. He hadn't missed a thing.

But he had changed his plans. He'd meant to leave her some coins and sail away after he dealt with Jewel. And then steal back, months later, to retrieve his treasure. Then sail away again, for good this time. But he could no more leave her than his heart. He'd known it the moment he'd joined his body with hers. Or it might be, he thought, sitting back on his heels, that he'd known it the moment he'd seen her, no matter what yarns he'd told himself. Else why would he have taken such care to take the pendant to the meeting with Jewel so that he could plant it in his coat when he killed him, and then bring it out to show the world who had stolen it? Or have it on his own body when he died, if he had lost the fight, so they wouldn't have to suspect any of the locals of taking the treasure?

He'd been tempted, lured, landed, beached, and what of it? He asked himself now as he stirred his hand through his hoard of bright coins. He'd leave most of it here, and build a stout house over it. He'd live in that house, and year by year the pile would dwindle as he invested it wisely, so as to grow another, bigger one in a proper bank. Kidd had been a man of business and had amassed a fortune before he'd become a pirate. He was easily as clever as Kidd, if not more so. Because he knew when to leave the sea. And could do the same work on shore. Because a land pirate, as he'd learned from Kidd, could steal as much money in his own way, and not risk his hide either.

"Pitheth of eight! Pitheth of eight!" the parrot warbled as it flew in the door and landed on the bed.

"Yes, so you say," Dancer said as he buried his hoard again. "And more than that, lad."

Then he set to cleaning his shack and preparing himself for the dawn. When he would set in motion what was necessary to enable him to bring home his real treasure—and keep it by his side until he left the land, the sea, and the earth itself.

Fathers and Daughters

by Patricia Rice

"I would like your permission to marry your daughter, sir." Lord Edward John Chatham stood nervously before the older man's desk. From his crisply immaculate white waterfall cravat to the elegantly tailored dove-gray pantaloons tucked correctly into a pair of gleaming Hessians, he was every inch the proper young gentleman. A thick head of burnished brown curls cut fashionably to fall forward over his forehead did not disguise the bleakness of his eyes as he watched the other man turn his back on him and walk away. The fact that he had been offered neither brandy nor a chair spoke ill for his hopes.

"I've been expecting this, Chatham." A small, slenderly built man, Henry Thorogood opened a drawer in a nearby cabinet and withdrew a sheaf of papers. As an astute businessman who had turned his family's dwindling estates into an extremely profitable and lucrative career, Thorogood was always prepared for every eventuality. The neat study in which they stood bespoke his natural methodicalness. He came forward and threw the papers on the desk. "Your vouchers, Chatham. Do you have any idea of the sum total of their worth?"

"Considerably more than you bought them for, I wager," Lord Jack replied wryly, acknowledging Thorogood's shrewdness in obtaining large discounts on practically worthless pieces of paper. Some of those vouchers had been so long outstanding that his creditors would gladly have taken a ha'penny on the pound.

"Enough to have you called before the court, in any case." The older man came to stand behind his desk again. The Thorogoods were an old and respectable family, but no title attached to their name, and Henry's immersion in trade had tainted their welcome in the highest echelons of society. Chatham, on the other hand, was the son of an earl and younger brother of an earl, the current holder of the title, in direct line to the succession, and an eminently eligible bachelor. Henry was well aware of these distinctions and refused to buckle under to the dictates of etiquette and society. He neither sat nor offered his noble guest a chair.

The young man paled slightly at the threat, but he remained steadfast, clenching his hands at his side. "I realize I have overspent my income for some time, but I have already given up my expensive habits and begun to pare down my debts. Except for repaying what you hold there, my allowance from my late father's estate is sufficient to keep Carolyn comfortably, if not quite in the style to which she is accustomed. She understands and has no objections to the modest life we must lead."

"You have already spoken to her? That was unwise. She is much too young to know her own mind. You should have known that of all the wealthy young girls available to buy you out of penury, my daughter was the least suitable. I have no intention of further financing your extravagance at my daughter's expense." Thorogood's voice was harsh and cold as he glared at the lordly young man before him. "You will stay away from Carolyn or I shall have you in debtors' prison so fast your family will not know where to find you."

Or even care, the young man acknowledged to himself. His elder brother had more debts than anyone could repay, but no one dared charge an earl with unpaid bills. He was on his own, as he had been since his father's death, when he was still a schoolboy. The present earl couldn't fish him out of prison any better than he could save himself from going. Lord Jack's jaw tightened at this new obstacle to his happiness.

"I love Carolyn, sir, and I have reason to believe she returns my affections. I will repay those debts in time. You need settle nothing on Carolyn. I will keep her on my income. We will be able to live comfortably in my mother's dower house in Dorset. She will come to no harm at my hands, I assure you." Although he spoke with confidence, Jack was beginning to relive the doubts that had plagued him ever since he had realized his idle pursuit of an heiress had become something much different and totally uncontrollable. He meant every word he said, but he couldn't help remembering Carolyn's youthful innocence. Did she have any idea what a modest life in Dorset meant? How long would it be before she grew restless and bored, deprived of the extravagances her wealthy father had led her to expect of life?

"She will come to no harm at your hands because I will not allow you to lay hands on her!" Thorogood shouted. He had expected the young lordling to crumple with his first shot. This obstinate refusal to acknowledge the facts gave Henry some admiration for the lord, but not enough to surrender his eldest daughter into the young fool's hands. If the man thought his title and family name fair trade for Carolyn's dowry, he would learn otherwise. Carolyn's happiness did not rest on titles, but on character. Chatham's profligate habits did not display the kind of character required for Carolyn's happiness. Resolutely Henry pressed his point. "I will call my daughter in here and you will tell her before my face that you will not see her again. In return, I will not call in your debts. Should you so much as show your face at my door, however, I will hand your vouchers over to the magistrate. Do you understand me?"

Jack heard and understood. Beneath his fashionably pale complexion he turned a shade grayer, but his eyes hardened and took on a light of their own. "I understand you are destroying your daughter's life as well as my own. As you say, she is young and perhaps will recover. For myself, as long as you hold those vouchers, there is no hope for me. If you truly wish me to leave, I request a loan so that I may set about finding a means of repaying those debts." And of returning to Carolyn—but he did not say those words aloud; they held his last flickering hope of a life worth living.

The older man looked at the younger contemptuously, seeing the request as a bribe to ensure his silence. There were very few ways a gentleman could turn money into wealth without land and still remain a gentleman. The loan would be wagered at a card table in a mad attempt to win it all back and would never be seen again. If that was what it took, so be it. Henry nodded tersely. "You will sign a voucher for the sum."

Curling his fingers into his palms and feeling all his plans crumble to bitter ashes inside him, Jack waited for the servant to fetch Carolyn. They had known each other only a few brief months. Perhaps for her it had been a carefree lark, part of the experience of coming out into society. For him it was much more, but he had been careful not to let her see how deeply she affected him. He had never known such quiet, kind affection and cheerful joy as she had brought to him. It should be enough to treasure these few months of happiness they had shared. He tried to fix a careless expression on his face as he heard the unmistakable light patter of her small feet in the hall.

She floated into the room, a brilliant expectancy upon her face as she smiled into Jack's warm gray eyes. Her smile faltered somewhat as she met an unfamiliar cold barrier there, but she did not hesitate. All fragile grace clothed in pale green gauze and ribbons, her light brown hair piled artlessly above a slender throat and velvet eyes, she advanced bravely to kiss her father's cheek. In her hand she carried what appeared to be a red paper-and-lace heart. She turned and gave Jack another reassuring smile.

"Lord John has something he wishes to tell you, my dear." Henry rested a comforting hand on his eighteen-year-old daughter's shoulder. He had five daughters and no sons. Their mother had died giving birth to the youngest just two years ago. Carolyn had been his right hand and biggest comfort during those two years of grief and chaos. He would not surrender a gem such as this to a man who would not appreciate or care for the gift. The pain he was about to cause could in no way measure the misery of a lifetime of poverty and depravity. Someday she would understand that.

Carolyn turned the trusting blue of her gaze to Jack's irregular but handsome features. She knew the story behind the crook of his once-patrician nose, knew the tiny scar above one arched dark eyebrow had been earned during a childhood tantrum, knew he had inherited the Chatham pugnacious jaw and his mother's sharp Spanish cheekbones. She knew him with all her heart and soul and was ready to give the words that would allow her to share his life forever. The promise appeared in her smile as she waited for him to speak.

"Carolyn, I just wished to tell you that I am going away and won't be able to see you again."

She continued staring at him as if he hadn't spoken, waiting for the words that would surely follow. The light had left her eyes, so she had heard him, but she wasn't accepting what she heard. The red-and-white heart in her hand crumpled a little beneath the pressure of her fingers.

Steeling himself, telling himself it was for her own good, Jack tried again. "Your father has refused to give me your hand. I cannot keep you in the manner to which you are accustomed."

That, she understood, and the light quickly returned to her eyes as she turned to her father. "That does not matter, Papa! You must know that I have no care for silk gowns or balls or jewels. I should love to live in the country and will be quite content attending village affairs rather than London society. I know you mean well, Papa, but you must see that I love Jack too much to allow so small a thing as money to stand between us."

Henry turned a threatening look on the paralyzed young man. "Tell her, Jack. Do one decent, manly thing in your life."

Realizing he was being asked to cut his own throat, Jack threw the older man a murderous look, but as Carolyn turned questioningly to him, he ruthlessly whipped out the knife. "You don't understand, my dear. My debts are such that I would have to sell my home to pay them. Your father refuses to give you a dowry if you marry me. Without your dowry, we cannot marry. I must seek my fortune elsewhere."

Twin spots of color tinted Carolyn's cheeks as she

absorbed this self-serving speech, and the blue of her eyes hardened to a more crystalline color similar to his own. "You are saying you courted me for my dowry? That you only meant to save yourself from debt and never meant any of those promises you made? That your pretty words were nothing but lies?"

Jack said nothing, but remained stoic as she wielded the knife he had given her. Carolyn could by turns be pensive and gay, serious and flirtatious, but never had he seen her in a temper. At his lack of reply, her anger seemed to boil and explode, heightening her color, making her eyes more vivid, but not once did it remove the ladylike melodiousness of her voice.

"They were all lies, weren't they? The courtly gestures, the sweet flattery? Did you go back to your friends and laugh at how easily I fell for them? Did they wager on how soon you would woo my wealth? All those promises . . ." Her voice broke and her eyes glittered with unshed tears when he did not deny her charges. To compensate for her lack of words, she stalked across the room to stand in front of him and waved the fragile confection of red and lace before him. "I don't even want to know how much my father had to pay you to do this. You must have realized I would have run off with you anywhere. I loved you. *Loved* you!" Her voice cracked again, but temper had loosed her tongue and she could not stop now. "Fool that I am, I believed your lies! I gave you my heart, and you had no idea what you possessed. You will never know now. No one will ever know. I'll not be such a fool ever again."

Before his stony gaze she ripped the paper heart in half, then tore it again and again until it was in tattered pieces on the floor at his feet. She flung the last few bits at his snowy cravat. "There's my heart. See what good it does you now."

Carolyn stormed from the room, her large store of reserve severely depleted by the tantrum she had never indulged in to such extremes before. She slammed the door, rattling the precious Meissen vase on the hall table, and halted in the shadowed doorway to compose her face and hastily wipe away her tears.

Even as she stood there, she heard her father's low voice through the door. "I'll have the money for you on the morrow. I'll send my man around. I don't want to see your face here again."

Shuddering with dry sobs, she raced toward the stairs, no longer caring who saw her. It wasn't just a lovely valentine lying in torn pieces at the feet of the man behind her, but her heart. There would never be any repairing it.

Behind the closed door, the tall lord bent to pick up the flimsy pieces of paper heart that he had not deserved. He could see snatches of the fine penmanship of the child he had loved on the pieces as he gathered them. In his own heart, he knew they would never be whole again.

Grimly he pocketed the torn valentine, nodded curtly at his nemesis, and strode out, his long legs carrying him away as quickly as the laws of physics and nature allowed.

"I cannot get it to look lacy like the picture." Frustrated, Blanche threw down the tattered paper amongst the scraps already littering the library table. An unexpected ray of sun gleamed through the open curtains, catching her golden hair in a coronet of light that illuminated this dusky corner of the library as she bent over her task.

Smiling gently at the lovely picture the sight portrayed, the woman in the corner chair set aside her book and rose to see what task her younger sister had set herself now. Pale brown hair arranged unfashionably in an elegantly simple chignon, she moved with quiet grace and sureness as she came to stand beside her sister.

Blanche glanced up in relief as slender, competent fingers took up the misshapen piece of paper. "It is not at all like what you and Mama used to make. I thought I could follow the instructions in this magazine, but it is not the same. Show me how to make it lacy."

Carolyn held the tattered valentine, glanced at the magazine, and drawing on the strength she held in reserve for just such occasions, calmly sat down and picked up the scissors and a clean sheet of paper. "You have to cut the heart first, if I remember correctly."

Blanche watched in expectant silence as the plain square of paper shaped itself into a heart finely threaded with intricate designs and elegant scrollwork. Breathing a sigh of happiness, she eagerly took up the scissors when her sister laid them aside. "It is beyond everything, Lynley!" Her newly discovered grown-up manner disappeared briefly to let this childhood appellation escape. "Will you make one for George?"

Carolyn carelessly set the beautiful lace heart aside. "George would not know what to do with it. Whom are you making a valentine for?" Hoping to encourage her sister's confidences, she lingered to help fold the paper correctly and to pencil in cutting lines. Blanche had come out during the Little Season last fall, but she had shown no preference among the many suitors who swarmed around her.

"Why, for the first bachelor to appear at my door on St. Valentine's Day, just like the magazine says!" Laughing eyes lifted to meet her older sister's. "Why don't you make one too? Wouldn't fussy old George have a proper fit if you gave a card to someone else?"

"He is Lord Hampton to you, child. He would swallow a maggot if he ever heard you talk so. And one does not play childish tricks on her suitors. The marquess would have every right to be peeved should I start handing out love notes to someone else."

Instead of being chastised, Blanche laughed gaily at her sister's admonitions. Five years her senior, Carolyn still managed to combine her motherly advice with just enough humor to keep the camaraderie of their sisterhood lively. "I think you should have married when you were my age, Lynley. You have grown as crusty and dull as old Lord Hampton. You deserve each other. I can see the two of you on your wedding night. He will bow stiffly at the waist and offer you his arm to take you to bed, and you will make a deep curtsy and ask, 'Are you certain this is proper, my lord?' and the two of you will debate it until dawn."

"Blanche!" Equally mortified and amused at her eighteen-year-old sister's unruly imagination, Carolyn bit her tongue and began improving the lacy confection she had created earlier. "You should not even be thinking such things. Besides, Lord Hampton and I are not even officially betrothed. If you are going to do that properly, you must learn to make smaller cuts." She pointed the tip of her pen at the offending design in her sister's hand.

Blanche shrugged and reached for a new sheet of paper. "Everyone knows you will be as soon as his curmudgeon mother comes back from the Continent. And it's about time. You are twenty-three, Carolyn. Gossips will have you on the shelf. And just think what grand balls you can have when you are Lady Hampton! I think I shall have another Season just so I might meet all the noble gentlemen I have missed this year. Then, when I have found a duke or a marquess, we will both be able to bring out Alice and Jane. Why, with such high connections, we should find them princes, at least. Then they can introduce Penny to society, and she shall have to marry a king."

Carolyn smiled at these high-flying flights of fancy. "I cannot think of a prince I would allow in the same room with Alice and Jane, and while I will admit not having consorted with many kings, I daresay they will all be a trifle derelict for Penny. At the tender age of seven, she may have difficulty finding a king who will play at patty-cake and hobbyhorse with her."

Blanche made a rude noise that one of her suitors would find quite startling from so demure and innocent a miss. "You didn't used to be so prim, Lynley. I remember when you first came out and you and that fellow with the broken nose made up the most horrendous tales to tell when you knew I was listening. Whatever happened to that gentleman? He was quite fun. Much more the thing than stuffy old George."

Proud of her hard-won self-control, Carolyn smiled and laid aside her pen and valentine. "We both grew up. Now, if you need no further—"

A gentle rap at the door signaled an intruder, and Carolyn swung around to greet the footman bearing a card.

"The gentleman's come to see Mr. Thorogood, Miss Carolyn." He held out the card for her inspection. "He asks that he be made known to the ladies while he waits."

When Carolyn's expected reply did not come, Blanche looked up in time to see her sister's face turn pale and her lips compress in a manner she had not seen in years as she stared at the card in her hand. Before Blanche could inquire as to their visitor's name, Carolyn regained her composure. "Tell the gentleman we are not at home," she announced firmly.

Blanche gave her sister an odd look. Carolyn very seldom stood on ceremony with their visitors. She was friendly to young and old alike. Who could this be that she would refuse him? Smitten with curiosity, Blanche waited for Carolyn to return to her reading, then excused herself to disappear down the hallway after the footman.

Garbed in a heavy sable-lined cloak against the January cold, the gentleman waited in the salon doorway. As the servant repeated his message, the man bent his top-hatted head in acknowledgment and removed himself to the privacy of the salon until the master of the house could see him.

Curiosity thoroughly whetted now, Blanche slipped into the small family parlor behind the salon. The connecting door between the rooms had not been recently used and creaked slightly as she pulled it ajar, but a quick glance told her the stranger had not been disturbed from his pondering by the noise. He evidently did not mean to linger long, for he had not surrendered cloak or hat but held them on one arm as he stared at a porcelain figurine on the mantel. She could see by the dim light that his hair was sun-streaked and his complexion weathered, as if he were one of her father's ship's captains, but his richly tailored clothes were of the finest cut and not those of a poor seaman. The sable cloak alone bespoke his lack of commonplaceness. When he finally turned at the entrance of a servant, Blanche barely concealed her gasp of surprise. The man with the broken nose!

She had no opportunity to learn more. The man followed the servant out and up the stairs to the master's private study.

Five years older, Henry Thorogood still retained his slender build, although there was now a hint of a stoop to his shoulders and threads of gray in his dark hair. Lord Edward John Chatham observed these changes as he entered the book-lined study. Little else had changed in these last years, in this room, at least. He wondered at the refusal of the ladies of the house to see him, but his had been a whimsical gesture at best. Thorogood could have remarried by now; his new wife would not know his name. Carolyn's younger sisters were not likely to remember him. He could not expect to find Carolyn unmarried and still in her father's home after all these years. He had just been curious and tempted to find out what he could.

With the self-assurance of an older, more experienced man, Jack seated himself without his host's permission. He noted the older man's brief look of surprise and the trace of amusement in the slight lift of his brow, but he had only one purpose here and he was eager to get on with it. He waited for Thorogood to take a seat before he spoke.

"I have come to repay my debts, sir. I have brought the sum of the loan, plus interest. You will need to name me the amount due on the vouchers you bought."

Thorogood appraised the sun-darkened stranger seated across from him. In the ensuing years since their last encounter he had not forgotten the arrogant young lordling; in fact, he had had good reason to remember him. The changes wrought by the years were dramatic, but he would have recognized those stony gray eyes and that arrogance anywhere. Lord John had come into his own, it seemed. The question remained, had his character improved with time?

Ignoring his visitor's demands, Henry responded with coldness. "I will not accept tainted money. I have not heard of your brother's estates improving or of any of your family dying and leaving you a fortune. I would know from whence your payment comes."

Jack made an elegant sneer and withdrew a large purse. "Thank you for your confidence, but my money is honestly earned. You may speak with my superiors in the East India Company. It is not tainted, that is, unless you consider trade a taint. I don't believe you are in any position to quibble about that. Name me the sum I owe you."

Thorogood weighed the bag of coins thoughtfully in his hand as he contemplated the young lord. He would be nearing thirty now, not young any longer, actually. Whatever he had been doing, it had taught him a new authority and assurance that the callow spendthrift had not possessed. He propped his fingers together in an arch and named a sum that would have made royalty flinch.

Jack gave him a look of disgust. "That would more than cover the full sum of the original markers plus interest at a rate to make the shylocks cringe. If you think that is what I owe you for five years of my life, you are sadly mistaken. I will pay it, but I will have every marker I ever wrote in return. Should any more turn up at some future date, I will return them to you for payment."

Henry concealed his surprise with a brief nod. "I did not anticipate immediate payment. You may pay it as you are able."

Chatham rose abruptly. "I will give you a draft on my bank today if you can present the vouchers. I will not have your threats hanging over my head any longer than is necessary."

Fully astounded, Henry hurried to the drawer where the markers had been kept all these years. Something in the way Lord Jack had phrased that sentence gave food for thought, but he would savor it later. He would step cautiously for now. He wondered if the careless name he had gone by in his youth still applied. "Lord Jack" no longer suited this imposing stranger.

The transaction completed, Jack threw the sheaf of papers in the fire and watched them burn before striding out without a polite word of courtesy to his host. Five years of waiting for this moment had left him expecting an elation he could no longer feel. The deadness inside remained even with the burden of all those old debts lifted. He needed to seek some new stimulation now to keep his spirit from dying entirely.

Only recently arrived in London, he'd not had time to seek out old friends in familiar places. With his business accomplished, he felt ill-at-ease and restless. It was time to rejoin society and see how his reputation had fared over the cleansing solution of time.

Jack walked into White's and found little different in the decor other than a mellowing of additional age. Perhaps the faces behind the newspapers were slightly different or older, the youths behind the gaming tables seemed younger, he knew fewer than he had expected, but on the whole, the changes were slight. He moved easily toward the group in the corner of the back room, using his leisurely pace to identify vaguely familiar features. One of their number looked up and gave a whoop of recognition. Jack grinned at this irrepressible greeting. Peter's hair might have retreated slightly from his sloping forehead, his yellow waistcoat might be tighter over his paunch, but the cheerful beam of his round face remained unchanged.

"Chatham, as I live and breathe! Back from the dead, old boy? Have you come to haunt us in these dismal corridors?"

They drew him back into their circle without reproof, either glad of this diversion on a dull day or unaware of his fall into trade. Jack ordered drinks, joined in the genial jesting, and tested the waters carefully. Many of their former number were not evident in this gathering place. Some younger, newer faces watched this homecoming with disinterest or an eagerness to be amused but he found no disdain. Yet.

Settling into a comfortably upholstered chair, Jack turned the conversation away from himself and encouraged gossip about those faces among the missing. His companions eagerly grasped the opportunity. In this time-honored fashion he learned how little things had changed beyond the names and the faces.

"And Beecham? Has his father stuck his spoon in the wall and left him all those barrels of gold yet?"

The slender young toff with the diamond stickpin, sitting beside Peter, waved his hand lazily. "The old Judas will never die. Last I heard, he was swearing to leave everything but the entailment to some young niece. Beecham's out courting her right now. She's a

Friday-faced female if ever I saw one, not even been presented yet."

"The last lot of lovelies seem sadly lacking compared to those when we first came down, don't they, Harrison? They're all so demmed . . . green, somehow," Peter completed his sentence weakly.

General laughter ensued at this assessment, but it gave Jack an opening to the topic closest to his well-concealed heart. "And the Incomparables of all these years past? Where are they now? What of our number have shackled their legs for beauty?"

This regenerated the conversation as they sought to remember the reigning toasts of other years and who had carried them away into marital bliss or discord as the case might be.

Peter summed it up best after a fevered discussion. "They're all married and surrounded by whining brats is what they're doing. Seems a demmed shame to waste all that loveliness."

The gentleman with the stickpin shook his head in disagreement. "Not all. The Tremayne wench married some ancient baronet with a pot of gold, who popped off a few months later. She's sitting in splendor over on St. James's now, entertaining lavishly. I hear Bulfinch has been dipping his pen there."

Peter brightened at a renewed memory. "And the Thorogood eldest, what was her name, Jack? You used to be smitten with her. She's leading her young sister around this Season. She ain't never been wed that I know of. I'm surprised she ain't wearing caps by now, though she's still a lovely lass."

Before Jack could respond or even untie his tongue and allow his heart to drop from his throat after the shock of this news, Harrison made a deprecating gesture. "Hampton has her claimed. She's a smart one. She hung around for a title to remove the stench of trade. Wait and see, she'll have that brood of her father's married off to the cream of the crop as they come along. Watch your legs, men, they'll be in her trap before you know you're caught."

Jack peeled his fingers from the arm of the chair and reached for his glass. "George still unwed? He's older than any of us. How did the little Thorogood snare him?"

"He ain't snared yet. There's been no announcement. I wager it waits on his mama's approval, but if he don't come up to snuff soon, the chit will have her comeuppance. The ladies are raising eyebrows at his marked attentions without a ring on her finger. I daresay that devilish father will force the matter soon enough. Hampton was a fool to dabble in those waters. Thorogood's a shark."

Jack heard the stem of the glass crack beneath the pressure of his fingers. Forcing himself to relax and look bored, he rose and prepared to depart. "Maybe someone ought to warn Hampton what he's getting into. Good night, gentlemen. It's been entertaining, but there's a certain little lady who's expecting me."

He walked off and was gone before they realized he never had said where he'd been or what he'd been doing these past years.

"No, don't add the gold pins, Blanche! They are very lovely, but you will have to save them until you're older. The pearls will do just fine. You will be prettier than any other girl there."

"Fustain!" Blanche glared in the mirror at her reflection. "I shall look a simpering idiot like all the rest.

Why can I not wear cloth of gold like yours? You look like an angel just down from heaven. I look like a frumpy mushroom."

Carolyn smiled gently at her sister's nervous starts. Admittedly, virginal white tended to be tedious, but the extravagant gauze and lace of Blanche's ball gown were not exactly the common touch, and the lavender sash and embroidery enhanced her slender charms daringly enough. She would be a sensation, as usual, but she would not be persuaded.

"I don't have wings and you're not edible. You already have more suitors than you need. I don't know what you're worried about. Is there someone special you wish to impress?"

Carolyn's practicality always put a damper on any nervous hopes. Swinging around to observe her sister's elegantly draped gown, Blanche offered a reluctant smile. "No. I just thought it might be a pleasant change if I could be as beautiful as you. Your suitors are so much more interesting than mine."

Carolyn laughed. She had not spent half the attention on her own preparations as she had on Blanche's. She had bidden her maid merely to loop gold twine through her smoothly arranged upsweep, added a chain of silver and gold to her throat, and, wearing a gown she had worn the year before, called herself ready. Admittedly, her maid had teased a few loose tendrils into curling about her ears and shoulders, but they did that normally enough before the evening ended. She had no illusions about the men she would meet tonight. They had been attending her over five years now, and she was as heartily bored with them as they were with her. At one time or another, as fortunes waxed and waned, one or another of them would grow amorous and make an offer, but she had learned how to let them down lightly. Among the older set, it had become a game of nothing ventured, nothing gained. Wagers had been won or lost in earlier years. Lately, there were few takers on a sure thing. The eldest Thorogood girl had set herself firmly on the shelf. Few had any interest in being rejected in an attempt to remove her.

That was why Hampton's suit had caught everyone concerned by surprise. He had been an eligible *parti* on the Marriage Mart for a decade but had never shown any interest in indulging in the favors waved before his nose in attempts to catch his jaded interest. Wealthy, titled, and young enough to be considered well-looking, he made many a young girl weep with envy when he escorted one of society's more mature widows onto the floor. The gossip about his misalliances with these more worldly women was discreet. He never gained the epithet of rake, for he seldom spared a second glance to the innocent.

His studious courtship of Carolyn Thorogood had the *haut ton* all agog. She was neither worldly nor a widow. Not a hint of scandal attached to their relationship except in the fact that the courtship had lasted a good six months now without an announcement. That in itself was a record of sorts. Hampton had never assiduously courted any woman, young or old, for that length of time, and Carolyn had never allowed any courtship to go on so long without a firm rejection. Wagers once more were rife over whether the elusive toast would finally be snared.

Well aware of the tongues flapping behind her back, Carolyn did nothing to encourage them in either direction. She concentrated on bringing out her younger sister and seeing that Blanche was properly attended.

George Hampton's suit did not interfere with her goals, and aided it in many ways, so there was no reason to discourage him. She was well aware he had finally decided he needed an heir and had settled on her as older and more mature than the fresh crop of young innocents on the Mart. His less-than-romantic courtship caused her no pain. If she finally agreed to his proposal, it would be because she had finally decided she wished a family of her own too, and he was wealthy enough for her not to fear he wanted her for her dowry. It seemed a good, stable way of venturing into the treacherous waters of matrimony.

But Blanche was still filled with romantic illusions and Carolyn had no desire to remove the misty film of fantasy from her eyes yet. The time would come soon enough when the more objectionable suitors were weeded out and Blanche began to realize that marriage was a financial proposition and not a romantic one. For now, let her believe in love. It might happen. Even fairy tales came true upon occasion.

Blanche and Carolyn entered the ballroom that night on their father's arms. As a wealthy widower, Henry Thorogood was much sought after himself, and he had no difficulty in amusing himself while keeping an eye on his two beautiful daughters. Still, it was on Carolyn that he relied to act as chaperone for Blanche's high spirits. He seldom need interfere himself. Carolyn was immensely capable in dealing with overardent young gentlemen and advising her sister on propriety. Thorogood watched her through half-lowered lids as she smilingly refused one notorious rake and deflected a debt-ridden young lord with a request for some punch. Carolyn had learned propriety too well. Her natural happiness had become something much less animated, an artificial facade of smiles and gentle words that fooled the rest of the world but not her father.

Sipping his drink, he watched Carolyn's smile fade in weariness as she was momentarily left alone. The daughter he had known from infancy had been exuberant in her joy, passionate in her beliefs, dramatic in her sorrows. She had wept and laughed and infuriated alternately, until her eighteenth year. That was the year she had grown up, and he had not seen that girl again. As dutiful and pleasant as this new woman was, he rather missed the tempestuous girl. His eyes narrowed thoughtfully as he observed the two young men approaching her now.

Instantly aware that she was being watched, Carolyn raised her head with a renewed smile and sought George Hampton's properly attired figure bearing down on her. Garbed in sober black tailcoat and pantaloons, his immaculate cravat a masterpiece in simplicity, his stride one of noble arrogance and authority, he looked the part of wealthy aristocrat without need of the hauteur marring the faces of many of the nobility with whom she was acquainted. He seldom smiled, but she sensed a pleased look on his face now as he caught her eye.

In idle curiosity, Carolyn turned her gaze to the man at the marquess's side. She knew George frequented White's and several other of the gentlemen's clubs, but he seldom introduced her to his male friends. She wondered occasionally if it was out of embarrassment because he had attached himself to a female without title whose wealth came from trade, but she did not let the question concern her much. He made a pleasant companion and they got along well enough. Still, she couldn't help wondering about the stranger he evidently meant to introduce to her.

At this distance Carolyn could tell only that the stranger was unfashionably weathered in a startlingly attractive manner. His rather longish brown hair had light streaks from the sun, and his eyes seemed much lighter than the rest of his bronzed face. His gray swallow-tailed coat fit comfortably to unfashionably muscular shoulders, and his impeccably tailored matching trousers did not hinder his long, eager stride. Dressed for comfort more than style, he exuded a self-assurance she found instantly compelling. Unnerved by this sudden unexpected attraction to a stranger, she raised her gaze to search his face as they came closer. Shock brought her hand to her middle as if suddenly assaulted by a hideous pain, and her face paled a shade whiter.

Her plight did not go unnoticed by the newcomer. Cold gray eyes swept over her without demonstrating any emotion, finally lifting in dark acknowledgment at judging himself to be the cause of her distress. At his side, Hampton seemed oblivious of her lack of response as he introduced his companion.

"Do you remember Chatham, Carolyn? I daresay he was before your time. He's been in India practically since you were in short skirts."

Carolyn managed a weak smile and extended her hand. "I am not so young as that, my lord. I remember Lord John from my first Season." As his callused brown hand closed around hers, she wanted to jerk away, but that would be demonstrating a childish emotion she no longer felt. She forced a more pleasant expression to her lips.

"He's a bit out of touch with the current crop of lovelies. I told him you would be happy to surrender a dance or two and introduce him to a few suitable misses. That sister of yours might be just in his style."

Carolyn's aghast expression went unnoticed by the nobleman pleased with his helpfulness to both friend and would-be fiancée. Jack read her dismay without compunction and refused to release her hand.

"I believe the musicians are beginning a waltz, Miss Thorogood. You were reluctant to try it when last we met. Shall we?"

With her intended standing by affectionately rewarding her with his smile for her compliance, Carolyn had little choice but to follow Jack onto the dance floor. She remembered a time when she had stubbornly refused to indulge in the decadent dance sweeping the fast set, even when the man she loved offered to teach her. After he left, it seemed scarcely a point worth defending. She had been waltzing for years, but that same defiance returned with just the touch of Jack's hand. She wanted to stomp her foot and slap him and tell him to behave. It would have been apropos back then when he had been whispering sweet nothings in her ear all night. Such behavior now would be singularly inappropriate.

"You cannot kill me with looks, Carolyn. Smile and put a pleasant face on it before someone remembers old gossip and reminds George." Jack slid his arm around her slender waist with the possessiveness of familiarity, swinging her effortlessly into the steps of the dance as he spoke. "You're more beautiful than I remember," he added thoughtfully, searching her face when she did not respond.

"And you're more arrogant," she retorted heatedly. Under the intensity of his scrutiny, she felt a flush staining her cheeks for the first time in years. Her fingers itched to smack him, but his long masculine physique held her firmly, and the familiar sensations of years ago swarmed alive and well through her rebellious body. He could hold her like this for the rest of the night, and not a muscle would stir in protest.

"I see your temper has not cooled with the passage of time. I suppose you are the one who refused to see me yesterday. I did not expect to find you still in your father's house. I thought you would be married by now."

She hated the speculation in his eyes. The arrogant fool was wondering if she had waited for him. She would disabuse him of that notion immediately, if only she could find her tongue. "I have grown choosier with age," she finally gritted out between clenched teeth. She could feel the heat of his hand even through his glove and her gown. She hated him for reminding her of sensations better forgotten.

"So it seems. George is quite a catch. You cannot fear he is a fortune-hunter. When do you set the date?"

He asked that agreeably enough, and Carolyn glared up at him with suspicion. He seemed taller than she remembered, but then, George was nearly her height and she was accustomed to dancing with him. The white flash of Jack's teeth against his sunburned face irritated her, and she answered with as much aloofness as she could muster, "We have an understanding that suits us both, my lord."

"An understanding? How formal that sounds. Has he kissed you, Carolyn, or is that not part of the agreement? It would be damned hard to court you for long without stealing a few kisses, particularly for a man of George's inclinations. How much longer before that understanding leads to something else, Carolyn? I'd like to lay my wagers on the winning side."

Rage rose in her, a blinding rage that made Carolyn want to scream and shout and kick and cause a scene right here in the middle of this elegant dance floor. Jack had always been able to rouse her ire with a word or a wink, but he had always appeased her quickly afterward. The memory of those tender scenes added fuel to the fires of anger. His insults this time would get no response from her.

"You have become an insufferable boor, Jack. It is lucky for us that my father intervened in time."

Carolyn's haughty disdain made Jack furious, and at the same time, her words pierced him like shards of hell. Five years he had worked and waited, abstaining from society, from the luxuries of civilization, from everything he had ever known, just so he might come back and look her in the eye once more. He had been prepared to find her happily married with babes around her feet. She deserved that. He would never have wished her unhappy. But he had never imagined her like this, cold and bitter and haughtier than any princess. Something wasn't right here, and he'd be damned if he would let her slip through his fingers again without knowing why.

He deliberately ignored her harsh words. "When George spent hours raving about your pleasantness and agreeableness, I thought he'd got the wrong sister. Agreeableness is not what I remember most about you. I can see you haven't changed, so who is this Carolyn that George is talking about?"

His spiteful remark deserved no reply, and as the dance ended, Carolyn dropped his hand like a hot coal. She turned stiffly in search of George and grew tense at the sight of Blanche waiting with curiosity at his side, watching her and Jack. When Jack attempted to take her elbow to lead her back, she shook him off.

"Stay away from Blanche, Jack. I'll not have you spoiling her life." She could have added, "as you spoiled mine," but she would never admit that out loud.

He sent her a swift look, as if he heard the unspoken end to that sentence, but her lovely blue eyes had grown cold and stony and he found no evidence that he had heard aright. He turned his gaze to the young blond beauty waiting beside Hampton and shook his head. "By Jove, it's hard to believe we were ever that young. Are you certain she ought to be out of the school-room?"

Carolyn flashed him a look of irritation. "She's eighteen." Just as she had been when she had fallen head over heels for this unscrupulous rake, but again, she left the words unsaid. He knew them as well as she.

Had she turned to see Jack's face, she would have seen the fleeting look of pain in his eyes, but she was hurrying across the floor, eager for escape and heedless of the pain she left behind. She had once been as young and innocent as that vision in white. The similarities between that young girl there and the woman running toward her were so strong as to shake Jack to the core. Once Carolyn had looked at him with that wide-eyed dewy look that made his heart pound and his palms sweat. The palpitations now weren't for the young girl, though, but for the memory of the girl he had known. Blanche's glorious smile was nearly the same as Carolyn's had been, but the eyes were more cautious. She distrusted him much sooner than the young Carolyn ever had. Jack wondered what she knew of him, but suspected it was only curiosity that kept her gaze in his direction.

He felt Carolyn's tension as the introductions were made, and even George was looking at her with curiosity when she made no pleasantries but immediately insisted that she and Blanche must repair to the powder room. The stunningly demure woman Jack had observed from across the dance floor earlier had lost her composure, and the war of emotions in her eyes was plain to see for all who looked. Fortunately for her, George was blind to the nuances of female expressions. Politely Jack made his excuses and departed before he could drag Carolyn off to a corner and shake her until he received some explanations. If he needed time to gather his scattered wits, so must she.

Carolyn watched with a cry in her throat as Lord John's proudly straight back retreated. How could he be even more incredibly handsome and wicked than she remembered? She had never known him for the devil that he was until that last night, but she had just seen him looking at Blanche in that same way he had once looked at her. He wouldn't! Heaven help her, but she would kill him with her bare hands if he so much as held Blanche's little finger. Surely he was not so beastly arrogant as to believe he could win this second round by using her sister?

By the time she got home that night, Carolyn's head pounded with the thunder of her memories and fears. For nearly five years she had maintained her composure, playing the part of doting older sister, loving daughter, and society maiden. For five years she had refused to think of Lord Edward John Chatham. Just as she had thought herself fully recovered and prepared to consider marriage from a more sensible viewpoint, he'd reappeared like some demon straight from hell. What was wrong with her that he could still make her feel like this after all these years? She *hated* him. How could he stir her into this writhing agony of need and chaos and uncertainty after all he had done?

It wouldn't do to ponder the thought too long. Soon George's mother would return from the Continent and they would obtain her approval and Carolyn would be wedded and safe. With both her father and George to protect her, Blanche would be out of Jack's reach. There were too many other girls on the market for Jack to try his hand at another Thorogood.

Still, as she drifted off to sleep, Carolyn could not keep from dreaming of warm gray eyes and long legs striding eagerly toward her. So light those eyes had been, almost as if illuminated from within when they gazed on her. She felt them even in her sleep, warming her to the marrow.

When the enormous bouquet of impossible roses arrived early the next day, Carolyn nearly refused to accept them. Jack had ever been given to such extravagances, even when he hadn't a ha'penny for food. She knew they had to be from him, but telling herself that there was some chance that George might have grown sentimental, she read the card. The words "I need to see you" had scarcely grazed her mind when she heard Jack's voice in the doorway.

"I told the servant not to announce me. I didn't want to be turned away again." His wide shoulders filled the narrow space of the salon door. The expensive tailoring of his deep blue frock coat emphasized the breadth of his chest and the narrowness of his hips in their tight pantaloons, and Carolyn had to force her gaze to his sun-bronzed features. That was no relief, for the dizzying lightness of his eyes made her throat go dry, and her fingers longed to caress the blond streaks in his burnished curls.

The footman hastily disappeared, leaving Carolyn clinging to the roses. Jack properly left the door open, but they both knew there was no one but the servants to hear them, and they would not interfere. She tried to pry her tongue from the roof of her mouth as she measured the astonishing knowledge that he was here, in her house, in the same room with her after all these years, but she couldn't shake her disbelief. She felt as if she were still dreaming.

Dressed in a frail muslin of sprigged lavender, her hair carelessly tied in loose curls at the crown of her head, she had the grace and the startled velvet eyes of a gazelle. A hint of lavender scented the air around her, speaking of springtime and wildflowers and the beauty of an English rose. Jack could not take his eyes away, and all his carefully prepared speeches disappeared in a misty haze of yearning. For five years he had dreamed of this. He still could not believe he was so blessed as to find her unmarried. His hands actually shook as he reached to set the roses aside.

"We need to talk, Carolyn. I have so much I want to say to you, I don't know where to begin. I caught you by surprise last night. I'm sorry. I didn't mean those things I said. I had been listening to George sing your praises until I wanted to plant him a facer. That's why we have to talk. I want another chance, Carolyn. Will you listen?"

She flushed hot and cold hearing that deep, seductive voice again, feeling it wash over her with lingering promises of passion. She hated him for doing this to her again. She was old enough to know better. He had no right to come here and disturb her life all over. She wouldn't let him. She steeled herself against the impassioned plea of his voice, refused to see the pain and hope in his eyes. He deserved to suffer for what he had done. It was her turn to hand out pain.

"Get out, Jack," she told him coldly, meeting his eyes without flinching. "If I never see you again, it will be too soon. If you ever dare perpetrate this underhand trick again, I will have the servants bounce you out on your ear. You may take your vulgar flowers with you when you go. Try them on some poor cit who is desperate for a title. Don't ever try them on me again."

She swung around and started for the far door to the parlor. Stunned, Jack could utter no word of protest. In all these years of envisioning this scene, he had never imagined the coldness of her reception. The iciness penetrated his lungs, making it difficult to breathe. Too many hot summers, he thought wryly and erratically to himself as he felt the chill of the unheated room begin to take over and shudder through him. He heard the door close after her and still he could not move. He kept waiting for the blessed numbness that came with time, but it eluded him. He shook as if with fever.

He had expected anger at worst. Carolyn could be docile and patient and loving and eagerly understanding, but when she felt threatened, she retaliated with a temper that left scars long after. He could still feel the sting of her words from that night they had parted. They had lingered under his skin like some insidious poison for years. Those torn pieces of heart she had thrown at him had bruised as if they were stone, but her words had caused permanent damage. He had feared she would never forgive or forget, but never had he thought it would be like this. She had meant it when she said he would never know her heart again. The woman who had just left this room had no heart. That was what he had sensed missing last night. All that loving, trusting innocence he had once known had disappeared, bricked up behind a brittle facade of composure and disinterest. The Carolyn he had known had ceased to exist.

Aching as if with cold, Jack turned and slowly retraced his steps to the front door. The roses lay, forgotten, in the icy salon.

Blanche watched covertly as her sister paced the library, ostensibly in search of some volume of verse appropriate for the valentine they were making. It had been days since the ball where the man with the broken nose had made his appearance, but Carolyn's complaint of the headache had kept them confined indoors ever since. Blanche had little reason to object, since her suitors were overflowing the salons with their flattering lies of missing her, and flowers spilled over the furniture as reminders of their attentions in her absence. The social whirl was amusing, but she had spent most of her life in her father's country home and knew well how to entertain herself without need of constant attention. Her concern was more for Carolyn.

Blanche had learned nothing about Lord Edward John Chatham from discreet inquiries of her callers, but she had found his abandoned flowers and note in the salon the day after the ball. The fact that Carolyn had refused to appear in public ever since was serious cause for concern. She had never seen Carolyn troubled or discomposed. The time Alice had fallen from the tree and broken her arm had thrown the entire household in an uproar, but not Carolyn. She had directed servants, comforted Alice, and had everything calm before the physician arrived. Even their mother's death had not caused this withdrawal from family and friends. Carolyn had grieved terribly, but she had been the mainstay of the family throughout that tragic period. She had not bolted herself behind closed doors and refused to come out.

"Perhaps I shall write a poem of my own," Blanche suggested to divert her sister's attention from pacing. "Am I allowed to make personal allusions in poetry?"

Carolyn clamped her fingers into her palms and pulled together her distraught nerves as she turned back to her sister. She was being ridiculous. After what she had said, Jack would never cross their portals again. There really was no cause for concern. Blanche was a sensible girl beneath her frivolous romantic fantasies. She would listen to reason should the opportunity be needed. Mouthing these platitudes to herself, she forced a serene smile to her face.

"What personal allusions can you make when you don't know whom the card will go to? An 'Ode to His Shining Eyes'?"

Blanche grinned in appreciation of this sign of Carolyn's returning humor. "I can refuse to come down until someone meeting the description arrives. It's only the first man I see that day that counts. I shan't have to see anyone if I don't wish."

"Horrible child, that takes all the fun out of it. What if we had no servants? You would have to answer the door and accept the first man who came in."

"I should sneak around and see who it was before I answered. If it was someone unacceptable, I should just pretend I was not at home. I'll not give my favors for a year to a man with no wit to appreciate them."

"You are spoiled beyond redemption." Carolyn inspected the lacy creation of ribbons and paper that

Blanche had painstakingly put together. "It is quite good without a poem. Do not give them any ideas." She set the heart down and squared her shoulders decisively. "It is quite pleasant out. Would you care to accompany me for a stroll in the park?"

Blanche shuddered at the thought. Carolyn's idea of pleasant weather was a day without rain. Never mind that icicles still hung from the eaves. And "stroll" translated as a fast gallop on foot through deserted lanes at a hideously early hour, when there was no one to attend them. It did not strike Blanche as a particularly elegant way to spend the morning.

At Blanche's blunt refusal, Carolyn shrugged and went in search of her wraps. She had been confined inside for too long. She needed exercise to disperse these nervous fits and restless urges. A bruising horse ride would be more suitable, but that was not permitted in the crowded city parks and streets. A brisk walk would be just as beneficial.

Fetching her resigned maid to accompany her, Carolyn wrapped herself in a blue velvet pelisse lined with a fur that nearly matched the color of her own rich tresses, had she been vain enough to notice. Instead, her thoughts were far removed from her own looks as she set out to circumambulate the park.

A thaw had set in and the last patches of snow were disappearing into the grass and the icicles were dripping rivulets from bare tree limbs. The Serpentine still held patches of ice glinting in the sunlight, and Carolyn turned her mind to the beauty of the day. It felt good to stretch her muscles and breathe fresh air again. She had been quite childish in hiding from the ghost of her imagination.

A bright red ball bounced across her feet, nearly

causing her to trip, but she was adept at eluding such objects. With four younger siblings underfoot at various times of the year, she had learned to keep a tremendous store of patience. With a smile at this simple pleasure, she turned to find the runaway ball and return it to its owner.

With the object firmly in her gloved hand, she sought the youngster who had thrown it. To the side of the road and down a slight embankment stood a tiny figure garbed head to foot in warm furs and velvet, her pitch-black hair streaming out from a fur cap framing a strangely tawny face. She held back shyly, not willing to come forward to retrieve her toy from the grand lady.

"Shall I throw it to you?" Carolyn offered, quite content to be playing at simple childhood games for a time.

When the girl made no move but a timid nod, Carolyn gently heaved the ball toward her mittened hands. They sprang up instantly to catch the gently thrown ball, an adeptness that signaled someone had played this game with her with frequency.

As the child smiled shyly and clasped her ball, a dark figure unfolded from its relaxed position against a tree trunk and came forward. "Thank the lady, Amy."

The voice smote her with the swiftness of a rapier, and Carolyn stepped backward instinctively. "Jack!"

Only then did the top-hatted head lift to peruse the elegantly feminine figure on the path. Gray eyes shuttered cautiously, and a leather-clad hand protectively reached for the small shoulder of the child. "Carolyn." He nodded warily.

An awkward silence fell, of which the child showed no awareness as she held out the ball. "T'ank you, m'lady," she lisped carefully. "Will you play?"

As shaken by Jack's presence as by the dilemma of

the child's accompaniment, Carolyn could make no reply. Dazedly she tried to orient herself, to find some perspective to approach the situation, but she could not. She only waited in bewilderment for Jack to rescue her.

Caught unaware, Jack, too, had difficulty surmounting a meeting that he had never anticipated. He had never intended to keep Amy a secret, but there had been no opportunity to mention her. His fingers squeezed his daughter's shoulder reassuringly as his tongue summoned some form of polite introduction.

"This is my daughter, Amy. Amy, say hello to Miss Thorogood."

As the two exchanged shy greetings, Jack regained some of his assurance, and he glanced expectantly around. "Are you with someone, Carolyn? Surely you did not come out here alone?"

Briefly puzzled by this return to the mundane, Carolyn glanced around for some sign of her maid. "Florrie was right behind me. I do not know where she is got to."

Knowing Carolyn's galloping idea of a walk from old times, Jack shifted his daughter to his shoulder and climbed up the small embankment to the path. "There are still some dangerous patches of ice. We'd better look for her."

Somehow, it seemed perfectly natural to be walking along at Jack's side, his shoulder marching at the same height as her eyes, blocking half the view, but without disabling her in the least. She knew his sharp eyes would find Florrie first, and she need only concentrate on watching her step, since his arm was occupied keeping his daughter in place.

His daughter. How peculiar to think of Jack with a daughter. He must have married soon after he left London, to judge by the age of the child. Perhaps he had had someone else with a wealthy dowry waiting behind stage in case his first offer fell through. It pained her still to think these unkind thoughts of Jack, but she had to face reality. She had known he was in debt and would have to leave London. Now he was back and seemingly in funds again. There simply was no other explanation.

"That must be Florrie over there on the bench." Jack pointed out a woebegone figure in heavy wool and bedraggled bonnet. The figure looked up at the same time that he spoke, but she made no move to rise, and her expression became even more pitiful.

Carolyn broke into a quick stride. "Florrie! What has happened? I only just missed you. Why did you not cry out?"

By the time Jack trotted up, Carolyn was already kneeling in the mud, ruining her pelisse and velvet walking gown as she examined the maid's outstretched ankle. She glanced up as Jack set his daughter down and crouched beside her.

"She has twisted her ankle pretty severely. It's beginning to swell. I must get her home."

"My carriage isn't far. Will you be all right waiting here? You won't be too cold?"

His concern did not seem in the least feigned. Perhaps that was why she had believed in him so thoroughly. He should have been on the stage. Carolyn quelled the haughty words that came to her tongue. Florrie needed help. She had no right to question from whence it came.

"I'll be fine. Why don't you leave Amy with us? You could fetch the carriage more quickly that way."

Jack helped her to rise and glanced uncertainly from

Carolyn's open expression to his daughter's childishly trusting gaze. She was right that he could move more swiftly without the necessity of carrying this small burden, but he had never left Amy with strangers before. He and her ayah and Mrs. Higginbotham were all he had trusted with the child. But this was Carolyn. He nodded quickly in agreement.

"I'll be back shortly. You'll take cold if you don't have a dry gown soon."

He strode off, leaving Carolyn to stare after his elegantly clad back with perplexity. Why should he be worried if she caught cold? She turned her straying thoughts back to her injured maid and the curious child. She had no business trying to read Jack's mind.

By the time Jack returned with the carriage, Carolyn and Amy were laughing gaily, and even the maid smiled at their antics. In her love for pretty and exotic objects, Amy had obviously charmed Carolyn out of the long, arched feather that had adorned her bonnet, and it now stuck absurdly from Amy's furred cap. They both looked like naughty children when Jack jumped down, and he couldn't help but laugh at their expressions.

"Had I dallied any longer, she would be parading around in your slippers with your pelisse flung over her shoulders and dragging in the mud behind her." He pretended to pinch Amy's nose, and the child laughed with the trill of a little bird. "She is dreadfully spoiled. Now, thank Miss Thorogood for playing with you and let me help Miss Florrie into the carriage, there's a good girl."

The pride and love on his face were plain to see and could scarcely be part of his theatrics. Carolyn felt a tug inside that she dared not recognize, and she turned away from Jack's uneven features to help Florrie to her feet. Had it not been for her father, that little girl could be her own, and Jack would be looking at their child like that. It would not do to think along such lines. It was over and done and best forgotten.

Jack discreetly held Carolyn's hand no longer than it took to help her into the carriage. He kept the conversation general as they drove the short distance to the Thorogood residence. Never once did he give any indication of the severed relationship between them. Carolyn was grateful for his discretion but left uneasy by it. He behaved the perfect gentleman. Could his disguise be so thorough?

He handed Florrie over into the care of one of the footmen who ran down the stairs to open the carriage door. He bowed politely over Carolyn's hand in parting, and he made no attempt to cross the portal from whence he had been barred. Carolyn stared after his departing carriage in something closely akin to shock. She had spent these last days thinking of him in terms of a devil in tailcoats. She could not easily twist her thoughts to consider him as a knight-errant.

The next day, however, she gladly accepted the call of a Mrs. Higginbotham and one miss Amy Chatham.

The child was primly garbed in layers of velvet and fur, as she had been the day before. Her hair had been pulled back in a coronet of braids and her hat no longer bore the swooping feather that had adorned it on parting yesterday. Mrs. Higginbotham held grimly to her hand as she plowed into the salon, and Carolyn held her breath anxiously, as she expected the powerfully built matron to sit on the tiny child as they both attempted to occupy the same love seat.

"Good morning, Amy. Did you find a better hat to fit

your feather on?" Carolyn offered the stiffly shy child a smile.

"That is the reason we are here, Miss Thorogood." The jarring accents boomed from the matron's massively built chest, vibrating several delicate figurines on the table. Carolyn tilted her head in curiosity to better observe this natural phenomenon. Satisfied she had her hostess's attention, the woman continued, "His lordship insisted that his daughter thank you for the gift of the feather. She is much inclined to take things she admires, and he hopes she has offered no harm to your apparel."

Carolyn heard this with mild astonishment. Too well-bred to show her amusement at the woman's artificial attempts at elegance, she nodded politely and turned her attention to the child. "I thought the feather much more becoming on you than on me, Miss Amy. I used to have a doll that liked to wear hats. Do you have one like that?"

Dark eyes immediately lit with delight, and she nodded with a shy smile. Before she could say a word, her companion intruded. "The child has far too many dolls, in my opinion. Her father spoils her, and she does not know her place. I've not had much time to take the matter in hand, but I assure you, it will be accomplished in time."

The woman's encroaching self-importance was a source of amazement, but Carolyn had met her sort before. It was interesting how people with no claim to name or fortune or accomplishment could adopt an immense snobbery when come in contact with people who had any. Perhaps it was a means of hiding a feeling of inferiority, but in this case, the child was suffering for it. Carolyn permitted herself a small frown.

"Miss Chatham seems singularly well-behaved to me, Mrs. Higginbotham. I have four younger sisters myself, and not one of them ever behaved so properly on a formal call at her age." With this mild reproof, she returned her attention to the child, who had instantly withdrawn her smile at the sounds of discord. "I would be pleased to have you to tea one day, Miss Chatham. I rather miss my younger sisters, and I should enjoy having your company. Would you like that?"

Again the dancing lights returned to the little girl's huge velvet eyes, and a smile illuminated her small brown face. Before she could utter the smallest word, Mrs. Higginbotham rose in a grand flutter of shawls and lace.

"You are too kind, Miss Thorogood, but I cannot let her be foisted off on respectable company. I came only at her father's insistence. We would not think of intruding again. Good day to you." She sailed from the room with Amy in tow.

Visibly annoyed by now, Carolyn held her temper in check until her guests had departed, then contemplated sitting down and sending Jack a scathing note on the unsuitability of his choice of governess, if governess she were. By the time she reached her desk, however, common sense prevailed, and she set the pen aside. She had given up any right of interference in Jack's life the day she had thrown him out of the house. He would only ridicule and ignore any message from her.

Still, the memory of her anger at the encroaching Mrs. Higginbotham and her concern for the timid child returned swiftly when next Carolyn saw Jack. It was inevitable that she see him again. She could ban him from her own home, but not from every house in the *haut ton*. A seemingly wealthy, eligible bachelor was welcome anywhere he went. That he would attend many of the same events as she was a foregone conclusion. Her decision to avoid him wavered under the burden of her anger and concern.

She looked absurdly sophisticated, Jack observed as Carolyn drifted across the music room, regally exchanging pleasantries with half the *ton* in her path. He could remember when she was just a charming girl with a delightful smile to single her out from the legions of young lovelies. It was hard to acquaint that young girl with this elegant young woman with her head held high and a polished smile affixed to her face, but he had seen glimpses of the girl the other day in the park. He pondered that anomaly as he realized he was actually Carolyn's goal in crossing the room.

"It's good to see you again, Miss Thorogood," he intoned formally as he bowed over her hand.

Concentrating on her purpose, Carolyn ignored the fact that Jack managed to make himself look thoroughly at home in any environment. Gold and jewels glittered at throats and wrists all around them. Diamond stickpins, gold watch fobs, and pearl shirt studs adorned the formal attire of all the gentlemen. In simple black with nothing more glittering than his pristine cravat and intelligent eyes, Jack still appeared the part of arrogant nobility.

"I'd like a word with you about your daughter, my lord," she said boldly. When his dark brow rose a fraction, she refused to retreat. "I know it is not my place to interfere, but you must admit that I have some experience with young girls, and you do not."

He nodded politely in acknowledgment of that fact. In truth, he could do little more. That faint scent of lavender and wildflowers enveloped him, and he had to focus his concentration on keeping his hands at his sides and his eyes on her face, when it seemed much more natural to encompass her graceful waist with his arm and feel her soft breasts pressed into his side. Even concentrating on her face wasn't helpful. He had reason to remember the passion and promise of those rose-pink lips. Unlike calculating young maidens, once Carolyn had given her heart, she was lavish with her affection despite the fact that there was no formal engagement. She had trusted him.

When Jack made no further effort to encourage or reject her observations, Carolyn cautiously phrased her complaint. "This Mrs. Higginbotham seems somewhat overbearing for a child as timid as Amy. In fact, I wouldn't be surprised if Mrs. Higginbotham isn't the cause of her timidity."

That elevated his attention to a more respectable level. Jack straightened from his casual position against the newel post to take Carolyn's arm and lead her toward a quiet alcove. When he had settled her on a backless velvet-upholstered settee, he frowned down at her anxious expression.

"I could not bring Amy's ayah out of India. Mrs. Higginbotham had only just lost her husband, and she offered to accompany me and care for Amy on the journey home. She has been quite indispensable. What rackety notions have you got in your head now about that proper lady?"

His harsh words brought a caustic reply. "She is no lady. She's an encroaching mushroom intent on crushing your daughter into a nonentity for some obscure reason unknown to me. I cannot know anything about your household, but Mrs. Higginbotham seems prepared to rule it. She as much as said that you spoil Amy and she will not allow it to continue."

To Carolyn's surprise, Jack's expression grew weary and unhappy instead of angry at this declaration. Rocking back on his heels, he stared at the garish painting over her head before replying. Aware that a room full of people could watch their every action, he kept his words curt.

"Amy is not legally my daughter. I daresay Mrs. Higginbotham has taken it upon herself to protect society from such scandal. I will have to speak with her." He held out his hand and gestured to the room behind them. "I can feel your father's eyes burning a hole in my back. Perhaps we should join the others?"

Carolyn reluctantly placed her gloved hand in his and stood beside him. He smelled faintly of sandalwood and some musky scent that was all his own, and again that feeling of comforting familiarity at his size and strength swept over her. Other men tended to make her nervous and uncomfortable when they stood this close. Not Jack. Never Jack. He fitted beside her as neatly as her glove fitted her hand. It was a most depressing thought.

"I did not mean to cause anyone trouble," she murmured as they stood there, unwilling to return to the milling crowd. "But Amy seemed to be such a sweet, eager child. When we are in town, I miss young Penny. I thought it would be fun for Amy as well as Blanche and me if she came to visit. Mrs. Higginbotham informed me in no uncertain terms that that wouldn't be permitted. If those were your orders, I shall understand, but Amy seemed dreadfully disappointed and intimidated. I hate to see a child unhappy."

Jack sighed and squeezed her hand before he realized he should no longer be holding it. He released her but made no effort to lead her back to her father. "Perhaps Mrs. Higginbotham is right. I cannot believe your family would approve of your associating with a half-Indian child from the wrong side of the blanket. It isn't done. I'll have to move her to Dorset, but she has been so frightened by all these changes in her world, I couldn't bear to send her away just yet."

Heat flared in Carolyn's cheeks as she realized the intimate admission Jack had just made. No gentleman ought to admit to illegitimate children or mistresses before a lady. Carolyn would have been shocked if any other man had said it. The shock she felt now had little to do with his scandalous admission and more to do with imagining Jack going from her arms to some stranger's and the intimacy involved in producing this child. She couldn't find her tongue to reply, and he glanced down at her with curiosity.

"Have I offended you? I thought you were already so furious with me that nothing further I did could offend you more. I apologize if I spoke out of turn."

Carolyn forced her tumultuous emotions into control and offered a brittle smile. "I'm not offended. Perhaps my pride is. You did not lose much time finding a mistress, if I'm any judge of a child's age. I shouldn't be so surprised, but even after all these years of knowing what you are, I find I am. But I do not blame the child for the father's faults, and neither will my family. She is welcome in our home at any time."

The smallest inkling of hope gnawed hungrily at his insides as Jack gazed down into Carolyn's flushed and averted face. She spoke with more sophistication than the young girl he had once known, but the raw emotions couldn't be entirely concealed by her poise. The frozen tundra he had met with earlier wasn't quite so thick as he had believed. Amy had warmed a hole through it in a single meeting. What would it take to melt the whole and discover the truth beneath?

If he wanted truth, he had to offer honesty. This wasn't the place or time, but he might have no other. Touching her elbow, Jack guided her toward the refreshment table, easily skirting the crowd. He kept his voice low, bending his head closer to her ear. For all anyone knew, he could be speaking sweet flattery.

"Carolyn, I have never been more than a man, never claimed to be. Perhaps I cannot fit the perfect ideal you have made of your father, but he has only somehow been more discreet than I am. Until you give me permission to speak as a lover, I cannot defend myself further. Should that time ever come, I will tell you all you wish to know of Amy. In the meantime, I can only thank you for your concern for her welfare. I am glaringly aware of my faults, and I doubt that forgiveness is possible, but I would cry friends, if only for Amy's sake."

She had forgotten how smoothly Jack could erase all transgressions with his words. In the same few sentences he could raise her ire and soothe her ruffled feathers. He was quite right, actually. He should not be talking to her of Amy's origins, but to suggest there might be a future time when he had that right was above and beyond all else. She ought to slap him right here in view of everyone, but his mention of Amy's need for friends diverted all anger. Obviously, if he loved no one else, he loved his child. For Amy's sake, he said these things.

For Amy's sake, she might possibly agree to them. He knew that. Carolyn looked up at Jack with suspicion, but there was no triumph in those gray eyes. They glowed with a strange intensity as he awaited her reply, but there was no indication that he knew it in advance. His anxiety was only for Amy.

She nodded slowly. "If you can tame the dragon lady, I would have Amy come for tea. I know she is much too young, but little girls like to play at being grown-up. She will learn to get on in society that way."

Jack halted and caught her elbow to swing her around to face him. "I thank you, Carolyn, but she is not likely to be part of society. Surely you must see that."

She met his eyes coolly. "If you legally adopted her, she would be accepted, but that is your decision. All I can do is entertain her for a few hours a day."

Jack stared down into Carolyn's porcelain face, willing himself to see there what he wanted to see. Amy needed a mother. How many women would accept him knowing they would have to accept his bastard daughter too? He had thought briefly of finding her a loving family willing to raise her as their own, but he had not been able to bring himself even to look for one. Now here was Carolyn telling him to adopt her. Surely she knew that would be condemning him to a life without a wife, Amy to living without a mother?

He dared not think further than that, although all his heart yearned to do so. He made a slight bow of acceptance to the truth of her words. "Send around a note as to a convenient time for you. I will make certain that she is there."

Amy arrived promptly at the time designated, the feather perched archly over her tiny nose from a bonnet otherwise decorated in roses. Her guardian dragon sniffed loudly as Carolyn greeted the child.

"His lordship said I might leave her here briefly while I do some shopping." The disapproval on her face was more than apparent.

Carolyn dismissed her without a glance. "She will do quite nicely with us. Thank you, Mrs. Higginbotham."

Without a backward look, she led Amy to the library, where Blanche waited impatiently.

At the sight of Jack's small daughter, Blanche exclaimed in surprise, threw Carolyn a swift look, then knelt to remove her bonnet and cloak. The little girl gazed at Blanche's blond curls with awe and obediently stood still under her ministrations.

"It is a pity our Penny is not here to play with you. I'm certain you would get on tremendously." As protective as Carolyn of her younger sisters, Blanche easily accepted this new arrival. Carolyn had only mentioned that the child seemed exceptionally timid and perhaps a little frightened by her new surroundings. Blanche had been curious and willing to satisfy her curiosity, but it was more thoroughly stirred than before at the sight of the child's brown features.

Once freed of her outer garments, Amy wandered to the table where Blanche had been working. Scattered bits of paper and pens and scissors covered the leather working surface, and her velvet gaze fastened on the elaborate valentine. "What's that?"

Carolyn laughed. Jack had mentioned that she had a penchant for lovely and exotic objects. To a child's eyes, that lacy red-and-white confection would seem quite exotic. She helped Amy into a chair at the table. "That's a valentine. It's a gift to someone you love on St. Valentine's Day. Would you like to make one?"

To Blanche's amusement, her prim-and-proper older sister sat down at the library table and proceeded to instruct a four-year-old in the intricacies of valentine making. She had not seen Carolyn so animated in years. Whatever was going on here, it was good for her. Blanche rang for tea to be brought in the library. If she remembered correctly, four-year-olds preferred sweets with their instructions.

Over the next few weeks, Amy came to visit on a number of occasions. Sometimes they persuaded her to listen to a story or go for a carriage ride in the park, but mostly her fascination led to the glorious array of ribbons and pretty papers scattered across the library table. Dissatisfied with her first attempts, Blanche continued to make more and more elaborate cards, and Amy's awe at their extravagance did not cease. Under Carolyn's tutelage, she painstakingly constructed one of her own. In showing the child what to do, Carolyn created a card for the first time since she was a child of Blanche's age.

Jack sometimes accompanied his daughter to the door, but conscious of Carolyn's earlier threats, he politely declined to enter until he had been specifically invited. Carolyn stubbornly refused any such invitation, although when they met at social affairs, she willingly spoke with him of his daughter's progress. Since often this was in the company of Lord Hampton, Jack could not put a favorable construction on their new relationship. She kept him firmly in his place, but he could not resign himself to believing he had arrived to find her still unattached, only to watch her marry another. He consoled himself into thinking it was only a matter of biding his time.

*   *   *

Time rapidly ran out one frosty February day, however. The unsettling news that George's mother was actually on her way home from the Continent was quickly
superseded by a more immediate calamity. Jack came
home to a household in an uproar and two physicians in
the nursery. In near-hysterics, Mrs. Higginbotham cow-
ered in a corner, exhorting the physicians alternately to
take care and to do something.

In a trice, Jack was pushing between the maids and
doctors around the tiny bed to find his daughter lying
limp and pale against the sheets. Hiding his terror, he
knelt beside the bed and touched his hand to her smooth
forehead. It burned with fever.

With a stricken look, he turned to the elder of the two
physicians hovering respectfully in the background.
Jack could not speak, but the medical man replied to his
expression without need of questions.

"The child was overexposed to the cold, and I suspect she has eaten something while outside that does
not agree with her system. She has been vomiting
steadily until now."

A murderous anger began to build as Jack turned his
icy gaze to Mrs. Higginbotham and the two nursemaids
he employed to look after one small child. The nursemaids chattered in tandem, making it impossible to decipher a word. He focused his ire on the massive
woman cowering in the corner.

Realizing it was a matter of self-preservation, Mrs.
Higginbotham drew herself up to her full height and
presented the woeful tale in the best light she could.

"She took my sewing scissors and cut up the fron-
tispiece of one of your books in the library, mangled it
dreadfully, she did. I caught her when she was cutting
the fine lace off one of her gowns. She's badly spoiled,

m'lord, if you'll forgive my saying so. I thought to teach her a lesson, so I sent her to an empty garret to reflect on her bad behavior. She weren't there no more than an hour or so."

Her composure was slipping badly, and with it, the artificial elegance of her speech. Jack continued to stare at her grimly, determined to have the whole tale before he ripped the nursery and everyone in it to tiny pieces.

At his silence, the woman took a deep breath and continued, "When Maisie went up to fetch her for her tea, she wasn't there. We looked everywhere, we did. There's not a bit of furniture in that room. She couldn't of hid. She just up and disappeared."

Since the garret she referred to was icy cold and accessible only by the back stairs, Jack found nothing mysterious in this. He was not blind to Amy's less-than-obedient nature. She wouldn't have stayed in that dull, cold room for long, and he doubted that there was a key to be found to fit the lock. Given the opportunity, she would have slipped back down the stairs. Where she had gone from there was anybody's guess.

"Where did you find her?" he demanded curtly when it became apparent the woman would not willingly volunteer any more information.

"Begging your pardon, m'lord," one of the maids interrupted when Mrs. Higginbotham seemed unable to reply. "Timmy followed her footsteps in the snow. They got kind of confused in the park, he said, and he came back to get some others to help him. They said they found her by the far gate. She didn't have no coat nor nothin' on—just her wet dress," she amended at the furious blaze in Jack's eyes.

The fury was as much for himself as for the servants. He had brought the child to a strange climate that her

small body could not easily endure and that her mind
had not learned to fear. He had left his only daughter in
the care of thoughtless servants and a woman he had
been warned did not approve of or even like her. He had
selfishly not even made any attempt to find Amy a better situation, not wanting to admit that he couldn't care
for her by himself, not wanting to be parted from the
one creature on God's earth who loved him for himself.
And this was what he had brought to her.

With a strangled cry, Jack gathered Amy into his
arms and ordered everyone else out. She would be well
again, if he had to pour his own life's blood into her.

When Amy didn't appear at her appointed time the
next day, Carolyn was curious and disappointed. She
had grown fond of the child and enjoyed watching her
blossoming with care and attention. Oddly enough, the
news that George's mother would arrive in London
next week did not excite her so much as watching Amy
master the scissors and paper to cut an almost perfect
heart. Reporting this progress to Jack seemed more
consequential than speculating as to whether the dowa-
ger marchioness would consider an insignificant but
wealthy chit as wife material for her son.

Unable to curb her curiosity and concern, Carolyn
sent a maid around to inquire as to the reason for Amy's
absence. When the maid returned with the news, Carolyn picked up her skirts and headed for the stairs.

"Send word to Nanny that I have need of her fever
medicine, the recipe for the cold posset, some of those
dried herbs we picked last summer for steaming, and
perhaps the purgatives. Just tell her what you have told
me. She will know what to do." The instructions
streamed behind her as she hurried down the stairs.

At the last sentence, Florrie nodded in relief. Even if she forgot part of these hurried orders, Nanny would know what was needed. She watched in concern as Miss Carolyn called for her cloak and a carriage. Surely she could not be thinking of going to a gentleman's house unescorted.

Carolyn wasn't looking at her flight in precisely that light. She had nursed her four sisters through all manner of childhood illnesses. She knew what Amy needed. Since Blanche was from home at the moment and her maid had to get word to Nanny, it seemed expedient to go alone. The only consequence she had in mind was seeing Amy back to health.

Finding herself suddenly confronted with the door to the town house Jack had taken for the Season, Carolyn experienced a momentary qualm, but when the door opened to reveal a frightened Mrs. Higginbotham standing in the hallway beyond the doorman, her resolution firmed. She announced herself and stepped across the portal without giving the servant time to refuse her entrance.

"Where is Amy?" she demanded firmly of the startled matron. The woman in all rights belonged in the nursery with her charge. Such scandalous breach of duty ought to be reprimanded. Jack certainly ran a loose household.

"She is ill in bed." Mrs. Higginbotham drew herself up defensively, prepared to fight on more even terms with this interfering female than she could with his lordship.

"I wish to see her." Ignoring the challenge in the woman's eyes, Carolyn started for the stairs. The nursery would have to be upstairs. She would find it for herself if necessary.

"You can't go up there!" Scandalized, Mrs. Higgin-botham lurched after her.

Carolyn blithely sailed upward. "Just tell me which room. I'll find my way. You needn't concern yourself further."

"You can't go in there!" the woman repeated with slight variation. "His lordship's in there!"

It had truly never occurred to her that Jack would be in the nursery with his ill child. Her own father had probably never seen inside the nursery doors, but he'd had a wife and daughters to see to the care of his younger children. There hadn't been any necessity for involving himself personally in childhood illnesses. Still, the thought of Jack sitting at his daughter's bed-side sent Carolyn's heart pounding, and she experienced a momentary hesitation about entering.

A door at the end of the hall opened and a nursemaid came out carrying soiled linen. Without another thought, Carolyn hurried in that direction. Mrs. Higgin-botham beat a hasty retreat.

Carolyn halted in the doorway to get her bearings. The room was lavishly decorated in flowered wallpaper and sprigged-muslin curtains and a narrow canopy bed in blue velvet. Toys stood on shelves everywhere, and an alcove to the side was obviously intended for the maid's cot. It looked undisturbed at the moment. The only signs of life were near the bed.

Her gaze fell on Jack's haggard face first. He had drawn a rocking chair from the fireplace to the bedside and rested with eyes closed and his head against the high back. Lines of weariness etched his handsome face, and his rumpled clothes bore the certain signs of having been slept in. He retained none of the self-assured, polished demeanor with which he met the world. His dark curls stood on end as if he had been raking his fingers through them. His immaculate cravat had been pulled loose and flung aside, and a day's growth of beard bristled along his darkened cheeks. Carolyn bit her lip against a sudden surge of longing and turned her gaze to the bed.

She caught her breath at sight of the pale, motionless figure beneath the covers. She looked so tiny and defenseless, and only the spots of fevered color on her round cheeks gave any indication of life.

Her gasp brought Jack's eyes open, and he stared in disbelief at Carolyn's elegant figure posed in the doorway. She had not disposed of her pelisse or muff, and her cheeks still bore the fresh color of the cold outside. He fixed his gaze on her terrified eyes, and denying himself the relief flooding through him, said, "Carolyn, you have no business here. You must leave, at once."

She ignored his words. Unfastening the frog at her throat, she laid her pelisse and muff on a nearby chair. It was easier if she kept her gaze on the child in the bed and not the haunted man at her side. "You need some rest. Go get something to eat and lie down for a while. I'll sit with her."

Jack rose and clasped her arms before she could go closer. "For God's sake, Carolyn, go home before someone finds you here."

Carolyn's gaze finally swerved to meet his, and the heat flooding through her from the love and anguish she found there melted her insides. She had never experienced anything quite like this before, and she resisted the desire to fall into Jack's arms and hang on for dear life. She was disappearing into his eyes, and the feeling terrified and thrilled her. Nervously she looked away again, and recovered her strength as she remembered her purpose.

"I've sent to Nanny for her basket of nostrums. They seem to be more effective than most of the medicines the physicians use. We've certainly tested their efficacy often enough. Go rest, Jack. I'll come to no harm sitting here. And I do have considerable experience at nursing children."

Jack clung to her arms, staring down at her bare head with soaring despair and hope. She had no right to be here, but he needed her desperately. Just her presence had brought a return of hope. He felt the strength of her resolve, knew the magnitude of the character behind it, and knew beyond any doubt that if anyone could nurse Amy to life, it would be this woman in his hands. But in allowing her to do so, he would almost certainly be destroying her life. Unless . . .

He let the possibility of that one exception wash through him like a soothing balm. If she still cared, if she could possibly choose . . . He daren't let his thoughts wander to the borders of the impossible. He hadn't had any sleep in thirty-six hours. He was merely dreaming with his eyes open.

"I'll have Mrs. Higginbotham come up. Then I'll send for your carriage. You can't stay."

Carolyn gave him a brisk look, pulled from his grasp, and began removing her gloves, all traces of wavering gone. "You would do better to send that woman packing. If it eases your conscience, send one of the nursemaids up. We'll need a constant supply of fresh water. Has the cold settled in her lungs?"

Jack was too weary to fight both Carolyn and himself. He felt singularly helpless staring at the lifeless features of his daughter night and day. He had no notion of how to go on. Carolyn did. He grasped desperately at the offer.

Within minutes he had explained what happened, what the physicians recommended, and the results, or lack of them. Carolyn sat beside the bed as he spoke, touching gentle fingers to heated cheeks, avoiding looking too closely at the man behind her. He had been right when he had said he was just a man. Seeing him like this brought all her foolish fancies home. He was suffering in a way she had never experienced. The lordly rake she had condemned, the gentle lover she had worshiped—both were only small facets of his character. Men weren't so simply defined with a word or two. She had a lot yet to learn. Perhaps her father had protected her too well.

She felt him hovering uncertainly behind her, fearful of what would happen should he leave his daughter unguarded for even a moment. She turned and touched a hand to his sleeve, daring to meet his eyes just this once. "Go, Jack. You have done everything humanly possible. The matter is in God's hands now."

He needed to be reminded of that. Nodding, he pressed her fingers. Not daring to say more, he left hastily in search of a maid.

Telling himself he would nap only a few hours, Jack collapsed, still dressed, on a guest bed near the nursery. When he had fully recovered his faculties, he would decide what to do with the obstinate Miss Thorogood. She would certainly be missed by dinner. He had no illusions that she had told anyone where she was going, or she would have been prevented. Somehow, he would have to find a way to spirit her back into the safety of her own home. When he woke.

It was nearly midnight before he opened his eyes

again. It took a minute to recollect why he slept in a strange bed with all his clothes on. He hadn't been that drunk in years. When the memory came, it was with a rush of pain and fear, and he hastily swung his legs to the floor.

Amy's room was lit by a branch of candles. In their flickering light he watched Carolyn wring out a cloth in a washbowl and gently place it over his daughter's forehead. A worried frown lined Carolyn's brow as she worked, and he could see that she was biting her lip. In fear, he turned to observe Amy more closely.

She was tossing restlessly. As he came closer, he could see the fine sheen of perspiration on her small face. Even as he watched, he heard her low moan, and the bottom seemed to fall out of his stomach.

"What is wrong? What can I do?" he whispered hoarsely, coming to stand beside the bed.

Carolyn glanced up at him in relief. "Her fever is rising rapidly. We must keep it down. Call some of the servants and have them bring up snow to add to the washbasin."

Jack looked at the empty cot where the maid should be and shook his head in disbelief. Where in hell were his servants? Furiously he went in search of a maid. His daughter could be dying, and they all lay cozy in their beds. He would fire the lot of them on the morrow.

He forgot his temper a little while later as he cuddled his unconscious daughter on his lap while Carolyn applied the cold compresses to her brow. Amy seemed to lie quieter in his arms, and he felt better holding her close. She was so damned small and helpless. She needed him to protect her, and he hadn't done a very good job of it. Perhaps this was God's way of telling him he didn't deserve love. He'd certainly failed the child's mother. And Carolyn. He looked up to watch the grim lines of worry on her lovely face.

"I meant to send you home hours ago," he murmured more to himself than to her.

"I wouldn't have gone." Carolyn carefully packed the latest bowl of snow into a cloth. "You needed sleep, and Mrs. Higginbotham is useless. I'm afraid I yelled at her."

The idea of yelling at that redoubtable matron had never occurred to Jack. He lifted a surprised brow at this delicate lady beside the bed, gently applying compresses, and wondered what other secrets she hid. How much did he really know of her, after all?

"Did you yell at the maids too? I thought I specifically assigned them to helping you while I slept."

"They're sweet, but they haven't a brain between them. Mrs. Higginbotham dismissed the one who spoke up earlier, and she told the other to go on to bed. Then she went off to bed herself." Carolyn offered a small grin. "I gave her her marching orders, but she didn't seem to think they were final."

"Did you, now?" Jack leaned back against the wooden headboard and made Amy more comfortable in his arms. Carolyn's proximity and the faint scent of wildflowers soothed him. Under other circumstances, they would have aroused him, but not when his daughter lay ill in his arms. He just needed Carolyn's reassuring presence close at hand to let him know all would be well in a little while. "You're developing quite a nasty temper, my love."

Carolyn didn't even give him a second glance at this endearment. She'd heard his honeyed words before. She had yet to see proof of them. "I've always had a nasty temper. You just never came across it before."

"I think I've encountered it once or twice of late, and I remember a particularly brilliant tantrum that haunted my worst nightmares for years. Had you shown Mrs. Higginbotham that, she would be out of the house by now."

That caused Carolyn to meet his gaze. In this light, she could discern little of Jack's expression, but what she saw made her vaguely uneasy. His light words had a peculiar intensity. Ignoring his reference to another time, she kept to a safer subject. "I'm sorry I did not let my tongue fly, then. She is your servant, so I held back."

Amy stirred in his arms, and Jack returned his gaze there, brushing a strand of ebony hair from her dark complexion. "She will have to go. I just didn't know how to go about interviewing governesses or nannies. I don't know very much about children, I suppose."

Carolyn sat in the rocker and replied softly, "You know how to love them. That is what counts most."

At the gentleness of her voice, Jack relaxed slightly, and closing his eyes, leaned back against the bed. "I don't know what I would have done these last years without her. She is the only softness, gentleness, that I know. I hold her, and she smiles at me with all the love and trust in the world. I needed her faith to keep from losing mine."

Tears came to her eyes, and Carolyn had to look away from the man on the bed. He was so large sprawled across the child's narrow mattress, but he looked perfectly natural like that. She wondered how many nights he had sat just like that, rocking his infant daughter to sleep. "Her mother?" she heard herself asking.

Jack didn't look up. His mouth tightened into an

ironic curve. "If you wish more evidence to cast me aside, that tale ought to do it." When she made no reply, he shrugged lightly and continued. "The poverty in India is excruciating. Many times worse than you see on a London street. Servants can be had for the offer of a roof over their heads and food in their bellies. I was saving every brass farthing I could put a hand to, so I led a very simple life, two rooms and one old ayah to look after me."

He felt Carolyn rise to change the soaking compress, but he didn't open his eyes. He would have this story told and done with. There would be no more illusions between them. "With nothing better to do in the evenings, I was drinking heavily. I won't go into details of what life is like down there, but drink kills a lot of us. I suppose my ayah feared losing her lucrative position, or perhaps she sought a second income or a measure of comfort for another. Whatever her inscrutable reasoning, she brought a young girl to me one night when I was half out of my mind."

Jack opened his eyes then to watch Carolyn's expression at this revelation. He was going far beyond the bounds of propriety to speak these things, but he wanted Carolyn to know all that he was. He had fooled her when she was younger, filling her head with romantic fantasies while concealing the harsher side of his life. It had been an act of desperation at the time, just as the truth was now. Perhaps he was older but no wiser. Carolyn's expression told him nothing, and he took that as permission to go on, though he felt as if he were cutting his own throat once again.

"She became my mistress. There is no polite way to state it. I had no intention of marrying her. She filled a place in my life that was empty, but we scarcely spoke the same language. She was young and ignorant and became pregnant immediately. It made her happy, so I suppose that was what she wanted. She knew it would give her a position of comfort for the rest of her life in my household. That's the way things are done down there."

Carolyn made a small noise that sounded almost like a sob, but he couldn't stop now. It all had to be said. "She died shortly after giving birth to Amy. It was only then that I learned my mistress was also my ayah's daughter."

A soft exclamation indicated Carolyn heard and understood, but she made no other reply to this tale of Amy's origins. It was a tawdry tale, at best. He could have done as so many others had and left the child behind, but just as he had been unable to send the old woman and babe away at birth, he could not do it four years later. With a sigh, Jack snuggled his daughter closer, clinging to her warmth.

"I'm glad you told me," Carolyn offered once she recovered her composure. She hoped he couldn't see the tracks of her tears down her cheeks. The thought of his loneliness in that horrible place of exile and the mother willing to sacrifice her child to a life of infamy rather than allow her to starve tore at her heart. She was glad he had saved Amy from such a life. "Will you adopt her?"

Jack looked up and caught her eye. "I think that depends on several things," he answered slowly. The telltale blush did not rise to her cheeks and he saw only curiosity in her eyes. His hopes plummeted, but he clung fiercely to their remains. "Yes, I will probably adopt her," he answered shortly.

Carolyn did not understand the sharpness of his

words, but she was not given time to consider it. Amy began to shake and moan, and perspiration poured freely from every pore, drenching her tiny night shift. There wasn't time to do anything but act.

Afraid to expose her to the chilly night air, they wrapped her in blankets until she lay still once more. Then, hastily removing wet garments and finding dry ones, they returned to the previous routine of applying compresses. Within the half-hour she was shaking again. Steadily they worked throughout the night.

Shortly after dawn the kitchen sent up tea and toast, and Jack sent for the nursery maid and Mrs. Higginbotham. The maid arrived hurriedly and applied herself to changing the linen, giving the master and the lady surreptitious looks in the process. Both looked haggard but vaguely triumphant. The little girl seemed to be breathing easier.

Mrs. Higginbotham didn't arrive until an hour later. She gave Carolyn a small smirk and turned her full attention on Jack. His rumpled clothes of two days before set her slightly aback, but the snarl on his face made her visibly quail. She turned immediately to the offensive. "I beg your pardon, my lord, but I was told in no uncertain terms that my services weren't required. I will be more than happy to sit with the child while you get your rest. You shouldn't have the burden of nursing an ill child. I'm certain you have much more important things to do. Shall I ring for your bath to be sent up?"

Jack's lips tightened, but he held his temper with remarkable aplomb. Carolyn admired his performance. She would have scratched the woman's eyes out. More important things to do, indeed!

"We'll no longer be requiring your services, Mrs. Higginbotham. I will speak with my secretary when he arrives, and he will advance you six months' salary. I would like you to remove from the household before day's end."

The woman stared at him in astonishment. "On what grounds, my lord? Have I not cared for the wee one like one of my own, dressing her in all that is fine and seeing that she is properly instructed in conduct? I cannot be blamed that her kind cannot learn simple obedience. I have done my utmost to teach her."

Jack rose to his full threatening height and the woman stepped backward. "Out, Mrs. Higginbotham, before I lose my patience. I recommend that you do not seek any other position requiring understanding or compassion, for you have none. Leave us, at once!"

He practically roared this last, and the woman gave a squeak of alarm and rushed to the door, throwing Carolyn a malevolent look in parting.

Jack collapsed into himself, but a sound from the bed quickly returned his attention there. Amy sneezed, then opened her eyes. "Papa?" she inquired weakly as he scooped her into his arms.

Jack's shining eyes and radiant smile brought tears to Carolyn's eyes as she met his gaze. Touching her hand to the child's cheek and ascertaining that it was considerably cooler than before, she felt relief flood through her and felt the same in him. They needed no words of understanding.

"Nanny's basket will have arrived by now," she murmured. "I will go home and fetch it."

Jack's smile faded. "Not yet, Carolyn. Wait until I can come with you. I would not have you face the consequences alone."

She had not given much thought to consequences. She had possessed the freedom to come and go at will for some years now. Her father trusted her to do the proper thing. In all probability, he did not even know she wasn't at home. She offered Jack an uneasy smile. "That isn't necessary. My maid is the only one who knows, and she won't talk. You needn't worry."

Amy's fit of sneezing, followed by her hungry complaints, distracted them both for some while. Jack became frantic when she cried and spit up her toast. Carolyn soothed him and the child, offering apple juice and tea laced with honey and slicing the toast up into soft, buttery strips dotted with cinnamon. Between Jack shouting orders at an army of servants racing up and down the stairs and Carolyn patiently doctoring the food brought to suit an invalid, they succeeded in getting the first decent meal into Amy that she'd had in days.

Their triumph did not last long. Just as they got Amy into another clean gown and asleep, a roar in the lower hall warned that still another hurdle awaited. They exchanged glances at the familiar cadence of furious words. Carolyn's father had discovered her whereabouts.

She paled slightly at the unexpectedness of this visitation, but held her head high as she heard his angry strides outside the door. Not daring to compromise her further by touching her, Jack kept a respectful distance as the door burst open.

Henry Thorogood quickly took in his daughter's wrinkled walking gown and weary expression, Jack's rumpled clothes and defiantly protective air, and the tiny child lying curled beneath the covers. The vulgar message that had brought him flying here had no basis in fact; he knew his daughter too well to see anything else in this scene but what it was. He concealed his sigh of relief and turned his furious gaze on the young man who had so successfully turned his comfortable world inside-out.

"I will see you in my study in one hour, Chatham. Come, Carolyn, we will go home."

Stiffly Carolyn looked from one man to the other. Had they been tomcats, they would have their backs arched, their hair on end, and they would be spitting. That was an odd way to picture Jack, and she threw him a second look. His fingers were curled around the chair back while he engaged her father in a duel of glares. The tension mounting between them was too electric to bear. Silently she picked up the pelisse and muff she had thrown over the chair the day before and walked out of the room.

Angry shouts echoed up and down the hallways, vibrating the normally quiet air of the sedate Thorogood household. Blanche sent her sister a speculative look as she sat reading in the far corner of the library. Carolyn's air of indifference didn't fool her this time. She looked like one who hadn't slept in weeks, and the book she held was upside-down. Something was going on, but no one had given thought to informing Blanche.

Carolyn didn't seem surprised when the footman came to fetch her. She shook out the warm yellow skirts of the fine wool gown she had hastily donned, wasted no time tidying her loose arrangement of curls, and proceeded out, as if walking to her execution.

Her father at least had the decency to leave them alone for this interview, she observed as she entered the study to find only Jack waiting there. He had that haunted look on his face again, but his eyes were warm as they took in her appearance. He made no attempt at an improper embrace, as he might have in earlier years, but Carolyn felt his desire to do so. She was grateful for his restraint.

"How is Amy?" Although she had left the child little more than an hour ago, it seemed much longer. She would hear this news before the argument to come.

"Sleeping when I left her. Your maid brought the basket of remedies. I thank you for your concern."

His formality indicated uneasiness. Carolyn could understand that. Her father could have that effect on heads of state. Nervously she took a seat and clasped her hands in her lap. "You needn't look like that, Jack. He doesn't bite."

Jack made a wry smile. "I wouldn't swear to that. He's in the right of it, though. I have compromised you beyond repair. I'm obliged to offer for you."

She had hoped he would phrase it a little less bluntly. It would be soothing to her injured feelings to hear him mouth a few of the pretty phrases he was so good at saying. Just for a little while she would like to cling to the illusion of those long-ago years.

Her smile matched his as she replied, "I am obliged to refuse."

Jack's shoulders slumped imperceptibly and he turned to play with the candlesticks on the mantel rather than reveal his expression. "You cannot, Carolyn. That Higginbotham woman is spreading word far and wide. I could slit her throat, but the damage will already be done."

She had not expected that. Wildly, Carolyn contemplated her alternatives, but her ability to think straight had flown out the door when Jack entered it. She shook her head in hopes of freeing it from cobwebs. "We can deny everything. I'll not be forced into marriage."

"I knew you would say that." Bleakly he turned back to face her. "Can you not even consider it, Carolyn? Would it be so horrible a fate? I'm quite wealthy now, you know. I can support you in any manner that you choose."

Carolyn rose and gave him a cold glare at this insult. "What does wealth have to do with it? I would have married you when you were penniless, but you preferred gold to me. Go wed your gold, Jack. I'll not have any part of your lies."

She swung to leave the room, but he stepped forward and caught her wrist, his face a mixture of despair and desperation. "Is it George? Do you love him? I will go speak to him today and explain all that has happened. If you love each other, this misunderstanding can't come between you."

Carolyn gave him an icy look and refused to reply until he dropped her wrist. "Explain what you wish to whomever you wish if it eases your conscience. Good day, Jack."

She swept out in a trail of lavender and wildflowers, leaving him bereft. The fury in Thorogood's expression when he returned did not ease Jack's pain. He had lost her. The terrible emptiness that followed this realization could only be filled with silent screams of anguish.

Despite her lack of sleep, Carolyn did not find rest easy that night. She couldn't erase the look in Jack's eyes when she refused him. Surely he had not expected her to agree after what he had done to her? What did he stand to gain by offering now?

Amy. That thought came instantly to mind. He needed a mother for Amy. That much was obvious. She must have filled him with confidence when she had so foolishly taken the child under her wing. Instead of pretty words, he meant to woo her with his daughter.

Why did that notion not ring true? She was quite old enough and experienced enough by now to know when she was being manipulated. She had no more romantic illusions. George, at least, had the sense to treat her as an intelligent human being capable of making decisions without having to be wooed and won with silly words and gestures. Would Jack ever consider her in such a light?

That thought made her even more restless, and she got up to put on her robe and pace the room. George's polite note had only said that Jack had been to see him and that he understood all. What did he understand? Did he understand that she needed the reassurance of his presence, of hearing his voice say the words? Obviously not. Jack had, or he wouldn't have been so quick to go to George to explain it. Had it been Jack she had been considering instead of George, he would have been at her door within the time it took to receive the message. Jack had never stinted her in his attentions.

Nor did he now. There was another bouquet on her dressing table with a note telling her how Amy fared. She had nearly cried when she had seen it. All day she had felt isolated. Her father wasn't speaking to her. George's stilted message hadn't helped. And no one had come to call. Only Jack's thoughtful note bringing news of his concern for her had come to break her loneliness.

She was mad to be thinking like this. In a few days George would be escorting her to the usual social functions, the gossip would subside, and everything would be back to normal. Why should she place any consequence on a few flowers and kind words? Jack had always been lavish in his attentions. That was just his way. It didn't mean anything.

But, may the heavens preserve her, she wanted it to mean something. She wanted to know that bouquet meant he cared for her. She wanted to know he offered for her because he loved her and didn't wish to be parted from her again. She wanted to believe that he had come to her that day after the ball to explain his undying love and the misery he had suffered in those years apart, the same misery she had suffered and was suffering still.

Flinging herself weeping on the bed, Carolyn finally found comfort in repose. Only in her dreams could she believe that the warmth in gray eyes and the eager caress of browned hands meant something more than selfishness.

The days slipped away like the steady drip of the icicles outside the windows. Carolyn retreated inside herself just as Blanche remembered her doing those years ago during her first Season. Back then, she had at least continued to attend social functions, although with an icy brittleness that displayed little pleasure. This time, she refused to go out at all, putting a severe damper on Blanche's own social life. Something drastic had to be done, and swiftly.

The litter of paper and scissors and a crudely cut heart on the library table made Blanche smile in anticipation. Glancing surreptitiously around the room to be certain Carolyn was nowhere to be seen, she carefully completed the larger card with a few pen strokes, added the one Amy had made, wrapped both in a length of vellum with a scribbled note, and summoned a footman. St. Valentine's Day was for lovers. The gentlemen who had appeared at their door earlier this day weren't lovers, just men playing at games. Her romantic heart hoped she had made the correct surmise in sending this particular valentine.

Jack opened the slender package in his study, where he was working over long-neglected correspondence. The sight of the two lavishly decorated cards brought back such a painful memory that he nearly threw them aside as someone's idea of a malicious joke. But the crudity of the one card caught his interest, and he cautiously picked up the message accompanying it.

After reading the brief note, he more carefully studied the two hearts. Both were made with loving hands, one pair childish and uncoordinated, the other talented and gentle. He remembered well the poem inscribed inside the larger heart. He remembered the occasion when he had last quoted it. His hands shook and tears sprang to his eyes as he read it again. Surely, after all these years, she would have forgotten so silly a verse had it not meant something to her? Why, then, would she not say the words to his face?

Pondering this peculiarity, Jack took the smaller heart in his hand and went up the stairs to where a rapidly recovering child was wreaking havoc with her impatience to be out of bed. At the sight of him, Amy leapt from beneath the covers to hold her arms out and bounce upon the bed.

Her joyful cry of "Papa" brought a smile to his weary face, and Jack caught her up in a hug, careful not to crumple the paper in his hand. When he set her down, he presented the childishly beautiful card with a flourish.

"Do you remember this?"

Dark eyes lit with excitement. "Lynley helped me! It's for you."

"Lynley?" Jack sat on the edge of the bed and smiled at the childish name for so gracious and lovely a woman as Carolyn Thorogood. As Amy pointed out the card's many and varied features, he could hear Carolyn speaking in the voice of his daughter. Loneliness and a desperate need for her company welled up inside of him. He could not keep on living this half-life. Something had to be done, but he had run out of ideas. How did one go about wooing someone he had courted once, only to slam a door in her face? What he had done was unforgivable. How could they ever go back to that time again?

Something Amy was chirping caught his ear, and he turned his attention back to her. "What was that, love? Lynley said what?"

"Don't break it, she said," Amy gave him a look of disdain at his lack of attention. "You got to keep it forever and ever and ever," she admonished in a tone that reflected the adult she mimicked.

Don't break it. Jack thought of the torn pieces stored all these years in an ivory music box of his mother's. He had carried that broken heart halfway around the world with him as a reminder of how low he had fallen. If only he could put those torn pieces back together again and start all over.

The vague stirrings of an impossible idea came to mind, but nothing was too impossible to try in this desperate gamble for a love he had lost and wished to win back again. Giving Amy a kiss and thanking her with a hug for his beautiful valentine, he rose and went in search of the music box.

Many tedious hours later he had pasted and pieced

dozens of torn bits of lacy paper on a large sheet of vellum. Giving the ragged result a wry look, Jack admitted to himself that his chance of winning this gamble with such feeble backing was slim, but it was all he had.

Forgetting cloak and hat, he set out into the fast-growing darkness of the winter streets, gripping the forlorn fragments of an old valentine. He carried no roses or candy or trinkets as a proper valentine lover should. Instead, he carried his heart in his hand.

When notified she had a visitor, Carolyn refused to see him, as she had refused all visitors this day. She didn't have the heart to exchange witty sallies with friends or suitors on the state of her love life on this day for lovers. Tomorrow, maybe she would venture out again. George had been remarkably silent this past week, but the combination of the scandal and his mother's arrival would explain that. He had sent another reassuring note, but it hadn't reassured. She hadn't even finished reading it.

The footman returned some minutes later with a large bit of paper on his salver. Carolyn gave him a look of irritation for thus interrupting her morose thoughts again, but she took the awkwardly large message he offered. Her eyes widened in surprise and she rose to carry it to a brighter lamp to better peruse what she wouldn't believe she was seeing.

Carefully pieced and pasted back together was the valentine she had created five years ago for the man she had meant to marry. The faded ink still bore the words of the poem Jack had written for her when he had asked if she would marry him, the same poem she had written on the valentine she had left downstairs in the library, writing the words as if it had been only yesterday when last she heard them.

Tears poured down Carolyn's cheeks as the feelings of that long-ago time flooded through her, unlocked by this tattered heart that Jack had so painstakingly recreated. He had kept it all those years. Why?

Without a word to the waiting servant, Carolyn swept out of the room and half-ran to the front salon, where visitors waited, the tattered valentine clutched possessively in her hand. She had to see him face-to-face, to hear his reply. She had to know why he had kept this shattered heart for all these years. And why he had put it back together now.

Jack glanced up as she ran into the room. His weathered face had a lined and harried look to it, and there was a wariness in his eyes at her abrupt entrance, but he moved toward her as steel draws toward a magnet.

"Why?" She waved the forlorn heart beneath his nose.

He didn't need to understand the question. The answer was in his heart. "Because I love you. Because I've always loved you. Throw it back in my face if you will. I deserved it then. I've worked hard not to deserve it now, but that's for you to decide. I can't bear this loneliness any longer, Carolyn. I've worked and waited these five years in hopes of winning at least your respect, but what I want is your love. Can you ever forgive me and start anew?" He was not too proud to beg, but he desperately wished he dared take her in his arms while doing so. The cold air between them chilled his heart.

Carolyn stared at him in disbelief, not daring to believe the words. He had destroyed her with just such words before. She couldn't let him do it again. Her gaze faltered at the smoky gray intensity of his eyes, and she dropped it to the valentine in her hand. Her fingers instinctively smoothed the crumpled paper.

"I can't. How can I?" she murmured, almost to herself. "You sold my love for money. It's gone. There can be no love where there is no trust."

His heart ached, and he finally gave in and reached for her. Whether he hoped to prevent her escape or pour his love into her, he couldn't say, but the contact was electric. They both jerked with the jolt, and Jack couldn't have moved away if his life depended on it.

Holding her arms, he poured out his feverish response. "I paid him back, Carolyn. I paid your father back every cent I ever took from him. He was right. I had no right to ask you to share a life of penury with a careless spendthrift. I do not condone his methods, but he did what he had to to protect you. I didn't take his money in exchange for your love. I never wanted his money. He gave me no choice. Please understand that, Carolyn. Turn me away if you will, but not without understanding that I have never stopped loving you, that everything I have done has been for love of you."

Carolyn wanted desperately to be enfolded in Jack's embrace, to accept his words unquestioningly, to feel his strong arms around her and hear his heart beat beneath her ear, but she had learned her lesson at his hands too well. She shook her head blindly, refusing to meet his eyes.

"I heard you that night. Father paid you to turn me away. Don't lie to me anymore, Jack. I can't bear it."

Jack felt anger for the father who had allowed her to continue to think these things all these years, even after the debt was repaid. But the plea in Carolyn's voice called to him, and he gently pulled her into his arms. He rejoiced when she made no effort to fight him. The scent of lavender wafted around him, and he inhaled deeply. He could easily spend the rest of his life drowning in that fragrance.

"I've never lied to you, my love. Please believe me. Every word I've said is true, although I once put them cruelly to drive you away. I didn't want you wedded to a man lounging in debtor's prison. I didn't deserve you then, and I knew it. Your father's ultimatum only made it clear to me. I hated him for making me face the facts, but he gave me the opportunity to redeem myself, and I took it in hopes of one day being able to look you in the eye again. The money he offered was a loan, my love. I repaid it with interest. You may ask him if you have doubts."

Carolyn tried to make order of her swirling thoughts, but enveloped in Jack's arms, she could only drink in the radiant heat of his body and the ecstasy of his hard strength beneath her hands. She didn't wish to think of anything else.

She didn't need to think of anything else. A door slammed, and a harsh voice exclaimed, "What is the meaning of this? Damn you, Chatham, haven't you caused enough scandal—must you create more?"

Carolyn jerked and would have fled Jack's arms, but he held her firmly, entrapping her in his protective hold as they both faced her father together.

"If you'll excuse me, sir, I am asking your daughter to marry me. I do not believe I need your permission anymore."

"You do not need my money anymore, is what you mean! She refused you, Chatham. I'll not see her made unhappy. Get out of here before I call the constabulary."

Carolyn straightened at this threat, and without a second thought to her words, she answered her father's furious glare steadily. "Jack will leave when I want him to. If you throw him out, I go with him. You tore us apart once before, but I'm older now and know you are not infallible. Had you but trusted my judgment then, we neither of us would have had to suffer all these years. This time, the choice is mine. You cannot force it." She felt Jack's arm tighten around her, and this time she allowed herself to lean into his embrace.

"Shhh, Lynley," Jack whispered placatingly in her ear as her father's face grew suddenly ashen. "Save your temper for another time. I'm a father now too, and I know what it is like to protect a daughter. It is easy to think the safe thing is the right thing. No one wants to take chances with the ones they love."

Carolyn turned eyes brimming with love up to Jack's face, and her smile was one of joy and acceptance. Her words, however, had the ring of a woman who had set aside childish fancies. "You are not my father, John Chatham. If it's marriage you want, you had better learn I am no longer a gullible child to be swept away by your facile tongue. I can fight my own battles, thank you."

The warm chuckle in her ear made her heart quake. "Anyone who can simultaneously rout Mrs. Higginbotham and capture my daughter has my full respect, my love. I do not doubt your abilities. It is your temper I fear."

Henry Thorogood watched this display with bemusement but had the sense to hold his tongue. The young lord had a quick way with words, but perhaps that was what Carolyn needed. He certainly couldn't fault the loving attention the young man showered upon her, although he certainly could fault his methods.

With a loud throat-clearing to remind them he was in the room, he interrupted what could easily have become a rather intimate exchange. "I cannot leave the room unless I know a formal betrothal has been formed."

Carolyn turned her smile from Jack's loving gaze to her father's stiff figure. "Leave the room, Papa. Jack may talk with you later."

She felt the joy rocketing through the man holding her as her father glared and stomped from the room. She wasn't certain what she had done, but in her heart, it felt right. She turned her gaze expectantly back to Jack.

"I love you, even if you are as spoiled and obstinate as Amy." Jack's mouth curved lightly as she moved more fully into his embrace.

"Don't forget bad-tempered and willful," she reminded him, standing on tiptoes to reach his lips with hers.

"And mine." Firmly and resolutely, Jack covered her mouth with his, drawing her possessively into his hold so she could have no uncertainty as to what he meant.

"I never said yes," Carolyn gasped some minutes later when he gave her time to gulp for air.

"Yes you did, five years ago. It's been a long betrothal, my love. Shall we make it a hasty wedding?" Jack held her eyes with desperate intensity.

"Will you explain to George?" Carolyn asked, postponing her acceptance of this joy Jack offered her with open hand. She still could not quite believe it. She needed time.

Jack smiled. "I've already explained to George. He's a very understanding man. He's willing to let you choose."

"He'd give me up without a fight?" she asked in mock incredulity.

"He knows I'll put him six feet under if he stands in my way. Give me a date, my love."

"Christmas," she said firmly.

Jack bent his head closer and spoke inches from her lips "Try again."

"Easter," she murmured, rising to the temptation.

And as that holiday was little more than a month away, Jack said, "Done," and closed the compact with a kiss.

Although the sun shone and the guests wore their spring pastels for the occasion, the ebony-haired flower girl wore red velvet and the blond bridesmaids wore white lace and carried valentine roses when the bride walked down the aisle that balmy Easter Day.

When the ceremony ended and the groom's sun-darkened face bent to take the kiss he had earned from his shining bride, he gave no sign of surprise as their audience broke into gales of laughter rather than happy tears.

There at the foot of the altar two dancing cherubs in white and red cavorted to the sweeping swells of organ music, heedless of the solemnity of the occasion. The bride smiled softly into the groom's eyes, and the look they exchanged bespoke the distinct possibility that another cherub would be on the way before year's end.

Precious Rogue

by Mary Balogh

Holly House, Summer 1818

She had so little time to herself. It seemed unfair that her peaceful solitude should be shattered after a scant fifteen minutes. Nobody ever came to the lily pond, since it was a full ten-minute walk from the house and inaccessible by carriage because of the trees. She had come to think of it as her own special hideaway—whenever she could get away by herself, that was. That was not very often.

She was high up in the old, gnarled oak tree that she had appropriated as her own, sitting comfortably on a sturdy branch, her back braced safely against the trunk. She had not brought a book with her as she usually did. She had learned by now that she would not read it anyway. When she was at the lily pond, surrounded by the beauties of nature and filled by its peace, she liked nothing better than to gaze about her and allow all her senses to come alive. And sometimes she merely set her head back and gazed upward at branches and leaves and sky and went into a daydream.

There was so little chance to daydream. Night dreams were not nearly as pleasant, since one could not control them—or even remember them half the time. She daydreamed about—oh, about many foolish things. About being beautiful and charming and witty, about having pretty clothes and somewhere special to wear them, about having friends and beaux, about loving and being loved, about having a home and a husband and children. All foolish things. She always reminded herself as she climbed nimbly downward back to the ground and reality that she was well blessed, that it was downright sinful to be discontented, that there were thousands of women far less fortunate than she—and that was an understatement.

But today she had only just begun to relax. She was still enjoying the sight of the pond with its large lily pads almost hiding the water and of the trees surrounding it and of the blue sky above. She was still enjoying the smell of summer greenery and the sound of silence—oh, blessed silence. Though the world about her was anything but soundless, of course. There were birds singing and insects whirring and chirping. But they were natural sounds, sounds to which she did not have to respond.

And then an alien sound. A man's voice.

"Ah," he said, "a lily pond. How charming. I do believe Mother Nature threw it down here this very minute in a desperate attempt to rival your beauty and distract me. She has failed miserably."

A trilling, female laugh. "What absurd things you say," the woman said. "As if I could rival the beauties of nature."

There was a pause as the two of them came into sight beneath the old oak tree and stopped beside the lily pond. Mr. Bancroft and Mrs. Delaney—two of the guests from the house. The house was full of guests, Nancy having just completed her first Season in London but not having quite accomplished the purpose of that Season. Oh, it was true that she had found her future husband. Everything was settled except for one minor detail. The gentleman had not yet proposed.

It was a mere formality, of course. The two of them had a clear understanding. Mr. Bancroft was young, unmarried, heir to a barony, and thoroughly eligible in every possible way. He had paid court to Nancy quite persistently through the spring, dancing with her at a number of balls, accompanying her to the theater one evening, driving her in Hyde Park one afternoon, and generally hovering in her vicinity as much as good manners would allow. And he had accepted her invitation to spend a few weeks at Holly House.

Two facts about him particularly recommended him to Nancy and her mama—or perhaps three, if one took into account the indisputable fact that he was excessively handsome and elegant. Nancy sighed over the fact that she was about to net one of London's most notorious rakes. All the female world loved him, and half the female world—or so the rumor went—had had its heart broken by him. It was a singular triumph for Miss Nancy Peabody to be the one to get him to the altar. Not that she had him there yet, of course. But she would before the summer was out. He had made his intentions quite clear.

The rather strange fact that recommended him to Mrs. Peabody was that he was poor—as a church mouse, if gossip had the right of it. Mr. Peabody, on the other hand, was enormously wealthy and had only his daughter on whom to lavish his riches. It might have been expected that the Peabodys would wish to ally their daughter with wealth, but far more important to Mrs. Peabody was to see Nancy move up the social scale. As Mrs. Bancroft she would be a baroness-in-waiting, so to speak. And until that day when Mr. Bancroft would inherit his uncle's fortune as well as his title, he would have to rely upon the generosity of his father-in-law to keep him in funds. He would be a husband kept firmly to heel.

It all seemed wonderfully perfect to Mrs. Peabody.

And now he was down below the oak tree telling Mrs. Delaney that nature could not rival her beauty. What a ridiculous untruth, the young lady in the tree thought. Mrs. Delaney was too fat—though she had to admit that it was the type of fatness that some men might find appealing. Mr. Delaney was not one of the guests at the house, though apparently he was not deceased.

And Mrs. Delaney had fished for further compliments. Mr. Bancroft did not disappoint her.

"In you, ma'am," he said, "the beauties of nature have combined with breeding and taste to produce dazzling perfection. How can I appreciate the scene around me when you are here with me? I do protest that you make your surroundings appear quite insipid."

The young lady in the tree held her nose.

Mrs. Delaney tittered. "I do not believe a word of it," she said. "You flatter me, sir. I wonder why." She reached out a lace-gloved hand and rested her fingertips upon his sleeve.

Mr. Bancroft possessed himself of the artfully offered hand and raised it to his lips. "Flattery?" he murmured. "You have not looked in your glass recently, ma'am, if you believe that. I have had eyes for no one else since arriving here three days ago. And I have had sighs for no one else."

"Now, that is a bouncer, sir," she said, allowing him to return her hand to his lips for a second kiss. "Everyone knows that you have come here to court Nancy

Peabody. She is a remarkably pretty girl, it must be admitted."

"Girl," he said. "Ah, yes, *girl*, ma'am. You are in the right of it there. A pretty girl can please the eye. It takes a beautiful woman to stir all the senses. A mature woman of your years. A woman who has passed the age of twenty."

It appeared to the young lady in the tree that Mrs. Delaney had passed her twentieth birthday long since, but it was a clever way of paying a compliment, she supposed.

"Sir," Mrs. Delaney asked, "are you flirting with me?"

The girl in the tree held her nose again.

"Flirting, ma'am?" His voice was like a velvet caress. "I do protest. Flirters have no serious intentions. Mine could not be more serious."

"Indeed?" The lady's voice too had become hushed and throaty. "Do you intend to tumble me on the ground, sir, when I am wearing my favorite muslin?"

The watcher stopped holding her nose. She felt sudden alarm.

"Ah, no," he said. "Such charms should be tasted and feasted upon in the privacy of a locked room, ma'am. And worshiped. They should be worshiped on a soft bed."

The lady withdrew her hand from his and tapped him lightly on the arm with it. "I have heard it said that you have some skill in—worshiping," she said. "Perhaps it would be amusing to discover the truth of the matter for myself."

"I am, ma'am," he said, making her an elegant bow, "your humble slave. When? I pray you will not tease me by keeping me waiting."

"It would please me excessively to tease you," Mrs. Delaney said with her trilling laugh, "but I really do not believe I could bear to tease myself, sir. The door of my bed chamber will be unlocked tonight if the fact is of any interest to you."

"I shall burn with unrequited passion and adoration until then," he said, and he bent his dark head and set his lips to the lady's for a brief moment.

"It promises well," she said. "Alas that only half the afternoon has passed. But we should return to the house for tea, sir. Separately, I do believe. I would not have it said that I dally with handsome strangers in the absence of my husband." She laughed merrily.

He bowed to her. "Far be it from me to sully the brightness of your reputation, ma'am," he said. "I shall remain here for a while and discover whether the beauties of nature will be more apparent in the absence of your greater loveliness."

"How absurd you are," she said, turning from him to walk back to the house in virtuous solitude. "And what a flattering tongue you have been blessed with."

The young lady who had been an unwilling witness to this tender love scene was partly amused and partly shocked—and wondered how long the gentleman intended staying at the lily pond admiring the beauties of nature. He sat down on the grassy bank and draped his arms over his raised knees.

Mr. Bancroft probably needed the rest and the solitude as much as she did. He was a busy gentleman. She had been passing his room quite early this morning, bringing Mrs. Peabody a second cup of chocolate, which by rights her maid should have been doing, when the door had opened and Flossie, one of the chamber-maids, had stepped out looking rosy and bright-eyed and slightly disheveled. Behind her as she closed the door there had been the merest glimpse of Mr. Bancroft in his shirtsleeves. It had not taken a great deal of imagination to guess that at the very least the two of them had been exchanging kisses.

At the very least!

And now he had made an assignation to spend the night, or at least a part of it, in Mrs. Delaney's bed, tasting and feasting and worshiping. It was really quite scandalous. When Nancy confided to anyone who was prepared to listen, evident pride in her voice, that her intended husband was a rake, she was making no empty boast.

And then an insect landed on the young lady's bare arm, and she slapped at it without thinking. The slap sounded rather like the cracking of a pistol to her own ears. She held her breath and directed her eyes downward without moving her head.

He had obviously heard it. He turned his head first to one side and then to the other before shrugging slightly and resuming his contemplation of the lily pond.

It amused him to break hearts. Oh, no, that was not strictly true. He supposed it might be mildly distressing to cause real suffering, real from-the-heart suffering. He always instinctively avoided any entanglement in which it seemed likely that the lady's heart might be seriously engaged.

It would be more accurate to say, perhaps, that it amused him to deflate expectations. Many of his acquaintances avoided eligible females as they would avoid the plague, terrified that they would somehow be caught in parson's mousetrap no matter how warily they stepped. Not he. He liked to live dangerously. He liked to see how close he could come to a declaration without ever actually making it or feeling that honor compelled him to do so.

He enjoyed watching young ladies and their mamas setting about entrapping him, believing that their sub-tleties went quite undetected by him. He liked watching them tread carefully at first and then become quite vis-ibly triumphant as they preened themselves before less fortunate mortals. He was never quite sure what the full attraction of his person was, since he always pleaded poverty into those ears whose accompanying mouths were most sure to spread the word. A baron's title was not exactly equivalent to a dukedom, after all, espe-cially when it was a mere future expectation. His uncle was not yet sixty and was the epitome of health and heartiness. And one could never be quite certain that his uncle would not suddenly take it into his head to marry again and start producing sons annually.

But he knew that he was considered a catch. Perhaps his reputation and his elusiveness was the attraction. Just as men felt compelled to pursue women with rep-utations for unassailable virtue, even if they were not wondrously beautiful, he supposed that women might feel a similar challenge when presented with a rake.

And so after paying casual court to the rather pretty and definitely wealthy Miss Nancy Peabody for much of the Season, he had accepted the invitation to spend a few weeks at Holly House, even though his friends had made great sport of both the invitation and his decision to accept it, pulling gargoyle faces and making slashing gestures across their throats and pronouncing him a sure goner. They all clamored loudly and with mar-velous wit for invitations to his wedding, and one of them volunteered to be godfather to his first child nine months after that event.

The pretty and wealthy and conceited Miss Peabody amused him, as did her gracious and pompous mama and her silent father, who appeared to be a nonentity in the Peabody household.

This visit, after all, afforded him a few weeks of relaxation in the country with congenial company and prospects enough with which to satisfy his sexual appetites. He might have made do with the buxom and eager maid who had made herself very available to him both yesterday morning and this morning, hinting of her willingness even before he had thought to sound it out. But Flossie was of that lusty breed of females who invited him with raised petticoats and parted legs to the main event without any preamble and then bounced and bucked with unabashed enthusiasm while he delivered. Just as if they ran a race. He doubted if it had lasted longer than two or three minutes either yesterday or today. And then she had been up and straightening her clothes and pocketing his sovereign and going on her way to continue with what she had been busy at, almost as if there had been no interruption at all.

He needed more. He would get more—considerably more—from Mrs. Delaney, whose reputation was quite as colorful as his own, though he had never yet had her himself. Tonight he would, and he would feast on her as he had promised, slowly and thoroughly, and several times more than once. He had no doubt that he could expect little sleep of the coming night, but sleep was always worth giving up in a good cause.

He would have her for perhaps a week and then be overcome with an onslaught of conscience over her married state before sounding out one of the two or three other prospects that the guest list had presented to his experienced intuition. Two for certain. The third probable.

Oh, yes, it would be an amusing few weeks. Not the least amusement would be that derived from looking into the faces of Miss and Mrs. Peabody on the day he took his leave of them, his leg still quite, quite free of a shackle. It was perhaps unkind of him to look forward to the moment. Undoubtedly it was. But then, what did kindness have to do with anything?

It was as he was thinking along these rather uncharitable lines, enjoying the quietness of his surroundings and the rare interlude of solitude and relaxation, that he heard the sound. He could not identify it, but it was unmistakably a human sound. A glance to either side showed him that no one was coming through the trees toward the lily pond, but the edge of his vision caught the lightness of some fabric up in the old oak tree close by. It was a dress. Worn by a woman or a girl. Someone who had just been entertained to the events leading up to an assignation. He was very tempted to punish her by sitting where he was for an hour or more. But he was too curious. He had not looked directly at her. He did not know who she was.

"Are you not getting cramped up there?" he asked after five minutes, not looking up. "Would you not like to come down?"

He expected confusion, stuttered apologies, a scrambled descent. A cool voice answered him without hesitation.

"No, thank you," it said. "I feel safer where I am."

"Do you indeed?" he said. It was the voice of a young woman. A light, pretty voice—a cultured voice.

"Are you afraid I will pounce on you and ravish you here on the ground?"

"I imagine," she said, "that you expended enough energy in that direction this morning with Flossie. And I would expect you would wish to conserve energy for tonight with Mrs. Delaney. But I would rather be safe than sorry."

He felt a gust of very genuine amusement. The voice was very matter-of-fact, neither frightened nor accusing. He was reluctant to look up. He was very afraid that the person would not live up to the voice.

"Ravishment is not in my line even when my energy is neither expended nor being conserved," he said. "You are quite safe from me. You may descend without a qualm. And it might more accurately be said that Flossie seduced me than that I seduced her. Mrs. Delaney, as you must have witnessed, was quite as eager as I to acquire a bedfellow for the night."

"I thought," she said, "that you were going to worship her."

He chuckled and looked up. She was tucked snugly between the massive trunk of the tree and a sturdy branch, her knees drawn up, her arms clasped about them. She was dressed quite unfashionably in drab gray. Her light brown hair was pinned back in a knot at the neck without any nonsense of curls to soften its severity. Her face was thin and rather pale and quite unpretty. Except for the large gray eyes, which looked unblinkingly down into his.

"Little bird," he said, "you have a sharp tongue. Who are you?" She looked like a governess, except that there were no children at the house. He got to his feet and strolled to the foot of the tree.

"Patricia Mangan," she said. "It was a foolish question, was it not? You are none the wiser and must either ask another question or walk away."

"I'll ask the question," he said, feeling wonderfully diverted. "Who is Patricia Mangan? Apart from a little bird who likes to eavesdrop on private conversations, that is."

"Oh, yes," she said. "I rushed from the house to this spot an hour ago just so that I might listen to all the private conversations that go on below. It must be the busiest spot in all England, sir. But I must express my gratitude to you for insisting upon a private room and a soft bed for your feasting and worshiping."

He grinned at her. "Would you have been thoroughly embarrassed if I had been less cautious and less patient?" he asked and was rewarded by the sight of Miss Patricia Mangan blushing rosily. He grinned again. "Or perhaps envious?"

"I cannot tell you," she said, having abandoned the momentary weakness of the blush, "how unspeakably thrilled I would be to be told that the beauty of nature quite paled beside my own. Your sincerity would bring me tumbling out of the tree to comply with your every demand."

"Ah," he said, "but I would never say such a thing to you, Miss Mangan. It would be patently untrue."

"I believe," she said, "I would prefer the quite ungentlemanly setdown, sir, to the ridiculous flattery to which I was just the unwilling witness. At least the setdown was honest."

He chuckled. "A woman immune to flattery," he said. "Almost challenging. Who are you, Patricia Mangan? You still have not told me."

"You have seen me a dozen times," she said. "Well, half a dozen, at least. I am the shadow to be seen frequently behind the shoulder of Mrs. Peabody. It is my function in life, sir, to be a shadow. It can be vastly amusing. I hear and see all sorts of things because people do not realize I have eyes and ears. Indeed, people do not even realize I exist. I am Mrs. Peabody's niece, only daughter of her brother, the Reverend Samuel Mangan, who committed the unpardonable sin of dying without a penny to his name. My aunt rescued me from destitution, sir."

"And took you to her bosom as if you were her own daughter," he said. Was she speaking the truth? Had he seen her before? Was she frequently in Mrs. Peabody's shadow, at her constant beck and call? He had not noticed her.

"Yes," she said. "Or so she tells me several times each day—whenever I do something to displease her."

"Dear me," he said. "Are you really so disagreeable and so disobedient, Miss Mangan?"

"Oh, more so," she said. "I pretend to be obliging just so that I will not be turned off and have to beg my bread in the streets. You ought not to be dallying with either Flossie or Mrs. Delaney, you know. You are to marry Nancy—or so she and Mrs. Peabody say."

"Am I?" he said. "But I am not married to her yet, little bird. Perhaps I am sowing my wild oats before settling to a sober and blameless married life. Or perhaps I am an incurable rake and will continue with my wicked ways until my life is at an end. And perhaps it is none of your business."

"Nothing ever is," she said. "But I would remind you, sir, that you are the one who chose to talk to me. I was quite content to sit in silence and watch the clouds scud by. That is why I came here, you know."

"You escaped?" he asked. "You flew the nest?"

"Perhaps Mrs. Peabody went into the village with some of the lady guests," she said. "Perhaps I had finished the tasks she had left me and had an hour or so to myself. And perhaps now I will be late back at the house and will be scolded. And perhaps it is none of your business."

"Touché!" he said. "Come down from there, Miss Mangan. We will walk back to the house together."

"So that I may be seen in your company and be thought to be setting my cap at you?" she said. "I would be scolded for a week without a pause for breath, sir. I can escort myself back to the house, I thank you."

"Come down!" he commanded. He had the notion that she was a small female and wanted to confirm the impression. He did not like small females, being rather on the tall side himself. He liked tall, generously endowed women.

"Oh, yes sir, right away, sir, if you are going to use that tone of voice on me," she said. She came down the tree with sure, agile movements, as if it was something she was quite accustomed to. She had trim ankles encased in white stockings, he could not help but see. Not that he had been even trying to avert his gaze. "You had better stand well back if you do not wish to be bowled over. I have to jump from the bottom branch."

"Allow me," he said, making her his most elegant bow and then reaching up and lifting her down before she had a chance to tell him if she would allow him or not.

His hands almost met about her waist. She was as light as the proverbial feather. When he set her down, the top of her head reached perhaps to his chin. Not the width of one hair higher. She was slender almost to the point of thinness.

Those large eyes of hers looked up into his. "Certainly," she said. "Yes, do please help me down, sir. I may slip and sprain an ankle if left to myself. But now that you have done so, you may remove your hands from my waist whenever you wish."

From sheer principle he took his time about doing so. "Tell me," he said, "do you have to use a knife with your meals, or is your tongue sharp enough without?"

"I could almost pity Nancy," she said. "You are not really a gentleman, are you?"

"I have been severely provoked," he said. He offered her his arm, which she took after a moment's hesitation, and began to lead her slowly through the trees in the direction of the house. "You could always save poor Miss Peabody by warning her about my, ah, expenditures of energy this morning and tonight."

"Ah, but she already knows you are a rake," she said. "It is your greatest attraction in her eyes. Well, almost the greatest."

The greatest being that he could elevate her to the rank of baroness at some distant time, he supposed.

"Of course," she added, "she will expect you to be a reformed rake once you are married."

"Ugh!" he said.

"Reformed rakes are said to be the best, most constant of husbands," she said.

"Best as meaning most experienced?" he asked. He was enjoying himself more than he had since leaving behind his male cronies in London. "Constant as meaning most constantly able to please in—You are steeling yourself not to blush again, are you not, Miss Mangan?"

"And you are thoroughly enjoying trying to make me do so, sir," she said. "I would have you remember, if you will, that I am the daughter of a parson."

"Why are you so different from your cousin?" he asked. "Why are you dressed so differently? Why were you not with her in London for the Season? *Were* you there?"

"I was in London," she said.

"But were not brought out with her?" he said. "Why are you not mingling with your aunt's guests now?"

"I live in greater luxury here than I knew at the parsonage," she said. "All my needs are seen to. Mrs. Peabody is to find me a suitable husband."

"Ah," he said. "That must be a delightful prospect."

"Yes," she said firmly, "It is."

The trees were thinning. He was not sure he wanted to be seen with her any more than she wished to be seen with him. He stopped, took her hand from his arm, and raised it to his lips.

"My dear little bird," he said, "we must not be seen consorting in clandestine manner like this. With the greatest reluctance I must part from you. Your beauty makes the sunshine seem dim, you know."

"Oh." She fluttered her eyelashes. "I was dreadfully afraid you would not have noticed, sir. I shall go this way. You may go that. So much for my lovely solitary hour." She sighed and turned to hurry across the grass toward a door at the side of the house.

He watched her go before strolling off in the direction of the terrace at the front of the house. Her step was light, her stride rather long. He could almost picture her with a basket over her arm, delivering food and clothing to the poor in her father's parish.

What a very amusing and refreshing little creature, he thought. There appeared to be no artifice in her at all. He felt no sexual stirring for her, but he stood and watched her nonetheless, a half smile on his lips. He rather believed he liked her. Liking was something he rarely felt, or thought of feeling, for a woman.

It was very true what she had always thought about the relative merits of dreams and daydreams. Dreams could not be controlled, and they were not always pleasant. Sometimes they were quite the opposite.

She woke up in the middle of the night aching with grief, and she realized that she had actually been crying in her sleep. Her cheeks were wet, she found when she touched them, and her nose felt in dire need of a good blowing. She felt beneath her pillow for a handkerchief, blew hard until she could breathe more comfortably, and tried to remember what had made her so miserable. That was the trouble with dreams. They were often hard to remember even when they had aroused such a real and deep emotion.

Mama's death, perhaps, and Papa's following it a scant year later? The contrasts between her life then and her life now? The almost total absence of love from her life now when it had used to be so filled with it? No. She turned back the sheet neatly to her waist and crossed her hands over her stomach. No, she would despise herself if she ever allowed self-pity to rule her. It was such a negative, such an unproductive emotion. She had long ago done all her crying and tucked her memories away into the past. That was the past; this was the present. Perhaps the future would be different again. That was life. In her twenty-two years she had learned that life was unpredictable and that all one could do was live it one day at a time, always refusing to give up hope when times were bad, always consciously enjoying the moment when times were good.

Except that these days there were so few good times.

It was a thought not to be dwelled upon. It was too bad that dreams could not be controlled, that one must wake up in the middle of the night bawling like a baby and not even knowing exactly why one wept.

He would be in Mrs. Delaney's room now, she imagined, her thoughts flitting elsewhere, either sleeping the sleep of the justly exhausted in her arms or else doing with her what would make him exhausted. Was that what had grieved her and then awoken her—the fact that he was not doing either of those things in her bed?

What a strange, shocking thought! And yet her breasts felt uncomfortably taut, and when she reached up one hand she could feel that the nipple she touched was hard against the cotton of her nightgown. And there was an aching throbbing down between her legs.

"Oh, dear God," she whispered into the darkness. It was a prayer. She followed the introduction with confused apologies for sin and pleas for forgiveness. And then she apologized for her insincerity and promised to enter the Presence again when she was truly sorry and could truly expect forgiveness.

"What must you think of me?" she asked God.

God held his peace.

For the first time in a long while she had stopped being a shadow. Just for a few minutes. He had talked to her and looked at her and laughed at her and insulted her and kissed her hand and mocked her with that silly compliment about the sunshine and called her his little bird. And what had she done? She had talked back and matched wits with him and scolded him and set her arm through his and—oh, yes, she might as well admit the ultimate humiliation.

She had gone and tumbled headlong in love with him.

Stupid woman. Idiotic woman. Imbecile.

She had despised Nancy for wanting him when she knew that he was a dreadful, unprincipled rake. Yet now she was being as bad as Nancy. Horrid, ghastly thought. He was here at the house to court Nancy. He would be married to her before the end of the summer in all probability. And yet he had tumbled Flossie yesterday morning—Patricia was not so naive as really to believe that he had merely kissed the girl. And tonight he was feasting upon the almost fat and definitely voluptuous Mrs. Delaney—a married lady. And beneath the roof of his future father-in-law's house.

Was there ever such an unprincipled rogue?

Yet she was besotted with him because he had asked who she was and then demanded further details. Because he had a handsome face and compelling dark gray eyes and a manly muscular figure and elegant costly clothes. And because she had felt his lips and his breath against the back of her hand. Because for a few minutes she had come out of the shadows and had been dazzled by the sunshine. She made the sunshine look dim, he had said, deliberately teasing her with the lavishly untrue compliment, knowing that she would have some answer to amuse him.

Idiot. Imbecile. Fool. She set her mind to thinking of a few other names to call herself. And she fished the damp handkerchief from beneath her pillow again. She was going to need it when she had finally scolded her snivelings to a halt.

She hated him. He could have played the gentleman and pretended not to have seen her up the tree. He could have gone away and left her to enjoy the pattern the branches made against the sky. But oh, no, he had had to talk to her and make her fall in love with him.

Oh, she hated him. She hoped that he was not finding Mrs. Delaney enjoyable after all. She quite fervently hoped it.

He was finding Mrs. Delaney something of a disappointment. Oh, she was quite as voluptuous without her clothes as with them, and she was quite as skilled as she was reputed to be and quite as eager to give whatever pleasure he demanded and in whatever manner and at whatever pace he chose. If she had been able to keep her mouth shut, he might have found himself thoroughly contented to bed only her for the remainder of his stay at Holly House and to forget about the other three prospects he had in mind.

But the lady liked to talk. While he undressed her and she undressed him. While they were engaged in foreplay. While he had her mounted. And after they were finished. He never minded a certain amount of eroticism whispered into his ear or even shouted out to him at the most crucial moments of a sexual encounter. It could be marvelously arousing. He liked to do it himself.

What he did not particularly enjoy—what he did not enjoy at all, in fact—was having the events of the previous day mulled over when his body was clamoring to shut down the workings of his mind or to have gossip repeated and commented upon while he labored to make the lady as mindless as he. He did not expect love from her—heaven forbid!—but he did expect a little respect for his famed prowess as a lover. The woman came to lusty climax each time he mounted her body, and it seemed genuine enough, but he never knew quite where it came from. It was almost as if, like Flossie and her ilk, she needed only the last couple of minutes for her own pleasure but was quite willing to grant him all the extra minutes provided he would allow her to make free with his ears while she waited for the good part.

During the second night and perhaps the seventh or eighth encounter all told, he loved her almost languidly in his tiredness and actually opened up his ears to hear what she was saying. She was planning the rest of their summer—*their* summer. He was to go to Brighton, where Mr. Delaney was a minor player in Prinny's court. They would have to be moderately discreet, but Mr. Delaney would not make any great fuss anyway. Mr. Delaney, it seemed, had a greater love for clothes and gossip than he had for any exertions of the body. In the autumn they would go to Bath, where Mrs. Delaney had an aged aunt. It was unclear where Mr. Delaney would be, but regardless the affair was to flourish in Bath until the winter drew them back to London. Mr. Bancroft, Mrs. Delaney knew, owned a very superior love nest there where they could meet once or twice a week. Or perhaps more often—she nipped his earlobe with her sharp teeth as an inducement to him to make it three or four times a week.

He finished what he was doing to her, having the good manners to allow her to shout out her own completion first, disengaged himself from her, reluctantly shook off the need to try to doze for a while, and promptly decided it was time for his crisis of conscience.

"It is a dream utopia, love," he said, regret in his voice. "It cannot be done. Your husband—"

Mrs. Delaney cozied up to him in such a way that if he had not already had her seven or eight times during the past one and three-quarter nights, his temperature might have soared. As matters were, it stayed exactly where it was.

"It weighs heavily on my conscience to have usurped another man's rights," he lied after she had protested. "You are too beautiful for your own good, my dear, and I am too weak for mine. But we must not continue. Let it end here, and let me be able to remember that for two all too brief nights I knew heaven on earth."

The lady, he thought as he tiptoed to his own room in some relief several minutes later, did not know the rules of the game for all her reputed experience. He wondered in some alarm if after all she was smitten with him. Surely she did not put up this much fuss every time a lover shed her. Or was she more accustomed to doing the shedding?

It did not matter. He was free of her. He would give himself tomorrow night in which to recuperate and then see what he could accomplish with Lady Myron, widow. She was a quiet lady, tall and nicely shaped, older than he at a guess, and unknown to him before this week. He had no tangible reason to believe that she was not a perfectly virtuous woman apart from certain looks she was throwing his way. More than once—he was certainly not imagining them. Come-hither looks if he had ever seen any. Well, he would try coming hither and see what came of it.

In the meantime he felt as if he had at least a week of sleep to catch up on and only a few hours in which to do it, unless he slept until noon, as some of the ladies were in the habit of doing.

But the annoying thing was, he discovered over the coming hour as he lay in his own bed, at first flat on his back, and then curled on his right side and then stretched on his left and then spread-eagled on his stomach, that sleep just would not come. He was beyond the point of exhaustion. That damned woman was inexhaustible. She was always ready to settle for a good gossip when his body was screeching for sleep. Of course, she never expended her energy as recklessly as he did. She must have learned that from experience. Now whenever he seemed in some danger of nodding off, he found that he was bracing himself for her next sally into conversation—even though she was a few rooms away.

Damn the woman. Damn all women. They would be the death of him. Sometimes he wondered if all the pleasure to be derived from them was worth the effort. And he must be exhausted to the point of death if he was starting to feel that way, he thought, kicking off the bedclothes and levering himself off the bed to go and stand naked at his window. Dawn was graying the landscape already. He ran the fingers of one hand through his hair and blew out air from puffed cheeks.

Maybe it was just that he was getting old. Twentynine on his next birthday, though it was still more than eight months away. Almost thirty. Time to be settling down. He could almost hear his mother saying the words in her sweet and quiet voice. He grimaced and wondered if he should stagger back to bed or get dressed and go for a vigorous ride.

And then he leaned forward to peer downward. A shadow flitted out from below him and darted across the lawn leading to the trees and the lily pond. A shadow that looked as if it was clad in a gray cloak and hood. A shadow that looked female. And small.

He found himself grinning. She had not lied. He must have seen her at least half a dozen times before he had caught sight of her up in the old oak tree. Almost wherever Mrs. Peabody went in the house, her little gray shadow went with her. The little shadow was made to carry and fetch—stools and shawls and embroidery and vinaigrettes and a dozen and one other things. She did it all with a quiet grace and downcast eyes. And it was true—incredibly true—that no one else seemed aware of her existence. Just as one could stand in the large hall of a grand house, he supposed, and think oneself alone when all the time there were perhaps a dozen silent footmen lining the walls, waiting to open doors or run errands.

In the day and a half since he had become aware of her, he had not once—not once!—been able to catch her eye. But knowing that she had eyes and ears and intelligence and a sense of humor and a quick wit, he had set about amusing her by being lavish in his attentions to Mrs. Peabody and untiring in his flattery of Miss Peabody.

She had brightened that day and a half for him. She was not at all pretty, especially since he could get no glimpse of her eyes, and she was far too small and had a figure that was trim but not in any way luscious. Her clothes were abominable, and the best that could be said of her hair was that it shone and looked clean and healthy. And yet it amused him to know that he was one of the few people at Holly House who was even aware of her existence. And to know that she was hearing every lying, flattering word he uttered and was silently scolding him.

And now she was off to her retreat again, fleeing the nest before her day of drudgery was to start. Poor girl. He felt an unaccustomed wave of compassion for her. He was not famed as a compassionate man.

He looked back at his rumpled bed with some distaste. If he lay down again, he would not sleep, he knew, especially now that daylight was beginning to replace darkness. And there was nothing worse than lying in bed, tired and unable to sleep. Much better to get dressed and stroll down to the lily pond to tease a certain little bird. He remembered her sighing and lamenting the lost hour of solitude—*lovely* solitude, she had called it. But he shrugged his shoulders.

He was not famed as a considerate man, either.

He walked through to his dressing room and lit a candle.

Sometimes she walked in the early morning down to the crescent-shaped lake. It was always deserted and lovely at that time of day. But there was something just a little too artificial about it. It had been constructed and landscaped to be lovely and it was, but it was a man-made loveliness. Sometimes she took the longer walk back to the hill behind the house so that she could see the surrounding countryside. She liked to do that particularly if there was likely to be some trailing mist in the lowland to add drama to the scene. But almost always, at whatever time of day she was able to get away by herself, she went to the lily pond. It was secluded and rather neglected. It was hers.

There had been no dew last night. She tested the grass with one hand, brushing it hard back and forth. Her hand remained dry. She sat down on the bank, drew her knees up, wrapped her cloak more closely about her for warmth, and clasped her legs with her arms.

It was the time of day she loved most—early dawn, even before the sun rose. She was not quite sure why she liked it, since it was a gray time of day. Perhaps it was the knowledge that there was a whole new day ahead. Perhaps it was the hope that the sun would rise to a cloudless sky and that the whole day would be correspondingly bright. Perhaps it was just that she knew this early in the day that there were still several hours to go before her aunt would summon her and begin the constant demand for service. Not that that in itself was something to be dreaded—Patricia had always led a busy life and did not enjoy endless idleness. But she could never please. There was always irritability in her aunt's voice when it was directed at her. If she set the second cup of chocolate of the morning on the left side of the bed, she should have set it at the right. And if she set it at the right, then it should have been placed at the left. It never failed. And the rest of the day always proceeded accordingly.

Patricia sighed and rested one cheek on her updrawn knees. She had had that dream again last night, whatever it was. She had woken up again with wet eyes and aching heart. She would be glad when all the guests were gone. Though of course then there would probably be a wedding to prepare and the certain knowledge that soon Nancy and he . . .

She closed her eyes. No, she would not think of him. How very amused he would be if he knew . . . And how irate her aunt would be. And how contemptuous Nancy would be.

He was quite shameless in his flattery of both her aunt and Nancy. It amazed her that they both seemed to lap it all up as a cat would cream. Could they not see that the man was all artifice, that he never spoke a true word? And had they not seen the complacent looks of Mrs. Delaney yesterday? The fact that she had spent a very satisfactory night in bed with Mr. Bancroft seemed to be written large over her whole person. And had they not noted the looks Lady Myron and Mr. Bancroft were exchanging? They were lascivious looks, to say the least.

Was he spending half a night in each lady's bed? And devouring Flossie for breakfast? Patricia hoped that he would drop dead of exhaustion. Oh, yes, she really did. Men with such low morals ought not to be allowed to live on to enjoy them. And any woman who allowed herself to fall into his clutches was quite as bad as he and quite as deserving of a bad end.

Oh, dear.

And then she heard the unmistakable sounds of someone approaching. She tensed though she did not move. No one ever came here. Not at this time of day especially. She did not want to be disturbed. She had so little time to herself. Perhaps it was one of the gardeners come to cut the grass around the pond. Perhaps he would go away again when he saw her. She was not one of the great personages of the house, but then she was not a servant, either.

The footsteps stopped. "Ah," a voice said. "Little birds who fly down from their branches are in danger of being devoured, you know. Big bad wolves—or more probably sleek stealthy cats—are likely to creep up on them unawares and pounce on them."

Her heart performed a painful somersault, and she wished she had gone to the lake or to the hill—anywhere but the lily pond. "If I were you," she said, not moving, "I would not apply for the position of big bad wolf or sleek stealthy cat. You would starve. I believe that on your way here you stepped on every twig that was available to step upon and brushed against every branch that could be brushed against."

"Did I?" he chuckled. "But you did not fly up to the safety of your branch, little bird?"

Her head was turned away from him, but she could hear that he was seating himself on the grass beside her.

"So that you might order me down and lift me to the ground again?" she said. "No, thank you, sir. When a pleasure has been tasted once, it quite loses its savor."

"What an alarming thought," he said. "What are you doing up and out so early?"

"Seeking a solitary hour at the lily pond," she said. "*Vainly* seeking, that is. And you, sir? Has Mrs. Delaney tired of being worshiped? Or is it Lady Myron? And has not Flossie yet appeared to perform any of her morning duties?"

"I see that your tongue and a whetstone have been no strangers to each other's company during the past two days," he said. "Would you not agree that despite my nocturnal adventures I have been behaving with faultless gallantry to my intended and her mother? Come, you must admit that."

"Where I was brought up," she said, "we were taught that it is a sin to lie. I do not know where a hot enough corner of hell will be found for you when you die, sir."

"I prefer not to dwell upon the prospect at the moment, thank you," he said. "But come, Miss Mangan, would this not be a dreadful world and would not gallantry die an ignominious death if we all spoke the truth without fail?"

She smiled, but he could not see her expression since her face was still turned away from him.

"Well, that at least has silenced you," he said. "Just picture it, my little bird. 'Madam, you are plain and totally lacking in any shape that might be called feminine. Silks and muslins appear lusterless when hung on your person. Looking at you is a pain only intensified when you open your mouth and speak. Madam, would you dance with me?' or 'Madam, would you care to shed your clothes and jump into bed with me? You appear to have been formed expressly for the purpose of satisfying my lust.' Would I gain myself a place in heaven and a golden harp to play upon if I spoke thus honestly to a lady?"

"Your lack of tact would doubtless make it impossible for you to indulge in any other sin," she said. "No woman would allow you within a five-mile radius of her. You might well find yourself living a spotless existence, sir."

"Ugh!" he said.

She could resist no longer. She still wished herself a million miles away, but he was close by. She could tell that by his voice. He was sitting very close to her. She turned her head to rest the other cheek on her knees, and gazed at him. He was wearing a dark cloak. He was bareheaded. He was sprawled on the grass beside her, propped on one elbow. And his eyes were laughing at her. She remembered then what it was that had caused her great stupidity in the first place. It had happened when he had smiled and laughed at her. Nobody ever smiled at her these days.

"Little bird," he said, "your eyes are too big for your face."

"Am I to thank you for your honesty?" she asked.

"If you wish." He grinned. "The thought has just struck me. Did you have a tryst here? Is there some burly and impatient swain hiding in the bushes waiting for me to make myself scarce?"

"There are probably half a dozen of them," she said.

"But no matter. They will all come back tomorrow. It is my eyes, you see. They slay men by the dozens."

"Mrs. Peabody is choosing you a husband," he said. "Is he chosen yet, little bird?"

She thought she detected mockery in his voice. "Yes," she said. "He is a tenant farmer. A *prosperous* farmer," she added, emphasizing the adjective.

"Is he?" He plucked a blade of grass and set it between his teeth. "And ruddy and rotund and sixty years of age?"

"He is handsome and slender and only two years my senior," she said.

He smiled slowly at her. "And how old is that?" he asked. "Twenty-three? Twenty-four? And already a prosperous tenant farmer? He is an industrious man, or a fortunate one."

"His father died young," she said, "and left him everything."

"Ah." He chuckled. "I have heard that even the coolest corner of hell is a mite uncomfortable, little bird."

"You will never know, will you?" she said. "You are going to turn virtuous and spend your time on useful accomplishments, like practicing the harp."

He chuckled again and stretched out on the ground, one arm behind his head. With the other hand he reached out to touch her arm and ran it down to her elbow and then down to her wrist, which he encircled so that he could draw her arm away from her knees and down to the ground. He clasped her hand firmly and closed his eyes.

"I am weary," he said. "And don't tell me that you know the cause, little bird, and that I deserve to be. One day, when you are married to your young and virile tenant farmer—your *prosperous* farmer—you will discover that the cause of the weariness can be worth every sleepless moment. Talk to me. Tell me about your life at the parsonage. At a guess I would say you were happy there. Were you?"

"Yes," she said. "Yes."

He opened his eyes and turned his head to look up at her. "Tell me about it, then," he said. "Tell me about all the sinners you led back into the fold. I am sure there were many of them. You would have scolded them with your sharp tongue and made them stubborn, and then you would have gazed at them with those too-large sorrowful eyes and melted away all their resistance. Is that how you did it?"

"Yes," she said. "Every Sunday morning before service all of Papa's parishioners had to file past me outside the church and gaze into my eyes for thirty seconds each. The church was always full of weeping penitents afterward."

He chuckled and squeezed her hand. "Tell me," he said. "Who was Patricia Mangan before she came here?"

She was the much adored only child of parents who had both been in their forties when they were blessed with her, as they had always put it. They had been married for almost twenty years before she came along. Her father had always likened himself and her mother to the biblical Abraham and Sarah. She had played a great deal, both alone with her imagination and with the other village children, and had gone to school with them to be taught by her father, the schoolmaster. But there had been work too—household chores set her by her mother, parish chores set her by her father. She had never been idle.

She had never really thought about her happiness until everything came crashing to an end. She had not been conscious at the time that she was living through an idyll. It had seemed to her a normal, plodding, unexciting type of existence if she ever thought of it. She rarely did. She had just lived it.

And then when she was seventeen Patrick had been killed in Spain.

"Who was Patrick?"

She had been hardly aware that she was talking aloud, that she had an audience. Patrick was the younger son of a gentleman who lived in a small manor outside the village. He had gone to the wars as a young ensign and been killed in his first battle. Patrick had been her childhood sweetheart, the boy she had loved. They were going to be married when he came home, a great hero. In her naiveté she had not really considered the strong possibility of his dying.

But she had learned a swift and thorough lesson about death. Her mother had died less than a year later of a fever, and her father of a chill a year after that. At one moment it had seemed that she had everything—everything to bring her contentment and a continuation of the world as she knew it. And at the next it had seemed that she had nothing. Though that was not true, of course. She must not complain. Her father had had a sister who had done very well for herself by marrying Mr. Peabody, a prosperous gentleman. Patricia had been offered a home with them.

"Little bird," Mr. Bancroft said, first squeezing her hand again and then lifting it to his lips. "I am sorry. Life often seems a very unfair business, does it not?"

"Not to me," she said untruthfully. "Many women

who are left destitute are forced to sell themselves, sir. I have not been brought that low."

"And there is always your future with your lusty farmer to look forward to," he said. "Tell me about your future. What will constitute a happy life to you?"

A husband and a home. A gentle and a kindly man. A good friend and companion. She did not care about good looks or social prominence or unusual physical strength or intelligence. Just an ordinary, honest, constant man.

"A rake would not do you, then?" he asked.

No, certainly not a rake. Someone she could depend upon. And a home of her own. It would not have to be very large or very grand or even very lavishly furnished. Just so that it was her own with a garden for her flowers and vegetables, and perhaps a few chickens. Oh, and dogs and cats. And children of her own. More than one if it was possible. Loneliness could be hard on children even when there were loving parents and plenty of village children to play with. Children should have brothers and sisters if it was at all possible. And she wanted to hold babies in her arms. Her own babies.

Nothing else really. She did not crave wild adventure or excitement in her life. Only contentment. She would wish too that her husband would live long, that he would outlive her—and that she would not lose any of her children in infancy, as so many women did.

It was not a very ambitious dream. But it was as far beyond her as the sun and stars. She was not speaking aloud now. It was an impossible dream. Her aunt would never let her go. She was too useful. And she had no dowry. And no beauty. Perhaps if she went away and tried to find employment . . . But as what? A governess? A housekeeper? A lady's companion? She was a lady's companion already. None of those types of employment, even if she could find any without any experience or recommendations, would find her a husband.

If only Patrick had not dreamed of the glory of being a soldier. But that was long in the past. He had become a soldier and he had gone to war and he had been killed. There was no point in indulging in if-onlys.

Mr. Bancroft was sleeping, she realized suddenly. His hold on her hand had loosened, and his breathing was deep and even. His head was turned toward her.

He was so very beautiful. She let her eyes roam over his perfect features, over his thick, dark hair. Patrick had been blond. The folds of his cloak hid the shape of his body, but she knew that he was both slender and muscular, that a broad chest tapered to narrow waist and hips. One of his legs, encased in pantaloons and Hessian boot, was raised at the knee and free of his cloak. She could see his thigh muscles through the tight fabric. For all his attention to women, which had led her to imagine that he must spend most of his life in bed, he must work hard at keeping himself fit.

He was so very beautiful. She could feel the warmth of his hand about hers and told herself with great deliberateness that she would always remember this moment. He was a dreadful and shameless rake, and she must be thankful that her lack of beauty and charm and fortune had led him into treating her like this, like a younger cousin, perhaps, when he might have been trying to seduce her. She had had these quiet minutes with him and would be able to treasure them in memory for the rest of her life.

She was glad she had no beauty with which to tempt him. She was glad he had never tried to make love to her. She bit her lip and tried to believe her own very deliberate thoughts.

It was full daylight. The sun was probably springing over the eastern horizon, though she could not see it here among the trees. She must go back to the house and prepare herself for the day. She was tempted to sit here until he awoke. Perhaps it would be hours later. But she did not have hours to spare. Besides, she did not want to talk with him anymore. She did not believe she would be able to keep up any of their usual banter. She felt a little like crying.

She wanted to kiss him. She wanted to lean down and touch her lips to his forehead or one of his cheeks. Or perhaps even his own lips. But she might wake him. She would die of humiliation if he awoke while her lips were touched to his.

So she merely raised his hand slowly and dipped her head to meet it and set her cheek to the back of it. And she turned her head and brushed her lips against the back of his wrist. Then she set his hand down carefully on the grass, got quietly to her feet, gazed down at him for a few moments longer, and walked softly away into the trees—far more softly than he had approached a half hour or so earlier.

He was not sleeping. He merely did not want to continue his conversation with her. He did not want to have to walk back to the house with her.

She had let him into her world, a very ordinary world, but one so alien to him that he did not know how to respond to her. Life had been cruel to her—viciously cruel. And her dreams, though humble ones, were quite, quite beyond her grasp, he knew. He did not for one moment believe in the young and handsome and prosperous tenant farmer or in the ruddy, rotund, elderly one, either. She was too valuable to Mrs. Peabody. Mrs. Peabody was the type of woman who needed someone more than a personal maid to fetch and carry for her, and someone who was always there on whom to vent her spleen. Someone who could not answer back.

Patricia Mangan would never hold any of those babies in her arms. It was such a humble ambition for a woman to have. She did not crave silks and jewels and fashionable beaux—only a kindly, constant husband and a small and cozy home and some babies of her own.

It was not pity he felt. He did not believe it was pity. His little bird was too sensible and too courageous a woman to be pitied. It was rage he felt. A rage against Mrs. Peabody, perhaps. A rage against God, certainly. Though he was not sure that God could be blamed for what people did to one another when they had been given the infinitely precious gift of free will.

He wanted to draw her down into his arms, to hold her against him, to warm her soul against his body. But to what end? He knew of only one thing to do with a woman's body when it was against his own. He knew nothing about giving comfort. And she did not need comfort anyway. She did not seem to pity herself, or if she did, it was something she fought in the quiet of her own heart.

He felt humbled by her.

He could not talk to her. And so he conveniently fell asleep and waited for her to go away. It was his answer to anything troubling in his life—close his eyes and wait for it to go away.

She did go away eventually—after lifting his hand to her cheek and kissing the back of his wrist.

God! Oh, Lord God!

He did not know what she meant by it. A mere tender affection because he had listened to her—and fallen asleep while she spoke? Or—or something else?

Hell and a thousand million damnations!

The guests had been at Holly House for two weeks and were to stay for another week. Patricia did not like their being there even though there was one distinct advantage to her in that Mrs. Peabody was frequently engaged in outings with them and left her with more than usual freedom. But she did not like their being there nevertheless.

She did not like *his* being there. She wanted him to go away. She wanted to be free of him. Since the morning at the lily pond she had been alone with him only once, for a mere few seconds and they had exchanged only seven words, four of his and three of hers. But she wanted him gone anyway. His presence in the house and frequently in the same room as she occupied with her aunt weighed heavily on her spirits.

The only time they met face to face, or almost face to face, was one morning when she was hurrying along the upstairs hallway with Mrs. Peabody's second cup of chocolate and he came out of his room just ahead of her. He closed the door and waited for her to draw level with him.

"Good morning, little bird," he said quietly.

"Good morning, sir." She did not raise her eyes and she hurried on past him. But she was upset for the rest of the day.

Mrs. Delaney was annoyed with him. Patricia could

tell that from the way the lady flirted so ferociously with all the other gentlemen who made up the party—including even Mr. Peabody. Lady Myron was Mr. Bancroft's current favorite and probable bedfellow. The lascivious looks they had been exchanging more than a week ago had become considerably hotter. And when the lady was passing him one day in a doorway, Patricia saw that she leaned deliberately forward and slid her bosom across his chest—as if the doorway was no more than six inches wide. His eyes had smoked down at her.

It amazed Patricia that no one else noticed such things. Perhaps one observed more easily when one lived the life of a shadow. Everyone else was perhaps too busy living. And everyone else seemed to assume that a betrothal announcement would be made before the final week drew to an end.

They could not be blamed for thinking so, Patricia thought, and undoubtedly they were right. He was markedly attentive to Nancy, leading her in to meals, standing behind her to turn the pages of her music when she played the pianoforte, walking out with her, strolling on the terrace with her after dinner before the evening entertainment began, dancing with her if that was the order of the evening, partnering her in cards or charades. He smiled at her and talked with her and devoured her with his eyes and made it appear that he was smitten to the very heart.

Most of them could not be blamed for not knowing that he had spent his nights with Mrs. Delaney at the start and was now spending them with Lady Myron and was also exchanging interested and assessing glances with Mrs. Hunter and had tumbled Flossie on at least one occasion.

Why should they know or suspect when a very obvious courtship was developing before their eyes and when Mrs. Peabody and Nancy were so very openly in expectation of an event to be celebrated before they sent their guests on their way?

Patricia was usually excluded from the social events that took place beyond the confines of the house. But she was informed that she was to accompany Mrs. Peabody on the picnic out to the hill one afternoon. She could make herself useful for a change, she was told, instead of being idle and indolent. She was going to have to revise her lazy ways after the guests had gone home. There was going to be dear Nancy's wedding to prepare for, after all. And perhaps she did not realize that her keep was costing Mr. Peabody a pretty penny. It was time she did something to earn it.

And so Patricia found herself on a warm and only slightly breezy summer afternoon seated in the open barouche beside Mrs. Peabody, Nancy and Nancy's young friend, Susan Ware, opposite them, Mr. Bancroft, riding like the other gentlemen, close to the other side of the conveyance, heaping gallantries on the ladies—on the three ladies, that was. Patricia was merely the shadow of one of them.

That morning at the lily pond had had results. Talking about her past and putting into words her dreams— as she had done to no one before, or not since Patrick's departure for Spain, anyway—had set her to thinking. And realizing what an abject creature she had become. What a victim. Could she really be quite this helpless? Was it possible that her aunt really owned her for the rest of her life, just as if she were a slave? Was it so impossible to try to shape a life of her own?

The new parson at home, the one who had taken over

from Papa, had been a friend of his. Patricia had met him once or twice before her father's death. She had heard since in the letters she sometimes received from the Misses Jones that he did not like teaching at the village school, that he considered it to be outside the limits of his responsibilities. He did it only because there was no alternative.

What if she presented him with an alternative? Patricia had been thinking it over during the past week. What if she offered to teach at the school? She did not know how she would be paid and she did not know where she would live, unless it was in that rundown cottage that no one had wanted to live in for the past ten years or so because the former owner had hanged himself inside and his ghost was said to linger there. But what if something could be worked out?

She had written to the parson, and she was waiting hopefully and anxiously for an answer. If only . . . Oh, if only something could be worked out. She would not need a fortune, only enough with which to clothe herself and feed herself and keep herself warm.

"Girl!" She could tell from Mrs. Peabody's sharp tone that it was not the first time she had spoken. "My parasol."

Mrs. Peabody's parasol was at her side, at the side farthest from her niece. Patricia had to lean across her to reach it. She handed it to her aunt.

"And it is to shade my complexion as it is?" Mrs. Peabody said. "Lazy girl."

Patricia raised the parasol and handed it to her aunt.

"Really, Patricia," Nancy said, "you can be remarkably dense. Oh, Susan, do look at the darling bonnet Lady Myron is wearing. I am positively *green* with envy."

"My dear Miss Peabody," Mr. Bancroft said, leaning down from his horse's back and setting one hand on the door of the barouche, "the bonnet would be wasted on you. The beholder would look into your face and not notice the beauty of the hat at all. You see, it is only now that I deliberately look that I realize how exquisitely lovely is the one you are wearing."

"Oh, such things you say, Mr. Bancroft," Mrs. Peabody said and laughed heartily.

Miss Peabody blushed and twirled her parasol and looked triumphantly about her to see who had heard the compliment.

Patricia would have held her nose if she could have done so without being observed. She did not look up at the gentleman, though she had the feeling sometimes that he indulged in such extravagant flattery partly for her amusement. She wondered if he would continue to say such things to Nancy once he was married to her.

Blankets had been spread on the grass at the foot of the hill. Mrs. Peabody had seated herself in the middle of one of them, Patricia slightly behind her, while most of the guests amused themselves in slightly more energetic ways until tea was served.

Most of them climbed the hill in order to gaze admiringly at the prospect Mrs. Peabody had promised them from the top, though she did not go up herself to display it to them. Mr. Bancroft led the way, Nancy on one arm, Susan on the other. A great deal of trilling laughter wafted down the hill after them. And then some of them strolled about the base of the hill while others walked the half mile to the east to look at the Greek folly that Mr. Peabody's father had had built years ago in the form of a temple. Still others wandered to the west to lose themselves among the trees that hid from view the river winding its way down in the direction of the crescent-shaped lake.

Mr. Bancroft went with the last group, though Nancy, who had elected herself leader of the expedition to the folly, appeared somewhat chagrined. He walked with Lady Myron and two other couples.

Patricia sat on the blanket the whole while, opening and closing her aunt's fan in concert with the passing clouds, fanning her aunt's face when the sun shone for too long, arranging a shawl about her shoulders when a cloud took forever to pass over, carrying messages to the footmen who brought the food, first to wait awhile and then to hurry along instead of standing idle for all to see.

And then when the footmen were busy setting out the food, which had been prepared in such variety and such abundance that it surely would have fed the five thousand with more than a dozen baskets of crumbs to spare, Mrs. Peabody decided that the wine should have been served first. Everybody would be thirsty from the heat and their exertions.

"Go and help, girl," she said impatiently to Patricia. "Make yourself useful. Go lift the wine basket from the wagon and take it over to Gregory. Instruct him to open the bottles immediately."

Patricia went to make herself useful. But the wine must match the food in quantity, she thought as she tried to lift the heavy basket down from the wagon. It must weigh a ton. And it was an awkward size. She wormed her hands beneath its outer edges and slid it to the edge of the wagon.

"Here, I'll take that," a hearty voice said from behind

her. "It is almost as big as you are, little lady, and probably twice as heavy."

Patricia turned her head gratefully to see Mr. Ware, Susan's father, hurrying toward her, smiling jovially.

"Thank you," she said, standing back as his hands replaced hers beneath the basket. But the basket was teetering on the edge, and she withdrew her hands a moment too soon. Mr. Ware roared out a dismayed warning, Patricia's hands flew to her mouth, and the basket came crashing to earth, bursting open and spilling its contents as it did so.

Perhaps one bottle alone would not have smashed since the wagon board was not particularly high off the ground and the ground itself was carpeted with grass. But bottles and glasses tumbled against each other and smashed with a glorious crashing and flying of glass and spilling of wine.

Everyone's attention was drawn—it was such a magnificent disaster. Mr. Ware first swore and then apologized—but whether for his language or his clumsiness was not apparent—and then started to look sheepish. Patricia kept her hands pressed to her mouth for a few moments and then started to assure the gentleman that it was not his fault, that she had withdrawn her hands too soon.

And then Mrs. Peabody was there.

If it was really possible for anyone to turn purple in the face, Patricia thought, then her aunt had just done so, and her bosom seemed to have swelled to twice its normal buxom size. If Patricia's own mind had been working coolly, she would have realized perhaps that her aunt for once in her life had forgotten her surroundings and her audience and the impression she was about to make on them. But it was not a cool moment.

"Imbecile!" Mrs. Peabody shrieked at her niece. "You clumsy oaf! Is this the gratitude I receive for opening my home to you when my brother left you without a farthing to your name, and for clothing you and feeding you and treating you like my own daughter?"

"Oh, I say, ma'am," Mr. Ware said with an embarrassed cough, "I am afraid the fault was mine."

Everyone else was still and silent, as if posing for a painted tableau. They had all returned from their various walks.

"I saw it all," Mrs. Peabody said. "It is good of you to be so much the gentleman, sir, but you need not protect the lazy slut."

"Aunt!" Patricia's voice was hushed and shocked. There was a faint buzzing in her head.

"Silence!" Mrs. Peabody's palm cracked across one of Patricia's cheeks, and she turned away. "Now, what is to be done about this? Gregory, back to the house immediately for more wine."

The lady seemed suddenly to remember who she was and where she was. She smiled graciously about her and set about soothing her guests and tempting them with all the edible delights spread out before them and assuring them that the wine would be brought and served in no time at all.

"Oh, I say," Mr. Ware said ineffectually to Mrs. Peabody's regal back. "Oh, I say." He looked helplessly and apologetically at Patricia.

But Patricia was stunned, hardly even aware yet of the stinging of her cheek. She had been called a slut and she had had her face slapped—in public. Everyone had been watching and listening. Everyone!

She turned suddenly and began to run. She did not

know where she was going or what she was going to do when she arrived there. She knew only that she had to get away, that she had to hide. Instinct took her in the direction of the trees. But even when she was among them, panic did not leave her. She turned north, away from the house, and ran recklessly among closely packed trees and hanging branches, heedless of slashing twigs and threatening roots. She could hear someone sobbing and did not even realize that it was herself.

And then she remembered the other folly, the little ruined tower down by the river, with the circular stone seat inside. She could collapse onto that. She could hide there for a while. For longer than a while. Forever. She could never go back to the house.

She had stopped running. She approached the folly from behind with quiet, weary steps and rounded the circular wall to the opening and the seat.

Mr. Bancroft was sitting on it, a lady with him. Patricia could not even see who she was until he raised his head, startled, from kissing her. Mrs. Hunter. Her dress was off her shoulder on the left side and down to her waist. He had his hand cupped about her naked breast.

Panic hit again. Patricia went fleeing away with a moan, crashing through trees once more until her breath gave out and a stitch in her side had her clutching it. Her cheek was hot and throbbing. She set her forehead against the trunk of a tree and closed her eyes. When the pain in her side had dulled, she wrapped her arms about the tree and sagged against it.

He was getting bored. Three weeks was too long a time to spend at one country home in company with the same twenty or so people. He would be thoroughly glad when the remaining week was at an end and he could get back to normal life.

And what was normal life? He would follow the fashionable crowd to Brighton for a month or two, he supposed. There was always plenty happening there, plenty of congenial male company and wild wagers with which to fill his days, plenty of bored and beddable females to add excitement to his nights.

And then where? A duty visit to his mother and his uncle? Yes, he supposed so. He loved his mother dearly. It was just that her reproachful glances and accusing silences made him uncomfortable at times. She always gave the impression that she was waiting patiently for the day when he would have finally sowed the last of his wild oats and that she was perhaps giving up hope that he would ever be finished with them.

And then where? Bath? London?

He was getting bored, he thought in some alarm. Bored not just with the present reality but with the general condition of his life.

He had been conducting a heated affair with Lady Myron for more than a week. She was everything he could possibly ask for. She had a body that could arouse him at a glance, and she made that body and all the sexual skills she had acquired over the years fully available for his pleasure all night and every night. She had an energy to match his own and was eager to learn new skills from him and to teach him those few he had never before encountered. She made no demands beyond the moment.

But he was bored. And puzzled. After a week he was tired of such a desirable lover? Why? He could not think of anything wrong with her beyond the fact that they had nothing in common except a zestful enjoyment of a good tumble between the sheets. Her conversation—on the few occasions when they talked—was all of horses and hounds and hunting. He had no particular interest in such country pursuits. But that could not matter, surely. A woman's body and her sexual prowess were all that mattered—and Lady Myron passed muster on both counts.

But he found himself eyeing Mrs. Hunter appreciatively during the days and wondering how she compensated herself for the fact that Mr. Hunter, not present at the Holly House gathering, was a septuagenarian, and by all accounts a frail one at that. He began to suspect that somehow she did it and that she would be only too willing to do so with him before the party broke up.

And so she maneuvered it and he maneuvered it that they spend some time alone together on the afternoon of the picnic, both Lady Myron and Mr. Crawford, Mrs. Hunter's escort, having been shed somewhere along the way. And they discovered the convenience of the little folly by the river and sat inside it by mutual but unspoken consent.

The lady did not waste time on conversation or other preliminaries, he was delighted to find. She turned her face to his and kissed him. And when he had fully accepted the invitation and got his arms about her, she reached up a hand and drew down her dress to expose one breast many minutes before he would have got around to doing it for himself.

He was, he realized with pleased certainty, about to feast upon the full delights of the woman in the middle of the afternoon on a hard stone bench. And he was being given the distinct impression that she was ravenous.

Interesting!

It was at that moment and just as he had got his hand on the woman's breast and was listening to her throaty murmur of appreciation that he knew someone else was there. Lady Myron, he thought as he lifted his head, and he had a momentary vision of the two women going for each other's hair with clawed fingernails—or else both going for *his* hair.

But it was Patricia Mangan. She stood there only for a moment before she moaned and disappeared, but he had the instant impression of a torn dress and a bonnet-less head with hair pulled loose from its confining pins, and of a wild, unhappy face, one side of it red and swollen.

"Good Lord!" he said, relinquishing his hold on Mrs. Hunter's breast and jumping to his feet. He could hear the loud crashings of a panicked retreat.

"It is just that strange drab little creature who hangs about Mrs. Peabody," Mrs. Hunter said crossly. "She must be playing truant. It would have served her right if she had seen more. She will not dare return. Come!"

When he turned his head to look down at her, she was smiling invitingly up at him from beneath lowered eyelids and pushing down the other side of her dress.

Strangely, he thought afterward, he did not hesitate, even though the feast was being laid out before his eyes and was ready for instant devouring.

"Something has happened to her," he said. "I had better go and find her. Can you make your own way back to the picnic site?"

"What?" The lady sounded incredulous and looked magnificent bared to the waist.

"I shall see you back there," he said and strode away. And another strange thing, he thought later, was that his mind did not linger on the abandoned feast for even a single moment.

He could think only of the fact that his little bird seemed to have broken a wing and that he had to find her. Fortunately, she was doing nothing to hide the sounds of her progress through the dense forest of trees.

Gray was a drab color, but it was a light gray and a light fabric. It was just as visible against the trunk of a tree as it had been up in the branches of the old oak tree at the lily pond. He paused for a moment, looking at her. And then he moved up behind her and set his hands lightly on her shoulders.

She did not react for a moment. She must have heard him coming, he decided. He had been a little afraid of startling her. And then she turned, her head down, and burrowed it against the folds of his neckcloth while her arms came about his waist and clung as if only by doing so could she save herself from falling.

"Little bird?" he murmured and was answered with a storm of weeping.

Weeping women had always embarrassed him. He never knew quite what to do with them. He closed his arms tightly about her, lowered his mouth into her hair, and murmured mindless nonsense to her. He might have been holding a child, he thought, except that she was not a child. She was a warm, slender, soft woman.

"What happened?" he asked her when she had fallen silent at last.

"Nothing," she said, her voice muffled against his chest.

"Ah," he said. "My neckcloth has been ruined for nothing. My valet will be thrilled."

"Give him my apologies," she mumbled. Her teeth were chattering, he could hear.

He leaned back from her a little and lifted her chin with one hand, though she tried ineffectually to push it away. Her eyes and cheeks—and nose—were wet. Her face was red and blotched all over from crying and a uniform red on one side. Most of her hair was down and hanging in tangles about her face and over her shoulders. She looked wretchedly unpretty. And inexplicably and startlingly beautiful to his searching eyes.

He drew a handkerchief from his pocket, dried her face and her eyes with it, and handed it to her. "Blow," he said.

She drew away from him and blew. And bit her lower lip as he took the handkerchief away from her again and stuffed it back in his pocket.

"Tell me what the nothing consisted of," he said.

"I smashed all the wine bottles and glasses," she said.

"Over someone's head?" he asked. "How spectacular! I am sorry in my heart that I missed the show. Tell me what happened."

She told him.

"And found yourself in massive disgrace with Her Majesty, I suppose," he said.

"Yes." She was regaining her composure as he watched.

"What happened to the one side of your face?" he asked, feeling fury gather like a ball in his stomach. He knew with utter certainty what had happened.

Her face trembled almost out of control again. "She struck me," she said. "She called me a slut."

Pistols at dawn. How he itched to be able to challenge the woman to meet him. Right smack between the eyes. That was where he would place the bullet. He would let her shoot first and then make her stand there in frozen terror waiting for him to discharge his own pistol. And he would.

He reached out to set an arm about her slim shoulders and drew her against him again. She did not resist. She was shivering.

"I will avenge that for you, little bird," he said. "My honor on it. Do you believe I have any honor?"

She did not answer his question. "I suppose I overreacted," she said. "It was my fault, after all. It is just that I have never been struck in my life. And the face seems a particularly insulting place to be hit. And in public."

She pulled back from him and smiled at him.

"It does not matter," she said. I will not be staying here long. I am going to teach in a village school. My home village. I will be among people I know. And I think I will enjoy teaching children. I shall be going soon."

"What has happened to the young, handsome, virile, prosperous farmer?" he asked. "Has he withdrawn his offer?"

She hesitated for only a moment. "I do not love him," she said firmly. "I do not believe it is right to marry without love, do you? What a foolish question. You do not believe in love. But for me it is not right. So my future is all settled. My *happy* future."

"Is it?" he asked her. "You have been granted the employment?"

"I am just waiting to hear from the parson," she said. "It is a mere formality. He is bound to say yes. He was a friend of Papa's."

Ah. Another impossible dream. Another humble, impossible dream. He smiled at her, picturing her for no fathomable reason seated in a rocking chair, her head bent to the baby suckling contentedly at her breast. The dark-haired baby.

She was fully recovered. "I am all right," she said. "You had better return to Mrs. Hunter. I am sure she did not enjoy being abandoned at such an interesting moment. She will, I do not doubt, be growing cold. In more ways than one, sir."

He smiled slowly at her.

"You are going to come to a bad end, you know," she said. "What if I had been Lady Myron? Or Mrs. Delaney? Or Flossie? Or Nancy?"

He could feel amusement bubbling out of him.

"You think it is funny," she scolded. "It is not. Someone is going to get hurt. With any luck it will be only you with a broken head."

"That's my little bird," he said appreciatively. "Tongue sharpened at both edges and pointed at the tip. Take my arm. I am going to take you back to the house."

"Mrs. Hunter—" she began.

"—may go hang for all I care," he said. "I am taking you back home. It can be either on my arm or slung over my shoulder. The choice is yours."

"Well, if you put it in that gentlemanly way," she said, "I shall make my free choice. Your arm, I think."

"Now," he said, guiding her around overhanging branches, "let me regale you with my life history, shall I? You told me yours early one morning a week or so ago. I shall return the favor if you think you can bear it."

And so he did what he had never done with any woman before. He let her into his life.

He did not even fully realize he had done it until he thought about it later, standing at the window of his room in unaccustomed solitude, waiting for everyone else to return from the picnic. He talked without stopping, knowing that despite her spirited efforts to pull herself together, she was in reality very close to collapse and still to a certain extent in shock. She leaned against him as they walked in a manner that would have been provocative in any other woman or under any other circumstances. But he knew that she leaned because her legs were unsteady and her head dizzy.

And so he talked to her and knew that despite her distress she listened. She even asked him some questions about his mother and about his two married sisters and their children, his nieces and nephews.

He took her up to her room when they reached the house after instructing a footman in the hall to have a hot drink and some laudanum sent up to Miss Mangan.

"You will throw them into consternation in the kitchen," she said. "I do not have maid service."

Fury knifed into him again. "Well, then," he said, having taken her to her room and into her room, despite her look of surprised inquiry, "I will perform one service of a maid for you myself. Hand me a brush. Your hair looks rather like a bush after a severe wind storm."

"What gallantry," she said, but her eyes looked wary.

"Sit down," he instructed her, gesturing her to the stool before a dressing table mirror. He drew out the remaining pins from her hair and began to brush it, teasing the brush through the tangles at first. He kept brushing even when her hair was smooth. He could remember doing the same for his mother numerous times as a boy. She had suffered from bad headaches and had always claimed that it was soothing to have someone draw a brush through her hair.

Patricia Mangan had beautiful hair, he noticed. Thick and wavy and shining and waist-length and actually more blond than brown. The style she normally wore it in was doubtless her aunt's idea. Though perhaps at the parsonage too she had been advised to tame its wantonness.

The hot tea and the laudanum were a long time coming. Flossie gawked when she came flouncing in with them. She left with considerably more respect in her step and with a shiny half sovereign in her pocket.

"I really do not need the laudanum," Patricia said, rising from the stool and turning to him a face that was blushing charmingly.

"But you will take it," he said. "And you will lock your door after I have left and rest. You will refuse to be roused for the rest of the day. Will that give you time enough to recover?"

She nodded.

"I shall take my leave of you, then, little bird," he said.

It was something he did by instinct, without the medium of thought. Something he might have done to a sister who had been hurt and whom he had comforted. He cupped her face with his hands, pushing his fingers into the silkiness of her hair and lowered his head to touch his lips to hers.

Except that with a sister he would have raised his head after the merest touch, not lingered there, feeling the trembling of her lips beneath his own.

Except that a sister would not have looked at him afterward with huge unblinking eyes.

Except that with a sister he would not have stood

outside her closed door a few moments later, gulping air, waiting for his knees to reform themselves beneath him so that they might assist his legs in getting him to his own room.

A stupid thing to have done, he told himself. Remarkably stupid.

Life for the next week was not as bad as it might have been. Patricia guessed that her aunt was embarrassed by the memory of her outburst at the picnic—it would doubtless appear ungenteel to her. And so she said nothing to her niece about it. Patricia was left alone to sleep for the rest of that day, and in the days to come she became her aunt's quiet shadow once more.

No one else paid her any attention with the exception perhaps of Mr. Ware, who went out of his way to avoid her. Not even Mr. Bancroft took any notice of her, for which fact she was profoundly thankful. She was very much afraid for the first day or two that he might make a public scene, demanding that her aunt apologize to her or something horribly mortifying like that.

On the contrary. He appeared to redouble his attentions to Nancy and Mrs. Peabody, sending them into a positive flutter of expectation. If he was still carrying on with Lady Myron or Mrs. Hunter or Mrs. Delaney, there were no outward signs of it during the days following the picnic. He seemed to have put all else aside in order to concentrate on bringing his courtship to happy fruition.

Patricia refused to allow herself to mourn. He had been kind to her. Yes, amazingly for such a man, he had been. And when he had taken her face in his hands and kissed her lips—no man had done that since Patrick had smacked heartily at them the night before he left to join his regiment—he had been giving comfort as if to a child or a younger sister.

Oh, yes, she had no illusions. And so there was no point at all in allowing herself to become heartsick. That she loved him was her own foolishness. It was something she would not fight, because she knew it was something she would keep with her for a long time to come, and his kiss was something she could relive perhaps for the rest of her days. But she would not allow it to upset the quiet equilibrium of her days.

Something else did that. She had a reply from the parson at home. He wished he had known sooner of her interest in teaching the schoolchildren. He had recommended the hiring of a teacher just two months ago, and one had begun her duties just last month. He remembered Miss Mangan with fondness and wished her happiness and God's blessings on her future.

Oh, yes, it upset her. She had counted upon this new idea of hers so much. She had dreamed of the escape it would bring her and the independence and sense of worth and self-respect. But she would not give up. Now that she had thought seriously of taking employment, she was not going to crawl back into her shell. She would try again—somehow. Perhaps her uncle would help her. He was quiet and totally dominated by his wife, but he was a sensible and a kindly man, she believed. Perhaps he would know how she might come by employment. She would ask him after the guests had gone home.

And then there was the other upset, the one she had thought herself fully prepared for. The betrothal. Nancy to Mr. Bancroft.

Patricia was in the drawing room after dinner two evenings before the party was to end, though she had not been at dinner. There was no space for her at the dining room table while their guests were with them, she had been told three weeks ago. But she had a function in the drawing room. She was seated behind the tea tray, pouring tea.

When the gentlemen joined the ladies after their port, Mr. Bancroft made his way immediately to Nancy's side and proceeded with the customary gallantries. Patricia, as usual, insisted upon feeling only amused at what she heard. And then, when Mrs. Peabody had joined them and when somehow he had gathered about them almost all the ladies—Patricia had the strange impression that he had maneuvered it so, though she did not know how he had done it—he took Nancy's hand in his, raised it to his lips, and gazed with warm intensity into her eyes as he spoke.

"I have asked for and been granted a private interview with your father tomorrow morning, Miss Peabody," he said. "I doubt I shall have a wink of sleep tonight, such is the anxiety of my heart. It is my fondest hope that by this time tomorrow I will be the happiest of men."

Nancy knew just how to behave. She blushed very prettily, lowered her eyes, opened her fan and fluttered it before her heated face and answered in a voice that was little more than a whisper—but since everyone was hushed, it carried to the farthest corner of the room.

"I do not know what can be so important that you must speak to Papa in private, sir," she said. She allowed herself a peep upward. "But you deserve to be happy, I am sure."

He was returning her hand to his lips when Patricia decided she could be of no further use behind the tea tray. Everyone had been served with a first cup, but someone else must pour the second. With the present steadiness of her hands—or lack thereof—she would doubtless fill the saucers as well as the cups. She slipped quietly from the room.

And lay fully clothed on top of her bedcovers for long hours into the night, staring upward at the canopy, a pillow clasped in her arms.

He had coldly plotted his revenge. No, perhaps not quite coldly. It had never been his way to hurt anyone more than that person deserved to be hurt, though he had never pretended to be either a considerate or a compassionate man. His first idea would have brought too great a humiliation to someone whom he had intended only to embarrass. His desire was to punish the mother, not the daughter.

Until the daughter gave him good cause to be added to his black list, that was.

No one at the dinner table the evening after the picnic mentioned the incident that had happened there. He guessed that the memory of it was an embarrassment to all of them. Indeed, conversation seemed somewhat strained and over-hearty. Calling even a servant a slut in public and slapping her face hard enough to cause swelling was not considered genteel behavior among members of the *ton*.

He took Nancy Peabody for a stroll out on the terrace after dinner, as he often did.

"Did you hear what happened after you were forced to return to the house with a nosebleed, sir?" she asked him.

"Did I miss something?" he asked. "Beyond a precious hour of your company, that is?"

"Oh, that." She tittered. "I am sure you must have

seen more than enough of me in the past few weeks, sir."

He returned the expected answer.

And then she proceeded to tell him about the breaking of the wine bottles. His little bird, it seemed, had been sent to lift down the wine basket from the wagon. It must have weighed as much as she did. And she had dropped it after summoning Mr. Ware and demanding that he carry it for her—and then had tried to put the blame on him. Poor Mr. Ware, like the gentleman he was, had been quite prepared to accept responsibility.

"And then when Mama tried to reprimand her gently and smooth over the situation," Miss Peabody said to his interested ears, "she was impertinent and Mama was forced to be quite sharp with her and send her back to the house. Poor Mama. It quite spoiled her afternoon. And mine too, sir, you may be sure. You would not believe all Mama and I have done for Patricia. Mama has been a second mother to her, and I have been a sister to her despite the fact that her own mama was nothing more than the daughter of a curate who was hardly even a gentleman. But she has returned nothing for all our kindness except sullenness and sometimes open impertinence. Mama is a veritable saint for putting up with her."

"And you too, Miss Peabody," he said, patting the arm that was resting on his. "There are not many young ladies who would watch another taken to the bosom of their mama without losing the sweetness of their disposition as a result."

"Oh, well." She tittered. "It is not in my nature to feel jealousy, sir. And one must be charitable to indigent relatives."

He led the conversation into more congenial channels, and they talked about her for the remaining ten minutes of their stroll on the terrace.

He gave her a second chance. Two days later, they all went to church in the morning. He took Nancy up to ride beside him in his curricle. They drove the mile home from church in a slow cavalcade, his curricle behind the barouche that carried Mr. and Mrs. Peabody, Patricia, and Mrs. Delaney.

"I see," he said, "that your cousin has been forgiven and taken back to your mother's bosom."

Patricia Mangan had been granted the honor of carrying Mrs. Peabody's parasol and her prayer book.

"Oh, yes," Nancy said, tossing her head so that the feather on her bonnet nodded appealingly. "Mama is too forgiving by half."

"And you are not?" he asked, looking at her with raised eyebrows.

She perceived her mistake immediately. "Oh, yes." She laughed. "To my shame I must confess to an excess of sensibility, sir. I am even more tender-hearted than Mama—or so Papa always tells me. But she ought not to have been forgiven, you see. By her carelessness she smashed a dozen bottles of Papa's best wine and twenty of the finest crystal glasses. And she did not even apologize or shed a single tear. She has never shown any gratitude at all for all we have done for her. I hate ingratitude more than almost any other vice, sir."

"It is disturbing to know that some of our acts of charity go unobserved and unappreciated by those whose sole function in life should be to make us feel good about ourselves," he murmured soothingly.

"Yes." She looked dubious, as if she had not quite grasped his meaning. "I believe she should have been turned off, sir."

"Even though she has nothing else to go to?" he said.

"Well, that is her problem, is it not?" she said.

"Even if she was to end up on the open road with nowhere to go?" he said. "Or in the nearest town with nothing to do and nothing to sell except . . . Well, what I was about to say is not for such delicate ears as yours. And of course, you would not really turn her off, would you? You were merely telling me what you would do if you did not have such a tender heart."

She sighed. "You are right, sir," she said. "Papa says he does not know how I will manage servants of my own when I find it impossible even to think of disciplining them when they break things or do not do things as they ought to be done."

Mr. Bancroft turned the conversation again. But he had heard what he needed to hear and what he had fully expected to hear. He had given her two chances and she had squandered both.

He plotted his revenge quite coldly. All his attention was concentrated upon it for the remaining days of his stay at Holly House. He lost interest in all else. He terminated his affair with Lady Myron with one pretty speech and neglected to develop the affair with Mrs. Hunter that had had such an extremely promising beginning. His nights were spent alone. He did not sleep a great deal more than he had done during the first two weeks of his stay—though he doubtless expended a great deal less energy—but at least he was alone. He tended to spend many hours of each night lying on his back with his hands clasped beneath his head, thinking. And reliving a certain kiss, which had been easily the least lascivious he had ever given, even as a green boy.

His plot approached its culmination two nights before the guests were to leave Holly House. After the

ladies had left the dinner table and after the gentlemen
had drunk their port and risen and stretched and decided that the moment of rejoining the ladies could be
postponed no longer, he spoke quietly to Mr. Peabody,
asking if he might have a private word with that gentleman the next morning on a matter of some impor-
tance.

And then he proceeded to the drawing room to tell
Miss Nancy Peabody about his hopes and anxieties,
though with the skill of long practice he succeeded in
gathering about him almost all the ladies before he
began to speak and soon enough all the gentlemen were
listening too.

It had been well done, he thought in self-congratula-
tion as the evening proceeded. And tomorrow would
come the denouement. There was only one part of it
that he was unsure about—totally unsure.

And so he had a largely sleepless night again.

He had noticed her slipping from the drawing room,
unseen and unlamented by everyone. No, not by everyone. And even Mrs. Peabody missed her when guests
had talked up the thirst for second cups of tea and there
was no little shadow seated behind the tray to pour
them.

Well, tomorrow, he thought with grim satisfaction,
his hands clasped behind his head. Ah, yes, tomorrow.
But his heart thumped with unaccustomed nervousness
when he thought about part of tomorrow.

All the ladies were gathered in the salon by late
morning. All of them without exception. Even Mrs. Delaney, Lady Myron, and Mrs. Hunter were there, and
even those ladies who usually slept until noon and then

spent another hour or two in their dressing rooms with their maids.

The air positively pulsed with excited expectation. Mr. Bancroft had been closeted in the library with Mr. Peabody since shortly after breakfast. Nancy and Mrs. Peabody had explained to everybody who had been unfortunate enough not to witness it for themselves—though in fact there was no such person, except Patricia—that before leaving the breakfast room Mr. Bancroft had bowed over Nancy's hand again and lifted it to his lips again and gazed at her with adoring eyes—the adjective was supplied by Mrs. Peabody, Nancy being too modest to use it herself—and murmured to her that he had one hour of excruciating anxiety to live through before putting the question to *some lady*—he had emphasized the words, not naming her—the answer to which would determine the happiness or misery of the whole of the rest of his life.

Nancy was becomingly flushed. Her eyes shone. She looked about her with slightly elevated nose as if she pitied all the other lesser mortals who were not about to receive an offer from Mr. Bancroft. She was dressed in her very best muslin, though it was still only morning, and her hair was a glorious and intricate mass of carefully constructed ringlets and curls.

She looked, Susan declared, faint envy in her voice, like a princess.

They all waited for the moment when the door would open and someone—surely the butler himself and not a mere footman—would summon Nancy to the library to receive the addresses of her beau.

Patricia sat quietly on her chair just behind Mrs. Peabody's, thinking determinedly about her own planned talk with her uncle during the afternoon if in all the excitement she could get him alone. She was going to ask him if he knew how she would go about applying for employment as a governess or schoolteacher.

And then the door handle was heard to turn and all the ladies fell instantly silent and turned toward the door, awaiting the summons. Nancy sprang to her feet, her hands clasped to her bosom. Mrs. Peabody smiled graciously about at her gathered guests.

It was neither a footman nor the butler who opened the door and stood in the doorway for a moment, looking impossibly handsome and elegant, before proceeding inside the room. It was Mr. Bancroft himself. Nancy's lips parted and she leaned a little toward him. Mrs. Peabody clasped her own hands to her bosom.

"Ma'am," Mr. Bancroft said, proceeding across the carpet toward Mrs. Peabody, smiling at her, and then turning his gaze on Nancy, "my meeting with Mr. Peabody has been brought to a successful and happy conclusion. It seems that at least some of the anxieties that kept me awake and pacing last night have been laid to rest."

Mrs. Peabody sighed. "Of course, my dear sir," she said. "Mr. Peabody has never been a difficult man with whom to deal. He would certainly not find it difficult to deal with a future baron."

But his eyes were upon Nancy, devouring her. "Miss Peabody," he said, "may I be permitted to compliment you on your appearance this morning? Your taste in dress is, as always, exquisite. But as always the loveliness of your person quite outshines the finest muslin."

"Oh, sir." Nancy's eyes were directed quite firmly on the floor.

"And so." Mrs. Peabody's voice had become hearty.

"You will be wishing to step into another room or perhaps outside—"

"Outside, with your permission, ma'am," Mr. Bancroft said with a bow. "It is a lovely day for a lovely lady and for what I hope will be a lovely conversation."

"And you have a lovely way with words, sir," Mrs. Peabody said regally. "You will wish to step outside, then, with my—"

"Yes, ma'am," he said, smiling his most dazzling and charming smile. "With your niece, if you please."

Mrs. Peabody's mouth hung open inelegantly. Nancy did a fair imitation of a statue. So did all the other ladies. Patricia's head snapped up and all the blood drained out of it at the same moment. Mr. Bancroft continued to smile at his hostess.

"With my—?" she asked faintly.

"With your *niece*, ma'am," he said, transferring his gaze and his smile to Patricia. "With Miss Mangan. I have your husband's permission."

"With—Patricia?" Mrs. Peabody stared at him in disbelief.

"Thank you, ma'am," he said, bowing to her once more and stretching out a hand toward Patricia. "Miss Mangan, will you honor me with your company for a stroll outside?"

She merely stared at him, quite as dumbfounded as everyone else until his eyes warmed and one eyelid closed in a slow half wink. And she understood in a flash. She understood what he had done and was doing and why.

The—oh, the *precious rogue!*

She got to her feet and, when he stepped close enough, placed her hand in his. Her own was icy, she realized when she felt the warmth of his.

"Thank you, sir," she said, allowing him to place her hand on his sleeve and lead her from the room, in which a pin might have been heard crashing to the carpet.

It was, Patricia decided, quite the most delicious moment of her life.

It had worked beautifully. He had feared that perhaps she would not be in the salon with the other ladies, that perhaps she would have to be sent for. That would have spoiled the drama of the moment a little. But she had been there and everything had proceeded according to plan, almost as if he had written the script and all the players had learned their lines and actions to perfection.

And here she was, tripping along at his side, the top of her head reaching barely to his chin. His little bird, who had kept him awake for a weekful of nights, though not in the usual way.

"To the lily pond?" he suggested when they were outside the house and down the marble steps. "It seems the appropriate place to go, does it not?"

"To the lily pond." She smiled up at him, tying his stomach in unfamiliar knots. No one had told him that when she smiled she was pretty even by objective standards. Not that he could really see her by objective standards any longer.

He had expected her to be quiet, serious, wary. Puzzled. Reluctant to come with him. But she was still tripping along.

"Well, little bird," he said, "did you like it? Was it appropriate?" He did not expect her to understand his meaning. He thought he would have to explain.

"It was quite the most fiendish scheme I have ever been a witness to," she said. "It was cruel in the ex-

treme. You will certainly fry for this one, sir. They are
going to have to construct a particularly fiery corner for
you in hell. I *loved* it."

He chuckled. "Did you?" he said. "I expected that
after I had confessed all to you, you would lash out at
me with both sharp edges of your tongue. Have I
pleased you, Patricia?"

She darted a startled look up at him. "Yes," she said.
"Thank you. Doubtless my life here will be made a
misery once I have returned to the house and once you
have gone on your way tomorrow, but it will be worth
every moment. Perhaps I am cruel too, because undoubtedly Nancy will suffer dreadful mortification, but
I cannot help feeling spiteful and glad. And I will not
have to suffer for long. Soon I will be leaving here to
teach."

"Will you?" They were among the trees already, and
he was parting branches for her so that her face and
arms would not be grazed. "You have heard from the
parson who has your father's living?"

He watched her hesitate and then smile. "Someone
else has that appointment already," she said. "But it will
be better to go somewhere new anyway. My uncle is
going to help me find something. It will not take long,
I think. I am looking forward to it."

They were at the lily pond, and he gestured for her to
sit down before seating himself close beside her.

"Are you?" he said. "I am disappointed."

She turned her head to look at him.

"It was common knowledge why I went to talk to
your uncle this morning," he said.

She smiled with bright mischief. "What did you talk
to him about?" she asked. "You certainly deceived
everyone quite spectacularly."

"I went to talk about a marriage contract," he said.

"Oh." Her smile faded. "I see. I misunderstood. You are merely teasing her, then. Punishing her for a little while. You will ask her later today or tomorrow. Well . . . Well, it is good enough. It still felt good."

"Little bird." He took one of her hands in his and held it tightly. His heart was thumping like a hammer. This was the part he had been unsure about. He was still unsure. "It was you I talked to your uncle about. It is you I intended—and have intended for all of the past week—to ask to marry me."

She stared into his eyes, her own huge. Was she trying to drown him? She was succeeding.

"Will you?" he asked. "I can think of every reason in the world why you would say no, but I must ask anyway. Will you marry me, Patricia?"

"Why?" He saw her lips form the word though he heard no sound.

"Because I love you, little bird," he said. "Because you flew down into my heart from the branch up there that first afternoon I saw you, and have lodged in my heart ever since. Because you have wrecked the life with which I have been quite contented for the past ten years and have got me to thinking of constancy and a permanent home and a garden and cats and dogs. And babies, my love. And you, darling."

"You feel you owe it to me," she said. "You think this is the best way to spite them. And you feel sorry for me. You don't need—"

He dipped his head and kissed her. And brought one hand behind her head to hold it steady while he did it more thoroughly, parting his lips over hers, licking them and teasing his tongue through to the flesh within.

"And you are a rake," she said.

"Guilty," he said. "But past tense, not present or future, my love. I don't know how I can be sure of that, and I certainly don't know how I can convince you that I am. But I know it is true. I know it *here*, darling." He held his free hand over his heart. "I will be a model husband, as reformed rakes are reputed to be, I believe. Or so someone once told me."

He kissed her again. And coaxed her backward to the ground so that he could do so without having to hold her head steady. Her arms came about him as he slid his tongue past her teeth into her mouth.

"I have not a farthing to my name," she said, twisting her face away from his after a heady couple of minutes. "You have to marry money because you have squandered your own fortune."

"Tut," he said. "Where did you hear such a malicious rumor, little bird? It is one I put about myself quite deliberately at regular intervals in order to discourage fortune-seeking mamas. On this occasion it seemed to work the other way, I must admit it. I believe your aunt expected to have more power over a poor man than she would have had over one who was independently wealthy."

"You are not poor?" she whispered.

"Not at all," he said. "Gambling has never been one of my vices, my love, though almost everything else you might name has. Will you marry me now that you know I am almost indecently wealthy?"

"But I am not," she said.

He kissed her again—her mouth, her eyes, her temples, her chin, her throat. He touched her breasts through the cotton of her dress and found them small but firm and well shaped. Perfect for his babies—and for his own delight.

"I cannot," she said, pushing first his hands away and then his face. "I do not know—"

"I will teach you," he said. "It will be my joy to teach you, Patricia. Little bird, I have not slept in a week, fearful that you would say no, knowing that I am unworthy of you, knowing that I have nothing to offer you but security and a fortune and my love. I am not going to let you say no. I was going to be very noble and honorable about it, but I have changed my mind. I am going to use all my expertise on you here, or as much of it as becomes necessary until you are mindless enough to say yes. Say yes now so that I will not have to live with guilt afterward. Why are you laughing?"

Gloriously, wonderfully, she was laughing up at him. Giggling up at him, her arms about his neck.

"You lifted me down from that tree without waiting for my permission to do so," she said. "And you took me home from the picnic last week with only the choice of whether I would go on your arm or over your shoulder. Why change things now? Why wait for my acceptance? You might as well marry me and be done with it."

He was sure of her suddenly. All anxiety fled, leaving not a trace behind. He grinned down at her. "Parsons can be sticky customers, though, little bird," he said. "They wait to hear the bride say yes and will not proceed with the marriage service until she has done so. Unreasonable of them, I always say, but that is the reality. Are you going to say yes when he asks?"

Her eyes were huge again. "Are you quite, quite sure, sir—Mr. Bancroft?" she asked.

"Josh," he said. "It is my name, you know. Joshua. My father was rather fond of the Bible. My sisters are Miriam and Hagar."

"Joshua," she whispered.

"Or darling for short," he said, grinning at her again. "As with Patricia. Little bird for short. Will you marry me?"

"If you are quite, quite sure," she said.

"I am quite, quite sure," he said against her lips. "Will you?"

"Yes," she whispered. "Joshua. Darling."

"And three words more, if you please, little bird," he said, closing his eyes and brushing his lips lightly over hers. "I have said them to you already."

"You precious rogue," she said out loud.

He threw back his head and shouted with laughter. "Well," he said, looking appreciatively down at her, "you have asked for it now. I am going to have to live up to your expectations, am I not?"

"Yes, please, Joshua," she said.

"Starting now?" He smiled tenderly at her.

"If you please, darling," she said.

"Starting now, then," he said, lowering his head.

PENGUIN PUTNAM

online

Your Internet gateway to a virtual environment with hundreds of entertaining and enlightening books from Penguin Putnam Inc.

While you're there get the latest buzz on the best authors and books around—

Tom Clancy, Patricia Cornwell, W.E.B. Griffin, Nora Roberts, William Gibson, Robin Cook, Brian Jacques, Catherine Coulter, Stephen King, Jacquelyn Mitchard, and many more!

PenguinPutnam Online is located at
http://www.penguinputnam.com

• •

PENGUIN PUTNAM NEWS

Every month you'll get an inside look at our upcoming books and new features on our site. This is an ongoing effort on our part to provide you with the most interesting and up-to-date information about our books and authors.

Subscribe to Penguin Putnam News at
http://www.penguinputnam.com/ClubPPI